# HEAT WAVE

# HEAT WAVE

## TJ KLUNE

**TOR TEEN**

A TOM DOHERTY ASSOCIATES BOOK
NEW YORK

HEAT WAVE

Copyright © 2022 by Travis Klune

A Tor Teen Book
Published by Tom Doherty Associates
120 Broadway
New York, NY 10271

www.tor-forge.com

Tor® is a registered trademark of Macmillan Publishing Group, LLC.

The Library of Congress Cataloging-in-Publication Data
is available upon request.

ISBN 978-1-250-20373-1 (hardcover)
ISBN 978-1-250-87867-0 (international, sold outside
the U.S., subject to rights availability)
ISBN 978-1-250-20375-5 (ebook)

Our books may be purchased in bulk for promotional, educational, or business use. Please contact your local bookseller or the Macmillan Corporate and Premium Sales Department at 1-800-221-7945, extension 5442, or by email at MacmillanSpecialMarkets@macmillan.com.

First Edition: 2022

Printed in the United States of America

0  9  8  7  6  5  4  3  2  1

*For queer kids everywhere.*
*I am in awe of all that you are because*
*you are the true superheroes.*

# HEAT WAVE

HEAT WAVE

**Fic: A Pleasure to Burn**
**Author**: PyroStormIsBae
**Chapter 37 of ?**
**138,225 words**
**Pairing**: Pyro Storm/Original Male Character
**Rated**: R (Rating is finally going up!)
**Tags**: True Love, Pining, Gentle Pyro Storm, Happy
   Ending, First Kiss, More Than First Kiss, Fluffy Like a
   Cloud, So Much Violence, Evil Shadow Star, Bakery AU,
   Private Investigator, Anti-Rebecca Firestone, Hands Going
   Under Clothes, !!!, Naked Party and You're All Invited

........................................................................................................................

### Chapter 37: Not a Chapter

**Author Note:** Hey, hi and hello! Sorry if you got excited for
a notification of an update. I never want to leave my readers
hanging, and I know that abandoned fics are the bane of all human existence. Like, is there really anything worse than finding
a story you love only to see that it hasn't been updated in six
years? *I hate that so much.* So, to reiterate: I'M NOT ABANDON-
ING THIS STORY!!!! I promise. A lot of things have happened in
the past few months, and I haven't felt like writing much. It
can be really hard to focus on a fic about solving serial murders
and falling in love with an Extraordinary when . . . well. When
things get a little too real.

   I don't have a lot of time these days to sit down and write.
School's out for the summer, but I'm busier than ever. I'll

hopefully get back to this sooner rather than later, so please keep your notifications on for this fic. I promise when I return, there will be explosions of the fiery *and* the sexual kind, so stay tuned!

PyroStormIsBae

........................................................................................................

## Comments:

**FireStoned 09:25:** DID YOU SEE REBECCA FIRESTONE ON THE NEWS??? ISN'T SHE THE MOST WONDERFUL THING THAT HAS EVER HAPPENED TO HUMANITY? AND BEFORE YOU SAY NO, SCREW YOU!! SHE IS GOING TO BE THE BEST MAYORAL PRESS SECRETARY THAT HAS EVER MAY-ORAL PRESS SECRETARIED. AND I WON'T BE RESPONDING TO ANYONE WHO TRIES TO ARGUE WITH ME!! DIE MAD ABOUT IT!!!

**LostDreamer 09:27:** Are you Nick Bell in Nova City??? The one who wrote that Shadow Star slash fic that never got finished?? Please say hi to Seth/Pyro Storm for me!

**ExtraExtra 09:29:** This has to be Nick Bell. He talks *exactly* like Nash does. Had I known this was self-insert fanfic, I would've read something else rather than wasting my time with some teenager's hormonal power fantasy.

**PyroStarLover 09:30:** You're going to leave us hanging right before they finally have sex? The only reason I've put up with hundreds of thousands of words was because you promised butt sex. You can't dangle anal without delivering! Also, are you really Nick Bell? What happened on prom night? Who were those other Extraordinaries with you?

**WTF6969 09:31:** If you're Nick Bell like everyone thinks, then why the hell are you so anti-police now? Your dad is a cop! Do you hate your own father?

**Anonymoose 09:32:** Did you get my message? See you soon!

**TacosAreFun 09:39:** I'm so sick of WTF6969. GET A LIFE, YOU FREAKING LOSER. Aaron Bell quit the force! It was all over Twitter.

PyroStormIsBae, write whatever you want. I don't care if you're Nick Bell or someone else, you do you.

**SoundOfJazz 09:42:** These comments are getting a little stalkery. Lmk if you want me to handle it. I got new Louboutins to replace my other heels, and guess what? The soles are red just like the BLOOD OF OUR ENEMIES. Fun! Gibby says hi. She also said some other stuff, but we need more positivity in our lives. Bye!!

**JazzFan12345678 09:49:** I did *not* say hi. Jazz forced me to make this account. Your followers are weird and make me uncomfortable.

# 1

Near dusk, shadows stretched like reaching darkness, the heat from the summer day like molten claws to the chest, digging into the beating heart of a city under siege. Steam (and brown water) leaked from manhole covers, creating a wet fog that smelled like desperation and a complete lack of infrastructural understanding.

People scurried on the sidewalks, sweat dripping down their faces in streaks like tears, silently crying out for someone to save them from themselves. Horns honked in steel gridlocks, fists shaking angrily out the car windows. Darkened buildings loomed, towers of the rich and powerful, holding the populace in the palms of their diabolically malevolent hands. Neon lights snapped and crackled, burning against the coming dark, illuminating the faces of the damned and the forgotten. Wavy heat lines rose from cracked asphalt, a reminder of the extreme temperatures that had descended upon a city of steel and glass.

"Who will protect us?" the people wailed as they darted their gazes up toward the darkening sky in fear. "Who will be the champion we so desperately need? If only there was someone out there who could be the hero we deserve! Nay, the hero we *require*."

This was a city filled with disease, tumors growing in the bones and connective tissue, spreading with no hope for a cure. This was a city trapped in a war for its very soul, a thin sliver of light threatening to be smothered by the shadows of evil, the scales of truth and justice tipping dangerously toward chaos.

But the city was not alone. She had someone who loved her,

someone who would lay down his very life to ensure her survival.

Atop a small building that had once been a yogurt shop but was now a hipster coffee lounge with logs instead of chairs because *what,* a figure sat perched on the ledge like a stone gargoyle watching hundreds of years of history pass by in the blink of an eye. This figure shifted slightly, the white lenses on his helmet flashing as the exposed mouth twisted into a furious snarl. "This is my city," he growled dangerously. "And I will do everything I can to protect her people." His head jerked up at the sound of a scream in the distance. "Hark! There's crime afoot." The figure looked off into the distance, the light of a nearby cell tower blinking red as if to say, *I am the pulse of Nova City, weak and thready. If only my light could burn forever.*

"Yes," the amazing figure breathed. "I hear you. I see you." He rose slowly, the strong muscles of his body shifting sexily underneath the costume, a symbol of freedom and hope and justice. He breathed in deeply. "And I can smell you . . . but also . . . taste? Oh my god, what the hell *is* that? Holy crap, it's *everywhere.*" He gagged. "It's coating my throat. Did someone die and then their body fell in the water and now it's a bloated mess filled with gases and ballooning organs that will soon explode in a burst of—no. Focus. Darkness has found its way into—"

"Seriously," another voice said. "I love you, but you've been narrating out loud for the past fifteen minutes, and while I appreciate your creativity, we probably should get a move on before the thieves get away with all the jewels."

The Extraordinary known as Guardian squawked as he lost his footing and fell off the ledge backward onto the roof. He landed roughly on his back, blinking up at the night sky. A moment later, the sky disappeared as a familiar face appeared above him, curls of dark hair hanging down around his face. He wore a sleek costume, black with red piping that ran up the length of his legs and torso. Across his chest, a symbol of a flame, the mark of a hero.

"Pyro Storm," Guardian growled, voice modulated deeply

through his cerulean-blue helmet. He pushed himself up off the ground, ignoring the helping hand reaching toward him. "I knew you'd be here."

Seth blinked. "I should hope so. We came together. It'd be weird if I wasn't here."

"Would it be weird?" Guardian hissed. "Or would it be all part of your plan to get me alone so you can have your way with me?" He took a step back away from the Extraordinary. And another. And another. And then the back of his legs hit the ledge of the roof. He turned around, bending over, hands flat against the ledge as he looked back over his shoulder. "You've trapped me, Pyro Storm. I answered a call thinking it'd be a citizen in need of saving, but instead, it's you. You, with your righteousness and your face looking like it does. My body is tense with pleasure and thrumming arousal."

"Uh-huh," Seth said, a black-and-red helmet dangling from the fingers of his left hand, the lenses dull in the low light. "You sure seem to be shaking your ass a lot for someone who's not sure."

"Villain!" Guardian cried. He moaned loudly, arching his back. "How dare you speak to me as if you have any right to!" He gasped dramatically, the voice modulator making it sound as if he smoked fifty cigars a day. "Don't you *dare* think of using your fire powers to burn away my costume, leaving me nude and helpless, though more than willing to participate because consent is important, even during role-play, and I don't want you to think I don't want this when I actually do. Also, my safe word is *charcuterie,* and no, you don't get to ask why."

"Because you like varied meats and cheeses served to you on a cutting board?"

"*Exactly.*"

"Nick, you can't just—"

He coughed.

"Nicky, you need to—"

He coughed again, this time much more forcefully to make

a very serious point. He hoped Seth got it this time because it was making his throat hurt.

Seth rolled his eyes. *"Guardian."*

Success! "That's better. Thank you. Remember, we talked about this. When I've got the costume *and* the helmet on, I'm not Nick anymore, I'm Guardian. But if I have the costume on and the helmet *off,* I'm Nick because you can see my face. Or, if I'm not wearing the costume *or* the helmet and am very, very naked, you can call me whatever you want."

He winked over his shoulder.

And then remembered Seth couldn't see his eyes because he was wearing his helmet.

"I just winked at you," he said. "In case you were wondering."

"Oh," Seth said. "I wasn't, but thank you for telling me. That changes everything."

Guardian lifted the helmet off his head, the sharpness of the world around him fading. The lenses inside his helmet were strong, letting him see farther and more sharply than he could without it. He never wanted to take it off, but apparently he wasn't allowed to wear it whenever he wanted, which was bullshit. Setting the helmet on the ledge, Nicholas Bell turned and faced his boyfriend. "It wasn't fifteen minutes."

"You're right," Seth Gray said, a quirk to his lips. "It was actually closer to twenty. I'm not sure if a hero should spend that much time narrating his plans out loud. What if there was someone listening in?"

Nick winced. He hadn't thought of that. As per his usual, he'd been so wrapped up in being Guardian that he'd let it go to his head a little. Probably more than a little.

It'd only been a month since he'd come home after Gibby's graduation and found a package waiting for him on the kitchen table. Inside had been a note from Miss Conduct, the drag-queen Extraordinary with acerbic commentary known to fry a man as thoroughly as her electric powers. She wore bangles and had legs for days. Nick could never pull off bangles, and his own legs were pasty and thin, with knobby knees and that one weird hair on the left side of his right knee that grew obscenely long, which was *bullshit,* seeing as how he couldn't get any hair to grow on his chest.

The note, while sweet and wonderful, hadn't been the best thing. No, that had been the costume she'd created for him with help from Nick's friends. A costume of blue and white with a helmet to match.

And here he stood in said costume in all his glory, though *glory* might have been a bit of a misnomer. You see, when one decides to become a real Extraordinary, one must wear a skin-tight costume to be taken seriously. The *problem* with that, however, was that Nick had learned his body was strangely shaped, and things that *should* have bulged—arm muscles, chest muscles, and yes, the groin—did not bulge at all.

(The second time Nick had tried the costume on, he'd stuffed a folded sock down the front of the tights and nodded in the mirror. "Oh, this?" he'd said to his reflection, nodding down at his crotch. "Don't worry about that. Just my penis. Yeah, it's big."

His father had come in without knocking. The silence that had followed had been absolute before Dad backed out of the room slowly. They had never talked about it, and Nick hadn't tried to put a sock over his junk again.)

So: there was a reason Nick didn't like wearing what amounted to a full bodysuit of spandex. It left nothing to the imagination.

"Bend over," Nick demanded.

Seth squinted at him. "What?"

"I want to show you something. This isn't about sex stuff. Trust me."

"Yeah, see," Seth said, "the last time you told me to bend over and said it wasn't about sex stuff, you said, and I quote, 'It looks like someone ordered cake from a sexy bakery.'"

Nick snorted. "I'm funny. *And* erotic."

Seth sighed. "It would've been funnier and maybe more erotic if you hadn't said it while my aunt and uncle were standing three feet away."

Nick scowled, grateful the encroaching dark hid the furious

heat blooming on his cheeks. "How was I supposed to know they were going to be in the living room of their own house? Martha really didn't need to get out sandwich baggies and begin to make dental dams right then and there. That was uncalled for. I blame her. And Dad." Mostly his dad, though, because he'd been the one to show the Grays the wonders of DIY sexual safety.

Seth shook his head. "Just be grateful she hasn't started crocheting the harness she wants to make for some horrific reason. Ever since she went to that sex shop for *learning purposes,* she hasn't been the same."

Nick groaned. "Oh my god, I hate *everything.* Now stop distracting me and bend over."

Seth hunched his shoulders, his chest and stomach making a half circle. "Like this?"

Nick nodded. "Now rub your hand along your chest and stomach."

Seth's eyes narrowed. "This sounds like a sex thing."

It really did, but he wasn't to be deterred. "Get your mind out of the gutter, Gray. You'd know if this was a sex thing."

"O . . . kay." Seth ran his hand along his sternum, down to his stomach, stopping just above his groin before going back up to his chest. "Now what?"

Nick—always and forever Nick—short-circuited a little at the sight of his Extraordinary boyfriend touching himself, the tip of Seth's black-gloved fingers pausing against his broad chest. All the porn Nick had consumed in his life paled in comparison to the sight before him: Seth with his dark curly hair and a jaw that could cut glass. Nick knew that objectification could be seriously problematic but come on! *Look at him.*

"Yeah," Nick muttered. "Just like that."

"Nick," Seth said pointedly.

"I'm not thinking sexy thoughts!" Nick said. "I'm just . . . admiring the scene before me!" He frowned as he bent over the same way Seth had, rubbing a hand over his chest and stomach. "See? What the hell!"

"Uh, what am I supposed to be looking at?"

"This!" Nick said, glaring as he hunched over. "When *you* bend over in your Extraordinary costume, your stomach is flat because you're ripped. When I do it, you can't even see the abdominal muscles that are probably there even though they weren't this morning. I thought being an Extraordinary was supposed to make me have noticeable washboard abs!"

"Hoo boy," Seth said. "That's not how any of this works."

"Says *you*," Nick retorted, glaring down at the gentle swell of his stomach as if it had betrayed him. "You became an Extraordinary and you turned into a sex god. *I* became an Extraordinary and it gave me body issues. Yes, I had nachos for dinner last night, and *yes*, there wasn't enough cheese so I added more, but still! I ran last week, Seth. For a quarter of a mile. And I only had to stop twice to catch my breath."

"I know," Seth said. "I was there, remember? You complained the entire time."

Nick sniffed. "Yes, well, running is pointless and you should feel bad for making me do it." He poked his stomach a final time before standing upright. "I may need to consider a redesign of my costume. What do you think about layers? I took a test in *Cosmo*, and the result said I have a body made for layers." He frowned. "It also said that I was a free-spirited woman who won't be constrained by society, but still. Layers."

Seth chuckled, walking toward Nick with a strange heat in his eyes. He set his helmet next to Nick's on the ledge before leaning in. Nick's heart sped up a little. It always did when Seth was around, but when he was so close Nick could count the faint freckles across his nose and cheeks? Man, did Nick enjoy the hell out of it.

Seth kissed him slowly, lips slightly chapped. Nick returned in kind, his tongue sliding against Seth's as sweat trickled down his neck. The heat wave that had settled on Nova City a few weeks ago hadn't let up. After a bitterly cold winter with storm after storm of heavy snow followed by a wet spring, summer had come to the city with a vengeance: blazing hot, the humidity almost unbearable. If Nick wasn't destined to become an Extraordinary, he'd have stayed inside with the air-conditioning on until senior year started up in the fall.

Senior year, he thought distantly as Seth's lips worked over his. The end of one life, and the beginning of another one entirely. On his best days, Nick wasn't a fan of change. His ADHD—while mostly under control with the new meds he was on—required routine in his life, order to keep things from spinning out of control. Sure, chaos often reared its head and laid waste to his plans, but Nick was trying, something he'd decided he had to do in order to live a double life of a mild-mannered student who moonlighted as an Extraordinary.

Sort of. In the month since he'd been gifted the costume and become Guardian, he hadn't done much with it. Dad said he wasn't ready to save the day on his own. No matter how much Nick begged to go out as Guardian, Dad stood firm, telling him he had to ease into it, to take things slowly. "Besides," Dad said, "you're still the leader of Lighthouse. That's just as important."

Being a hero was vastly more complicated than he'd expected it to be. Not only did he have to worry about saving-the-day shit, he also had to focus on being Nick Bell, too. He didn't understand how the comics made it look so easy. He was supposed to wear a skintight costume while also worrying about getting into college? He needed to fret over the fact that Seth might not get to go back to Centennial High (home of the Fighting Wombats!) because he revealed himself as Pyro Storm while at the same time figuring out how the hell he was supposed to take AP History and survive? Gibby was going to NCU in the fall, so they were already down one person. Was it just supposed to be him and Jazz at school for months on end, all while rumors swirled around them about what had happened the night of the prom?

He didn't know how he was going to do it. Everything felt too big. While grateful it was June, he knew that eventually he'd have to face the very real fact that things were changing, splintering, and there wasn't much he could do to stop it.

"You're thinking too hard," Seth murmured against his lips.

Nick sighed as he pulled back. "Yeah, I know. Sorry. You know how it is. I have thoughts and then *those* thoughts have thoughts."

Seth smiled. "I know, Nicky. Anything you want to talk about?"

"Just the same crap as always. Everything and nothing all at once."

"We'll figure it out," Seth said, reaching out and squeezing Nick's gloved hands. "But we can talk more about it later. Tonight, we focus, all right?"

Nick nodded as he relaxed. "Right. Focus. I'm with you." He had something to prove tonight, to show that he was capable.

Seth stepped around him, going to the ledge and looking down at the alley below. "Good. Now, tell me what you think we should do."

Nick turned and stood next to Seth, hands resting on top of his helmet. He followed Seth's gaze down to the alley. Across the alley was another building, a little shorter than the one they stood on. An old air conditioner rattled and groaned next to a metal roof-access door.

"Could go through the roof door," he said. "Avoid any windows that could give us away."

"Door's bolted and locked," Seth said. "How do you get in if you want to avoid as much property damage as possible?"

He paused, looking at the air-conditioning unit. His gaze traveled along the length of the roof, toward the side of the building closest to them. Sitting near the top was a vent covered in a metal grate. "There," he said, pointing. "Could go through the vent."

Seth nodded. "Think you can fit?"

"Rude."

Seth rolled his eyes. "You know that's not what I meant." He bumped his shoulder against Nick's. "You don't want to try something like that, only to get stuck. Think, Nick. What should you do when you have to enter a building you've never been to before?"

"Powers," Nick said automatically. "Make my own door." Images flooded his brain of him standing before a brick wall and waving his hand, causing the bricks to shift and break apart, making a door.

But Seth nipped that right in the bud, shaking his head and saying, "*Without* powers. You can't always count on them. There may come a time when powers could work against you." He paused, considering. "Or, when you don't quite have control over them."

Nick scowled at him. "I totally have control of my powers. Watch." He looked around, trying to find something he could use. Near the far corner, a plastic bucket sat as if forgotten, the handle rusted, the side cracked. Taking a deep breath, Nick raised his hand, and in his head, a light sparked, warm and sweet. He held on to it as tightly as he could and *pushed,* a shiver of not-quite-pain rippling through him.

The bucket wiggled from side to side before rising slowly off the roof, floating five feet in the air. "See?" Nick said, a trickle of sweat sliding down his forehead. "Easy. I got this. I'm so good at—"

The spark pulsed in his head, and the bucket shot through the air, arcing high before it landed three roofs away with a faint clatter.

Nick sighed, dropping his hand. "Okay, so there might be a few kinks to work out, but still! What's the point of being an Extraordinary if I don't get to *be* extraordinary?"

"There's more to it than that," Seth said, and it wasn't the first time he'd told Nick this, or the tenth. "While having powers is all well and good, you can't always rely on *just* your powers. You have to think, too, Nicky. And since no one thinks like you do, you've got this. Come on. Can't go in through the front or the roof access. Doors locked. How do you proceed?"

Nick brightened. "Lighthouse."

"Exactly." Seth nodded toward his helmet. "Get to it."

Nick lifted his helmet from the ledge and put it on. The moment the helmet settled on his head, bright lights exploded inside as his vision sharpened. Lines of code ran like cascading water before they disappeared, replaced by two words, blinking in cerulean blue.

## WELCOME, GUARDIAN.

He grinned despite himself. That would never not be the coolest shit he'd ever seen. Gibby was a goddamn genius when it came to all things tech, and she'd outdone herself.

"Lighthouse," Guardian said, voice once again modulated. "Do you copy?"

Nothing.

Guardian frowned, tapping the side of his helmet. "Lighthouse, this is Guardian. Do you read me?"

Silence.

"What the hell," he muttered. "They're supposed to be—"

"Lighthouse here," Jasmine Kensington said in his ears, voice crackling. "We read you loud and clear. Sorry about that. Gibby was punching the bag Seth has hanging in the basement, and then she started sweating and you *know* what that does to me."

"They're having sex in the secret lair," Guardian told Seth.

Seth threw up his hands.

"We are *not*," Gibby snapped. "It was just foreplay. Trust me, Jazz would sound more out of breath if it was sex, because I can do this thing with my fingers that—"

"What in the good goddamn *shit*, Gibby," Guardian growled. "Stop fornicating when we're supposed to be stopping a jewel heist! I need the schematics of the building."

"On it," Jazz said, ever the professional. "What's the—Gibby, you're going to get us in *trouble*. Oh. *Oh.* That's . . . wow. Do that again!"

"*Schematics!*" Guardian bellowed.

Seth sighed. "So much for the element of surprise."

"Schematics," Gibby said, and Nick could *hear* the eat-shit grin in her voice. "We'll get them for you. What's the address?"

Guardian looked at Seth, who shrugged and said, "What is it? You need to pay attention to these things, every single little detail. You'll never know when you need to call for backup, and you shouldn't always rely on the tracker in your suit. What if something disrupts it? An Extraordinary who could cause a blackout and knock out your locator as well as the comms? What do you do then?"

"Right," Guardian muttered. He moved to the ledge to his right, looking down at the street below. People walked along the sidewalks, unaware that an Extraordinary watched them from above. Cars lined the road, traffic backed up, horns honking obnoxiously. There wasn't any place like it in the world, and though Nova City had bitch-slapped him more than a few times, he'd always do what he could to keep her safe. "We're at the corner of Tenth and Marketplace." He glanced at the numbers on the buildings across the street. All even. Numbers going up to the left, down to the right. He thought back to their arrival. He'd seen the street number of the building, hadn't he? He'd glanced at it. What was it? Think, think, *think*—ah! He grinned. "1757 Marketplace. No, wait, that's the building we're on. 1759 Marketplace."

Seth squeezed his shoulder. "Good. Nice one, Guardian."

"1759 Marketplace," Jazz chirped in his ear. Through the speakers in his helmet, he could hear her fingers flying over the keyboard in the basement of the Gray brownstone. "And here . . . we . . . go."

Guardian blinked against the brightness of the screen in his helmet. The light faded slightly, and when he could see clearly again, a three-dimensional schematic of the building they needed to infiltrate appeared before him, spinning slowly. "Any way in that doesn't involve doors?" Guardian asked. "And would avoid alarms?"

"Gibby, you got anything?" Jazz asked.

"There," she said. "You see a vent near the top of the building?"

"Yeah," Guardian said, heart thumping in excitement. "Big enough for us to get through?"

"Should be," Jazz said, and the schematic zoomed in to focus on the venting system. "Might be a tight squeeze, but both of you should be able to get through it. Hold on. Gibby, do that line thing."

"That line thing," Gibby said with a snort. "I love you so much. Yes, I can do the line thing." A moment later, a red dot appeared at the start of the vent before extending in a line through the ductwork. It took a right, a left, two more rights, before it stopped in the middle of the building. "There, that should lead you to a grate in the ceiling. Gives you the drop on anyone inside."

"Security system?" Guardian asked, staring at the vent access.

"Old," Jazz said. "Looks like a simple system that only registers the front door opening after hours. Hasn't been updated since 2004."

Guardian nodded. "Good. The city calls for me. I hear her cries and will do whatever I can to save her."

Silence.

Guardian tapped the side of his helmet again. "Did you get that?"

"We did," Jazz said. "We didn't know if there was going to be more like there normally is. Don't you usually say something about diseased hearts and the writhing morass of—"

"No time!" Guardian cried. "It's time to take out the—no, I can't use that one, because I already used the word *time*. Dammit. Okay, hold on. I've . . . almost . . . got . . . it. Just . . . one . . . more . . . second and—ah!" He squared his shoulders. "You want to try and take jewels that don't belong to you? See how well you do when I *kick* you in the jewels!"

He waited for thunderous applause.

None came.

Guardian deflated slightly. "Oh, come on, really? That was awesome."

"Is that what we're considering awesome now?" Gibby asked. "My bad. Gay gasp! You're *so good* at this superhero thing. I've never seen such a—"

"I hate everyone," Guardian mumbled.

Seth slid on his own helmet, the lenses flashing an ominous red as he too came online. "Lighthouse, this is Pyro Storm. We're going in. Be ready. It's time to burn."

"What the—I *wrote* that catchphrase. Why does it sound so much cooler than mine? I demand you come back and give me compliments about kicking thieves in the jewels!"

Apparently, some vents weren't built big enough for people to fit inside easily. After they saved the day *again,* Guardian decided the next bit of Extraordinary business would be to propose a citywide mandate that all vents be made larger so certain situations (such as the one Guardian was currently in) could be avoided in the future.

"Shove my ass *harder,*" he said, the pressure against his shoulders and chest from the surrounding vent causing him to wheeze. His legs dangled out into nothing, kicking empty air. He'd wanted to fly up to the vent on his own, but aside from the one time he'd floated after jumping off a building (long story), he hadn't quite got the hang of flying. Or floating. Or even jumping really high.

Guardian sucked in his stomach, wishing he didn't have ribs. Pyro Storm pushed him again, and just when Guardian thought he'd be stuck forever, he shot forward, the top of the vent rising slightly to give him more room. He was able to pull his legs inside, and rose to his hands and knees, back bumping against the metal above him.

"I'm in," he panted. "Lighthouse, would you—Oh, crap, sorry. Sorry."

"What happened?" Jazz asked.

Pyro Storm groaned. "He kicked me in the face."

Guardian squirmed a little farther into the ductwork to give

Pyro Storm room to climb in after him. "It was an *accident*. It's not my fault I've got long legs like a dancer."

"Yeah, no," Jazz said. "I've seen you dance. For a queer man, you dance like your joints are fused together."

"That's *bullshit*," Guardian snapped, sweat trickling down the side of his head to his ear. "How dare you perpetuate harmful stereotypes about queer people and their ability or lack thereof to shake their asses in a way that suggests sexiness. What's next, you're going to comment on how well I dress?"

"Have you *seen* your clothes?" Gibby said.

"Gibby!"

"Yeah, yeah. You need to turn right . . . there."

The ductwork opened up off to his right, and Guardian crawled through it, Pyro Storm close at his heels. Guardian paused, panting, wishing he could use his powers to make the vents wider. Just a little push, and he could walk in a crouch instead of on his hands and knees. But that would make too much noise and give away their position. He couldn't take the chance. Not with the villains somewhere below them.

"Left," Gibby said in his ear when he came to another opening.

"On it," he said, turning left and crawling as quietly as he could. Which, of course, meant that his knees hitting the metal sounded as if a herd of cows was running through a swap meet that sold nothing but highly breakable glass figurines.

As they continued on, Pyro Storm spoke behind him, whispering, though his voice came through clearly from the speakers in Guardian's helmet. "We counted four of them. Armed. What should you do to avoid getting shot?"

"Don't engage them face-to-face," Guardian whispered back. "If we can come from above, or behind, it'll give us a chance to take them out without a shot being fired."

"Correct. Even if it takes a little longer, it's always worth it to avoid any potential injuries or loss of life. What if there are innocent bystanders? Say, a security guard they've taken hostage. What do you do then?"

"Protect them at all costs," Guardian replied, his excitement building once more. "They're the first priority. The jewels are most likely insured, and it's better to save people than rocks that some weirdos put value on because they're shiny."

"Right. People first, property second, though we need to re-member that if there is any kind of damage done, someone has to clean that up, and we don't want to make more work for others if we can avoid it."

Guardian winced as he banged his funny bone against the wall of the duct. "Being altruistic is so hard. It'd be easier if we didn't have to care about everyone and everything."

Pyro Storm chuckled. "That's what being a hero means."

"I know. But what if—"

The metal underneath him creaked dangerously. Guardian looked down slowly in horror as the duct began to sway side to side. "Um," he said. "Should it be doing that, or . . . ?"

Guardian—meaning Nick—was exceptional at falling. Off a bridge. Off a roof. Hell, out of bed. So it shouldn't have been surprising when the ductwork underneath him collapsed with a loud shriek of metal, causing him to plummet face-first toward the ground ten feet below him. "Oh, crap, oh, crap, oh, *crap!*"

He raised his hands as the cement floor hurtled toward him, and in his head, that spark like a star exploded. He closed his eyes, hoping he'd be intact enough for an open-casket funeral where everyone would sob and wail that he'd been taken far too soon, that he was the best of them, how can we go on without Nicholas Bell?

For a moment everything faded around him. The building, the metal falling with him, the fact that he had wanted to prove himself tonight, all of it. The only things in existence were Nick and this exploding light, this light that never quite did what he wanted it to do. He reached for it.

*Please,* he said, either out loud or in his head, he didn't know. He brought the light to his chest, curling around it, holding it close. *Please.*

When he didn't end up as a pile of bones and exposed brain matter, he opened his eyes and found himself floating a few feet above the cracked cement floor, pieces of metal from the duct swirling around him. He stared in wonder, reaching out and pushing his finger against a piece of metal, watching it slowly spin away. He heard voices in his head, his friends demanding to know if he was dead. "I'm doing it," he whispered in awe. "Hell yes! Suck on that, you stupid—"

Guardian fell the remaining distance to the ground, landing hard, metal clanging against the cement and bouncing away. "*Ow*," he groaned against the floor. "Oh my freaking *god*, it hurts. Everything hurts. Lighthouse, Guardian is down. I repeat, Guardian is down and is grievously injured. Send a medic and potentially a priest to perform last rites!"

He rolled over onto his back, grimacing at the aches in his chest and knees. Above him, Pyro Storm appeared at the edge of the collapsed duct. Guardian waved at him weakly.

Even through his pain, he could still appreciate Pyro Storm rolling out of the vent, somersaulting in midair, and floating gently toward the ground, landing on his feet.

Pyro Storm knelt down next to him, cupping his face. "You're fine. It was only three feet."

"Against a hard surface," Guardian said. "Look. Look how hard the floor is."

"I can see," Pyro Storm said. "It's probably the hardest floor ever made."

Guardian shoved Pyro Storm's hands away. "Yeah, yeah. You've got jokes. Hysterical." He pushed himself up from the ground, grimacing. But then all was forgotten when he remembered what he'd just done. "Dude, I *floated*. Did you see that? And *yes*, I know it only seems to happen when I'm falling, but *still*."

"You should probably change your name to Floating Man," Gibby said in his ear. "That's sure to strike fear into the hearts of our enemies."

"You good to go?" Pyro Storm asked, looking Guardian up and down. "Or do you want to call this off?"

Guardian shook his head. "I'm fine. Let's keep going."

He looked around to see them standing in a large room that

appeared to be used for storage. Shelves lined the walls on either side of him, filled with cans of paint and cleaning supplies, their stench thick and harsh. Behind them, a door that led out into the main floor of the building. He rushed toward it, planning on bursting through and spouting off a kickass catchphrase that would cause the armed goons to tremble in fear. He skidded to a stop before he could think of one, remembering what Seth had taught him.

Guardian pressed the side of his head against the door, trying to determine if anyone on the other side had heard him. He barely flinched when Pyro Storm appeared beside him, lips curving into a small smile.

"Good," Pyro Storm said as he leaned against the door, and Guardian warmed at the praise. "You're thinking ahead. Rather than shoving the door open and startling someone, you're taking it slow. It won't always be like this, but when you get the chance to take your time, it'll make things easier in the long run. What do you hear?"

"Nothing. No voices. No movement."

"What does that mean?"

Guardian stepped back from the door. "Either they're farther in the building and didn't hear us, or they're waiting to spring a trap."

"Exactly," Pyro Storm said. "Gibby, the schematics again, please. Interior only. Show us where we are. Looks like a storage closet."

Inside Guardian's helmet, the building formed once more. The image zoomed in, showing two blinking dots in the west corner of the building. "Found you," she said. "You're a little off course, but . . . hang on." Through the speakers came the sound of fingers flying over a keyboard. The image spun one hundred eighty degrees, a white dot blinking on the south end of the building. "There's where you need to go. It's where the jewels are supposed to be. Thieves, too, if they haven't heard you."

The image collapsed. "Through the door," Guardian said. "Down the hall. Last door on the right out to the showroom." He reached for the doorknob and began to turn it, only to have Pyro Storm's hand fall on his, stopping him from opening the door.

"Careful," Pyro Storm said as Guardian looked at him. "You know this. Slow."

Guardian nodded as Pyro Storm stepped back. "This would be so much easier if we had flash-bang grenades. Just toss one of those suckers out there and *blam*! Everyone is blinded."

"We talked about this," Pyro Storm said patiently. "And we all agreed that the idea of you with a grenade of any kind was extremely terrifying."

"You'd probably end up having it blow up in your face," Jazz said. "And I happen to like that face as it is, so."

"Yeah, yeah." He turned the doorknob as quietly as he could. Once he heard the latch click, he pulled the door open just a sliver, peering out into the darkness on the other side of the door.

The hallway appeared empty. Closed doors, three on the left, two on the right. Lights off. No movement, no sound. He glanced at Pyro Storm and grinned. "Is it bad I almost want the thieves to be waiting for us? How awesome would it be for us to have a hallway fight scene?"

Gibby snorted. "You have a hard time fighting in wide open spaces, so I think a hallway fight would probably only see you getting your ass kicked."

Guardian scoffed. "I don't get my *ass* kicked. I sometimes appear to lose so it just *looks* like I have no idea what I'm doing only to then gain the upper hand."

"Oh," Gibby said. "Well, if that's the case, you're really good at it."

"Thank y—wait, what."

Pyro Storm cleared his throat pointedly.

"Right," Guardian said. "We're in the middle of doing stuff. On it."

He pulled open the door, walking swiftly out into the hall. He kept eyes on the closed doors, Pyro Storm following him, watching his every movement. Though he knew his boyfriend was in his corner, Guardian wanted to make him proud, to show Pyro Storm he could be counted on to have his back.

He tried the first door. Locked. Same with the second. The third. He barely turned the knob on the fourth, knowing it would also probably be locked.

He stopped at the last door on the right. It had a rectangular window, and he pressed himself against the wall near the door, craning his neck to look through the glass.

His breath caught in his chest.

Three figures were dressed head to toe in black, ski masks covering their faces. All had guns and flashlights, the beams crisscrossing as they took in the room around them. Two of the figures stood next to each other, heads close together as if in conversation, facing away from the door. Perhaps they still had the element of surprise.

And then the third figure moved to the side, revealing what they'd come for.

There, sitting in a glass case, was a large diamond, glittering atop a stand covered in red velvet. A single light shone down on the jewel, causing the light to refract in rainbow arcs. The third figure bent over, one hand on their knee, gun pointing down as they stared at the diamond.

Three jewel thieves. There were supposed to be four.

Guardian looked at Pyro Storm, who cocked his head in question. "Where's the fourth one?"

Pyro Storm nodded, sounding relieved when he said, "Perfect. Sometimes you have to make decisions on the fly, and whatever repercussions follow are on you. You know there's four, and you can only see three. What do you do?"

Guardian looked back through the window. All three goons now stood around the diamond. They looked like they were waiting for something. Guardian was about to tell Pyro Storm that they should just take the chance the fourth guy was somewhere else when, out of the corner of his eye, he saw the shadows shift beside him. Panic reared its ugly head, squeezing his throat, making it hard to breathe.

*Owen,* he thought, the word rising like a dark star in his head, causing his vision to tunnel. *Oh my god, it's—*

It wasn't Owen.

He'd made a mistake.

The last door on the left was open, the one he'd barely checked. And there, standing with a gun pointed at Pyro Storm's head, eyes narrowed behind the ski mask, was the fourth man, his mouth twisted into a terrible smile. "Well, well, well," he said, voice rough and gravelly. "What do we have here?"

"Shit," Guardian said.

H e stumbled through the door when the man pushed him hard. He managed to stay upright as the three others surrounding the diamond turned toward them.

"Look what I found, boys," their captor said, gun against Pyro Storm's head as the goon forced him into the room. "Seems as if we got a couple of interlopers."

"Interlopers?" Guardian retorted. "I don't even know what that *means.*"

"Not helping," Pyro Storm muttered as the man made them stand side by side, circling them slowly, gun pointed in their direction. The others joined him, all guns raised and trained at Guardian and Pyro Storm.

The fourth man laughed maniacally. "You've fallen right into our trap."

Guardian glared at him. "What the hell are you talking about?"

The man in front of them laughed. "We don't care about the diamond. You're worth far more than that stupid rock will ever be. Trust me when I say that our boss can't wait to get his hands on the both of you."

The man behind them leaned his head next to Guardian's, the gun at the base of his spine. "Let me at him," he whispered. "Come on, what do you say? I wanna peel the skin from his bones and see what kind of sounds he makes."

"Wow," Guardian said. "That was a little dark, even for me. Maybe dial it back a bit? You sound psychotic."

"That's right," the man said. "I *am* psychotic. In fact, that's what everyone calls me. Psycho. Wait. The *Cannibal* Psycho."

"Enough," the man in front of them said. "It's time to end this." He raised his gun again, this time pointing it at Pyro Storm's head.

"Try it," Guardian snarled. "It'll be the last thing you ever do."

The man glanced at him before shrugging. "Okay."

He pulled the trigger.

Time slowed down around Guardian. Blood rushed in his ears as the colors of the world melted like so much wax. The air between the heroes and the goons rippled as if on the surface of a lake. Guardian jerked his head, and Cannibal Psycho flew back against a wall, crumpling to the floor. Guardian paid him no mind, all his focus on the death warrant signed for Pyro Storm.

The spark in his head pulsed brightly as he closed his mind around it once more, familiar, safe, *his*. The bullet slowed, spun around, pointing toward the man who'd fired the gun, the man who had tried to take everything from Guardian.

"Suck on *this*," Guardian snarled, and the bullet hurtled back toward the man, striking him right between the eyes.

# 2

The man blinked as the bullet—really a green foam dart with a plastic suction cup at the end—bounced off his head and fell to the ground.

"You *murdered* me?" the man said, sounding aghast. "What the hell, Nicky." Aaron Bell frowned as he pulled off his ski mask, his dark hair slick with sweat, sticking up at odd angles. "We talked about this. Many, many times. I can't believe I have to repeat this, but I will: We. Don't. *Kill*."

Behind them, a man groaned as he pushed himself away from the wall. "Oh, sweet lord, my bones. My actual *bones*." Guardian glanced over his shoulder to see Miles Kensington pull off his own ski mask with a grimace. "When Jasmine asked me at our daddy-daughter date if I would help out with Nick's training, she didn't mention being flung against a wall."

Guardian rolled his eyes. "Yeah, maybe you should've thought of that before you called yourself Cannibal Psycho."

"Okay," Trey Gibson said, lifting his ski mask until it revealed his face, letting it rest on the top of his head. "So, here's the thing: holding the gun sideways is useless. You can't aim at anything. Movies lied, and they should be ashamed. Gibster, did you know about this?"

"Did I know movies weren't real life?" Gibby asked through the comms. "Yes, Dad."

"A*ha*!" the last man shouted, pointing his own foam-dart gun at the others, swinging it wildly. "Now I will betray *all* of you and—"

"Seth?" a voice said through the comms. "It's Martha. Sorry to interrupt, sweetheart. You sound like you're having fun, but can you ask your uncle to pick up toilet paper after he's done with his betrayal? I forgot to grab some when I went to the store earlier. And you tell him if he comes home with single-ply again because it's cheaper, we're going to have words."

Bob Gray removed his mask and said, "Darn. My betrayal was going to be so neat."

"Wow," Miles said, jumping up and down. "I think . . . I think that cured my back pain. Who knew all it would take was being thrown by telekinesis against a wall? Take *that,* over-priced chiropractor!"

Guardian threw up his hands in disgust. "You are the worst pseudovillains who have ever pseudovillained. Training exercise over. Guardian out." He removed his helmet, glaring at his dad, who tossed the foam dart up and down.

"Your son killed you," Trey told Dad. "That's some Shake-spearean shit right there."

Dad sighed. "Yeah, we'll have to work on it more, I guess. You would think not murdering anyone would be a given, but here we are."

Before Nick could issue a devastating retort that Dad would most likely end up having to tell his therapist about, Seth pulled off his helmet and said, "Nick, you figure out where you went wrong?"

Grumbling under his breath, Nick nodded. "The last door. I didn't check it."

"I was hiding inside," Miles said, sounding rather gleeful. "You know you were supposed to be quiet, right?"

Nick groaned. "It's because I don't have abs yet. And no, you don't get to ask how that explains anything. It just does."

"You should consider doing stadiums," Dad said. "Run-ning stairs will get you in fighting shape. Just don't ask me to do it with you because my knees are shot to hell and I don't want to."

Nick stared at his father in horror. "Dad, *no*."

"Dad—"

"Aaron," Miles said. "I've got this." He walked around Nick and Seth, eying them up and down before stopping in front of the others, crossing his arms over his chest. The others seemed to take that as a signal to also pose, Trey's hands on his hips, Bob tapping the Nerf gun against the side of his head, Dad tossing the dart up and down without even looking at it.

Miles nodded, squared his shoulders, and said, "Dad, *yes*."

"Dad Squad," Trey said, fist-bumping Bob without even looking at him, which, *what*.

Nick groaned. "I'm all for the elderly trying new things, but did you really need to make shirts that said that?"

"We're wearing them right now," Dad said cheerfully, and sure enough, they all unzipped their thin coats to reveal matching shirts that had the same stylized lettering: DAD SQUAD.

"Mine has glittery letters," Trey said, stroking the sparkles on his chest fondly. "Aysha said they bring out my eyes. But I think I'd still wear it even if they didn't. We don't believe in toxic masculinity in our house. Glitter is for everyone."

As if he was a little nervous, Bob said, "I hope you don't mind I have a Dad Squad shirt too, Seth. I know I'm not—you know." He frowned down at his shirt. "Thought about making it Uncle Squad, but . . ."

Seth went to him, and Bob grinned when his nephew hugged him tightly. "It's perfect," Seth said quietly. "More than, even."

"Yeah?" Bob said, face in Seth's hair. "I hoped it would be."

Nick left them to it, going to the diamond still sitting in the glass case. "Where did you get this? It's not real, is it? Ooh, it's so *shiny*." He pressed his face against the glass, causing it to fog up. "I want it."

"Miss Conduct," Dad said, coming to stand next to Nick. "Mateo uses it as part of his drag show. Something about a diamond being a girl's best friend."

Nick sighed. "I think he has a crush on you."

Dad nodded solemnly. "Makes sense. I'm very attractive."

Gagging, Nick said, "Gross!"

"Thanks, kid."

"You can't date Miss Conduct," Nick said, starting to panic. "I get to be the only queer in this family. How dare you try and usurp my throne."

"Or," Dad said, "I can love who I want to, and if that happens to be Mateo, then—"

"As if you could ever handle a drag queen. She'd chew you up and spit you out." He glared at Dad. "And don't tell me if that's something you'd enjoy. I'm scarred enough as it is."

Annoyed, Nick glanced at the others. Miles was doing jumping jacks while exclaiming that his chiropractor wasn't going to believe this, Trey was—for *some* reason—still stroking the glittery letters on his chest, and Bob had an arm wrapped around Seth's shoulders, holding him close.

Momentarily forgetting his father's crimes against humanity, Nick was struck—not for the first time, but perhaps seeing it clearer than he ever had before—by how lucky he was. Ever since the parental figures had been told the truth about their kids, there hadn't been a moment when Nick hadn't felt loved, validated. Even if that meant spending a Friday night in a vacant building that Bob had secured for them to use through his job connections as a super.

His irritation over his father's ridiculousness faded as quickly as it'd arrived. Because here Dad was with the rest of the dumb Dad Squad, working to help Nick become the best hero he could be. He didn't have to be here. None of them did. But they were, and Nick was absurdly touched by their faith in him. If his mom had been here, too, it would've made everything even better.

And Dad was trying. He really was. Ever since he'd resigned from the force and gone to therapy, he'd seemed . . . lighter, somehow. Perfect time for him to grant his son's deepest desire. And really, he'd tried to shoot Seth—with a foam dart, but the point remained the same—so Dad owed Nick.

"What do you say, Pops? Think I'm good enough to go out on my own?"

Everyone else fell silent as Dad's brow furrowed before smoothing out. He laid his hands on Nick's shoulders, hesitating a moment. "I know you think you're ready. And I've seen how hard you've been working in these last weeks."

"But," Nick said, knowing it was coming.

"But," Dad said, "we have to be careful, kid. You've seen what's happened since Seth revealed himself. Are you ready to take the chance that the same thing happens to you?"

"It's gotten a little better," Bob said. "Not as many death threats now that we've changed to an unlisted phone number. And our house hasn't been vandalized in a few weeks, so I count that as a win. The security cameras help."

"It's not just about that, either," Trey said, nodding at Dad as he walked over to them. Dad took a step back, dropping his arms. "I won't speak for your dad, Nick, but you know as well as we do it's not only vandals we're facing."

"Burke," Nick spat, feeling that old familiar anger washing through him.

"Burke," Trey agreed. "Ever since he announced his mayoral run and that he could cure Extraordinaries . . ." He shook his head. "No, not cure, because that implies there's something wrong with you and Seth and others like you."

"I know," Nick said. "But that doesn't mean I can hide forever."

"I get that, kid," Dad said. "I swear I do. But are you ready for the moment it all becomes real? When there are actual bullets instead of foam darts? Forget the bridge. Forget the prom. This is different. Can you stand there and tell me this is something you're *really* ready for?"

Nick was about to open his mouth and say *yes* emphatically, but he stopped himself. His telekinesis was finicky, and he was still trying to get the hang of it. He'd taken on villains Smoke and Ice when they'd attacked Centennial High at prom, but how could he be sure he could do the same thing again?

Nick sighed, shoulders drooping. "I don't know." He scuffed his boot against the ground.

Dad slung an arm around his shoulders. "Don't kick your-self too much over this, okay? We'll figure it out. I'll make you a deal. Let's get through the summer, and we can talk again be-fore you go back to school."

"Fine," Nick grumbled. "But I'm holding you to that. End of summer, we'll talk again." He looked down at the floor. "We could, I don't know, still do these exercises, if you want. I like . . . doing stuff like this with you."

"Me, too, kid," Dad whispered in his hair. "And in case I haven't said it today, I'm proud of you."

"Thanks, Dad," Nick whispered back.

"I love us," Miles announced when Nick and Dad pulled away from each other. "We're the best. Screw Simon Burke. Whatever he's got planned, he won't make it far, not with our daughters, Pyro Storm, Guardian, and the Dad Squad."

"Dads, *no,*" Nick moaned.

"Dads, *yes,*" the men said.

Good people, all.



The Dad Squad had plans to go get a beer or two to celebrate a somewhat successful training session. They left Nick and Seth outside the building, everyone promising they wouldn't stay out too late. Miles reminded them that they were expected promptly at six the following afternoon at the Kensington house for Jazz's seventeenth birthday party. "Don't be late," Miles warned Nick and Seth. "You think Burke is scary? He pales in comparison to my daughter when something doesn't go her way."

Nick shuddered, the image of Jazz wielding her high heels shooting across his brain. No one was as terrifying as Jazz. "We'll be there," he promised. "Probably early to help her get ready, even though she says I shouldn't be allowed to dress any-one, even myself."

Miles looked him up and down, taking in Nick's ripped shorts, a tank top, and his beat-up black Chucks. "Yes, well.

At least you're . . . trying." He winked at Nick before leaving them to catch up with Bob and Trey, who waited at the corner down the street.

Nick hoped Dad would follow without saying anything they'd both regret, but since he was Nick's father, he apparently couldn't help himself. "Be good. What did we talk about?"

"We talked about many things," Nick said, trying to buy time to figure out how to make his father incapable of speech without harming him. "Nothing that needs to be rehashed here, of course, given that I listen to—"

"Public indecency laws exist," Dad said, as if Nick hadn't spoken at all. "I don't want to get a call that you and Seth are grinding up on each other because you can't wait until you're behind closed doors."

"Oh, no," Seth whispered. "I'm standing right here and I wish I wasn't."

"*Dad,*" Nick spat, face on fire. "You're doing this on purpose."

"And you'll never be able to prove it," Dad said. "See you at home? Don't stay out too late. You know she worries."

He ruffled Nick's hair before turning to catch up with the others. Miles and Bob led the way across the intersection, Trey and Dad walking a couple of feet behind them, heads close together as they talked.

Trey and Nick's father had a somewhat complicated relationship, what with Dad having done things while carrying a badge that he never should have. Nick didn't begrudge Trey his anger. He'd been right about the police's role in violence against the Black community, and ever since Dad had quit the force, Trey had softened, especially when Dad had started going to therapy. When it'd all come out into the open, it'd caused Nick to question everything he'd thought cops stood for, the idea of good versus evil, a clear delineation that allowed no room for shades of gray. Dad was trying, but Nick was, too. He still had a way to go before he could completely dismantle the idea that police deserved hero worship, an unearned idea that existed only because his father had worn a uniform. They both owed it to their friends.

"Does Dad . . ." He looked at Seth. "Does he seem different to you? Ignore him embarrassing me for the fun of it. I'm not talking about that."

Though the temperatures had lowered slightly, it was still disgustingly humid. Nick felt sorry for Seth, who wore a hoodie with the hood pulled up over his head, giving him a bit of anonymity. Ever since he'd removed his helmet and revealed himself to the world on prom night, Seth had a hard time going out in public, seeing as how his face had been plastered over every newspaper in the country, along with a never-ending cycle of coverage on 24/7 news channels. Nick had tried watching, at least at first, but it soon grew tiresome, what with certain pundits screaming that Seth was dangerous, that he could destroy the very fabric of society if he chose to. This was darkly hysterical, seeing as how Seth, while strong, was a marshmallow who always tried to avoid hurting others.

"Different how?" Seth asked as he started down the sidewalk, taking Nick's hand in his and pulling him along.

"I don't know," Nick admitted. "He seems . . . happier."

Seth arched an eyebrow, squeezing Nick's hand. "That's a good thing."

"I know." He struggled to find the right words to make Seth understand. "It's weird, though. I have this . . . memory." He scrunched up his face, thinking hard. "But that doesn't seem quite right because I don't have any context for it. It *feels* real, and not, all at the same time. You know how you're having a vivid dream right before you wake up, and when you do, it still feels like the dream is happening?"

"Sure," Seth said. "A waking dream."

"Right," Nick said. "Maybe that's it. Because I think I'd remember if I found my father crying in his room."

Seth frowned. "Crying? About what?"

Frustrated, Nick huffed out a breath. "I don't know. All I

remember is him sitting on the edge of his bed, and he didn't know I was there. But I was. And I wanted to go to him. I didn't. It felt . . . personal."

"It was just a dream, Nicky. You're probably overtired from working as hard as you have."

"Right," Nick said slowly. That had to be it. "Still, he smiles more."

Seth grinned. "Yeah, I saw that. It looks good on him. How's it going with him and Cap?"

"Good," Nick said as they stopped at an intersection, cars backed up across the crosswalk. He bumped the call button, waiting for the light to change so they could continue on. He did his best to ignore an old, ripped poster hanging just above the call button that read SAVE OUR CHILDREN. "It's still early days, but they got their license and are ready to start building their client list. Dad thinks Cap is having the time of his life. Said they should've opened their own private investigative agency years ago."

Rodney Caplan, the former chief of police, had resigned from his job a few months before. It was either that or be forced out, and Cap wouldn't give those in power the satisfaction.

"Sounds like things are going well, then."

Nick sighed as the light changed, and they crossed, walking around the cars still gridlocked on the street. A cabbie leaned out his open window, yelling at them as he honked the horn obnoxiously. Nick waved back. "A little too well, if you ask me."

Seth rolled his eyes. "Oh, boy. Nick, we're allowed to be happy."

"I know," he said quickly. "It's just . . . it's like we're waiting for the other shoe to drop. Burke. Owen. Stupid Rebecca Firestone, oh my god, just her *name* is enough to make me want to punch something." Regardless of all the villains they'd fought, Nick Bell's *true* nemesis was always going to be the reporter turned press secretary. At least when she'd been a reporter, he'd been able to keep track of her bullshit. Now that she wasn't on television every day, it made Nick nervous, wondering what fresh hell she was planning.

"We'll figure it out," Seth said. "Whatever happens, we'll handle it like we always have."

"With me complaining about everything and wondering why so many people seem to want to kill teenagers?"

Seth chuckled. "Together. We'll handle it together."

Nick grinned at him. "Damn right we are. Motherfreaking Team Pyro Storm and Guardian with Support from Jazz and Gibby. Okay, that name needs some work, but I've got ideas that I'm workshopping. I'll run it by you when I've got something concrete."

"Looking forward to it," Seth said dryly. "I'm sure it'll be as lasting as the first name, or the Twitter account you haven't touched in weeks."

Nick scowled, using his arm to wipe the sweat from his brow. "I turned off the notifications because *way* too many people were sending us nudes. Seriously, you find out the identity of an Extraordinary, and the first thing you do is send them pictures of your junk? Men are gross. And some women, too. The things I've seen. The last time before I quit checking it, a poly commune in Oregon sent a video inviting you to live with them and partake in their nightly orgies. Guess what the video showed?"

"An orgy?"

"An orgy," Nick agreed. "I guess that's the price of fame. You get famous enough, and people want you to see their genitals and invite you to cult sex parties. Explains a lot, if you think about it."

"No more," Seth pleaded. "Dear god, no more." He pulled Nick off the sidewalk, leading him through a gate to a small park. It was vaguely familiar, but for the life of him, he couldn't figure out why. An empty playground, the chains of the swings creaking in a hot breeze. A stone pavilion surrounded by trees, and for a moment, Nick thought he'd been here before, hiding behind a tree, listening as . . . someone . . . what. Talked on a phone? Who would it have been?

The hairs on the back of his neck stood on end as he pushed the thought away. "What are we doing here?"

Seth glanced back over his shoulder. "Do you know what today is?"

Uh-oh. Not Seth's birthday. That was in December. It was a Friday in June, so it wasn't as if he'd missed a holiday, or so he hoped. "Uh, yes?" Nick said, trying to keep his voice even while his thoughts whirred frantically. "Of course. Today is . . . today. A *special* day. The . . . best . . . day?"

"That's right," he said, and Nick *knew* Seth was giving him shit. "It is the best day. I'm glad you remembered."

Nick groaned as Seth led him toward the swings. Seth helped him take his backpack off, setting it on the sand under the swings before pushing Nick to sit down. He dropped his own backpack as Nick grabbed the chains, letting his feet make divots in the sand. "You should probably remind me what makes today special so we're both on the same page."

"Close your eyes."

Nick did. He heard Seth open his bag and pull out something that crinkled, like plastic. He felt Seth take his hand, tugging it away from the chain and turning his palm up. A moment later, Seth placed something in his hand.

"Okay," Seth said, sounding as if he were sitting on the swing next to Nick's. "You can open your eyes now."

Nick did, looking at what Seth had given him. As soon as he saw it, he knew. He knew that Seth was it for him. He didn't know how he'd gotten so lucky to have someone like Seth love him despite . . . well, despite Nick's everything, but he'd never take it for granted.

A package of Skwinkles Salsagheti. Watermelon flavored.

"Today, we've been together for seven months," Seth said. "Officially."

"Holy shit," Nick said in a choked voice. "I freaking love you, dude. Don't ever leave me."

Seth laughed, lifting his feet as he began to swing. "Deal, Nicky. And I love you, too."

Flustered—they'd gone from bros, to bros who kissed, to bros who kissed *and* were in love because *what*—Nick said, "I didn't get you anything. I suck. I'm sorry."

"Nah," Seth said. "The great thing about Skwinkles Salsagheti is that we can share it."

And so they did. For the next hour, they sat on the swings, laughing, Nick peeling off strands of candy and wiggling his eyebrows, putting one end of the candy in his mouth, holding the other out for Seth. His boyfriend didn't hesitate, leaning over and taking the other end between his teeth before sucking it in. Closer, closer, until they kissed, sticky, sweet, and oh, how Seth smiled against Nick's mouth, and for a moment, Nick could pretend that nothing else mattered. That they were just two queer boys without a care in the world.

*This is what I fight for,* Nick thought as he gave up trying to swing and instead tackled Seth to the ground, lying on top of him and deciding that making out in the park was pretty damn rad. *This is what's important. Not powers, not villains who want to kill us. This. Just this.*

No public indecency laws were broken, though not for lack of trying.

Seth and Nick parted ways an hour later, Nick promising Seth he'd text as soon as he got home. He waved at Seth as he shouldered his backpack and headed toward home, his Guardian costume a heavy weight, always reminding him it was there.

He entered his neighborhood, lost in thoughts of Seth and the noises he made when Nick bit down on the skin beneath his ears. It was the best noise, really. Light surprise with a darker undercurrent of something more, something they were building toward. Not there yet, but Nick thought he'd be ready sooner rather than later. It made him nervous and excited in equal measure.

As he reached the walkway that led to his darkened house,

he stopped and frowned. The skin on the back of his neck prickled, as if . . .

As if someone stood behind him. He didn't know how he knew, but he did. The neighborhood was quiet. No one else out on the streets. A perfect time to be attacked.

Gripping the straps on his backpack, he whirled around, teeth bared in a snarl, ready to kick whoever's ass had followed him home.

A figure stood on the sidewalk in front of the house, watching him. Black, bulky costume made up of heavy armor. Steel-toed boots. A helmet that covered the head completely, an opaque sheet of plastic on the front.

An Extraordinary, one of the most powerful.

He relaxed as TK lifted their hands to the sides of their helmet, pulling it off in one smooth motion.

There, standing with a quiet smile, was his mother.

"Hey, kid," Jennifer Bell said, running a hand through her short blond hair, glistening with sweat. "How'd training go? Your dad texted me and said you shot him in the head." She snorted. "Wish I could've been there to see the look on his face."

Nick groaned, heart slowing to a somewhat normal rhythm now that he knew he wasn't about to be attacked. "He's such a freaking drama queen. Did he tell you that he shot first? Because he *did*. What did he think I was going to do? *Not* protect my man?"

She grinned as she moved up the walkway, joining her son near the porch. She was approaching fifty but was in much better shape than Nick would ever be, lean and thinly muscled underneath all that armor. He took more after her than he did his father, his eyes exactly like hers. "And they say chivalry is dead." She kissed his cheek, her lips warm. "Don't worry, Nicky. I told him the same thing. If anyone came after you or your father like that, they'd be lucky if they were able to walk away on their own."

Nick made a face. "Oh, so you can say stuff like that, but when *I* do, I'm told that violence should always be a last resort."

"And it should," Mom said, tugging him up the porch steps. "I'm feeling like ordering takeout for dinner. Good with you?"

"Hell yes," Nick said.

She grinned as she unlocked the front door. "Thought as much. And if you promise not to try and shoot your father again, I'll tell you about the idiots I stopped from trying to rob a farmer's market tonight. Just rob a bank, cowards."

Nick stopped, swaying slightly. The words *rob a bank* echoed in his head, insistent yet faint, as if they too came from a far-away dream. A dream that tried to force its way to the surface, but then Mom squeezed his hand and the strange feeling melted away as if it'd never been there at all. He came back to himself, feeling right as rain.

"All right?" she asked, sounding concerned.

He shook his head. "Yeah, I . . . just got lost in my head for a second. Must be tired."

She watched him for a long moment before saying, "You've been working hard, so that's to be expected. Come on, let's get you fed and we can have an early night."

"Deal," Nick said promptly as he walked through the door, flipping the light switch just inside. "Did the robbers scream when you showed up? Please tell me they screamed."

Mom laughed loudly as she closed the door behind them, and Nick thought it was one of the best sounds he'd ever heard. He didn't know where he'd be without her, but thankfully, he'd never have to find out. Mom was here, just like she'd always been. Dad, too. They were good. They were healthy. Whole. They stood together so they didn't have to struggle apart.

Everything was fine.

# 3

After the Attack on Centennial High when Seth revealed himself as Pyro Storm, Nova City had captured the world's attention. Seth was at the center of it all. People who called themselves "experts" screeched the loudest, shouting at anyone who would listen that the students at Centennial High were in danger, that Seth Gray could kill them all if he wanted to. "What happens if he fails a test?" one such man asked, his eyebrows looking like they were trying to eat his entire face. "Is he going to hold the teacher hostage until they give him the grade he wants? Is *that* what we want for our children?"

"Do you have kids?" the newscaster had asked him. "A teenager, perhaps?"

"No," the man had replied. "Children are terrible, filthy creatures ruled by their hormones, and I had a vasectomy in 1997 to ensure I'd never have to suffer because of them. But I've *studied* Extraordinaries for the last two weeks, so I know what I'm talking about. They are going to *kill* you. They're going to kill your entire *families*. And even worse, they'll take your jobs! Who is going to want to hire a *normal* person when they can have someone who can shoot lasers from their eyes? Is *this* the America the Founding Fathers wanted for us? Let me answer that question for you: no, it's *not*."

(Which, of course, led Nick down a rabbit hole, but as far as he could tell, Thomas Jefferson hadn't been an Extraordinary, unless being the ultimate racist douchebag was a power.)

The fallout from Seth's big reveal had been tremendous: not

only was he kicked out of Centennial High, but the weirdos came out of the woodwork; people were obsessed with the idea of someone able to create fire out of nothing. Some called him the devil. Others called him a god. And more than a few sent their underwear in the mail, something that Bob and Martha had *not* expected, if the looks on their faces were any indication. "I suppose I could wash them and mail them back like the others," Martha said, lifting the tenth pair of boxer briefs they'd received with her thick, yellow cleaning gloves. "It's the nice thing to do. Darn, I'm all out of stamps. Silly me, what was I thinking?" She threw them away, removed the gloves, and then washed her hands with water so scalding, the kitchen filled with steam.

In the weeks before and after Gibby's graduation, Seth hadn't been able to go out in public without being accosted, either by reporters or by people who were after the million-dollar bounty. He'd spent the beginning of their summer break either in his house or in Nick's, the blinds drawn over the windows, everyone trying to pretend it would go away on its own.

Seth seemed to take it all in stride. Nick kept a careful eye on him, studying him, wanting to make sure that as soon as he saw *any* sign of regret, he'd be there, ready to help Seth work through it. He owed Seth that and more; after all, he'd successfully diverted attention away from Nick's part in the Attack on Centennial High, knowing Nick wasn't ready yet for the world to know what he could do. The guilt Nick felt over this was enormous. A good Extraordinary, Nick knew, was kind, just, and above all else, brave. Nick wanted to be brave. He really did. He owed Seth that much. But try as he might, he couldn't bring himself to do it. He saw the anger on people's faces, the way they spat and snarled about a *child* having the power Seth did. Sure, there were quite a few people who were on their side. It was mostly young people who took to the streets the world over in support of letting the Extraordinaries peacefully coexist, but the news seemed hell-bent on doomsday scenarios, letting guests on their shows or in op-eds give dire warnings about superpowered people and what it meant for the future of humanity.

At a meeting with all of them a few weeks back (the support group, something Nick had scoffed over at first but had begun to appreciate more and more), Mom had suggested they all limit their time online and avoid watching the news as much as possible. The other adults had agreed, and Nick had barely put up a fight, mostly relieved at the idea. He felt a little bad that his readers wouldn't be getting an update anytime soon on his fic, but every time he'd tried to write a new chapter, it always ended up as a stream-of-consciousness diatribe (with*out* paragraph breaks) about how some adults were a little too obsessed with a teenager.

Seth didn't go out as Pyro Storm as much as he used to and anytime Pyro Storm was needed, Mom went with him, while one of the other adults was in the secret lair with whoever was on comms.

It'd been going reasonably well until two weeks ago.

It should've been an easy call: a fire at a high-rise in midtown. A blaze had broken out due to faulty wiring on the fifteenth floor. The fire had spread quickly. Everyone below the fifteenth floor had been able to evacuate, but those above were trapped, the elevators fried, the stairways blocked by thick, noxious smoke, making it damn near impossible to see anything. Nick's mother—TK—had gotten there first, followed quickly by Pyro Storm, cameras tracking him hurtling across the sky, leaving a trail of flames in his wake. In a shocking moment that took over the news cycle once more, TK had shattered a window on the side of the building before moving out of the way. Pyro Storm took her place and had *pulled* the fire out, gathering it into a great, writhing ball above his head that rivaled the brightness of the sun. He'd then leaned back, horizontal to the ground, and hurtled the ball into the sky, where it dissipated safely high above Nova City. TK and Pyro Storm had helped people get out of the building, working in tandem with the Nova City Fire Department.

And when they'd helped the last person to the street—a six-year-old girl named Luciana with a soot-covered face and stars in her eyes as she looked up at her rescuer—the police had descended.

They'd tried to arrest Pyro Storm and TK.

The only reason they hadn't was because the people Pyro Storm and TK had saved formed a wall in front of them, arms linked, joined by others who'd stopped to gape at the fiery destruction from above and had seen the rescue. They were threatened with pepper spray and Tasers, but hadn't moved. In an image that had been exalted and condemned in equal measure, a photographer with the AP had captured the moment when little Luciana shoved her way to the front, her hands on her hips as she glared up at the cop before her, her dress slightly singed.

LEAVE THEM ALONE! the caption had read under the photo, her words like a battle cry that others picked up and began to chant. The only reason it hadn't devolved into complete chaos was because some of the firefighters had joined the line, telling the cops to get *back,* that Pyro Storm and TK had saved dozens of lives.

But by then, the Extraordinaries were already gone.

Seth didn't go out much after that, even though Mom had told him he'd done exactly what he was supposed to. In fact, the only time he suited up after was to help Nick with his training. He believed in Nick, in Guardian, and Nick didn't think he trusted anyone as much as he did Seth, not even Dad and Mom. Nick listened.

Because the nightmares he had were vicious things, filled with smoke and ice and shadows, the people he loved in danger, and Nick unable to do anything to help them. Sometimes it was Seth. Other times, Gibby and Jazz. Most times, though, it was Dad. Dad, a band of smoke wrapped around his chest.

Never Mom, though. He never dreamed she was in danger.

It was made all that much harder by Simon Burke's rising presence in Nova City ever since he'd announced his candidacy for mayor.

At rallies with thousands of people he stoked the flames of fear, playing the role of a grieving father whose son had betrayed him, all while condemning the actions of Extraordinaries, Pyro Storm in particular. "For any of them who say they want to help us, there will be a dozen more hidden in the shadows wanting to take away your lives and liberties," he said, working the crowds into a frenzy. "I know. Believe me, I know this better than anyone. I've seen firsthand what these people are capable of. I . . ." He blinked rapidly, looking away as his throat worked, people cheering, cheering. Burke raised his hand to quiet them down. "My son was—*is* one of them. I failed him as a father, and that is my greatest mistake, one I still grapple with. I will *not* fail Nova City. You have my solemn promise that if you bestow upon me the great honor of being your next mayor, I will do everything within my power to protect you, to protect your children so that you no longer have to cower in fear from those who want to destroy your way of life. We will take our city *back,* and nothing—not even Extraordinaries—will stop us. Elect me, and I will make Nova City the crown jewel of this great country once again!"

*"In Burke we trust! In Burke we trust!"*

Mom said he wasn't as dangerous as he seemed, that he was bloviating, talking himself up, wanting to stoke the fires of outrage to get people on his side.

"We can handle him," she said. "If it should come to that."

He trusted her.

She was his mother, after all.

I t wasn't all bad, Nick often thought. They were alive. They were together. They were a team, and nothing could tear them apart.

Jasmine Kensington, in all her resplendent glory, stood in front of the large oval mirror in the corner of her room. Her brunette hair had been styled in a bun wrapped in thin braids with green ribbons. She wore a white dress patterned with red flowers surrounded by leaves and vines of green, the hem stopping just below her knees. Her feet were bare, red toenails digging into the carpet as she turned this way and that, a quiet smile on her face.

Nick sat on her four-poster bed, back against the headboard, phone forgotten beside him as he watched his friend. Gibby and Seth were in Jazz's bathroom, their voices low as Gibby tried to smooth down Seth's unruly curls.

"What do you think?" Jazz asked, looking at him in the mirror.

"You look like a princess," Nick said honestly.

She laughed as she spun in a slow circle, her dress flaring around her legs. "Is that a good thing?"

"It is. You'll be the center of attention, just like you should be. Happy birthday, Jazz."

"Thank you." She nodded at herself in the mirror before turning around and going to her ridiculously oversized closet, rows of clothes on one wall, shelf after shelf of shoes on the other. She put her hands on her hips as she looked up and down the wall of shoes before settling on a pair of ballet slipper–type flats that matched the green on her dress and the ribbons in her hair. She came back out of the closet and dropped the shoes at the foot of the bed before sitting down against Nick. He spread his legs, letting her get comfortable, back to his chest, careful to keep her dress from getting wrinkled but still positioned so they could see Gibby and Seth. Nick snorted when Jazz pinched his thigh. "You look nice, too."

"Eh," Nick said. "I feel a little underdressed compared to you." He wore a pair of black jeans and a thin, baby-blue button-down shirt, the top few buttons unfastened, sleeves rolled up.

She shrugged as he rested his chin on the top of her head. "You tried. That's all that matters."

"Gee, thanks. Just what a guy wants to hear."

She snorted. "You can wear whatever you want, Nicky. I'm just giving you crap. It's not as if this is going to be a big party."

"It's catered," Nick reminded her. "And your dad hired a waiter. Mateo told me he's making more at your party than he does in a month working elsewhere."

"I told him he didn't have to," Jazz said. "I wanted him to be my guest, but he said he'd rather make rent than stand around drinking sparkling cider. I think he gets antsy when he doesn't have something to do. Sounds like someone else I know."

Nick sighed. "Can't argue with that. I tried to get a job for the summer, but Mom and Dad changed their minds. Said they wanted me to focus on training and school prep instead of trying to find seasonal work on top of it."

She titled her head back to look up at him. "Wasn't your mom talking about going back to work after your dad resigned?"

"Yeah, she mentioned that a couple of times, but I . . ." He frowned before shaking his head. For some reason, he'd had the momentary thought that his mom had always worked, but that wasn't right. She'd quit a few years after he was born, wanting to put all her focus on raising him. "She hasn't made any concrete plans yet. I think she was worried about Dad and Cap starting up with the PI agency, so I think she put that on hold for a little bit."

"Makes sense," Jazz said. "Maybe after you graduate. I bet she's waiting until you go to college before dusting off her law degree. She'll need something different to do that isn't raising you."

Nick sighed. "I hope that's not it. I don't like the idea of her putting her life on hold just because of me, you know? She needs more than that."

"Which is why she became TK," Jazz reminded him. "Remember?"

He did. That's right. He hadn't worked up the courage to ask her about that decision, at least not completely. She'd been there, standing on McManus Bridge next to Dad, watching as Shadow Star failed to bring Nova City to its knees. Though Nick hadn't known it then, it'd been her who'd saved him when he'd fallen from the bridge, the metal struts raining down around him. Well, sort of. It'd *mostly* been her, but Nick thought it'd also been his own latent powers manifesting, breaking through the haze of Concentra that coursed through his blood. Which, to be honest, didn't make much sense, but Mom had told him he still had a lot to learn about powers and being an Extraordinary. She would know, seeing as how she'd been at it for years.

And that had all come out later when he'd found the tape in the attic, the one that'd shown his mother as a telekinetic, manipulating a glass of water to the astonishment of a young Aaron Bell and Simon Burke. When he'd confronted his parents about what he'd seen, they'd broken down, revealing the truth of what she could do, who she'd once been.

Guardian, the protector of Nova City.

"I guess," Nick said to Jazz. "And she seems good with how things are now. She's helping me to figure out how to use my powers."

"She's good at what she does," Jazz said. "And between her and Seth, you couldn't ask for better teachers."

"Yeah," Nick said. They glanced at the open bathroom door where Gibby was telling Seth he should just shave his head, Seth grumbling that his head was too lumpy for that. Jazz dropped her voice near a whisper. "Gibby says her parents have calmed down a bit after everything that happened."

After the rightful honor of valedictorian had been unfairly stripped from her in the aftermath of the Attack on Centennial High, Nick wouldn't have blamed her for letting it all weigh her down. If he'd been in her position, he didn't think he'd have handled it with as much grace as Gibby. She'd been angry, sure, but hadn't let it hold her back. She was already looking beyond school to the future, and what she could do to effect change in Nova City.

Nick shook his head. "Enough serious stuff. Today is about you, and I need to apologize up front because I recently discovered I do *not* know how to wrap presents without using six feet of tape. It looks like a football, but I promise it's not."

She rolled her eyes. "You didn't have to get me anything. I

told you that. I'm just happy you're here. And besides, it's only going to be people in the know at the party, so if anything, we can try and piss you off to get your powers to work and you can unwrap it for me."

Nick groaned. "There has to be a better way for that shit to work. I can't believe I threw your dad against a wall."

Jazz snorted. "Yeah, well, he had it coming. Cannibal Psycho?" She grimaced. "That was a little much."

Nick laughed. "Nah. He was having fun with it. It won't always be that way, but we should appreciate it while we have it."

Jazz frowned at him. "That was uncharacteristically mature. Quick, think of something stupid for us to do that'll break at least four laws but doesn't involve you jumping into a river wearing drag-queen jewelry."

Nick shuddered. "Okay, so, here's a fun idea: let's never talk about that again and instead focus on other things that are much more important." He glanced at the bathroom before lowering his voice, going for nonchalant. "You and Gibby going to . . . you know?"

"Are we going to what?" she asked, tilting her head back to look up at him.

"*You* know," Nick said, waggling his eyebrows.

"I do," Jazz said, "but I just want to see if you can say it out loud."

"I can! I do it all the time!"

"Cool," Jazz said. "Then you should have no problem doing it right now."

"Why are you like this?" Nick muttered, face aflame. Then, because he refused to let Jazz win, he said, "Are you and Gibby going to make the sex?"

Jazz grimaced. "Never mind. I don't want to talk to you anymore."

"You *asked* me to elaborate!"

"And now I wish I hadn't," Jazz said. "People are allowed to change their minds."

Nick groaned. "That's what I get for asking a lesbian for sex tips."

"Is that what you were doing? Question: when you and Seth finally have sex—which, take your time, whenever you're ready—are you going to use your powers to like, float lube over to you? That's what *I'd* do if I was telekinetic." Her eyes widened. "Speaking of, what other sex things could you do involving your powers? Could you, I don't know, stretch your—"

Nick sat up in a panic, putting his hand over her mouth—carefully, so he wouldn't ruin her makeup and cause her to bite him. "Are you *insane*?"

She smiled against his hand. "Oh, please, like that hasn't crossed your mind."

"It *hasn't*!"

She shoved his hand away. "Liar. I bet that's one of the first things you thought of after we were done almost dying."

"It wasn't!" This was a lie given that, for least a night or two, Nick found himself alone in his bedroom, hand shoved down the front of his shorts, gripping himself as Fantasy Seth moaned in his ear, asking him if he wanted to prep himself with his powers. This, of course, led to an image of Nick doing just that, and then accidently going too far and turning himself inside out, Seth covered in gore. Nick did not masturbate for three days after that. It was the longest three days of his life.

"Riiight," Jazz said. "I totally believe you. At least when you guys get around to doing it, you'll be able to answer your dad's question if Seth can orgasm fire or not."

Nick crossed arms grumpily, eyeing her with disdain. "Why are you *like* this?"

"Because it brings me joy." She softened, patting his knee. "Condoms have an expiration date, Nicky. It's like, five years, or something. You should probably use them so you don't have to go back to the store and run into more doors while trying to flee."

"Yet again, not one of my better moments," Nick muttered.

Then, with a glance at the attached bathroom to make sure Gibby and Seth weren't coming out, he added, "We're getting there. We've got the making out thing down. It's just all the rest that we haven't quite worked our way up to." Hands *above* clothes was pretty damn good. Hands *under* clothes meant crossing a line he still wasn't sure if he was quite ready for. Seth seemed fine keeping things as they were, at least for now. Neither of them pushed for something they couldn't take back. It would happen, one day, but on their terms. As awkward as it was to talk about (at least for Nick), they were honest about this with each other.

"I'm just messing with you," Jazz said. "There's no rush. You'll know when the time is right."

"How did you know?" Nick asked. He frowned. "Is that something we can ask each other? It *feels* like something we can ask each other, but that might only be because we don't quite understand healthy boundaries."

"Don't I know it," Jazz said, smoothing down her dress so it wouldn't get wrinkled. "We talked about it a lot before we ever did anything. What we wanted, what we didn't want. And it was a lot of trial and error." She shrugged. "It wasn't perfect because we didn't know what we were doing. But we took our time and kept checking in with each other. Not exactly the most romantic thing, but it's better to ask than to assume."

"Sounds complicated," Nick admitted, uncomfortable, but pushing through it. "I . . . want to? And don't, at the same time. I don't know."

Jazz smiled at him. "You'll figure it out, Nicky. There's no deadline. You don't have to do anything until you're ready. Same with Seth. It's not a race."

"I know," Nick said. "But—"

"No buts," Jazz said. "You're either ready, or you aren't. It's that simple. And there's nothing wrong with not being ready to take that step. It's a big deal, Nick."

"Is it?" he asked. "Because isn't virginity just a construct used to—"

"Stop it," she said, and he deflated. "You don't need to make excuses, Nicky. It's okay to wait."

"What if we don't have time?" Nick asked dully.

Jazz hesitated, brow furrowing. Nick was about to make a joke, telling her he was just kidding, but something stopped him, the words on the tip of his tongue but going no further. Jazz opened her mouth, but someone else spoke instead.

"Time for what?" Seth asked, and Jazz and Nick jerked their heads toward him. Seth stood in the doorway to the bathroom, leaning against the frame, arms crossed. He wore black slacks and a red dress shirt, complete with a white bow tie with little red flames imprinted on it. Nick's breath caught in his chest at the sight of him and, not for the first time, he wondered how he'd gotten so lucky to have someone like Seth by his side.

"What were you talking about?" Gibby asked, pushing by Seth and coming into the room. Her tight pants were torn at the knees, wallet chain dangling on her hip. Her collared shirt matched Jazz's dress—white with red and green flowers—her head freshly shaved, skull gleaming in the low light. "It looks serious." She crossed the room, stopping next to the bed, leaning over and kissing Jazz on the forehead before sitting down next to her, feet on the floor. "Did something happen?"

"Nope," Jazz said before Nick could steer the conversation back to dangerous waters. "Everything is good. Just talking with Nick about the party. You both look wonderful." She squeezed Nick's knee, letting him know she understood.

"Thanks," Seth said, coming to the bed. He stopped next to it, standing above them. "It's . . . nice. Having a night off." He smiled down at Nick. "You good?"

Nick almost blurted *TAKE ME NOW,* but thankfully caught himself at the last moment. "I'm good. Jazz is right. You look hot as balls."

"Yeah?" Seth said, smile growing. "Exactly what I was going for. Good to know you approve."

"Tonight is going to be the best," Jazz said. "I swear to god, if anyone thinks of crashing my party and monologizing about how evil they are, I'm going to handle it myself. It will not be slow. It will not be kind. My wrath will be unending, and whoever comes will regret ever being born."

They all stared at her.

"What?" she asked primly. "Do I have lipstick on my teeth?"

"I'm so glad you're on our side," Nick said honestly. "Because you are terrifying in the best way possible."

"I'd make a pretty good supervillain," Jazz agreed. "You're lucky I don't plan on switching sides because it'd be over for you bitches if I did."

"Don't we know it," Gibby said, grinning at her girlfriend.

"You're right," Nick announced. "Enough with all of this. Tonight is about Jazz. And a-one! And a-*two*. And a— Haaaaappy birthday to you—"

The others joined, off-key and terrible. But Jazz didn't seem to mind. She blushed, looking away, obviously pleased. When they finished, she clapped, and Nick felt a little better. His friends were right. This was the important thing. Them, together, happy and alive and pretending, at least for one night, that they didn't have a care in the world.

# 4

The party was in full swing as they descended the stairs. Nick could hear the thrum of voices above the sound of Jazz's favorite pop travesties filling the air, the beat thumping. He peeled off from his friends at the large hallway closet near the front door, planning on grabbing lip balm from his backpack before joining the party. Nick reminded himself to take as many pictures as possible as he pulled open the closet door.

Only to see two people inside, stepping apart quickly, clothes in disarray.

Nick blinked, unsure of what he was seeing until it came into a sharp and horrifying focus.

There, on the left, wearing an ill-fitted suit and a guilty expression, was Chris Morton. Officer Rookie, the cop Dad had taken under his wing and worked with at the Extraordinaries Division before he'd resigned. The Rook's face was flushed as he coughed, looking anywhere but at Nick, lips shiny, hair in disarray as if hands had been running through it. He had grown out his beard, too, and it wasn't quite as patchy as it'd once been.

Nick turned his head slowly to look at the other person standing in the closet, a slender, tall figure with short black hair and dark eyes that sparkled with barely disguised mirth.

Mateo. AKA Miss Conduct.

"What," Nick said stupidly. "What. What. *What*."

Mateo grabbed Nick by the arm, pulling him into the closet and shutting the closet door behind him. Distantly, Nick wondered why the Kensingtons needed a closet large enough to fit three people—one looking like he wanted to sink into the floor, another gaping and sputtering in shock, and a third who was obviously trying not to laugh.

"Nicholas," Mateo said, failing to smother his laughter. "Thank you for joining us. So, I'm sure you have questions about what you just saw. You see, when a consenting adult meets another consenting adult, sometimes they—"

"You're a *homosexual*?" Nick hissed at Officer Rookie. "When the hell were you going to share *that* piece of important information? How dare you keep such a necessary thing from me!"

The Rook sighed, looking toward the ceiling. "You're going to make this a thing, aren't you?"

"My *existence*," Nick groaned, clutching his head in his hands. "It hurts. Everything hurts."

Mateo sobered slightly. "Nick, this may come as a surprise, but not everything has to do with you. Chris and I are—"

"Chris," Nick said. "You're calling him *Chris*."

Mateo squinted at him. "Well, yeah. That's his name."

"I know that! But you're saying it like . . . *Chris*. Like how I say *Seth*." His eyes widened, so much so that he thought they'd pop out of his head and land wetly on the floor. "Oh my god, you like him!"

"I do," Mateo said. "Quite a bit, in fact."

The Rookie shuffled his feet. "Ah. That's . . . um. So. There's—me, too," he managed to finish with a strangled gasp.

Nick narrowed his eyes as he glanced between the two of them. "This is real? Like, you're serious about this?"

"We are," Mateo said. "Still early days yet, but we're . . ."

"Doing this," Officer Rookie said firmly.

Nick glared at him. "If you do *anything* to hurt Mateo, I'll kick your ass."

He blinked. "Uh, noted. And that threat works a bit more now that you can . . . you know." He wiggled his fingers. Nick wanted to scold him for reducing his powers down to a finger wave, but he was on a roll.

"Good," Nick said, staring a beat longer before turning to

Mateo. "And you, you're wonderful and perfect and I still sort of wish I could be you when I grow up."

"As you should," Mateo said with a sniff.

"But if *you* do anything to hurt the Rook—*Chris*—you'll have to answer to me. He's one of the best people I know, and I'm really protective of him. He deserves everything good, especially after getting dragged into all this bullshit."

Chris softened, smiling as if relieved. "Thanks, Nicky. That means a lot, coming from you."

Nick nodded. "You deserve it." He looked down at his hands. "It . . . helps, you know? Knowing you don't care about Mateo being an Extraordinary." Then in a quieter voice, "You don't care about that, right?"

He relaxed slightly when Chris wrapped an arm around his shoulders, tugging him close. Nick went willingly, even if Chris's beard needed to make friends with a razor immediately.

"I don't," Chris said. "Never have, never will." He hesitated. Then, "If you're anything like me, you're probably a little worried about everything."

"Still a fan of euphemisms, I see."

Chris jostled him a little. "Nick."

"Yeah, yeah. I hear you."

"I hope so. Because I mean it when I say I've got your back, Nicky. I know a lot of things are still up in the air—"

"That was also a euphemism."

"—but life can't stop just because of it. I want to be happy, you know? And Mateo makes me happy. It's not about what he can do, but who he is as a person. And I happen to like that person a lot. The whole turning-his-body-into-electricity thing is just an added bonus."

Nick sniffled. Regardless of what else he was, he was still a ridiculous romantic. And he could hear the sincerity in Chris's words, so he had to ask the most important question. "Have you seen him perform in drag?"

Chris laughed. "I have. He's . . . well. He's something else. Both in and out of drag."

"Then you have my blessing," Nick announced magnanimously as he pulled away. "I know you were probably wondering about that, so rest easy in the knowledge that I approve, and you no longer have to hide in the closet. Shout your love from the rooftops, Chris."

Chris paled, eyes wide and frantic. "No one said anything about *love*—" A slow smile bloomed on his face. "Holy shit, you called me by my name. Twice."

"I did," Nick said. "You're welcome. Now, if you'll pardon me, I have a party to attend where I will most likely accidentally tell everyone what I've witnessed. I hope you didn't expect me to keep this a secret. I have ADHD, so I tend to hyperfocus on things that confuse me. And this is very, very confusing."

"You can't use that as an *excuse*—"

"That's ableist, and I won't stand for it. Of course I can." And with that, he turned and exited the closet, about to bellow that he'd discovered new love and that it was as frightening as it was celebratory. But right before he did, he glanced back over his shoulder to see Mateo cupping Chris's face, leaning forward to kiss him sweetly. They looked . . . happy. Stupidly, wonderfully happy.

Nick decided that maybe others didn't need to know about it, at least not yet, and probably not from him. Love, Nick knew, was like trust: a fragile thing that needed time to grow. But the more it did, the stronger it became, and he hoped they both found that in each other.

The backyard had been lit up with strings of lights hanging from the overhang on the back deck. The halogen lights from the large pool in the center of the backyard pulsed slowly, bright, then dark, bright, then dark. The air was sticky-warm, the coming night doing little to cool things down.

A long table had been set up at one end of the yard, covered in a white tablecloth, rows of flowers draped along the edges.

In the middle of the table sat trays of food piled high, cuts of meat, vegetables, fancy little sandwiches stacked on top of each other. Coolers of beer and soda and bottles of water were buried in containers of melting ice.

Nick stood in the small patch of grass next to the pool, sipping on water, not wanting the caffeine from a soda given how jittery he felt. He couldn't shake the thought that if there was someone out there who wanted to harm them, now would be the time to do it, seeing as how they'd all gathered in one place. If *he* were an asshole villain, he'd use this opportunity to his full advantage. The fact that the Kensington driveway was gated would do little to keep a determined person out.

"You all right?" Mary Caplan asked him, frowning as she brushed a lock of his hair off his forehead. She wore a pretty white dress that hugged her trim figure, her warm brown skin lovely in the low light. "You look a little pale." She pressed the back of her hand against his forehead. "You don't feel feverish."

Nick shrugged as she dropped her hand. "You know how it is. Just thinking too hard."

Rodney Caplan shook his head, his bushy mustache twitching, hands folded above the swell of his stomach pressing against the buttons of his dress shirt. It was still a little weird, seeing him out of uniform. "So, as per usual, then."

"You know me," Nick said, distracted. He looked around the backyard. Bob and Martha were filling their plates at the table. Seth and Gibby sat at the edge of the pool, pants rolled up, bare feet in the water, heads close together as they spoke. Jazz stood with her parents, who smiled at her as Jazz waved her hands excitedly. Trey and Aysha were with Chris, both of them grinning as the Rook watched Mateo moving between everyone, offering flutes of sparkling cider.

Nick pulled out his phone, frowning because he had no notifications. "Have you heard from Mom and Dad? They haven't answered my texts."

"Not since this afternoon," Cap said. "Aaron called and let

me know he had some paperwork to finish for a domestic abuse case we snagged. I'm sure your mom wanted to wait with him so they could come together."

That made sense. Mom and Dad were always together, and Nick was relieved to know that the past months hadn't changed that. "I'm sure it's fine," he said, trying to sound like he believed his own words. "She's probably getting him ready. Dad can't dress himself to save his life."

"Please say that to his face and let me be there when you do," Cap said.

"Done and done," Nick said. "His left eye will do that twitchy thing it always does when I'm right. It happens a lot because I'm right all the time."

Cap snorted. "Keep telling yourself that, Nick. I seem to remember when—

"There they are," Mary said, nudging her foot against Nick's. "See? Right as rain."

He followed her gaze, and there, coming through the double doors that led to the backyard, were Aaron and Jenny Bell, her arm hooked through his. They waved when they saw Nick, walking toward him. Dad wore a suit Nick had bought for him a few weeks back with his meager savings, with Mom's help. Dad owned a bunch of suits, but Nick wanted him to have something that was new, given his recent change in careers. The three of them had spent an entire morning at a suit shop (the proprietor of the store eyeing Nick with disdain, given the condition the dead magician's suit had been in when he returned it after prom), Dad trying on different outfits, Nick and Mom hissing and booing whenever he'd come out in a terrible suit, and they'd cheered when they'd found the right one. It was charcoal gray, the dress shirt open at the throat, tie missing. It'd cost more than Nick had expected, and Mom tried to say she'd help pay for it, but Nick was determined. Dad was trying, which meant Nick needed to as well.

Mom looked as beautiful as ever, her makeup sparse, her short blond hair artfully messy. She wore a summer dress, black that faded into the same charcoal gray as Dad's suit. They made a striking couple, and Nick thought of leaning on a railing overlooking the ocean, a lighthouse in the distance, something that came out of nowhere and made his throat constrict. He didn't know why. That had been a happy day. He had the photographic evidence sitting on his desk to prove it.

As they got closer, there was something on Dad's face that Nick didn't like, the set to his jaw, a tightness around his eyes. Mom was smiling, but it wasn't as bright as it normally was.

"Hey, kid," Dad said as Mom reached out and straightened Nick's collar. "Sorry we're late."

"What happened?" Nick asked as he accepted a side hug from Dad once Mom had finished fussing over him. "Work stuff?"

"I had to drag him home," Mom said. "You know how it is."

Dad chuckled, but it didn't seem like he found anything humorous. "Always something that needs attention." He looked around, waving at those in attendance, shouting happy birthday at Jazz, who grinned and thanked him.

"Everything all right?" Cap asked, and Nick didn't know if that made him feel better or worse. Cap had noticed something off, too, which meant it wasn't Nick overreacting.

Dad said, "Well, I think we need to—"

"Focus on the reason we're here," Mom said firmly, and she and Dad glanced at each other for a beat or two, having one of those silent conversations long-term couples seemed to have. "Tonight is for celebrating." She squeezed Mary's arm in greeting before leading Dad away toward Jazz.

"You caught that, right?" Nick said, staring at his parents. "It's not just me?"

Mary said, "I don't think that—"

"Yeah," Cap said, and Mary bit her bottom lip. "I caught that." He frowned, his mustache twitching. "Probably nothing, but with everything that's been going on as of late, I don't think they'd keep something from us." He looked at Nick. "From *you*. They learned their lesson after the whole . . . you know." He shuffled awkwardly as Mary sighed.

"Lying to me about what I could do and making me take medication that hid a major part of my life?" Nick suggested.

"That," Mary agreed. "And you won't hear either of us defending that decision."

"They love you," Cap said. "That's not something you should ever question. They did what they thought was right. We're not your parents, Nick, so I'm not sure how much we should get involved, but you're allowed to be angry at what happened."

"I don't know how to fix it," Nick admitted. "I think I'm getting past it, and then I'm reminded of what happened, and it starts all over again."

"Have you thought about therapy?" Mary asked. "It seems to be helping with your father." Jazz said something that caused both Mom and Dad to laugh loudly. "He seems happier, no?"

"Kind of hard to go to therapy and talk about anything real when people are trying to kill you and you can't tell them that part. Makes it difficult to trust anyone. And I can't take the chance that I'd let something slip."

Mary frowned, brow furrowed. "That shouldn't stop you, Nick. Doctor-patient confidentiality exists. It may take a bit of research to find a good therapist, but if that's something you think you need, I would hope you'd bring it up. Cap goes."

Nick glanced at Cap. "I didn't know that."

"Didn't like it at first," Cap said gruffly. "Felt weird talking to a stranger about things. It's gotten easier. I needed it, I think. As much as I try and tell myself I'm all right with how things played out with the NCPD, that's not exactly true. There's a lot of anger and betrayal to work through. Haven't said a thing about you kids," he added quickly, "in case you were wondering."

"I know you wouldn't, Cap."

"It's helping," Cap said quietly. "I think the same could be said about your dad. He's keeping up with it, just like he promised you and your mom. I know you three had a rough go of it, but never doubt the love they have for you." Cap held up his hand before Nick could interject. "Yes, I know they went about it in a terrible way, but I will always believe it came from a good place."

Nick nodded. "So he's happy, because he's in therapy, and that explains everything."

"What else could there be?" Mary asked.

To that, Nick had no answer.

T he rest of the party went off without a hitch. No one crashed the Kensington home, no villain tried to destroy them while cackling manically. It was just that: a party with people who cared for each other. They laughed, they danced, they ate until they could barely move. Mateo took a break, pulling Chris onto the dance floor, much to the surprise of Nick and his friends, but apparently not to anyone else. "We do have eyes," Aysha told Nick when he asked why she wasn't freaking out like he was. "It's pretty obvious. They're smitten with each other."

"I don't understand anything," Seth said faintly as Mateo dipped Chris so low his back almost touched the ground.

Jazz was the center of attention, and rightly so. The cake her parents brought out was massive, three tiers of thick white frosting over red velvet. They sang to her once again, and when they'd finished, she scrunched up her face for a moment before blowing out all the candles in one go.

He was on the makeshift dance floor—just a thick carpet on top of the stone patio—swaying side to side, holding Seth close, neither of them speaking. Nick was trying to keep track of his feet to make sure he didn't step on Seth, but he soon gave up, letting the music wash over them. Seth barely even winced when Nick messed up, and never complained.

He startled when he felt a tap on his shoulder and looked back.

Dad was there, smiling at them. He said, "Hey, you mind if I cut in?"

Nick blinked. "You want to dance with Seth? Uh. Okay?" He glared at his dad. "If you threaten him with more dental dams or fire extinguishers, we're gonna have words."

"Is that right?" Dad said, lips quirking. "Words, you say."

"So many words," Nick threatened. "Like, *all* the words. I

still haven't sufficiently recovered from you trying to destroy my life."

Dad winced, and Nick wished he'd kept his fool mouth shut. He hadn't meant it how it sounded, but now that it was out there, he wondered if there was a kernel of truth to it. Maybe therapy wasn't a bad idea after all. Being fluent in Nick, Seth squeezed his arms, letting him know he was there.

Nick sighed. "That's not what I meant. Sorry. You know how it is. My mouth moves before my brain tells it to."

"I know, kid," Dad said. "It's one of the things I love about you." He shook his head. "And I don't want to dance with Seth. Wouldn't want him to see that I'm the upgrade over you."

"Oh my god, why are you *like* this?"

"Cool your jets, kid," Dad said. "I'm not asking your boyfriend to dance. I'm asking you."

"Wait, really? You want to take all this for a spin, Pops? Sure you can handle it?" Yet again, he wished he could take his words back. "Okay, there was an implication there necessitating certain fic tags that would automatically make me ill, so let's move on from that."

"Too late," Dad said with a huff. He began to turn away when Nick laughed and grabbed his arm.

Dad's hands started to go to his waist, when Nick shook his head. "I get to lead." He settled Dad's hands on his shoulders and put his own on Dad's waist.

"Seth?" Dad called over Nick's shoulder. "Nick wants to lead, so can you have 911 dialed and ready? I have a feeling my feet are about to be broken."

"You're not funny," Nick said with a glare.

"I really am," Dad said, and they began to shuffle their feet awkwardly.

"So," Nick said after four seconds of silence, far more than he was comfortable with.

"So," Dad said.

"We're dancing."

"Sort of," Dad said, wincing as Nick somehow managed to kick him in the shins.

"Should I spin you?" Nick wondered aloud. "I feel like I want to spin you."

"Let's not and say we did," Dad said. Another bit of shuffling where Nick received empirical evidence that bony knees were hereditary. Then, "Good party."

Nick sighed. "We really need to work on your small talk."

"Yeah? Why don't you give me a few pointers since you seem to think you're so much better at it?"

"I don't think it," Nick assured him. "I know it. It's fact."

"Good to know, Nicky."

He was about to tell his Dad that a spin was *definitely* necessary, but his brain highjacked his mouth and something else came out. "Are you happy?" he blurted, wishing almost immediately he could take the words back. He didn't want to do this here. Now. Not in front of everyone.

Dad stopped, hands still on Nick's shoulders. He cocked his head, blinking as if trying to clear his vision. His brow furrowed momentarily, and he glanced around as if he suddenly remembered where they were. Weird. He looked at Nick again, and that faint confusion was gone. "Of course I am, kid. I'm with you. Nowhere else I'd rather be."

"And everything is . . . good?"

"Think so. Why?"

Nick shrugged. "I don't know. Feels like I haven't checked in with you in a bit."

"You've been busy."

"I know," Nick said. He let out a frustrated breath. "But that shouldn't matter. We're a team. You and me." He paused. "And Mom." Of course she was included. She was part of them. He glanced over Dad's shoulder to find her surrounded by Mary, Aysha, Jo, and Martha. But whatever they were talking about, she wasn't paying attention. All her focus was on Nick and Dad. She smiled when she saw Nick looking at her and gave a little wave.

"We are, aren't we?"

Nick nodded, though something tickled along his mind, a thought he couldn't quite grasp. Faint yet adamant: *Before. After. Before. After.* He didn't know what it meant, so he ignored it. "We are."

"You certainly have a way with words, kid. Speaking of, I wanted to talk to you about your fic. What's it called? *Burning Pleasure*?"

"It's *A Pleasure to Burn*," Nick hissed at him. "And why the hell were you reading that?!"

Dad laughed. "I wanted to see the darkest depths of my son's imagination." His smile faded slightly. "And it went much, much darker than I expected it to."

Nick groaned, tilting his forehead against his father's shoulder, the angle awkward. He hadn't done this in a long time, and he was startled to realize he was as tall as Dad. He didn't know when that'd happened. His father had always been the biggest person in his world, both figuratively and physically. Strange, then, that in the end, he was still just a man. "Please tell me you didn't read all of it. Because if you *did*, I need to figure out a defense for my depravity."

"That's what we're calling it, huh? Pretty good word for it, if you ask me. Yes, I read every word, and let me tell you, some of those descriptions of Pyro Storm were a little too close to—"

"Do you trust me?" He didn't mean to say it. He wasn't even sure where it came from. Too late now.

Dad stopped. Everything stopped. The music. The other people. All of it gone, because Nick could see his father's mind processing. Surprise, then something akin to suspicion. A flash of sadness, like grief. Nick knew his father. He knew him better than almost anyone could claim to. He watched as Dad tried to cover up his expressions, but he failed spectacularly.

"I trust you," Dad finally said. "To know what's right. To know what's not."

"But . . ." Nick said, knowing it was there, and hating it existed at all.

"But," Dad said, letting the word hang between them. Then, "But I . . . it's not that I don't trust you, Nick. It's not that at all. I'm . . . *we're* worried that you might not think the big things through."

"Like?" Nick asked, trying to keep his voice even.

"We don't have to do this now," Dad said. He took a step back, dropping his hands from Nick's shoulders. He opened his mouth but no sound came out. He closed it, shaking his head.

"Like?" Nick insisted.

"All right?" another voice said, causing them both to jump. Mom had appeared out of nowhere. Nick hadn't heard her coming over. "You look like you're being very serious over here. It's a party, guys. You're killing the mood."

"We need to tell him," Dad said, and a chill ran down Nick's spine. "Tell all of them. They have to know, Jen. They need to be ready for what's coming." His hands curled into fists, knuckles popping.

Mom nodded tightly, mouth curving down. "Wanted to give everyone a chance to enjoy themselves before we . . ." She looked away, blinking rapidly. "I thought we'd have more time, but you're right."

"What are you talking about?" Nick asked, a buzzing sound filling his ears. "What's going on?"

Mom raised her hand, twisting her fingers slightly. The music cut off midbeat, the silence deafening as everyone looked around as if waking from a stupor. Though Nick was sure no one else could feel it, he could. The energy from his mother. Her powers, so much like his own. It was strange, this feeling, like a heavy wave crashing over him, pulling him into the depths. Distantly, he thought, *Is this real? Is any of this real?*

*Yes,* a calming voice whispered in reply. *Of course it is. It's real. All of this.*

The feeling dissipated, though not completely. Gently, it brushed over his skin like an unwanted caress, soft and wrong. It was maddening and intoxicating all at the same time. A thought on the tip of his tongue, muddled, out of focus. Incapable of clarity.

He forgot all about it when Mom spoke, her voice raised so everyone could hear her. "I didn't want to do this tonight," she said. "Miles, Joanna, I just wanted this to be Jazz's night." She looked pale. Nervous. She glanced back over her shoulder at her son and husband. She held her hand out. Dad went to her, taking her hand in his. "But I need to." She squeezed Dad's hand. "*We* need to. Because sometimes, we can't wait for the fight to come to us."

Nick didn't move. He couldn't. His feet were stone, heavy, holding him in place.

A little flash of light in his head. A memory. But . . . not? Because it didn't feel real. It wasn't how it'd happened. They hadn't—

*Smoke and Ice unconscious, trapped behind ceiling struts embedded in the ground. Dad, Dad, Dad rushing toward him, shouting his name, lifting him up, hugging him tightly, face buried in his neck. It'd been close, so close yet again, death knocking on their doorstep, banging, banging, but they'd survived, they'd won, and Dad . . . Dad had asked—*

*Who was that?*

*TK. He's . . . like me.*

*He? Who is he?*

*Don't know. Never seen him outside of his costume.*

"He's like me," Nick whispered, gooseflesh prickling along his arms, defiant against the summer heat. "He's . . . like. Me."

"Nicky?" Mom said, and held out her other hand toward him. He went to her, moving as if in a dream, practically floating. He took her hand, and calm washed over him. He was tired. That's all it was. He was tired and remembering things that hadn't happened. TK wasn't a man. She was his mother. She'd always been his mother.

"I need you to listen," she told him. "This is important. Can you do that?"

Nick nodded slowly, blinking, trying to clear his head.

He looked away from her at the others, taking them in. Bob frowning, Martha's hand at her throat. Miles and Jo standing near the edge of the pool, arms wrapped around each other, flutes of sparkling cider clasped in their hands. Trey and Aysha, Gibby standing between them, eyes questioning. Mateo taking a step toward Nick and his parents, Chris stopping him, fingers around his wrist, brow furrowed. Jazz near the food table, a large steak knife gripped in her hand as if she thought she was going to stab the shit out of someone for interrupting her party.

And Seth, moving slowly toward them, head cocked in question. Nick knew his mind was whirring, trying to figure out what had changed, more than a little Pyro Storm in his narrowed gaze.

Seth, who spoke for all of them. "What's wrong?"

Jennifer Bell said, "Owen Burke has returned to Nova City."

An explosion of noise, chaotic, loud as the adults began to speak over each other furiously. Jazz's eyes narrowed, and Gibby scowled ferociously. Seth barely moved, face blank, though his hands curled into fists at his sides.

Nick's knees betrayed him, weak, loose, and he almost sagged to the ground. "What?" he whispered. He knew this was inevitable, that it was only a matter of time, but hearing his mother say it aloud showed him how much he'd hoped Owen would just . . . disappear.

"How do you know that?" Seth asked.

Gibby pushed through her parents, shaking them off when they tried to stop her. "How can you be sure?"

Jazz huffed out an irritated breath, bringing up the knife and, somehow, flipping it expertly in her hands. Nick didn't know when she'd learned that trick, but he took a moment to be suitably impressed by it. "Let me at him. I'll take care of him myself."

"Uh, Jasmine," Miles said. "Let's hold off on that for just a moment, if you don't mind. I don't think we need to commit felonies quite yet. You haven't even opened your presents."

Mom wasn't put off by Jazz's display, or the questions from Seth and Gibby. If anything, she looked almost . . . pleased?

There and gone in a flash, but Nick saw it. He knew he did. Gravely, she said, "Because I've seen him."

Seth stared at her for a long moment. "You're sure."

"Of course I am," Mom said. "If I'd been suited up, I'd have been able to get photographic evidence. I saw him in a crowd on the street this morning. And before you ask again if I'm sure, I was there when he and Nick were dating."

"We weren't *dating*," Nick mumbled, aghast, mind reeling. "It was just two people who happened to find each other attractive." He glared at his people. "And before anyone questions my tastes, I will remind you that I traded up to the most perfect specimen that has ever existed. Seth, I'm talking about you."

"Noted," Seth said dryly. He sobered as he looked back at Nick's mom. "Why didn't you tell us right away?"

"We didn't want to ruin Jazz's party," Dad said. "We wanted her and the rest of you to have one night without thinking about anything but being here."

"She's right," Chris said, stepping forward. Mateo looked stunned, but he covered it up quickly, face carefully blank. "Aaron, you need to tell him the rest."

Nick leaned forward to look past his mom to Dad. "Tell me *what*?"

Dad hung his head, mouth a thin, bloodless line before he exhaled sharply. "The day you got Mateo's gift. The costume."

"Uh," Mateo said. "I don't know what you're implying, but if you think I'm working with that asshole, you'd better have evidence to back it up. I already have enough twinks to deal with, I don't need another one."

"It's not that," Mom reassured him. "When you came to me and said you wanted to build Nick a costume, I knew Nick was in good hands. You're a good friend, Mateo."

"Right," Mateo said slowly. He blinked once. Twice. "You helped me with the costume." He smiled, but it didn't reach his eyes. "Since it was your mantle he was taking on and all. I don't know why I forgot that."

"What's Chris talking about?" Nick demanded. "Another secret? I thought we were done with that. You promised me." He stepped around his mother, stopping in front of his father. Dad's shoulders were hunched near his ears. "You *promised* me."

Dad scrubbed a hand over his face. "I did. And I wasn't keeping this from you, not like you think. We couldn't be sure it . . ." He shook his head. "We needed to be sure before we said anything."

"Your father wanted to tell you," Mom said gently. "If you're going to be angry at anyone, be angry with me. I was the one who asked him to hold off."

"Hold off *what*?" Nick asked as Seth came to stand slightly behind him. He rested his hand on Nick's shoulder, a calming presence. The fire in Nick's head and chest dampened, sparks and smoke rising.

"A note," Dad said, raising his head and looking Nick directly in the eyes. "It wasn't signed, but it was addressed to you."

Nick gaped at him. "You opened my mail? That's a felony!"

"Other things to focus on, Nicky," Seth muttered.

"I thought it was hate mail," Dad said. "We'd already gotten a couple of pieces after Seth revealed himself. Nowhere near as much as Seth and his aunt and uncle have, but some. And it was vile, kid. Awful stuff that you didn't need to see."

"We did the same for Seth," Bob said suddenly as Martha made a small, wounded noise. "We've gotten a bunch of that crap, and there was no point in bringing it up. We turned it all over to Chris, but aside from it having been posted in the city, there wasn't any way to track where it'd come from. People can be cruel, especially when they think they're anonymous."

Begrudgingly, Nick knew Bob wasn't wrong. He'd seen some of the comments left on his fics.

"But it wasn't like the others," Mom said. "Aaron showed it to me. It had Owen's Shadow Star symbol scribbled over it in black. We first thought it was a threat from someone working with Christian and Christina Lewis. That it was meant to be smoke. But it wasn't. It was—"

"A shadow," Nick whispered, the hairs on the back of his neck standing on end.

Mom nodded. "And it had three words underneath." She breathed in deeply, letting it out slow. "'See you soon.'"

Seth's grip on Nick shoulders tightened painfully, but Nick didn't try to shove him off. It kept the worst of the panic at bay, though not all of it. "You didn't tell me."

"We didn't," Mom said. "Because if we could have dealt with him ourselves, then there would have been no point."

Nick scoffed angrily. "No point? *No point?*" He glared at her and Dad. "We had *every* right to know. We've been out in the city on our own. He could have come after us whenever he wanted to, and we wouldn't have seen him coming."

"That's not exactly true," Gibby said, and Nick whirled around, tamping down on the hurt that bubbled in his chest. Gibby looked apologetic, but it didn't stop her from continuing. "We knew he'd escaped, Nick. And you know as well as I do that we've been keeping our eyes and ears open for any sign of him. You most of all."

"And we haven't found anything," Jazz said, moving until she stood next to her girlfriend. "Doesn't mean we didn't miss something, but it's not like we weren't already thinking about it."

Nick deflated. "Yeah, I know. But they still should have told us."

"We did," Dad said. He held up his hands before Nick could retort. "Just now, when we confirmed he's really here. And no, before you ask, none of the other parents knew. It was just me, your mother, and Chris."

Nick tried to focus, but his mind was a mess, hundreds—perhaps thousands—of thoughts screaming through his head all at once. He latched on to the first one he could. "So . . . what. He's here. We knew that he might come back. But what's he after? Me? Seth? It's not *our* fault he turned out to be a dick who stole my fanfiction wholesale and tried to pass it off as his own."

"I think he's after his father," Mom said, and whatever else Nick wanted to say died in his throat. "I'm sure he's not happy with all of you, but think, Nick. Really think. If you were Owen, who would you go after first? You and Seth? Jazz and

Gibby? Or would he want revenge against the one person who made him who he is?"

"Burke," Nick breathed.

Mom nodded. "You know what Burke did to him. He turned his son into . . ."

"A guard dog," Seth said grimly. "He experimented on Owen. Changed him. Made him an Extraordinary."

"But it won't stop with Burke," Nick said. "Even *if* that's what his plan is, it doesn't mean he isn't gunning for the rest of us. Burke may have done what he did to Owen, but *we're* the ones who defeated him on the bridge."

"Which is why we're telling you now that we know for sure," Mom said. "Your father and I didn't want to worry anyone without evidence. Isn't that right, Aaron?"

Dad opened his mouth, but then something crossed his face—a quick flash of what looked almost like confusion—and he nodded slowly instead.

"You still should have told us," Trey said, speaking for the first time. "Our daughters are just as involved in this. We've been here before, remember? With Nick and Seth and Jazz and Gibby? Turned into this whole big thing where we agreed we weren't going to keep secrets anymore? What the hell happened with that?"

"Trey's right," Aysha said. "We should've heard about this weeks ago."

"You're right," Mom said quickly. "But that's not on Aaron. If anyone's to blame, it's me. I asked that he hold off until we could be sure. I'm sorry. But believe me when I say your kids are just as important to us as Nick is. And they are safer *with* us than without us. I know you'd do anything to protect them, but sometimes, it takes something a little extra to ensure their safety. I have that. Mateo does, too. Seth. And Nick."

"We know that," Miles said. "But if we're going to do this, if we're really going to be part of this, then you can't keep stuff like this from us. Trey's right. We should have been told as soon as you got that note."

"What are we going to do?" Bob asked. "If he's here, we need to find out what he's up to as soon as we can. Do everything to prepare."

Martha looked older than Nick had ever seen her. "Does Simon Burke already know? What if this is all a ruse and he's working with Owen?"

"Owen hates his father," Nick said in a daze, flashbacks of being held up by shadows against a bridge rising through his head. "He wouldn't help him with anything. Unless that's what he *wants* Burke to think."

"Which is why you're not going to like what I have to say next," Mom said. "I wish there was any other way, but I don't know if there is. I'm open to ideas, but I can't think of how to get to Owen without showing our hand."

Nick rolled his eyes. "Great. More bad news. Fantastic. Just frickin' peachy. What is it?"

"We need to protect Burke. If Owen is going for him, then we need to be there when he does."

Everyone had an immediate opinion on this, and quite loud ones at that. They all began to talk over each other, their outrage palpable, but for what was perhaps the first time in his life, Nick didn't join in. He let it wash over him, mouth closed. He watched his mother, his father, the stiff set to their shoulders, the way they stood side by side. A team.

Of course, the very idea of doing *anything* for Burke grated against Nick harshly, but there was a sort of twisted logic to the idea. "Two birds, one stone," he said, raising his voice, and everyone fell silent.

Mom nodded, obviously pleased. "That's exactly right. If we get in with Burke, that might mean we can also get to Owen."

A sense of savage satisfaction rolled through Nick at the idea of saving Burke from his own creation, and then flinging it back in his face. How would Simon Burke do with his anti-Extraordinary propaganda if the only reason he lived was *because* of Extraordinaries? Sure, he'd probably try to spin it in his favor, but he'd already be revealed as the two-faced bastard he was.

"We don't have to decide anything right now," Dad said, scratching the back of his neck. "But we all need to be on guard, just in case. At least until we have a better idea of what we're facing. Chris will use the resources at his disposal—*carefully,*" he added. "Cap and I can do the same. We don't have the same access we once did, but there are still a few people loyal to us inside the NCPD in case we need something." He tried for a reassuring smile but missed completely. "And the rest of us. No one goes anywhere alone. Always have someone with you. Eyes and ears open. Be aware of your surroundings."

"Let him come," Aysha said with a sneer, her words like steel. "I'd like to see him try and hurt my daughter while I have her back. It'll be the last thing he does."

"Same," Miles said.

"On it," Jo said, and Nick knew she meant it. Jazz was evidence enough of that.

"We'll figure it out," Mom said. "We have to. All of us. Because it's easier to stand together than it is to struggle apart."

Their mantra, the words that Nick had heard for most of his life. Their gospel truth. A tidal wave of surety washed over him. Heartened—though still more than a little furious—Nick almost felt sorry for Owen.

He'd never see them coming.

# 5

It was a day like any other. A Friday, Nick thought, though he didn't know *how* he knew it. Faintly, he remembered being at Jazz's party, but that had been on a Saturday. Days had passed, days he couldn't remember.

Summer, he thought, but when he looked down at the calendar on his desk in his room, it said MARCH, and he promptly forgot about any party.

"Spring break," he said. "I'm on spring break." His voice cracked. Broke. But that made sense. He was twelve years old. Puberty had come with a vengeance for one Nicholas Bell. Hair in places where none had been before, a collection of zits on his nose and forehead. The urge to stare at shirtless men on the internet and the fear of getting caught.

"Staycation," he said, looking around his room. "We're—"

Skip. Jump. Flash.

He was on his bed. On his phone, feet kicking above his butt. He and Seth were texting back and forth. Seth, the boy whom Nick loved to look at, to see his bow ties, to see him smile. There was nothing better than Seth smiling. He knew what this meant, at least a little. He wasn't stupid, but he couldn't quite bring himself to give it a name, at least not yet.

The last days of Nick's spring break. Dad at work. He had a case that demanded all his attention. He left early. Came home late. Nick barely saw him.

Mom, though. Mom had taken the week off with him, and that was just fine with Nick. They didn't leave the city. They played video games, Mom spamming the buttons as colorful sprites jumped and smashed. She took him to the movies. She took him to lunch, to dinner. She packed a picnic for them to take to the park. They watched TV. They played Monopoly with cheater's rules, meaning anyone could hold up the bank whenever they wanted.

The bank. The bank. The bank.

"Nicky," Dad whispered, broken, destroyed. "Oh my god, *Nicky.* She's—"

Sometimes Seth was with them. Gibby, too. Jazz was in Europe with her parents, sending them photo after photo of waters so clear and blue, they looked unreal, as if from a dream. She said she missed them. She said while she was having fun, she couldn't wait to come home.

Friday morning. The last weekday before school picked up again and hurtled toward summer. Just before nine. On his bed, waiting for his phone to ping, for Seth to laugh at the text Nick had just sent. For the life of him, he couldn't remember what it was, but that was okay. Everything was fine, and he was thinking muddled thoughts about how nice Seth looked in a bow tie, the one with the little green frogs on it.

A knock at his door. *Tap. Tap. Tap.*

"You up?" Mom asked, voice muffled.

"Yeah," he said, and he thought *I've been here before,* but it was without context, a fractured piece of glass with a fuzzy reflection.

"Decent?"

He groaned. *"Mom."*

He heard her laugh before she pushed open the door, leaning in, her long hair pulled back in a messy ponytail. She grinned at him in that way she did, warm, happy, the lines around her eyes soft. "Can't be too careful. Don't want to interrupt you if you're having alone time."

Cheeks aflame, Nick pulled the comforter up and over his head. "That was *one time,* and you swore you'd never bring it up again."

"I swore I'd *try,*" she countered as Nick heard her coming

into the room. "And I lasted three weeks, so that should count for—dear *god,* kid. You need to clean your room. Clothes don't belong on the floor. I told you to put them in the hamper. It's literally right there next to . . . the . . . is that *milk?*"

It was. He'd gotten a glass last night while on his computer, munching on stale crackers he'd found in a drawer of his desk. Then he'd been distracted by a fic he'd been reading, glancing over his shoulder to make sure no one was spying on him, given how . . . well. Given how delightfully descriptive the fic was getting. Who knew people could be so bendy?

"Okay," Mom said, clapping her hands. "Here's how this is going to go. I've got to stop by the office real quick, and then the bank."

*Nicky. Oh my god,* Nicky. *She's—*

He blinked in slow motion.

Time snapped back into place, and she said, "Shouldn't take too long. While I'm gone, you're going to make your room at least marginally habitable."

"I have everything where I want it," Nick countered, still hiding under the blankets. "You're going to mess up my system."

"And I feel so badly about that."

"Liar," Nick muttered.

"Or, if you want, I can pick up your underwear for you, seeing as how you think it needs to be flung onto the floor. I could probably also take care of that crusty towel if you—"

"*Mom.*"

The bed shifted as she sat down next to him. He sighed when she pulled the blanket off his head. "Yeah, yeah," she said, pinching his cheek gently. He batted her hand away. "Rude. You should—oof, kid. What is that *smell?*" She grimaced as her nose wrinkled.

"Stop smelling me!"

"Shower," she said. "After you clean your room. And you need a haircut. You're looking a little shaggy. I'll make you an appointment. See if we can get you in today. Got your meds."

She leaned back, hand going to the pocket of her tan shorts. When she pulled it back out, there, sitting on her palm, was a little familiar pill. Concentra—*It'll help you concentrate!*

Nick looked away, huffing out a breath.

"I know, kid."

"You don't," he retorted. "Your brain isn't broken like mine is." He hated the pathetic whine in his voice, but he needed her to understand.

"Look at me."

He did. He was helpless to do anything but.

She wasn't smiling anymore. If anything, she looked angry, but Nick didn't think it was at him. "You are *not* broken. You never have been, and you never will be. I know you hate this. I know you wish you didn't have ADHD, but it's *not* a death sentence. You're still you, no matter what."

"Yeah, well," Nick muttered. "Maybe that's the problem."

"It's not. And you won't hear me trying to minimize how you're feeling about it. That wouldn't be fair of me. This is as real for me and Dad as it is for you. But I need you to know that it doesn't matter to us, and it's not your fault because there's nothing to find fault with. We'll take you any way we can get you because you're the greatest part of our lives."

Nick sighed. "Yes, counselor. You've made your closing arguments. The jury has reached a verdict in your favor."

She snorted. "Smart-ass." She looked down at the pill in her hand. "I know it's easier said than done to take what I'm saying to heart, but I mean it. Maybe it won't always be this way, but even if it is, I'm going to be there to remind you when you need me to. And even when you don't, I will because I'm your mother and I've earned that right."

He took the pill, swallowing it dry with a grimace. Obnoxiously, he opened his mouth, lifting his tongue to show he wasn't hiding it. She didn't give him more than a perfunctory glance. Trust, this. Layer upon layer of trust. She patted his arm before standing. "I mean it, Nick. Clean this room. If you haven't made any headway by the time I get home, you can forget pizza with Seth and me later today. I'll just take him out and leave you here to wallow in your filth."

"Seth likes me more than you," Nick grumbled.

"Of course he does," Mom said, heading toward the door, grimacing as she stepped over a pile of dirty clothes. She paused a moment, smiling at a familiar picture: Nick and her, standing at the edge of an ocean, a lighthouse in the distance. "And I can't wait for you to figure out what that means. Up, kid. Get your butt in gear. If you find mold because you live in squalor, we're putting you up for adoption." And then she was gone.

Like he hadn't heard *that* threat before.

He got up. He cleaned. He texted Seth as he shoved clothes in the hamper. He laughed at Seth's reply as he took half-empty cups down to the kitchen, including the milk. He turned up music and screamed along with the lyrics, the bones of the house rattling. He showered. He dressed.

He stood in the middle of his room and said, "I've been here before. I know what this is. The phone is about to ring." He dropped his voice to a lower register, gruff, like his father. "Nicky. Oh my god, *Nicky*. She's—" A tear trickled down his cheek, his heart thundering against his rib cage, and it—

His phone rang at 12:47 on a Friday in the spring, where the sun was shining, and everything made some sort of sense.

He glanced down at the phone screen.

*Dad,* it read.

He didn't want to answer.

But Nicholas Bell was not in control, and he could not stop himself from answering the phone and bringing it to his ear. "Hey, Pops. You should see my room. It's freaking clean as—"

Dark water poured from the phone, covering his fingers, his hand, his arm, working its way up his neck and down his chest. It swallowed him whole, and as he tried to scream, it crawled down his throat, choking him, filling him with darkness.

But it wasn't water, was it?

No.

It was *shadows*.

"See you soon," a garbled voice spat from the phone. "See you soon, see you soon, *see you*—"

"Nick."

He opened his eyes.

Darkness. All shadows, all smoke, holding him down, grip strong as he fought as hard as he could, legs kicking, hands slapping against flesh.

"*Nick*."

He stopped. He inhaled. He exhaled.

"There. Good, Nick. You're all right. I'm here. Breathe, kid. In. In. Good. Hold. One. Two. Three. And out. One. Two. Three. Again."

He did. Again and again and again.

When he came back to himself, throat raw, skin slick with sweat as he panted, focus returned. He was in his room. In his bed. It was dark out, the light from the streetlamps on the sidewalk below filtering in through his window. Blankets tangled around his legs. Hot and cold, all at the same time.

"That was a bad one. You all right?"

He jumped, making a strangled noise as he looked over. His mother sat next to him on his bed. She wore a loose old shirt. Sleep shorts. Her hair was swept back off her forehead.

"Yeah," he croaked out. "I don't . . . nightmare."

"Thought so." She ran her fingers over his arm, nails scraping against his skin. "Want to tell me about it?"

He didn't. For some reason, he didn't want to tell her anything. It wasn't real.

His brow creased. That felt like an untruth.

Right?

He said, "You died." Yes. No. Split, right down the middle, a clear division. It was Before, and then it was After, and she was in both places at once, on either side of the line, and it wasn't possible. "You *died,*" he said again, and began to shake.

She smiled, a hint of teeth behind her lips. "Of course I didn't. I'm right here. I've always been here." She leaned over him, her face inches from his own as her hand moved up his arm to his shoulder, his neck, stopping on his forehead. His skin crawled. He didn't want this. He didn't want *her*. When she spoke again, it was barely a whisper, her breath hot against his face. "I'm not going anywhere, *Nick*. You can count on that."

Then her hand moved to his forehead, and he felt a faint pulse wash over him, insistent, tendrils reaching, reaching, turning truth and clarity into nothingness.

Everything was fine.

He woke up the next morning and blinked up at the ceiling. He felt loose. Relaxed. He yawned, jaw cracking, before turning his face into his pillow. A good night's sleep. He hadn't had one of those in a while.

A voice shouted from somewhere below him. "Nick! Get your butt out of bed. Breakfast!"

He could smell it. French toast with vanilla and cinnamon. Bacon, fried to a blackened crisp. He jumped out of bed like it was Christmas morning. Wide awake, he pulled on a discarded shirt and hurried toward the door, throwing it open. Music, from downstairs. The King. Only fools rushed in. He laughed. Her favorite.

He moved down the hallway, right hand trailing on the wall. He thought, if he really wanted to, he could fly. He could rise from the floor and fly. The stairs creaked as he thundered down them, and there, in the back of his mind, another thought: *Before. After. Before. After. After . . . what?*

*Nothing*, a voice replied. *There was no Before. There was no After. Everything is fine.*

"Looks like someone's finally up," Dad said as Nick came into the kitchen. He leaned against the counter near the sink, wearing a pair of sleep shorts and a tank top. Ankle socks, a small hole in one of the toes. Mom was at the stove, pans sizzling, snapping. Next to the stove, a plate stacked high with French toast, more than they could possibly eat in one sitting. Nick would eat all of it.

She glanced back over her shoulder, eyes alight. "Hey, kid. Thought we were gonna have to drag you out of bed." She winked at him, and Nick thought about lighthouses against rough seas.

"Nope," Nick said. "Smelled breakfast. Didn't want to miss it. French toast is ass when you have to reheat it."

Mom laughed, and Nick relished the sound. "It is, isn't it? There's a little peanut butter left. Should be enough for your French toast. I'll go to the store later to stock up."

Nick grinned at her. Grocery stores on Sundays. Routine. Normal. "Sounds good. Think fast." He punched Dad playfully on his bicep. Dad winced, but it was just for show.

Mom tapped her cheek, and ever the dutiful son, he kissed her with a loud smack. "Looks good," he said, peering over her shoulder at the bacon on the stovetop.

"Of course it does. I am your mother, after all. Can you set the table?"

He did as asked. A carafe of orange juice already sat on the table, next to a bottle of syrup and a mostly empty container of peanut butter. He set down a plate for Dad and one for himself, with silverware for each. He was about to sit in his usual chair when Mom said, "Ah, aren't you forgetting something? I'm here, too, sweetheart."

He paused, looking down at the table. She was right. He'd barely been paying attention when he'd set the table. Why hadn't he included her? That didn't make any sense, and for a moment, something itched, deep and insistent. There were three of them, the way it should be. "Yeah," he said. "Sorry." He grabbed another plate and set of silverware, setting them on the table. Once done, he sat down.

"Your father and I were talking last night," Mom said, scooping up the bacon and placing it on a plate covered in a paper towel.

"About what? The Owen thing? The Burke thing?" He still didn't think protecting Burke was the right way to go about this, but he trusted his parents. They knew what was best.

Dad came to the table, carrying a mug filled with black coffee. He sat down in his usual chair across from Nick. The coffee spilled a little onto the table, and Nick tossed a napkin toward him. It was cloth. They didn't use cloth napkins, at least not anymore. They'd stored them away in the attic after . . .

He paused, frowning. After what?

"Both," Dad said, leaning back in his chair. "We'll want to bring the others in on it, but we need to make a plan." He glanced at Mom. "You want to tell him, or should I?"

Mom brought the bacon and French toast to the table. She kissed Dad on the forehead just as the doorbell rang. "I think that's for you," she told Nick. "Why don't you go see who it is? We'll talk when you come back."

He jumped up from his chair, hurrying toward the front door, bare feet slapping against the floor. A little arc of electricity—snapping, cracking—bowled down his spine at the familiar figure standing on his porch.

"Hey, dude," Nick said, flinging open the door. "I didn't know you were coming—holy *shit*."

Seth stood on the porch, wearing tan shorts and a black, short-sleeved collared shirt, complete with a red bow tie, his glasses slightly askew. "What?" he asked, looking down at himself as if trying to see what Nick was gaping at. "What's wrong?"

"How *dare* you come over so early in the morning looking so fine," Nick said. "Question. Can you be my breakfast? Fair warning: peanut butter might still be involved." He was a foodie, after all.

Seth rolled his eyes fondly, cheeks darkening. But that didn't stop him from crossing the threshold, gathering Nick up in his arms, and kissing him soundly. "Okay," he said, pulling back. "You want to know how I know you haven't brushed your teeth yet?"

Nick grimaced. "Let's not and say we did. Not everyone can be as put together as you this early in the morning." He stepped back as Seth closed the door. "I thought we were going to meet up later."

"Your mom invited me over," Seth said, hooking his pinkie finger around Nick's. "Said she wanted to talk to us about something."

Oh no. "If they pull out plastic baggies, we run. Deal?"

Seth nodded solemnly. "Deal."

"Besides," Nick said without thinking, "I already looked up dental dams online. They're cheaper than I thought they'd be. And your aunt was right. They're sold in bulk, so we won't run out when—okay. I heard what I said. Um. So. Huh. Yikes? Did I say that? Yikes."

"You just . . . threw that out there," Seth said faintly. "Like it was nothing."

Nick groaned, slumping against the closet door behind him. "Goddammit. I was going to surprise you with them."

"You were going to surprise me with dental dams."

"Inflection is a thing that exists," Nick reminded him. "And you gave me Skwinkles Salsagheti. I thought it might be nice to give you a present, too."

"That's not even remotely the same thing." But there was a heat to his eyes, something that had nothing to do with Pyro Storm. Nick gasped quietly as Seth crowded him against the closet door, their knees bumping together. Seth kissed him again, teeth and tongue. He turned his head to the side as Seth kissed his jaw, his ear, breath warm as he bit down gently on Nick's neck.

"Boy stains," Dad called from the kitchen, causing them both to jump. "Don't make me get the spray bottle."

"Welp," Nick said. "I guess I don't have to worry about *that* boner anymore. Hooray."

"Oh my god," Seth moaned, face aflame. "They can *hear* you."

"That we can," Dad said. "Get in here and eat before it gets cold. And no more talk about boners."

Mom laughed.

Halfway through breakfast, Mom said, "So."

Nick looked up, mouth full of bacon. He chewed quickly, wiping his chin with the back of his hand. "So."

"Your father and I were talking," Mom said, nodding toward his napkin pointedly. He picked it up and cleaned his hands. "With everything that's going on, we want to make sure the rules are clear."

"About what?" Nick asked, glancing at Dad. He was mopping up his last bit of French toast in the puddle of syrup on his plate.

"Being Guardian," Mom said, and *that* caught Nick's attention. Excitement began to build, but he did his best to keep himself in check.

Of course, he failed spectacularly. "I get to go out on my own? Hell damn, *yes*." The table rattled as his knees bumped the underside.

"Not on your own," Dad said. But before Nick could deflate, he added, "You'll either need to be with your mother, Seth, or Mateo."

"Why now?" Seth asked, ignoring the look Nick shot at him. "I mean, I know what Nick is capable of. He can handle himself."

"I can," Nick said firmly. Relief, then, when Seth reached over and squeezed his hand. Did he need Seth's support? Possibly, but not as much as he *wanted* it. There was a difference.

"You can," Mom said. "And we're proud of you and how hard you've been working." She sat back in her chair, right leg folded underneath her, the sun pouring in from the window above the sink. "This thing . . . with Owen. I don't need to tell you he's dangerous, but I think it helps to be reminded. He's killed people, Nick, and hurt many others. There's no telling what he might do now that he's here."

"Which is why I asked why now," Seth said. "I'm trying to figure out what's changed between a couple of days ago and this morning."

Nick studied his parents, cataloguing every fleeting expression, parsing through whatever he could latch on to. They looked resigned, and that didn't sit well with him. It felt like a last—or only—resort.

"We have to be prepared," Dad said finally. "Until we know exactly what Owen is doing, we need to tread carefully. While we think this has to do with his father, we can't know for sure until . . ."

"Until we find out ourselves," Nick finished for him.

Dad nodded. "Eyes open. Always be aware of your surroundings. We weren't kidding when we said we don't want any of you going off on your own, suited up or not. I just wish . . ." He looked down at the remains of his breakfast, the syrup congealing on the plate. "I wish it hadn't come to this." He laughed hollowly. "But it has, and there's nothing we can do to stop it."

Nick stood abruptly, chair scraping on the floor. Without looking at Mom or Seth, he circled the table, stopping next to Dad. Hesitating briefly, Nick settled his hand on the back of Dad's neck, pulling him against his stomach. Dad clutched him, fingers digging in. "I know you're scared," Nick whispered. "I am, too." More than, but he had a feeling Dad already knew. "I can do this. You know I can. Trust, remember? You and me. I've got your back if you've got mine."

"You and me," Dad whispered back. "Always."

"And me," Mom said, and Nick startled. He'd almost forgotten she was there. He looked over at her, and she wasn't smiling. She covered it up quickly, but Nick caught it before it disappeared. For a moment, she'd looked almost . . . angry? "I'll help you as best I can. After all, I'm the only one who's telekinetic like you, remember?"

"Right," Nick said. "You are." He stepped back away from his father. "So, what do we do first?"

"Your pill," Mom said, and there it sat on her palm. "Gotta

keep that mind moving like you want it to. Take it, and we'll decide on the best course of action."

"Yeah," he said. "Of course." He took it from her and swallowed it dry, making a face at the bitterness on the back of his tongue. Then, without thinking, he opened his mouth wide to show her it was gone, just like he'd done when he was a kid.

She said, "Close your mouth, Nicky. No one likes to see that."

A fly, fat and heavy, landed on Dad's plate, dipping its legs into the syrup. It buzzed loudly, and Nick thought of electricity crackling. Miss Conduct, standing in an alley, bangles clicking together. A memory, foggy, distant. A phone being smashed on the ground. His . . . phone?

*You're children. You're children. You're—*

*You don't know me. I don't know any of you. And it's better if it stays that way. Knowing people means getting hurt. And I'm not going to put myself into that position. Not again.*

"Nick?"

The voice echoed in his head as he looked over at Seth, a worried expression on his face. He'd risen half out of his chair as if he wanted to go to Nick. "You all right?"

Mom reached over and circled her fingers around Seth's wrist, tugging him back down. His face went slack for a split second before he smiled as he looked at her. "Thanks for inviting me over to breakfast, Mrs. Bell. I appreciate it."

"Anything for you," Mom said, letting him go. "Sit, Nick. Let's make a plan. Here's what I'm thinking."

# 6

The next morning—Monday, but then it was summer vacation, so the day didn't exactly matter—he stepped out of his house, shouting at Mom that he was heading out to meet up with Gibby. She called back, reminding him to text her if Gibby didn't show for some reason. She'd wanted to come with, but she'd relented when he promised her that he'd only be on his own for a few blocks in broad daylight. Gibby had already texted him that she was waiting at the Franklin Street station entrance.

He moved lethargically, swallowing down a yawn. Yesterday had been intense, Mom working him hard. They'd started small, with empty plastic cups. He'd been able to lift them with ease, still in awe that he could do such a thing. He'd moved them back and forth before spinning them in concentric circles. He'd managed to get up to ten at one time before they started to wobble.

Dad had been their victim (his word) for what came next. Sweat dripped from Nick's forehead as he'd lifted his father a few feet above the ground carefully, not wanting to hurt him. Dad had looked a little green as Nick bobbed him up and down, head almost bumping up against the ceiling.

"Good," Mom had said, watching from a few feet away. "It's all about control, Nick. Focus. No distractions." She'd circled behind him and clapped her hand hard right near his ear. Dad dropped a couple of feet, but Nick managed to catch him before he could hit the floor.

And on and on it went.

He knew this work was important, but he was relieved to get out of the house. It felt like he could breathe a bit better, even if the oppressive heat settled over him like a wet blanket. When he reached the sidewalk, he glanced back at the house. Mom stood in front of her bedroom window, watching him. He waved. Maybe she wasn't looking at him because she didn't wave back.

He left the house behind, moving down the familiar sidewalks, his backpack heavy with his Guardian costume, something his parents had at first kept locked up, same as his pills. They'd given it to him the night before, telling him that part of being prepared was having it near, just in case.

(If he'd slept with the costume in his bed, hugging the helmet . . . well, that was no one's business but his.)

The humidity was terrible, with the promise of worse in the hours to come. Wavy lines rose from the blacktop of the streets. People passed him by, most looking sluggish, wiping their brows. Some glanced at him, nodded in greeting, but no one tried to stop him. He ducked his head, not wanting to take the chance he'd be recognized. It didn't happen very often—at least not as much as it had even weeks before—but he couldn't be too careful. Some idiots out there probably thought they could still strike it rich with the bounty Burke had put out on Seth. He'd recanted in an interview with the worst person in the world, and had apologized, but Nick didn't trust him in the slightest. It rubbed him the wrong way that Mom seemed to think the only way to get to Owen was to protect Burke. After everything Burke had done, Nick almost wanted to let Owen at him, if that's what he was planning to do.

But being a hero didn't mean getting to pick and choose who to save. That was something the police seemed to do, and Nick wanted to be better than that. Better than *them,* even if it meant having to help an asshole like Simon Burke. Two birds, one stone.

He spotted Gibby at the entrance to the Franklin Street station, leaning up against the railing near the stairs that led down to the subway. She didn't see him, her phone pressed against her ear. She wasn't smiling. Nick hurried toward her.

She must have seen him out of the corner of her eye, because she nodded at him, speaking quickly into the phone before hanging it up and shoving it into the pocket of her black Dickies shorts, her silver wallet chain jangling. Her green tank top was low-cut, a black sports bra underneath.

"Hey," she said with a frown. "Why are you jogging? I thought you hated anything that wasn't walking."

"Or flying," Nick said. "But seeing as how I still haven't gotten the hang of that, I have to use my legs. Good thing they're sexy. At least, that's what Seth says. Apparently, he likes pasty white sticks covered in hair."

"No accounting for taste, I guess."

"Who were you talking to?"

"Jazz," she said. "She's with Seth at the secret lair. They were going to see if they could hack into CCTV cameras to try and find out if they could catch a glimpse of Owen. They'll meet up with us later."

"Our lives are so damn cool," Nick breathed. "Say *hack into CCTV cameras* again, only slower this time."

"Yeah, I'm not going to do that. You good?"

"Why wouldn't I be?"

"I don't know, Nick," Gibby said, as if *he* were the idiot. "This weekend was . . . a lot."

"Still a fan of hyperbole, I see."

She snorted. "You're lucky I love you because you're kind of a dick."

"Yeah, yeah. You wouldn't have me any other way. I'm . . . good." And he thought he meant it. Mostly. "You know, for someone who people want to murder."

"Our lives are too close to those dumb comic books you read."

He blinked. "What do you mean?" He startled when someone asked at him to move out of the way. He apologized as he stepped away from the front of the station stairs. The man nodded his thanks and descended.

"Former enemies coming back out of the blue for revenge like this is some self-serious sequel," Gibby said as she grabbed Nick by the arm, pulling him down the sidewalk. Her hand was hot—too hot—and Nick pulled his arm free. She didn't stop, and he had no choice but to follow her. "Doesn't that happen all the time in comics?"

She had a point. "Makes you think."

"About?"

"If comics have more basis in reality than people think. I'm not even talking about the social-justice angle. Like, what if there are Extraordinaries who're comic book writers? Taking real-life stuff and putting it into comics? Oh man, do you think someone will write a comic book about us?" He hurried around Gibby, stopping in front of her and posing, hands on his hips as he looked off into the distance. "Well, how do I look? They could use this for the cover."

She looked him up and down before snorting. "Could use a bit of bulking up. Your pasty sticks look like you've forgotten all about leg day."

He scowled at her as he dropped his hands. "It's not *my* fault I don't have muscle mass. It's genetics."

"Your dad has muscles. Your mom does, too."

He waved her off. "It skips a generation, like male-pattern baldness. It's *science*, Gibby."

"That's right," Gibby said. "Science." She lifted her arms and flexed. Her biceps were bigger than Nick's. She kissed both—first the right, then the left.

Nick was begrudgingly impressed. "Yeah, yeah. You're stronger than I am. That's . . . actually pretty damn cool. You go, girl. Maybe you should've been the Extraordinary instead of me."

She rolled her eyes as she dropped her arms. "Wouldn't want to steal your spotlight." She stepped around him and continued on down the street. Nick spun on his heels, hurrying to catch up with her. "You got what I think you do in the backpack?"

He nodded. "Yep. They're letting me have it, but there's a list of conditions a mile long."

"Probably for the best, knowing you. You'd wear it wherever you went."

"Only for my adoring fans," he said seriously. "Who am I to turn them down if they want a photo with a real live superhero? You may like crushing dreams, but I won't do that."

"I've seen your fans in the comments of your fics," Gibby said as they stopped at an intersection, waiting for the light to change. "Extraordinary groupies are weird and don't understand boundaries."

"You're one of my groupies, though."

She sighed, looking up at the sky as if praying for guidance. "If you ever call me a groupie again, I'll sic Jazz on you."

Nick shuddered. "That's a very realistic threat. Did you see that thing she did with the knife at her birthday party?"

Gibby smiled dreamily. "Right? She's so hot. I can't believe I get to love her."

"Your kinks are showing," Nick muttered. "But yes, it was very hot and for a moment, I questioned my sexuality, but then I remembered penises, and nope."

Gibby had a gleam in her eye that either meant a) she was going to be rude, or b) she was going so say something specifically tailored for Nick to make his soul want to depart his body. Unfortunately, she went with c) all of the above. "Would you look at that? I also say nope when I think of penises. They look like depressed little wrinkly men who sometimes wear turtlenecks while standing on top of hairy beanbags."

"Oh my god," Nick whispered fervently. "That was poetry. Disgusting, horrible poetry. You are a *goddess*. An evil one, but a goddess nonetheless."

"Damn right I am. You're welcome for gracing you with my presence."

"Notice how I didn't even put up a fight at the word *little*."

"I see you've accepted reality. Good for you, Nicky."

The light changed, and Nick and Gibby moved with the people around them as they crossed the street, ignoring the horns honking at them for no reason. It was a normal thing in the city.

"Where are we going?" Nick asked. "Not that I don't want to hang out, but your text was pretty cryptic."

Gibby glanced at him, looking as if she was choosing her next words carefully. "You said you wanted to be part of change, yeah? To help make things better?"

He had. After she and Jazz's parents had found out the truth about Seth, things had been . . . strained, to put it mildly. He could still remember how awkward it'd been to sit there, listening as Trey and Aysha read his father the necessary riot act over his involvement in police misconduct. Mom hadn't interjected, telling Nick to be quiet when he'd tried, saying that they needed to listen. And now that he thought about it, he didn't know why she hadn't told them about herself at the same time. Granted, Nick hadn't known then that she'd used to be Guardian. That would come later when he'd found the tapes in the . . . in the attic.

He stopped, swaying slightly, feeling like his legs no longer worked. That . . . was that how it'd gone? The tapes. One in particular, labeled THE TRUTH. He'd found it. Not alone. Someone had been with him. Who was—

Jazz. She'd been there. Worried about Gibby going away to Howard, something they hadn't known until recently. They'd watched the tape, saw a younger version of Nick's parents and Simon Burke. His mother was an Extraordinary. He hadn't known that. Grief, then. But over what?

Lies. His parents' lies. That was all it was. That was all it needed to be.

And then Jazz told him to try to move cups like he'd seen Mom do in the video. He had, and then *everything* had started moving in the house, forcing them to flee. They'd run to . . .

Somewhere. He couldn't remember. To Dad? To Mom? That . . . sounded right. He'd found them, confronted them, and they'd told him the truth. The pills. Simon Burke. Crushing him, *suppressing* him. It'd been a whole thing, anger and tears and accusations flung like grenades. But they'd moved beyond it. Mom had made sure of it.

Right?

"Nick?"

He blinked, the sounds and smells of the city crashing back into him. Gibby stood in front of him, frowning.

"You all right?" she asked, touching the back of his hand, concerned.

"Yeah," he said. "Just . . . I don't know. Tired from training, I guess. What were you saying?"

She watched him a long moment before nodding and turning back around and moving down the sidewalk.

"I got word last night on this message board I follow," Gibby said as he caught up with her. "There's going to be a protest at your dad's old precinct. Figured you'd want to come along and see why it's so important."

"Oh."

"You good with that? You don't have to go if you don't want to, but I think it's important for you to see—"

"You sure it's okay for me to be there?" Nick asked nervously. "I don't want to be a distraction."

She rolled her eyes. "Letting notoriety go to your head already? I knew you'd turn into a diva. So disappointing."

"No, it's not—that's not what I'm talking about."

"Then say what you mean, Nick. I can't read your mind."

"My dad worked there. He was . . ." He swallowed thickly. "He was part of the problem. Yeah, he's trying to make amends, but that doesn't mean it's all forgiven. I don't want that to try and take away from what's important if someone recognizes me. Put the focus on where it should be."

She blinked in surprise. "Wow, that's . . . really mature of you, Nick. Respect." She held out her fist, and he bumped it gladly. "But I think *if* someone recognized you because of your dad, they would see that you're trying to . . . well, not accept responsibility for what he did, because that's not your job. They would hopefully see that you understand how harmful his actions were, and that you're trying to learn all you can about what we mean when we say Black lives matter. And it's not about being Guardian or anything like that. I want you there as Nick, because we don't need a hero to save us, not in the way you're probably thinking. We need you to *listen* when we tell you what's happening because of police brutality."

"Then hell yes, I'll go with you," Nick said immediately.

"Really?" Gibby asked, and Nick's heart hurt a little with how relieved she sounded, as if she'd thought he'd try to weasel out of it. "That means a lot to me."

"You're one of my best friends. You've been there for me time and time again. Of course I'd do the same for you. I've got your back, no matter what."

She bumped her shoulder against his. "I know, but it helps to hear it every now and then. This isn't as sexy as being an Extraordinary, but—"

"It's just as important," Nick finished for her. "I'll follow your lead. If I seem to be getting in the way for any reason, call me out for it, yeah? I promise I'll do my best to listen." He looked around, recognizing where they were. The precinct was still at least fifteen blocks away. "Why didn't we just take the train?"

"We're queer. We walk fast because of our survival instinct."

He snorted. "Okay, that was funny in a really sad way. I feel bad for the heteros. They wanted us to run from them, and so we did, and now we evolved to be much quicker than they are. They really don't get anything aside from having all the rights they could ever ask for."

"The white people, anyway," Gibby said. "Thought about the train, but I figured if anyone tried anything, it's better to be out in the open than trapped in a metal tube underground. We're not supposed to meet until noon, so we have plenty of time to get there."

"You mean Owen," Nick said, shuddering at the remnants of a dream he couldn't quite remember. Shadows. All those shadows. He looked up, almost expecting to see the familiar figure of Shadow Star descending toward them. Nothing, just buildings reaching toward a deep blue sky.

"Yeah," Gibby said grimly. "I wouldn't put it past him to do something like that. Assholes are always going to asshole. Come on, in here. I want to get some water bottles to take with us." She pushed open a door without looking to see if he'd follow.

He stepped into the bodega after her, the man behind the counter nodding at them from behind a sheet of thick plexiglass before going back to his book. Behind him, an old television sat on a shelf, blaring a commercial that was either for mattresses or depression medication. He followed Gibby past rows of colorful packaging in various languages, including Skwinkles Salsagheti, to the back corner of the bodega. A large calico cat sat on top of one of the drink coolers, tail swishing as it watched them with bright green eyes.

"We should use bodegas more for secret meetings," Nick said. "It's very cloak-and-dagger. We could have code names. I'll be Mr. X. You can be Butch Fatale. Get it? Because instead of Femme Fatale, you're—"

She laughed. "Butch Fatale. I call dibs in case I suddenly get powers and need an Extraordinary name."

"Oh man," Nick said. "I'm already imagining your costume. Like, the entire thing is made of wallet chains." He frowned. "Wait. That's probably not the look you'd want to go with. You wouldn't be able to go through metal detectors. And if someone had magnet powers, you'd lose pretty quickly."

"And this is why you didn't get to pick out your own costume," Gibby said. "Because of ideas *exactly* like that."

Nick scoffed. "Oh, please. If you all hadn't helped Mateo make my Guardian costume, I still would've come up with something badass. And at least *that* way, I wouldn't have body issues because of all the spandex. Seth makes it look hot as hell. I look like someone filled a plastic tube with oatmeal and gave it arms and legs."

"And googly eyes."

"And googly eyes," Nick agreed. "Which, to be fair, is not my fault. I always look like I have googly eyes. That's why I wear a helmet."

She opened the cooler door, both of them crowding in front

of it, letting the cold air wash over them. Gibby grabbed a few water bottles, handing them over to Nick before grabbing a couple more. She closed the door, and Nick was about to turn and head toward the front when she said, "Hey, Nick? Can I ask you something?"

He stopped, looking over his shoulder. "What?"

She looked as if she were picking and choosing her next words carefully. He turned back around as she leaned against the cooler door, giving her his complete attention.

"This is going to sound stupid. I don't even . . ." She huffed out a breath.

"You're in the best company if that's the case," he told her. "Pretty much everything that comes out of my mouth is stupid."

She nodded, studying him for a long moment. "Okay. So. Just . . . let me talk this out, yeah? I swear I have a point."

"Go," he said. "I'm listening."

"Why doesn't your mom have a job?"

He blinked in surprise. Out of all the things he thought Gibby might say, he hadn't expected that question. "She quit so she could stay at home after I was born. Dad and she agreed that one of them wanted to be there so I wasn't a latchkey kid like they were. You know that."

"Right," Gibby said slowly. "But didn't she go back at some point? Like, it's weird. I keep thinking she's still a lawyer. I thought I remembered you saying that she went back when you started going to school."

"No," he said. "She never did." But even as he said it, a strange feeling of unreality washed over him, threatening to split him in two. "Maybe for a little bit when I was younger, but I . . ." He frowned, forehead scrunched up, tongue thick in his mouth, throat parched. "Huh. That's weird. Didn't she . . ." She was home. She was always there. When Nick got up. When Nick came home. Always there, always waiting for him with open arms and a smile on her face.

Gibby said, "I have two words in my head. Two words that I can't shake for some reason. *Before. After.* Always capitalized, like they're . . . I don't know. Important. But not to me. Does that mean anything to you? I don't know why, but it feels like they came from you."

"They didn't," he said, and this, too, felt like a lie, but he didn't know *why* that was. Hadn't he just had the same thought yesterday? "It's . . ." He looked off into nothing, unfocused, dizzy. The heat was getting to him. That had to be it. He shook his head, trying to clear out his brain. "Why does it matter?"

Visibly frustrated, Gibby said, "I don't know. I keep thinking she . . . your mom. For some reason, I remember a time when she wasn't there. With you and your dad. It's all foggy. And it doesn't make any sense because if she *wasn't* with you and your dad, then where would she have gone?"

"But she wasn't gone," Nick said slowly. "Maybe when she worked, if she had to go to a seminar or something. But other than that, I don't think she ever left."

Right? Right.

"Yeah," Gibby said, looking unsure. "You're right. I'm probably misremembering. Everything is fine."

"That's all right," Nick said. "A bunch of shit has happened in the last year. My head is all jumbled up with it, too." Then, because Gibby was being honest with him, he said, "Can I tell you something, too?"

"Of course," she said, pushing herself off the cooler door.

He gnawed on the inside of his cheek until it was ragged. "This whole . . . Burke thing. Protecting him from Owen. I can't . . . I don't know how to reconcile that, you know? He's done so much to try and hurt us, and it feels . . . wrong to step in and save him should something happen." He looked down at the floor. "I know we're supposed to help everyone we can. We're the good guys. We can't pick and choose who to save."

"But," she said, knowing there was more.

"But," Nick said. "Hearing my mom say that, and have Dad agree with her, doesn't sit right with me. They know our history with Burke. They have their *own* history. He's never done anything unless it benefits himself, and I don't get why they think we need to do anything for him. And even worse, I almost feel . . . sorry. For Owen." He winced, wishing he'd kept his mouth shut.

"Why?" she asked, and he loved her for the lack of censure in her voice.

Nick scrubbed a hand over his face, elbow knocking against an endcap of potato chips, the plastic crinkling. "He's not a good person. He lied to us. Hurt us. Tried to *kill* us. Hell, he *did* kill people."

"But," she said again.

"But would he have been like that if Burke wasn't his father?" He groaned, shaking his head. "I know how that sounds. If it comes down to us or them, I'm always going to side with us. Owen sucks ass. I want to make him eat his goddamn teeth the same as the rest of you, oh my god, I *hate*—"

"Nick."

He sagged, practically panting. "Thanks. That probably would have gone on for at least ten more minutes before I got to the point."

"I'm aware," she said dryly.

"It sucks," Nick continued. "Burke has hurt so many people, none more so than his own son, and now we're . . . what? Supposed to help him? After everything? How in the hell is *that* fair?"

"It's not," Gibby said quietly. "But then being an Extraordinary never really is. I may not know what it's like for you and Seth, but Jazz and I have been there for almost everything. We've seen how much it weighs on the both of you." Then, another strange question. "Do you trust your mom?"

He wanted to say yes immediately. He did. It was on the tip of his tongue, *right there,* and yet, he couldn't make the single word come out. Instead, he whispered, "I don't . . . know." The guilt that washed over him was enormous. Why shouldn't he? She was his *mother.* This felt like a betrayal. "I don't know," he said again, this time, a little louder. Another thought struck him, terrible, ridiculous. "I mean, it's not like she's working with Owen or anything. Or Burke. Or both."

"She already did," Gibby reminded him. "Remember? At least partially. It was a whole big thing. Your dad giving Burke info about Pyro Storm. The Concentra. And your parents were friends with Burke at one point."

"My dad's not like that," Nick snapped. "Yeah, he screwed up, but he promised me there'd be no more secrets."

"He kept Owen's letter from you," Gibby reminded him.

"He did," Nick admitted. "But I'm trying to give him the benefit of the doubt. He's worked his ass off to make things right. Also asked me to hold him accountable, and I've been doing that. We're all each other has."

Gibby looked spooked when she said, "You have your mom, too, though."

Shit. He'd forgotten her. Again. Why would he not have included her? It wasn't just him and Dad. It was the three of them. A team. Unnerved, he laughed. It sounded false even to himself. "Yeah. Of course. She's—"

His phone pinged. Gibby's, too.

They took a step away from each other. The cat above them hissed, ears flat against its skull, tail twitching. Nick pulled out his phone, looking down at the screen.

**BREAKING NEWS**

"Goddammit," Nick muttered. "I really hate these stupid notifications. They're never anything good. Like, why can't the breaking news be to say that everything is fine and nothing is exploding?"

"I don't think that's how it works," Gibby said, tapping out a quick message on her phone before shoving it back in her pocket. "Come on. There was a TV behind the counter. Bigger screen. I sent a text to Jazz in case she and Seth didn't see the notification."

The guy at the counter arched an eyebrow at them as they approached. Behind him, the TV. Another commercial, this time selling jewelry or an advertisement for a mariachi band, Nick couldn't be sure. He was about to tell Gibby that it couldn't be *that* important if Steve Davis wasn't already on the screen with his cheekbones and too-white teeth, but then the commercial cut away, replaced by the Action News banner.

"Can you turn that up?" Gibby asked, leaning on the counter.

"Are you going to buy anything?" the man asked. "This isn't a library."

Nick squinted at him. "What does a library have to do with—forget it." He dropped the water bottles on the counter, shoving them under the partition. Gibby did the same. "There. Now please turn up the TV."

"Would you also like to purchase a festive bandana?" he asked, nodding toward a small plastic stand on their side of the partition. On it, rows of rolled-up bandanas in a variety of colors. "Ten percent of proceeds go to saving the whales."

Gibby said, "Anything for the whales."

"Hell yeah," the man said. "Gotta keep those big fish swimming. Pick out a color you like. I'll get the TV."

"Whales aren't fish," Nick muttered as Gibby chose a green bandana with little white stars on it.

"And?" Gibby said out of the corner of her mouth. "It'll get us what we want. Who cares?"

"—and we're just getting word that . . . hold on." Steve Davis touched the tiny mic in his ear. "Yes, it seems as if mayoral candidate Simon Burke is getting ready to speak in front of the Tenth Precinct of the Nova City Police Department. This wasn't on any campaign schedule, so we don't know what sort of speech he plans to give."

"That's Dad's old precinct," Nick said. "Why the hell would he be speaking there?"

Gibby scoffed. "He probably found out about the protest and decided to insert himself where he isn't wanted."

The man behind the counter held out his hand. Not thinking,

Nick grabbed it and shook it. "Thank you for supporting the youth of this country. We are the future, and it's important to recognize—"

"Yeah, no," the man replied, tugging his hand free. "That's twenty bucks for the water. Ten for the bandana."

"Twenty bucks for *water*?" Nick exclaimed. "What the hell kind of racket *is* this? You know what? Never mind. I support local businesses. You're welcome." He dug into his shorts pocket and threw a couple of crumpled bills on the counter before turning back to the TV in time to see Steve Davis's face disappear, replaced by a podium set on a stage in front of a crowd, flags flying, people cheering, their arms waving in the air. The stage was lined with cops in uniform, standing at parade rest, eyes forward. An American flag hung limply next to a black-and-white flag with a single blue stripe across the middle.

"Does he really need eight cops up on the stage?" Nick asked. "Seems a little overkill."

"Not when you're trying to make a point," Gibby said darkly. "See the banners behind them?"

Nick did, long red banners with white lettering across the middle spelling out one word: BURKE. "That's . . . certainly a choice. Do you think they know Hitler had the same aesthetic, or . . ."

Gibby snorted. "Oh, I'm sure it crossed someone's mind at one point or another."

The camera panned over the crowd, a sea of white faces twisted in ecstasy. Behind them, blocked off by a line of at least twenty cops, were a smaller group of protesters, a Black woman at the front with a bullhorn, leading the chant of "NO JUSTICE, NO PEACE. NO JUSTICE, NO PEACE." The protestors with her looked like they came from all walks of life, but most of them appeared younger than those in the crowd in front of the stage. The woman with the bullhorn raised a fist into the air, holding it steady as she continued to shout into the bullhorn.

"They must have started early," Gibby said. "I bet they saw the stage getting set up."

The camera turned back toward the stage just as a familiar figure climbed the few steps. She was smiling, waving with both hands at the crowd, her light hair in curls on her shoulders, her lips slashed a furious red. She wore a skirt and heels, and a collared shirt, the top few buttons open to reveal tan skin.

He hadn't seen her in person since the night she infiltrated the prom. Though he didn't have proof, Nick knew she'd been tipped off by someone, and that someone was undoubtedly Simon Burke.

"Rebecca Firestone," Nick snarled as his archnemesis continued waving with an obnoxious grin, soaking up the adulation of the crowd.

"She's so hot," the man behind the counter said, glancing at the television. "Man, the things I'd let her do to me."

"You need a priest," Nick told him. "Someone with experience at performing exorcisms, because your soul being infested by a demon is the *only* reason anyone would say something like that."

"Or," the man said, "I have eyes. What. You don't think she's hot?"

"I do not," Nick assured him. "I'm gay as balls, so."

"She's hot," Gibby said. Nick started to sputter, and she added, "But only if you hate yourself."

"Oh, I do," the man said. "That's another story entirely. When I was seven, my grandpa ran over my pet chinchilla, and I—"

"I don't know what a chinchilla is," Nick said. "Also, not to be rude, but I'm trying to watch TV in your store."

The man muttered words under his breath. Nick chose to believe they were compliments. It made things easier, especially when Rebecca Firestone approached the podium and the crowd before her fell silent. The protestors continued to shout, but she ignored them.

"Nova City!" she said, voice booming. "How the hell are you?"

"Ugh," Nick said, making a face. "The audacity. Trying to relate to people as if she's not ten lizards wearing human skin."

"It is my great honor to stand before you today," Rebecca Firestone said, "to be able to introduce to you a man who loves this city with every fiber of his being. He *is* Nova City, born and bred, just like you, and that makes him a man of the people. He went to the same private schools—"

"Really relating to the common person," Gibby muttered. "Nothing says understanding the struggles of the everyman like private schools."

"—graduated from the top of his class at Nova City University—"

"Neat," Nick said. "He's an alumnus of the same school we're all going to. How fun."

"—built his company from the ground up all on his own." The crowd cheered as if Simon Burke hadn't come from a wealthy family, giving him opportunities most would never have. Why were people falling for this? Why couldn't they see Burke for what he really was? Nick understood the power of words, but he didn't know how anyone could hear Burke and believe what he was saying.

"I'm here to tell you that Simon Burke is the savior this city needs," Rebecca Firestone continued, voice raising over the boisterous noise flooding over her. "We are the normal people. We are the citizens who want to take our city back from those who think they're more than we are, those who think they can sit in judgment of the rest of us because of genetic abnormalities."

"What the hell," Nick breathed. "They're not even *trying* to hide it."

The man behind the counter scoffed. "Saying the quiet part out loud." Nick's approximation of him rose an inch or two, his lust for Rebecca Firestone be damned.

"—which is why I'm so thrilled to be able to introduce the man who won't let anyone or anything stop him from making this city the shining jewel it once was. My fellow Americans, I present to you the next mayor of Nova City . . . Simon *Burke*!"

The crowd went wild as Rebecca Firestone stepped back from the podium, clapping furiously. The noise rose to deafening levels as Simon Burke walked out in front of the stage, a wide smile stretched across his face. He wasn't alone; with him, holding his hand, was a woman Nick had only seen a handful of times: his wife, Patricia Burke. She shook hands with the officers as Burke pointed at the people gathered before them. Instead of his usual power suit, he wore jeans and a T-shirt. On the shirt across the chest were four gold letters: NCPD. Dad had the same shirt, though he didn't wear it anymore. Patricia was dressed similarly, her long black hair pulled back into a loose ponytail.

They stopped next to the steps leading up to the stage. Burke kissed her, said something lost to the noise. She nodded, and disappeared behind the stage as Burke climbed the steps. He reached Rebecca Firestone, taking her hands in his, leaning forward and whispering in her ear. She smiled blandly at whatever Burke was telling her, but right as Burke let her go and turned toward the podium, the smile dissolved into a grimace, there and gone again in a flash.

Burke stopped in front of the podium, letting the cheers wash over him. A deep chill ran through Nick, his spine a block of ice. It was easy to snark at Rebecca Firestone. *She* made it easy.

But Burke was something else entirely. Nick wasn't stupid. He knew Burke was, for some reason, popular, that most polls showed him leading the incumbent, Stephanie Carlson, by a healthy margin. The election was still a little over four months off and things could change between now and then, but what if it didn't? How the hell could no one else see just how dangerous he was? Yes, most people didn't know what he'd done or what he was capable of, and *yes,* Burke had a knack for spinning certain events in his favor, but that shouldn't have mattered, or so Nick thought. Burke had apparently perfected the art of manipulation, and it made Nick furious that so many people were falling for it, hook, line, and sinker.

Burke raised his hands to quiet down the crowd. He leaned toward the microphone, his perfect teeth flashing in a quick grin before he spoke. "Thank you for the warm welcome. It touches me greatly to know that so many of you have joined our movement to bring peace and prosperity back to Nova City. I stand before you today with the hardworking men and women of the Nova City Police Department, whose support I do not take for granted. They are the real heroes of this place we call home. They wear uniforms but they don't hide their faces behind masks. They are not vigilantes who take the law into their own hands. They protect. They serve. And they do it out in the open, without concealing who they really are, *as it should be*."

Gibby took Nick's hand in hers, squeezing tightly.

"Much has been made about the people who call themselves Extraordinaries," Burke said. His smile faded, but it looked intentional, practiced. "And I know that better than anyone. I was—no." He shook his head. "I *am* a father to one such person. His name is Owen. He is my son, and I know the harm he caused. The people he hurt."

"Killed," Nick spat, as Gibby made a wounded noise.

"And I think about him every day," Burke said, voice a little softer, as if it pained him greatly. "A father's love for his child is a beautiful thing, even when it shows us our own frailties. The mistakes we made. The mistakes *I* made." He sighed as the crowd cheered once again. "I am not a perfect man, but then I never claimed to be. I have learned from my own failures as a father and I will make you this promise: I will *not* fail you.

"The word *Extraordinary* is loaded, charged, given to those who can do things most of us couldn't even begin to dream about. It implies that they are, somehow, better than we are. *More* than we are. Why be ordinary when you could be extraordinary?" He bared his teeth as he practically swallowed the nearest microphone. "You are ordinary. *I* am ordinary. But we are still just as powerful. Perhaps we aren't pyrokinetic. Perhaps we aren't telekinetic, but together, we are going to make sure those who can do such things won't ever destroy our way of life."

The crowd exploded once more.

Burke spoke over them. "Which is why you have my solemn promise that, if elected mayor, in my first one hundred days, I will introduce legislation to make Extraordinary registration mandatory. We deserve to know who these people are, especially if they are our coworkers. Our neighbors. Extraordinaries in schools with our children. The only way to protect ourselves is to face the threat head-on. For too long, Nova City has allowed these people to act as they see fit without checks and balances. No more. The time to hide behind masks or in shadows is coming to an end, and I will lead the charge to ensure every single Extraordinary in Nova City is known to everyone."

Nick's phone vibrated insistently in his pocket, an incoming phone call. Without looking away from the screen, he answered the phone, putting it against his ear. "Hello?"

"Nick, I need you to listen to me. We don't have time for questions."

"Mom?" Out of the corner of his eye, he saw Gibby look at him with a frown. "What's going on?"

"Burke is speaking right now. He's—"

"I know. We're seeing it on TV. Did you know he'd be at Dad's old—"

"Nick," she snapped. "Stop. *Talking*. It's Owen. I've spotted him in the crowd. Do you hear me? He's *there*."

"Oh my god," Nick whispered, heart thudding against his rib cage. "No, no, *no*—"

*It's all about layers, Nick. My family tends to have a certain . . . flair for the dramatics.*

And:

*We're going to change the world, Nick. Of course I'd want to be a part of that. Don't you? Think about it. If you were given the power to make sure your dad would never be hurt again, wouldn't you take it?*

And, and, and:

*My name is* Shadow Star.

"Nick?" Gibby asked, sounding concerned. "What is it? What's wrong?"

"Listen to me," Mom breathed in his ear. "Get there as quickly as you can. I need your help. We have to protect them. I don't know what he's going to do, but we have to stop him. There are innocent people there. Hurry."

The phone beeped as she disconnected the call. Nick lowered his phone slowly, mind in overdrive.

"What is it?" Gibby asked again.

"Owen," Nick snarled, slamming his hand on the counter, the sound flat. The man behind the counter jumped, looking at Nick with wide eyes. "He's there. He's—"

"*What?*" Gibby said. She looked back at the TV. "Are you sure? Where? I didn't see anything."

"Mom saw him. She's heading there. I have to go. Get to the secret lair. Alert the others. Seth. Miss Conduct. Tell them to get to the precinct *now.*"

"The secret what now?" the man behind the counter asked, squinting at him.

Gibby was already shaking her head, looking determined. "We can tell them on the way just as easily. You're not going by yourself."

"I can't be distracted by—"

"I'm not a distraction," Gibby snapped. "I can handle myself. I don't need you to be my hero because *I'm* already my goddamn hero. We're a team, remember?"

"I get that," Nick said. "I'm not trying to say otherwise. But, Gibby, what if someone sees you? You won't be . . ." He glanced at the man behind the counter, who was looking at the both of them like they were the most interesting thing that had happened all day. ". . . covered, like I am."

She held up the bandana. "This will work, right? At least for now. You're not alone, so stop acting like you are. You're wasting time." She hurried to the door, stopping only a brief second to look at him and say, "You coming or what?"

"Dude," Nick said, suitably impressed. "Literal chills. That was almost a catchphrase. We'll need to work on it, but you're heading in the right direction."

She sniffed. "Damn right it was. Butch Fatale, ready to kick ass."

"What about your water?" the man called after him as Nick followed Gibby.

"Donate it to charity!" Nick bellowed over his shoulder. He paused before he went through the door, looking back at the man behind the counter, who stared at him with wide eyes. "Thank you, citizen. And remember what I always say." He posed heroically, hands on either side of the doorframe, chest puffed out. "It's time to take out the—"

The door swung shut, pinching his fingers painfully.

"*Ow!*" he cried, pulling his hands free and glaring at the door. "Motherfreaking *balls.*"

The man said, "It's time to take out the motherfreaking balls? What is that supposed to mean?"

"I hate everything," Nick mumbled, pushing the door open again and rushing out of the bodega.

# 7

He hit the street. Traffic backed up, the stench of exhaust thick and noxious. The precinct was at least ten blocks away, and Nick didn't think he could get there in time if he stuck to running. Regardless of how much he'd trained as of late, running was still the bane of his existence.

"Nick!"

He looked through the crowd on his left, seeing Gibby already half a block away, jumping up and down and waving her hands. "Here!"

He caught up with her, and she grabbed his hand, pulling him farther down the block. She skidded to a stop in front of a slim alley, blocked by a gate with a heavy lock. "You can change in here."

"On it," he growled. "I'll knock it down. Stand back."

"Why? Just use your—"

He threw himself at the gate, and immediately bounced off it, hitting the ground hard. He blinked as Gibby appeared above him, head silhouetted by the sun. "So," Nick grunted, grimacing at the jolt to his funny bone. "That didn't go like I thought it would. It must be made of the strongest steel ever created."

"Right," Gibby said, looking like she was trying to keep from laughing. "Let's go with that. Sucks you don't have powers. Oh, wait." She helped him up, turning him around to brush off his backpack.

"Yeah, yeah," Nick muttered. He raised his hand toward the gate and the pulse in his head flashed brightly. The gate shuddered as Nick jerked his arm back. The padlock squealed as it split right down the middle, falling and bouncing on the ground.

And because it was completely necessary (and because he didn't get to finish it back in the bodega), he growled, "It's time to take out the trash." He raised his leg to kick the gate open, putting all his force behind it, wishing he'd told Gibby to film it so he could replay it later to see how badass he looked.

In the end, though, it was a good thing she wasn't filming him, because the gate didn't open, the impact vibrating up his leg, causing him to almost fall down again.

Nick bounced around, hopping on one foot as he clutched his leg. "Why won't you *open*? I'm trying to save the damn city from my sort-of ex-boyfriend! Whoever invented gates is now my worst enemy, and I will—"

Gibby pulled the gate open with ease, staring at him as she did so.

"Yeah," Nick said. "That just happened."

"It did," Gibby said. "Good thing I'm with you. You'd probably have spent ten minutes pushing the gate before realizing you needed to pull it. And now I have some concerns."

"No time," Nick said. "Let's go. Thank you, Gibby. You might have just saved the day."

She rolled her eyes. "Glad to be of service."

He rushed through the gate into the alley, Gibby close at his heels. Jumping over wooden crates and overturned trash cans, he stopped halfway through, sliding his backpack off and setting it on the ground. He crouched next to it, pulling on the zipper.

It was stuck.

"*Why is nothing working?*" he roared. He gripped his backpack on either side of the zipper track and tore it open.

"You're such a disaster," Gibby said with a sigh as his helmet fell out, landing on the ground and bouncing a few feet away.

He ignored it for the moment, focusing on his costume. It was wrinkled. Jazz was going to kill him if he ended up on the news in a disheveled costume, but there was little he could do about that now.

He stood upright, beginning to pull his shirt up and over his head. He paused with it raised near his nipples, looking at Gibby. "Uh. Can you just . . . turn around?"

"Why?"

"Because I'm shy about nudity and don't want you to see my everything!"

She squinted at him. "Is this where I'm supposed to tell you that many people our age have body issues and it's important to—"

"*Gibby!*"

She sighed, but turned around, facing the opposite direction.

He waited a moment to make sure she wasn't going to peek before pulling his shirt the rest of the way off, letting it fall to the ground. Because his life was a farce, it landed in a dirty green puddle with bits of black *something* floating in it. Where the water had come from, Nick didn't want to know, especially since it hadn't rained in almost two weeks. He grumbled under his breath as he kicked off his Chucks and immediately stepped in a discarded container of what looked like days-old meatloaf, or at least that's what he told himself, because it could also be evidence of someone who'd *eaten* days-old meatloaf, only to have it evacuate their bodies into said container.

He should've listened to Seth when he'd said Nick should practice getting into his costume under a time constraint. Nick had told Seth he should show him how it was done first, innocently batting his eyes. This had been a mistake, because the moment Seth had stripped off his shirt, Nick had forgotten what they were supposed to be doing.

Wasting no time, Nick shoved his feet into the legs. He nearly brained himself against the wall as he pulled the costume up and over his shoulders, running his hand up the chest on a nearly invisible seam Mateo had come up with. That done, he grabbed his boots and practically jumped into them.

And last, the helmet, Gibby picking it up and handing it over. A familiar sense of *rightness* washed over him as the helmet settled on his head, vision growing sharper. A polyphonic tone played, light and happy, before the words WELCOME, GUARDIAN appeared before his eyes.

"Lighthouse," he said, voice deeper through the modulator in his helmet. "Do you read me?"

A beat of silence. Then, "Lighthouse here." Jazz. "What's going on? Why'd you come online, Nick? I thought you and Gibby were—"

Nick coughed pointedly as he picked up his clothes, putting them in his backpack and handing it over to Gibby, who slung it over her shoulder.

"Nick? You there?"

He coughed again as apparently the first time wasn't pointed enough.

Jazz groaned. "Seriously? You're really—fine. *Guardian*, I read you loud and clear, you absolute nerd. What's going on?"

"Owen," Guardian spat. "Burke's having a press conference at Dad's old precinct. Mom saw him and called me. I don't know what he's doing, but we can't let anyone get hurt."

"*What?* Why didn't she let us know through the app? We didn't get—hold on." Background talk, faint, muffled. Then Jazz's voice came back. "Seth is suiting up. He'll meet you there. You want me to put out the word for Miss Conduct?" He could hear her typing furiously in the background.

"Yeah," Guardian said as he looked up at the tall building next to him, trying to psych himself up for what would come next. He didn't know how he'd deal having Gibby with him, but he was a goddamn superhero. He'd figure it out. "Make sure she knows not to approach until we're all there."

"Will do." A beat. Then, "I've got your position. You're still ten blocks away. How are you and Gibby going to get there? Did you figure out how to fly since yesterday?"

Guardian took a deep breath, letting it out slowly. "I'm going to run up the side of this building and then leap from roof to roof. I'll carry Gibby with me."

Jazz and Gibby burst out laughing.

Guardian did not.

"Oh my god," Gibby said as she struggled to breathe. "You're *serious*? Nicky, what the hell, man. You're not going to carry me anywhere." She pulled out her phone, tapping on the screen quickly. Nick heard the familiar polyphonic tones as she entered their app. "Jazz, can you hear me?"

"Hi, babe! Don't let Nick carry you. I think he'll probably end up dropping you. I like your body shaped the way it is."

"Noted," Gibby said, still chuckling. "It might be quicker to just take a cab."

"Superheroes don't take cabs," Guardian growled dangerously.

"A Lyft, then."

"Gibby!"

"Don't yell at her," Jazz said. "She's right, which is why I've already ordered you a Lyft. Someone was close. It'll be there in a minute outside of the alley."

"That's my girl," Gibby said.

"Goddammit, *fine*. Lighthouse, we're heading for the Lyft. Keep us in the loop when you hear back from Miss Conduct." He ran-limped toward the gate that led back onto the street, Gibby mocking him by doing the same.

"On it. Your driver is named Gerald. He'll be in a . . . wow. A van that doesn't look like it has windows. But! He's got a really good rating, so I don't think he'll take you to his basement where he'll sing about wanting to wear your skin."

"Oh my god," Guardian mumbled as he crossed through the gateway. "We really need to find better ways to do this."

He reached the sidewalk and froze, Gibby bumping into him, causing him to stumble forward. The van wasn't there, but there were many, *many* people on the sidewalk, and they all stopped and stared.

He waved at them awkwardly. "Hey. How you doing? Good, I hope. Don't mind me. I'm just . . . doing my thang." Before he could stop himself, he pulled out his finger guns. *"Pew. Pew . . . pew."*

"This is the best day ever," Gibby announced to no one in particular.

A van screeched to a halt in front of them, rubber smoking, brakes wheezing. A lack of windows proved to be the least of their concerns, given the mural painted on the side of the van of a scantily clad, well-endowed woman riding a gigantic black seahorse surrounded by wavy green kelp.

"And somehow," Gibby said, "the day just got even better. Or worse."

The window rolled down, and a portly man with brown, curly hair leaned over, glancing down at his phone before looking back at Guardian and Gibby. "Jasmine Kensington?" he asked, arching a thin eyebrow.

*"Burrito Jerry?"* Guardian gasped. "What in the actual—"

Burrito Jerry, the man whom Rebecca Firestone had interviewed after their first clash with Smoke and Ice last winter. He'd apparently had his dinner ruined when Pyro Storm and Nick had been fighting for their lives. And here he was again, apparently their Lyft driver. Because *what*.

"Heck yeah," Burrito Jerry said happily. "That's me! I love being recognized. Always great to meet a fan. You want an autograph? Don't have any paper, but ever since that day, I get free burritos for life, so I've got a bunch of wrappers. That cool?"

Yes. That was probably one of the coolest things Guardian had ever heard of. But then he remembered what he was supposed to be doing, and he jerked open the passenger door. At least a dozen crinkled wrappers fell out onto the ground. "No time. Citizen, I need your assistance. It's life or death. We have people to save."

Gibby opened the sliding door, climbed inside, and settled on a bench seat that wheezed pitifully.

"Rock and roll," Burrito Jerry said, gunning the engine. "I

know this city like the back of my hand. I'll get you where you need to go before you can scream, '*Slow down before we die!*'"

Guardian and Gibby barely had time to shut the doors before Burrito Jerry slammed his foot on the gas, the van rocketing forward. Guardian did *not* scream, no matter what the noise that fell out of his mouth sounded like. He scrambled for a seat belt, only to find a rope. He heard Gibby curse and looked back to find her holding up a green bungie cord instead of her own seat belt, eyes wide.

Burrito Jerry glanced in the rearview mirror before looking at Guardian. "Yeah, sorry about that. Seat belts broke last week. Ferrets, man. They chew on everything, especially when there's fifteen of them. Just tie the rope around your waist. And you, miss. That bungie cord is just for show. But don't worry. I haven't been in an accident this week." He patted the dashboard as everything passed by them in a blur. "Don't want to hurt Matilda. Put too much work into her to mess her up. So. How are you?" He reached over and turned up his stereo. Guardian was sure heavy-metal music was about to pour from the speakers, guttural and angry. Instead, a feminine voice whispered, welcoming them back to her hair salon, that she was so happy to see them again. "Role-play ASMR," Burrito Jerry explained as if Guardian had asked. "Helps me sleep. Insomnia, you know? Hell of a thing."

Guardian's phone rang again. Mom calling. He answered and said, "Did you—"

"Where *are* you?"

Guardian sighed. "You wouldn't believe me if I told you. We're on our way."

True to his word, Burrito Jerry seemed to know Nova City better than most. Guardian didn't recognize half the side streets they turned down, but Burrito Jerry's phone affixed to the dash showed they were heading in the right direction. Somehow, it only took them six minutes to reach the street the precinct was on, though it was blocked off, police standing in front of blue wooden sawhorses with NCPD in white lettering. Behind them, in the distance, Nick could see a crowd of hundreds gathered in front of the stage, Burke's voice echoing unintelligibly.

Gibby leaned forward between the front seats. "Not here. We don't want them to try and stop us."

Burrito Jerry continued on down the road away from the roadblock. "Bad news, Jasmine. Things are weird lately. You feel it, right? It's in the air. Don't know why people are so gung ho about that dork."

"Burke?" Gibby asked.

Burrito Jerry nodded. "People like him, they think they know better than the rest of us. Throw enough money at a problem and it goes away. That's not how it works, though more than a few seem to fall for it. Rhetoric like his divides us. Makes us doubt each other and ourselves." He pulled up to a sidewalk half a block away from the roadblock. "Makes us angry. Hurt. And that's an awful combination. It makes you say and do things you don't mean." He shook his head as the van came to a stop. "We need to work together, you know?"

"Stand together so we don't struggle apart," Guardian whispered.

Burrito Jerry grinned at him. "You got it, man. We're so much stronger when we lift each other up and leave no one behind." He held out his hand to Guardian, who shook it gratefully. "Jasmine, it's been a pleasure. Anytime you need a ride, you let Burrito Jerry know. I got you." His phone pinged, and he blinked in surprise as he looked at it. "Holy mackerel. Now *that's* a tip. Thanks."

"I love him," Jazz breathed in his ear. "I want to protect him forever."

Guardian pushed open the door. Gibby did the same with the side door, stepping out onto the street before sliding it shut.

Before he shut his own door, Guardian looked back at his driver. "Hey, Burrito Jerry?"

"Yeah?"

"You're frickin' rad as hell."

Burrito Jerry held out his fist. Guardian bumped it with his gloved hand. "Thanks, Jasmine. You're pretty kickass yourself. Now fly, my sweet angel! Fly!"

"I can't fl—You're talking to the van, aren't you?"

"Who else would I be talking to?" Burrito Jerry winked, and then roared away, leaving Guardian and Gibby standing on the sidewalk, the passenger door hanging open. It slammed shut when the van screeched around a corner and disappeared from sight.

"Okay," Guardian said, ignoring the people stopping to stare at him, their phones up, taking photos and video. "Lighthouse, make a note for a team discussion. I vote we bring Burrito Jerry in on everything because he might be the greatest person who has ever lived." He grimaced as he pulled a burrito wrapper off the bottom of his boot. "Mostly."

"Noted," Jazz said. "You have my complete support in the matter. Gibby?"

"Agreed," Gibby said into her phone.

"That's three ayes," Jazz said. "We have a majority, but we'll run it by Seth later to make sure he's in agreement. Guardian, if he tries to argue, you'll need to threaten to break up with him to show how serious we are. Burrito Jerry is everything and should be celebrated as such."

"I heard that," another voice said. "Lighthouse, I'll remind you that threats don't work unless there's follow-through."

"I read you loud and clear, Pyro Storm," Jazz said. "And I've threatened more people than you have, so why don't we leave that to the professionals?"

"Goddamn," Gibby breathed. "I'm so turned on right now."

"Me, too," Guardian said. "It's very confusing. Pyro Storm, where are you?"

"See the building in front of you? East?"

"Uh," Guardian said. "Yes. Right. East. Exactly. Because normal people use cardinal directions rather than just saying right or left." He turned and looked across the street, ignoring the people gaping at them. "That's east. Right?"

"And you wanted to leave me behind," Gibby said. "For shame." She grabbed Guardian by the shoulders and turned him around. "That's east." She nodded toward the building in front of them, an eight-story thing of old brick and mortar that, according to the sign out front, housed different offices on each level—a law office, an architectural firm, and half a dozen others.

"Got it," Guardian said.

"On the roof," Pyro Storm said. "I have a view of the rally. Lighthouse, scanning the faces in the crowd. Should be up on your screen."

"It is," Jazz said, keyboard clacking. "Guardian, I have a way to get you by the cops blocking the road without being noticed. Incoming. Gibby showed me how to do the line thing."

A map appeared inside Guardian's helmet, a red line stretching through the building and out on the other side. It would put them on a back street to come up behind the precinct. Nick knew this area well. His dad had worked at this precinct since before he was born, and he'd gone there countless times.

"Line thing received," Guardian said. "Lighthouse, we're on the move."

"How do I look?" Gibby asked.

He turned toward her to see she'd wrapped the bandana around the lower half of her face, her nose a bump of green fabric. "Like it's 1867 and you're going to rob a train filled with rich people."

She snorted. "Exactly what I was going for. Let's go."

He jogged toward the building, Gibby at his side, the roar of the crowd and Burke's booming voice growing louder, people moving out of his way, eyes wide, phones following his every step.

"Thank you, citizens," Guardian called as he moved through them. "Have an Extraordinary day and remember: say no to drugs unless prescribed by your physician."

"Should've workshopped that one a little more," Gibby muttered as they reached the heavy ornate door. She pulled it open, and a wave of cold air washed over them.

Guardian stepped inside, lenses brightening slightly to make up for the difference in light from outside to inside. A security guard sitting behind a large desk said, "Welcome to . . . what?" His jaw dropped as he rose slightly from his chair.

"Just passing through," Guardian told him. "Continue doing what you're doing. I appreciate your cooperation."

The security guard nodded dumbly, sitting hard back down on his chair.

As Guardian and Gibby moved through the lobby toward a set of doors on the opposite side, Pyro Storm said, "I'm not seeing him. Lighthouse, anything?"

"No," Jazz said. "Are we sure he's there?"

"She said he was," Guardian said as they reached the doors. He opened the left one, leaning out to make sure no cops were standing outside. "If she saw him, then he's there. Keep looking."

"On it," Jazz said. "Let me see where she . . . huh."

"What is it?" Guardian asked, looking left, then right. This side of the building was mostly empty, used for deliveries to the back of the businesses. No sidewalks. One-way street with yellow arrows on black pavement.

"TK's tracker is off," Jazz said. "Why would she do that?"

"Might be a glitch," Gibby said, though she sounded unsure. "She's the one who saw Owen. She has to be here by now."

"She should be," Guardian said, opening the door all the way and motioning for Gibby to go through. She did, and he followed her out. "Don't worry about her right now. Focus on finding Owen. Have you heard from Miss Conduct? Where's—"

A snarl of electricity came from above, and Guardian raised his head in time to see crisscrossing power lines begin to shudder, blue arcs like lightning snapping. The air became heavy, stagnant, and Guardian grabbed Gibby by the arm, pulling her back just as electricity shot toward the ground. Guardian turned his head away from the bright light, the lenses on his helmet almost not enough to keep his eyes from burning.

A moment later, a powerful voice said, "Miss Conduct, reporting for duty and ready to save the day while looking fabulous."

"Her entrance is infinitely better than yours," Gibby said. "Full offense."

"Tell me about it," Guardian muttered as he looked at Miss Conduct standing before him.

The curls in her blue wig bounced, white mask covering her eyes, the corners of which turned up, almost like horns. Her bangles jangled as she came to them, the sequins on her black leotard glittering like a universe of stars. She grinned as she squeezed his wrist. "Look at you, honeybunch. You fill out that costume well. Looks like you've moved up to the ten-pound barbells. Good for you."

Guardian flexed, knowing the bumps in his arms *almost* caused the fabric of his costume to stretch. "Thank you for noticing. If all goes well, Seth said I can start using the heavier barbells. The *fifteen*-pound ones."

"Dare to dream," Miss Conduct said seriously. She nodded at Gibby—eyes widening slightly at the bandana around her face—before taking a step back. "Now, what's all the fuss about? Jazz didn't give too many details aside from telling me I needed to get my lovely posterior here."

"Owen Burke," Gibby said. "Supposedly at the rally."

Miss Conduct frowned, looking over her shoulder before clucking her tongue. "He is? How do you know?"

"Mom saw him," Guardian said.

Miss Conduct nodded slowly. "She thinks he's going for Burke. And remind me again, if you could, why are we protecting that man after all the shit he's pulled? Seems to me that if Owen wants to take him out, shouldn't we just . . . I don't know. Let him?"

"We can't," Guardian said. "It's not just about Simon Burke. There are innocent people in the crowd."

"People who want to see us drawn and quartered," Miss Conduct said. She held up a hand before Guardian could speak. "Yeah, yeah. I get it. Protecting people means protecting everyone. Still doesn't mean I like it. They wouldn't lift a finger to help us, but then I guess it falls on us once again to be the bigger people. And on my one day off, no less." She sighed. "Such is the life of a drag queen. Good thing I look amazing as per my usual."

"You do," Gibby told her. "Your costume makes the rest of them look like crap."

Miss Conduct grinned as Guardian and Pyro Storm spluttered. "I like you. You're a good one. What the hell are you doing hanging out with these nerds?"

"We'd be lost without her," Guardian said. "She's—"

"Pyro Storm," Jazz said. "Back of the crowd, left, in front of the protestors. Left. Keep going. Keep—*there*."

Guardian straightened, skin buzzing in tremulous excitement. "What is it?"

"Man," Pyro Storm said. "Wearing a hoodie. Hood up around his head. Bad angle. I can't see his face."

"In this heat?" Miss Conduct asked. "That can't be good."

"Pyro Storm," Guardian said. "Be our eyes. Keep him in your sights. We're headed for the rally."

"On it," Pyro Storm said. "Look up."

They did, and Guardian gasped when a figure leapt between the buildings, backlit by the blazing sun. He landed on the roof of the building on the opposite side and briefly disappeared from view before he leaned over the edge, waving down at them.

"Please ignore my erection," Guardian said. "It's not my fault."

"Ah, young love," Miss Conduct said, patting the side of Nick's helmet. "Come on. Let's get this over with so I can go back home and try to crawl inside my freezer. Drag queens aren't meant to survive in humidity like this. It's ruining my wig." She turned and hurried toward the rally, Guardian and Gibby close at her heels.

The street was awash with noise and excitement, flags waving side to side, people cheering. Burke droned on and on, his words at odds with the shouts of the protestors gathered behind wooden sawhorses, a row of cops standing in front of them.

Guardian pressed his back flat against the building, peering around the corner. "Pyro Storm, you have him?"

"No. Lost him. Lighthouse, you see him?"

"Negative," Jazz said. "Too many people. Are we sure about this? I can't get TK on the line. Tracker's still off."

"We can't take the chance," Guardian muttered. "We need to get to him before he tries anything."

Gibby looked like she was going to argue but sagged instead.

"Shit," Pyro Storm said suddenly. "I see him. The man in the hoodie. Lighthouse, do you copy? He's moving toward the front of the crowd. I repeat, he's moving toward Burke."

"Got him," Jazz said. "Can't see his face. His head is turned down toward—oh no."

"What is it?" Guardian asked, feeling jittery, his tongue thick in his mouth. "What's going on?"

"He's reaching for something," Jazz said. "In his pocket. I can't—there's too many people in the way. He's moving."

Guardian didn't hesitate. He pushed himself off the building wall and tore around the corner, legs and arms pumping, Gibby and Miss Conduct shouting after him, Pyro Storm growling in his ear.

He flinched when streamers shot out of a cannon, filling the air with colorful strips of paper. The sound of the crowd bowled over him, but all Guardian could think about was Owen whispering in his ear in the bowels of Burke Tower, telling him that all he needed to do was take a pill, and all his dreams would come true.

*Tiny things, aren't they? Though they'll surely pack a wallop.*

Seductive, this, so much so that Nick had almost fallen for it. It'd been close, more so than most people knew, even Seth. Yes, in the end, he hadn't, but what would've happened if Pyro Storm hadn't shown up when he did? Did he really believe he'd have refused?

*Someone like you wouldn't even be given a chance. And how is that fair? After all, it's your father who suffered.*

It *wasn't* fair, but not in the way Owen had meant. It was unfair because Owen had known just how much Nick had wanted it, so much so that he'd been *gagging* for it. Maybe if Pyro Storm hadn't arrived at the last moment, things might have been different, but Nick wasn't that person anymore, and it had nothing to do with the fact that he'd inherited telekinesis. He knew now what he hadn't before: he didn't need the pills to be extraordinary because he already *was* extraordinary, powers be damned.

He was going to stop Owen if it was the last thing he did. It had nothing to do with Shadow Star or Pyro Storm. It had nothing to do with Simon Burke or Mom and Dad. It certainly didn't have anything to do with the people who feared Extraordinaries.

He knew how it felt to have despair, to feel small and scared, and he didn't want anyone to feel that way. If he could help them from ever knowing—

*Nicky. Oh my god,* Nicky.

He stumbled, nearly fell, as he thought, *Before. Before and After. There was a Before and an After and I, I—*

He pushed through it. Not now. Not when he needed to focus. As if shaking off a terrible dream, Guardian lifted his head toward the mob.

A woman noticed him first. She stood at the edge of the crowd to the left of the stage, wearing a shirt with Burke's face on it under the words IN BURKE WE TRUST! She must have seen him racing toward them out of the corner of her eye, because she turned toward him, mouth dropping, eyes bulging.

She screamed.

The effect was instantaneous. People around her whirled around, following her gaze, beginning to shout as Guardian ran as fast as he ever had. He waved his arms, yelling at them to get out of the way. They scattered, shoving into each other. A little boy holding the hand of a man next to him was knocked to the ground as panic descended. Another man wasn't looking where he was going and was about to trample the kid when Guardian reached for him, fingers splayed, the spark in his head bursting in a furious explosion.

The man's foot fell toward the kid's legs, but before he could step on him, Guardian *pushed,* teeth grinding together. The air in front of him rippled and shot forward, hitting the man's foot, causing him to spin awkwardly, stepping hard on the ground next to the kid, missing him by inches. The kid's father scooped him up, holding him close even as he glared at Guardian.

"Where is he?" Guardian snapped. "Pyro Storm, you got him?"

"I'm coming," Pyro Storm said, and Guardian looked up in time to see Pyro Storm jump from the rooftop, hurtling toward the ground.

"Move!" Guardian yelled. "Get out of the way!"

People did as he demanded, the crowd parting even as Simon Burke was practically tackled by cops, pulling him back from the podium, standing in front of him, shielding him and Rebecca Firestone. For a moment, it looked as if Burke smiled, but then he was blocked by a large cop.

Guardian moved through the crowd, those around him creating a circle that collapsed and regrew the farther he went. Hands grabbed for him but he managed to pull free.

Off to his right. Black hoodie casting a face in shadow, but Nick saw the curve of his jaw, the jut of his nose, and he knew, he *knew* it was Owen.

He pivoted just as Pyro Storm hit the ground a few feet in front of him, the red lenses on his mask flashing. They moved in tandem, pushing their way through. The man—*Owen*—turned away, looking as if he was going to flee.

Pyro Storm reached him first, grabbing him by the shoulders and spinning him around.

The hood fell off his head.

It wasn't Owen. It didn't even look like him. The man was at least thirty years old, his skin pale white, brown eyes bright with fear. He pulled his hands from his pockets, and a camera fell out, bouncing on the ground. Pyro Storm let him go, and he fell back into a group of women who kept him upright.

"Oh no," Guardian whispered.

"Hands *up!*" someone cried, and Guardian turned his head to see three cops standing at the front of the stage, guns drawn and pointed directly at Pyro Storm. "You, there! Stand down *now!* Don't move, you hear me?"

Guardian took a step back and bumped into someone. He glanced over his shoulder to see Gibby, Miss Conduct bringing up the rear, both of them looking worried.

"Where is he?" Gibby asked, a sheen of sweat on her forehead. "Did you get him?"

"It's not him," Pyro Storm snapped as people in the crowd began to film them instead of running which, *what.* Did no one have a sense of self-preservation anymore? "He's not here."

"Ah, shit," Miss Conduct groaned. "Are you serious?"

Movement on the stage, cops yelling for Burke to get back, sir, get *back.* But Burke ignored them, approaching the podium once more, never once looking away from the Extraordinaries. Guardian felt a chill run down his spine at the look on Burke's face. If he didn't know any better, he'd have thought Burke seemed almost . . . pleased.

"And this is *exactly* what I'm talking about," Burke said into the microphone, voice loud through the speakers, causing almost everyone to look at him. "Here we are, peacefully assembling, as is our right, only to once again have our lives interrupted by *Extraordinaries.* Don't you see? They want you—*us*—to be scared. They want us to doubt ourselves. Our mission. Our way of life."

The crowd nodded as one, and if looks could kill, then Guardian, Pyro Storm, and Miss Conduct would sure as shit be dead right then and there. Maybe even Gibby, too.

"They may think they're gods, but we know better than that, don't we?" Burke said, a nasty curl in his voice. "Pyro Storm, as you all well know, is nothing but a seventeen-year-old *boy* named Seth Gray."

"You're right," Pyro Storm said. And then, without hesitating, he removed his helmet, causing the people around them to gasp dramatically, as if Seth hadn't already done this once before. What a bunch of freaking drama queens. "I *am* Seth Gray. And I may only be seventeen, but I've still done more to help this city than you *ever* will."

Burke, for his part, didn't seem fazed. His gaze crawled over Gibby and Miss Conduct dismissively before landing on Guardian. His smile widened. "And you there. I haven't seen *you* before." He leaned forward, practically swallowing the mic. "Who are you supposed to be?"

"Guardian," he spat, ignoring the loud whispers buzzing around him like a hive of angry bees. "And you know damn well that—"

"Guardian," Burke said, the echo bouncing off the buildings. *Guardian, Guardian, Guardian.* "Is that right? The same Guardian who once haunted the streets of our fair city? No. Of course not. You picked up a discarded mantle and tried to make it your own, like you have any right."

"Gibby," Seth muttered under his breath without looking away from the stage. "Get back."

Out of the corner of his eye, Guardian saw Gibby nod and melt back into the crowd, though she didn't go far. He took a step toward the stage, the cops shouting at him to freeze, their guns all trained on him. He did, but continued to glare up at Burke. "I have *every* right. Your son is—"

Burke scoffed. "My son isn't here. We have done nothing wrong, and yet here you are, trying to stop the inevitable. Perhaps you're working with the protestors. Is that it? Did they want you here to interrupt us?" He shook his head. He paused for a moment as Rebecca Firestone stepped forward, whispering in his ear. He nodded slowly at whatever she said.

The doors to the precinct burst open, more cops streaming out. Chris Morton was among them, shoving his way to the front and telling people to get out of his way. He barely glanced at Guardian and the others as he raised his hands, standing between Guardian and the stage. "Stand down!" he bellowed. "Put your guns away! Are you out of your damned minds?"

Guardian didn't see who threw it. Movement off to his right, and then something flew toward Seth's head. Guardian acted without thinking, sure it was a brick or something equally as heavy that'd crack Seth's skull, spilling blood. The spark in his head burst brightly, and the air rippled around him as he raised his hand, fingers crooked like claws.

Not a brick. A water bottle, spinning end over end until it just *stopped*, a foot away from Seth's head, hovering in the air, the shadow on the ground wavering as water sloshed back and forth.

Deafening silence, so thick Guardian could almost taste it. He dropped his hand, and the bottle fell toward the ground. It split as it bounced off the pavement, water splashing on Seth's boots.

"He can do *magic*!" someone screamed in the crowd. "He's a goddamn *witch*. *BURN HIM AT THE STAKE*."

Guardian whipped his head toward the sound of the voice. "Do you know what *century* it is? Also, that had nothing to do with witches and *everything* to do with religious misogyny that—"

An orange bounced off his chest, skin breaking, sticky juice splashing up on his lips before it fell to the ground with a wet *plop*.

Guardian raised his head slowly. "Did you bring *fruit* to a rally? Why the hell would you—"

He never got the chance to finish. More things were thrown at them, driving them back: water bottles, a half-empty soda can, a banana, an umbrella. Guardian yelped as a leather briefcase struck him on the shoulder, causing him to stumble. A woman who looked like a kindly grandmother began to smack Miss Conduct with her purse, bellowing, "Your hair isn't even *real*! I would know because I *also wear a wig*!"

Miss Conduct snatched the purse away from her. "Lady, I will see you put in a *home* if you hit me with your cheap knockoff one more time. You don't want to test me." She shoved the purse back into her hands.

"He's threatening an old woman!" someone cried.

"*She*," someone else corrected him. "Just because we despise them doesn't mean we can't respect their pronouns. Don't be a dick, Ernie. It's not a good look."

"Sorry. Sorry, everyone! I got caught up in the heat of the moment, but that's no excuse. I will take what I've learned today and try to be a better person. *She's* threatening an old woman! Get them!"

"Get *out of here*," Chris snapped at them as he moved in front of the surging crowd, waving at the cops to help him.

Someone grabbed Guardian's arm, jerking him back. He looked over his shoulder to see Gibby trying to pull him away. "We have to *go*," she said. "We can't stay here!"

Guardian tried to pull his arm out of her grasp. He knew she was right; live to fight another day and blah, blah, blah, but part of him—a dark, dangerously strong part—wanted to raise his hands toward Burke. To use his remarkable powers to lift Burke off the stage, to watch him as he begged for his life, as he choked, face turning purple. Eyes bulging. It wouldn't take much. He could do it. He knew he could. And if he did, it'd be over, finally, at last, consequences be damned. Burke could never hurt anyone again.

*We don't kill,* Dad whispered in his head.

He crashed back down to reality when Seth crowded against his back, urging him forward. "No, Nicky," Seth breathed in his ear, grunting as something *wet* slapped against his back. "It's not worth it. *He's* not worth it. Don't give him an excuse. It's what he wants. He *wants* you to lose control. Don't let him win."

Dazed, he let himself be pulled away, pushing through the people grabbing at them, their eyes feral, teeth bared.

"Miss Conduct!" Seth bawled over his shoulder. "*Move.*"

Guardian shot a look back over his shoulder and saw Miss

Conduct staring up at Burke. "We're trying to *protect* your stupid ass. What the hell is wrong with you?"

Burke looked on either side of him, where the cops stood, guns still drawn. "Does it look like I need your protection? I have the good men and women of the NCPD on my side. Nova City is no place for vigilante justice."

"Get out of here," Chris snarled, eyes ablaze. "*Now.*"

Miss Conduct looked unsure, but Gibby hurried back toward her, grabbing her by the hand and pulling her along.

"That's it," Guardian heard Burke say as they retreated, voice booming. "Run. Run as fast as you can. People of this city: you have my solemn promise that if elected your mayor, I will put an end to the Extraordinary menace once and for all."

The crowd roared their approval as Guardian and his friends ran away.

# 8

To call the fallout catastrophic was, perhaps, a bit of an over-statement, regardless of how it felt in the days that followed. While the news spread like wildfire throughout Nova City— local reporters breathlessly recounting the confrontation at five, six, and eleven o'clock, and then again the next day and the next—it barely made a blip on the national level. If it was mentioned, it was mostly as an afterthought, and always with shots of the aftermath of the Attack on Centennial High, Pyro Storm rising above the crowd, fire leaking from him as he removed his helmet and revealed himself to be Seth Gray.

That being said, of course, it set the internet on fire. One video racked up six million views within forty-eight hours, complete with comical sound effects of the orange hitting Guardian in the chest. It was on Reddit. Tumblr. TikTok. It trended on Twitter for almost ten hours (#VitaminC4UandMe) before a dog was found barking at a small sewer pipe, scratching frantically on the ground. It turned out she was trying to rescue her puppy who'd gotten stuck. Most everyone agreed it was touching to witness (#SewerPupIsAllOfUs).

A spokesperson for the protestors—a Black woman named Tasha—was interviewed by Steve Davis of Action News that night. She looked poised, in control, calmly responding to Steve Davis when he asked what she thought of Guardian, and Extraordinaries as a whole. "Why does it matter?" she asked. "I can't speak to the motivations of the Extraordinaries. Frankly, that's not up to me. We were there because Simon Burke is a fascist, and his policies show that clearly. Anything else is a distraction. He has aligned himself with the NCPD, an organization that has proven itself to be woefully unfit and unprepared to deal with the problems that face Nova City. He *says* he wants to rid this city of Extraordinaries. What if he does that? What if it's not enough? Who does he go after next? People who look like you, or people who look like me? I'll give you three guesses, and the first two don't count."

Steve Davis smiled blandly. "Surely you don't think he'd—"

"I *do*," Tasha said. "Men in power like Burke, men with unlimited resources and a desire to control everything, are not only a detriment to society, but a danger to us all."

"Thank you, ma'am," Steve Davis said. "That was certainly illuminating. When we return from the break, we'll confront an important issue that everyone is talking about. When will this heat wave end? Meteorologist Chuck Hendrix has your extended forecast. We'll be right back."

Dad was, in a word, furious at what had transpired, but not at Nick. He might not have been exactly pleased that Nick had suited up when he did, but he said he understood. Dad wrapped Nick in a hug in their living room when he came home, holding him tightly, rocking him back and forth on the couch, his face in his son's hair. "Screw them," he said fiercely. "Screw them all. I've got you, kid."

If a tear or two fell from Nick's eyes . . . well. No one blamed him for that.

The interior of the house was quiet.

"Where is she?" Nick asked, trying to keep his voice even.

"I don't know," Dad said quietly. "I haven't heard from her yet."

"She told us Owen was there," Nick said, standing up from the couch. "She said she saw him. She's the reason we were there in the first place."

Dad stared up at him for a long moment. "What are you saying, kid?"

Frustrated, Nick fisted his hair and began to pace. "I don't know. But Jazz said Mom turned off her tracker. She wasn't on comms. She wasn't *there*. Why would she do that to us? To *me*?"

"I'm sure there's an explanation," Dad said, though he didn't seem as if he believed his own words. He looked off into nothing, obviously struggling with what to say next. "She . . . she didn't call me." He frowned.

"Because I couldn't," she said, causing them both to jump and whirl around.

Mom stood in the entryway of the kitchen wearing jeans and one of Dad's shirts, the sleeves rolled up, the hem hanging down around her thighs. She looked tired, dark circles under her dull eyes. Taking a step toward them, she said, "I'm sorry, Nicky. I should've been there."

Before Nick could snap at her, Dad spoke. "Where were you, Jen?"

She sighed, shaking her head, the floor creaking with every step she took. "Following Owen. He *was* there. I saw him. But he must have known we were on to him because he left before you arrived. I went after him, but I lost him in the city."

No one spoke. The only sound came from the clock above the fireplace, *tick, tick, tick*ing.

Mom tried again. "I know that's not an excuse, but I had to make a split-second decision. Aaron, you've had to do the same. Nick, you, too. I know you're angry with me, but I did what I thought was right."

Dad nodded slowly. "You should've told them. You should've told *me*."

"I know," she said quietly. "I wasn't thinking. All I could focus on was stopping him from hurting anyone."

Dad relaxed slightly, but that only made Nick angrier. "Why did you turn off your tracker? Why didn't you tell anyone where you were going before we walked into that mess?"

She sighed, shaking her head. "I'm sorry I wasn't there when you needed me to be. But I promise I'm here for you, same as your father. You don't have to go through this alone. It's easier to stand together than it is to struggle apart." She came around the couch and held her arms open in invitation.

Nick took a step toward her, wanting nothing more than to feel her arms around him. Already, he felt calmer than he had just a moment before, almost intrusively so. Like he wasn't in control. His legs moved of their own volition, and his arms raised, ready to hug his mother, just like she wanted.

*The bank,* he thought deliriously. *Oh my god, Nicky. She's—*

He stopped a foot away from her.

She watched him, wiggling her fingers.

"No," he said, taking a step back, even if it felt like one of the hardest things he'd ever done.

She blinked, arms dropping back down to her sides. "What do you mean, *no?*"

"I'm pissed off at you," he snapped. "We're a team. We work together. We don't go off half-cocked alone. We keep each other in the loop. That's what being part of Lighthouse means. Seth knows that. Jazz and Gibby, too. Even Mateo. So why don't you?"

The skin under her left eye twitched. "I seem to remember a time or ten when you did exactly what you're accusing me of. Recently, even."

"Whoa," Dad said, rising from the couch, standing next to Nick. "Jen, I know things are heated right now, but that was uncalled for. Nick is seventeen years old, and we're the parents here."

Her expression softened as she looked at Dad. "I know, Aaron. But you have to believe me that I never wanted this to happen. I wouldn't do that to you." She glanced at Nick before looking back at Dad. "Or him. We're on the same side."

"Then why don't you act like it?" Nick retorted.

"You're overreacting," she said in a calm voice that made Nick's skin itch. "But I don't blame you for that."

"Overreacting," Nick said. "You think *I'm* overreacting. Cool. Hey, I have an idea. If it's not as big a deal as you seem to think I'm making it out to be, let me call some reporters. Have them come over for a family interview. Me. Dad. You. You can put on your costume and have a dramatic reveal where you tell everyone who *you* really are."

He pulled his phone out of his pocket. He wasn't *really* going to call a reporter—in fact, he didn't have a reporter's phone number—but he was trying to prove a point.

His phone flew from his grasp, floating toward his mother, whose hand was raised toward him. The phone landed on her palm, fingers wrapping around it. "That's quite enough," she said. "You can be upset with me all you want, but why would you want to hurt me like that?" She sniffled. "Nick, I'm your mother. I would *never* do something like that to you."

Guilt, then, clawing at his insides, tearing him to shreds. "I don't . . ." He glanced at Dad, whose face was pale, expression spooked. An apology tried to force its way out, but he swallowed it back down. Self-righteousness and Nick Bell were old friends. "You hid everything from me," he said, voice hard. "You both did. For all I know, you're still working with Burke."

As soon as he said it, he wished he could take it back, but it was out there now, in the open, a secret fear he'd carried with him ever since he'd learned Simon Burke was responsible for the pills that suppressed his powers for most of his life. He loved his father, more than anyone in the world. Dad had made mistakes—but Nick had chosen to believe they were just that: mistakes without malicious intent.

*Mom too,* a little voice whispered, intrusive, tickling his brain. *She's just as much as part of this as Dad.*

Dad's face crumpled, shoulders sagging.

Mom, though. Her gaze was unfocused, her hands twitching at her side, lips moving without sound.

*She's here,* the same strange voice told him. *She only wants to protect you. Why are you being like this?*

He groaned, shaking out the tension in his shoulders. "I didn't mean that. I shouldn't have . . ." He huffed out an irritated breath. "I know you both are trying to help. Trying to do the right thing after . . ." *(Before, After, Before, After)* ". . . after everything. But if you think I'm just going to stand here and let you make excuses then, man, are you in for a major disappointment. I trust that you love me. I trust that you only want what's best for me. But I don't think I trust you to know what that is."

"Nick," Dad said quietly. "That's . . . okay, that's fair. Let's take a step back, yeah? Cool our heads a little bit. I don't think any of us want to say something else we'll regret later."

But Nick was worked up. He stared at his mother dead-on, refusing to look away. "If you're going to be part of Lighthouse, then you need to treat us like we're on your team. If you'd told us that Owen was already gone, we wouldn't have looked like assholes at Burke's rally."

"You're right," Mom said evenly. "I screwed up. It won't happen again." She wiped her eyes and gave him a watery smile. "I'd really like that hug now, if that's all right with you."

He went to her. Of course he did.

Everything was fine.

The next few days were surprisingly quiet, all things considered. Mom, Dad, and Nick moved gingerly around one another, as if they thought one of them might explode with the slightest provocation.

Reporters once again camped out in front of the Gray brownstone. They only stayed for a couple of days before moving on. The city never slept, and since they weren't getting anything from Bob, Martha, or Seth, they turned their attention elsewhere. It didn't take long for the Ruckus at the Rally (also capitalized, as if it carried the same weight as the Battle at McManus Bridge and the Attack on Centennial High) to become old news.

For his part, Burke didn't follow through with his threats. He was interviewed almost nightly, and whenever questions were asked about Extraordinaries, Burke answered in generalities, pushing his agenda that Extraordinaries as a whole were dangerous and he was the only man who was in a position to do anything about it.

It certainly didn't help that the current mayor—Stephanie Carlson—almost seemed to *agree* with him, saying she believed that everyone had the right to support their candidate without interruption. "While I am against everything that Simon Burke stands for and believe that he's not the leadership Nova City needs, I call on the Extraordinaries of this city to allow him to speak to his supporters without fear of those who call themselves superheroes. If they had done the same to me, I know that Mr. Burke would've spoken out. He is—"

Nick scoffed as he stopped the video, Carlson's face freezing midword on the screen. While he knew there were good people in politics with the best of intentions, he was of the mind that the rest were most likely sociopaths, and that outweighed everything else. Just like with the cops.

It helped when he switched over to a different tab (one of at least a dozen—Nick's interests were wide and varied, his chaotic mind knowing no limits) and looked at Twitter. He found Burke's campaign account and was heartened to see he'd been ratioed on his last seven tweets, most of the responses coming from accounts with some variation of the word *Extraordinaries* in their handles. There were even a few fancams of Pyro Storm with clips taken from the news, glittering hearts raining down around him over washed-out filters backed by terrible pop songs. Nick approved wholeheartedly.

It was Wednesday morning, and Nick was supposed to be working on practice essays for his college applications. He grumbled, but it was half-hearted. He didn't exactly have the extracurriculars that would impress a college admission's office, and while not terrible, his grades didn't set him apart from the crowded field. Dad wanted him to not put all his hopes into Nova City University, saying that while he was confident Nick would get in, he needed to plan just in case that didn't happen. The idea of Jazz, Gibby, and Seth all being at the same school without him rubbed Nick the wrong way, and he swore to himself that he'd make sure his senior year went as smoothly as possible so as not to give anyone reason to reject him.

He'd worked on the essay for exactly thirty-seven minutes before deciding that a better use of his time might be to see if there were any hints about an Extraordinary in Nova City who could move shadows. Dad was out with Cap, and Mom was . . . somewhere. He didn't know. It wasn't like she had a job. Seth was with Gibby, both of them working out in the basement of the Gray home.

Jazz was working on her own essay, texting Nick photos of her word count every ten minutes as if to rub it in his face.

So here he was, alone, the house all to himself.

What would a seventeen-year-old virgin do with such a fortuitous event?

Masturbate, obviously.

He listened carefully to make sure no one had come home without him knowing. The house was quiet, the only sounds coming from Nick's open window. It was cooler outside today than it'd been in weeks, and the sounds of the city drifting in through the window calmed him as they always did. He got up and locked the door, just to be safe, before going back to his desk. He had a routine for such things. A bottle of lotion and a small towel hidden in a drawer.

He pulled up an incognito tab, silently thanking whoever would listen that Dad hadn't put stricter parental controls on the internet. He found his favorite porn site and considered his options. Extraordinary porn? Boner Boy and rough-and-tumble oil worker was an old classic, but he'd already rubbed himself raw to that one. Literally.

He perused the categories, trying to find one that caught his attention. Twinks (eh). Bears (rawr). Mature (yikes). Furries (which, okay, maybe not for him, but they seemed to be having a great time being wolves and cats and goats, so who was he to judge?). Groups (where did everyone put their feet and arms?) and Fetish (maybe later) and Vintage (where the mustaches were somehow bigger than the pubic hair).

He paused over one category he'd never explored before. "Huh," he said to himself. "That's . . . interesting."

*Power Bottoms,* the link said.

He clicked on it, and the screen flipped over to row after row of videos with men in all shapes and sizes. He clicked on the first one. A slender man was painting a wall, wearing a pair of blue-splattered overalls and nothing on underneath. For some reason, he already had a boner, and Nick wondered if being a power bottom meant getting turned on by sniffing paint. It certainly seemed plausible, the evidence in front of him abundantly clear.

"Oh no," the man said, sounding as if he had never heard the word *acting* before. "It's almost quitting time and I haven't finished painting this wall. My boss is going to be so angry with me. I sure hope he doesn't take it out on my ass like last time."

"Okay," Nick said. "You're not really selling this yet. Like, I don't *believe* you're worried about employer repercussions. But if that's at the forefront of your mind, maybe you should look into forming a union?"

Another man walked in, wearing a tight white shirt that showed off his muscular build. And, for some reason, he was wearing jean cutoff shorts that barely covered his thick thighs.

"You must be the boss," Nick said sagely. "I can tell because of your steely gaze and your stoic frown."

"It's quitting time and you haven't finished the wall," the bigger man said. "You know what that means."

The painter sighed the weary sigh of those trapped in the throes of capitalism, knowing that no matter what he did, he wouldn't be able to escape a society built around an economic system in which trade and industry were controlled by private owners for profit. Nick had memorized this fact in order to pass a test. It was good to know he could still retain information with his blood rushing south.

"Yes, sir," the painter said, dropping his paintbrush and—

"You're getting naked *already?*" Nick said. "He's your *boss.* Show a little decorum. Make him work for it, at least. Why don't you—wow. *Wow.* So you don't have a gag reflex. Good to know." Nick did. He could barely stop from gagging if his toothbrush went too far back into his mouth. That didn't bode well in case Seth was . . . bigger than a toothbrush.

Almost forgetting he was supposed to be squeezing out a little lotion, Nick leaned forward, face inches from the screen as he studied the acts performed in front of him. When they got to the main event, Nick was sweating profusely, and not necessarily because of raging hormones, though that was part of it.

He was mostly impressed by how *easy* Painter made it look. He took his boss's penis like a damn *champ,* and Nick didn't understand why there wasn't even the smallest amount of prep. Painter bounced, wooden filth streaming from his mouth—interspersed with classic phrases such as "Yeah" and "Give it to me" and "Now I'll *never* finish painting."

Nick paused the video, sitting back in his chair, ignoring his own dick, which seemed to appreciate what he'd just witnessed.

"Power bottom," he muttered, wondering if Seth would . . . if he'd . . .

Now, it should be said that Nick's power—even before he'd found out he had *actual* powers—had always been his brain. His strange, wonderfully chaotic brain. When he found something he didn't understand, he researched it until he became an expert.

With that in mind, he clicked over to a different tab and began to type.

DOES BOTTOMING HURT?

He nodded. That sounded right. He hit Enter.

Row after row of links popped up on the screen, and he clicked on the first one, already feeling at ease. WikiHow, one of his favorite places on the entire internet, which had never let him down before. It crowdsourced all the important questions one might have, such as HOW TO MAKE YOUR OWN CEREAL and HOW TO USE BAD LANGUAGE WITHOUT GETTING CAUGHT and HOW TO BE A NORMAL PERSON. Granted, none of these topics interested Nick, but there was something out there for everyone.

What made it even better was how most of the articles were illustrated, for some reason, as if brightly colored pictures helped to explain the contents. Fun fact! They mostly did not.

The picture at the top of the article showed a man rubbing his chin thoughtfully, a word bubble above his head. However, instead of words in the bubble, it was a picture of a bare butt with a question mark next to it.

"Perfect," Nick breathed as he began to read with interest.

So, you want to be a bottom! Congratulations on making such an important decision. Though some seem to think tops have all the power in a relationship, it's actually the bottom who is in control. Without them, tops would have nothing to insert themselves into. They need people just like you!

"I feel validated," Nick whispered.

There are many ways to bottom—and not all involve penetration—which we'll cover in greater detail later on. But the first thing a bottom must ask themselves is this: What do I want to get from bottoming?

"Sex," Nick said promptly. "All the sex."

If you said sex, then you're partially right! However, please remember that penetration doesn't need to come from another person. There are many sexual toys that could allow a bottom to experience the joys of bottoming without another party present. If you would like to learn more about these, click on the following link to be taken to HOW TO FIND THE RIGHT SEX TOY FOR YOU!

Nick almost clicked but stopped himself at the last moment. "One thing at a time," he muttered. He figured it was better to learn *how* to bottom before he found something to stick *in* his bottom.

> While this how-to is comprehensive and will provide you with step-by-step instructions on How to Bottom, we would be remiss if we didn't remind you of SAFETY FIRST. Always, always take precautions. Condoms. Dental dams. Knowing your partner or partners' health status, and your own. Sexually active people—no matter how they identify—should get tested regularly. In addition, if you're having sex, you should consider speaking with a medical professional about getting on PrEP, a medication that helps lower the odds of HIV transmission. The more you protect yourself, the safer you'll be.
>
> Now, let's get to it.
>
> Step 1: Enemas!

"Oh my god," Nick whispered fervently. "I have to do *what*?" The more he read, the more blood drained from his face (and from his groin). He'd never considered such a thing, and now that he knew it was out there, he wasn't quite sure what to do with this information. Yes, he could see why it might be critical (*No one likes fecal penis,* the article told him) but the very idea of having to . . . to . . . *clean* himself out before he had sex broke his brain in ways he wasn't sure he could recover from.

Throat dry, he pushed his way away from his desk, shooting to his feet and running to the bathroom. He turned on the faucet and splashed water on his face, trying to ignore his bulging eyes in the reflection, his skin tight and overwarm. Did . . . Seth know about enemas? What if they were *both* bottoms? How were they supposed to have a lasting relationship if neither wanted to top? Or did that even matter?

He jumped when he heard the front door open, and a voice called out. "Nick? You home? Forgot some paperwork."

"In the bathroom!" he yelled, voice cracking pitifully. "I'm not doing anything weird!"

A pause. Then, "Yeah, see, when you say that, it makes me suspicious."

"That's because you're *always* suspicious!" Nick bellowed, gripping the sink and wondering if he and Seth were doomed to Bottom Hell for the rest of their natural lives.

A moment later, Dad knocked on the door. "Do I want to know what you're doing in there?"

"Oh my god, Dad, I'm washing my *face*."

"Uh-huh. If you say so. Remember, that's a shared bathroom, so if you're doing anything . . . normal, then make sure you clean up after yourself."

Nick groaned, face in his hands as he lamented on the fact that his father was the most embarrassing human in existence.

"And I've got that basket of laundry I told you to put away that you still haven't done."

"Just . . . put it in my room," Nick said as he dropped his hands. "Please. Thank you."

Dad chuckled, and the floor creaked as he moved away from the bathroom door.

If he'd known how much worse it was about to get, Nick would've probably fled the house, moved to Canada, and spent the rest of his days living in a cabin while making maple syrup, or whatever it was Canadians did aside from being pleasant and supportive, most likely because they enjoyed the benefits of universal healthcare.

But since foresight wasn't in his wheelhouse and he was therefore unprepared for the terrible fate that awaited him, he pulled himself together and took a deep breath, forcing a smile on his face. It only looked slightly manic, so Nick counted that as a win.

It was about this time that Nick remembered what he'd been looking at on his computer. The computer in his room. The same room where Nick had just given his father permission to enter.

"Oh no," he whispered, the face of his reflection bone white.

He flung open the door, looking down the hall wildly. Empty. His parents' bedroom door was ajar. Hopefully, that meant Dad was in his room after having dropped the laundry off.

The basket of folded clothes was sitting on the bed, and Nick slammed the door behind him, relieved that Dad had been so distracted, he hadn't seen what was on the comp—

Dad said, "So. Enemas."

Nick screamed, almost falling over. The doorknob jutted painfully into his back, and Dad arched an eyebrow from his seat on Nick's chair in front of the open computer, the wiki-How page on full display.

"Wake up," Nick pleaded with himself. "Please, wake up. This has to be a nightmare. That's all this is. In a moment, I'll wake up in my bed, and—"

Dad leaned forward toward the computer. "Please notice how I'm ignoring the tab called *Painter Gets His Insides Painted By Boss.*"

"I don't know what that is," Nick said quickly. "It was there when I got home. Someone else must have been using my laptop."

"Sure," Dad said. "Let's go with that so we can avoid further embarrassment. Enemas."

"You just said we were going to *avoid*—"

"Seems like there's a few different kinds," Dad said, as if he weren't murdering his only child. "One you can attach to the shower. That seems a little advanced for someone just starting out. It also says that shower enemas can . . . huh. Burn your insides? Wow. Learn something new every day."

Nick stared in horror.

Dad nodded. "Let's not do that one, especially since I'd have to see it every time I used the bathroom. Oh, what about this one? It's a big plastic bulb that you—"

"No," Nick moaned, face in his hands. "No, no, no."

"Noted," Dad said. "Not a fan of the bulb. Okay." He pushed himself away from the desk, standing from the chair. "I'm ready for this. I didn't think I'd do this today, but I suppose there's no time like the present. I'll be right back." He paused at the door, glancing back at Nick, who stood in the middle of his room, wishing he'd never been born. "Don't you worry, kid. We'll figure it out."

"Why are you *like* this?" Nick bellowed after him.

By the time Dad came back, Nick was grunting harshly, trying to shove his desk in front of the door to barricade himself inside. The desk was much heavier than Nick remembered, and he'd only managed to cause a two-inch-long scratch on the floor.

Dad ignored him, coming back and sitting on the edge of his bed, a plastic shopping bag on his lap. "Okay," he said as Nick collapsed on the floor, back against the side of his desk. "So, I went to a store a couple of months back. The guy working there was really helpful. Said this was a good starter kit. He'd used it himself, so I trusted his opinion on the matter."

Life, Nick knew, was full of highs and lows, peaks and valleys. And sometimes, said valleys opened up revealing untold depths filled with fire and brimstone and terrifying possibilities better left hidden in darkness.

But alas, Dad seemed to be of the mind that it was better to drag the horror into the light, seeing as how he opened the shopping bag and pulled out a rectangular box with colorful lettering that read MY FIRST ENEMA KIT!

"Dad, *no*," Nick breathed, covered in instantaneous flop sweat.

"Dad, *yes*," Dad said. "It's better to do this right than to go into it unprepared. So, this is called a Fleet enema." He held out the box toward Nick so he could see the picture of a white, thin nozzle on the box. "You fill it with the saline solution and then . . ." He looked down at the box with a frown. "I guess you just put it up there and then squeeze it? That can't be right."

Nick banged the back of his head against the desk, trying to give himself a concussion so he could potentially cause brain damage and suffer the joys of short-term memory loss.

"Oh, good," Dad said, sounding relieved as he opened the box.

"It comes with instructions. Let me just . . ." The thin nozzle fell out of the box and landed on the floor. "Oops. We'll need to sterilize that before you use it. Okay! The instructions." He unfolded the paper like a map, nodding down at it as his eyes darted back and forth. "Right, right. I get it. It's supposed to act like a laxative. I guess . . . that makes sense."

"Nothing about this makes sense," Nick moaned. "Nothing."

Dad ignored him. "So, we put the solution into the bottle." He held up the bottle, wiggling it at Nick. "And then the nozzle goes right on top." He bent over, picking the nozzle off the ground, the instructions crinkling in his lap. "And then you put this inside your rectum and squeeze. Stuff goes in, stuff comes out, and voila! You're ready for . . . entertaining a guest."

"I'm not going to do *any of that*!" Nick snapped at him.

Dad nodded solemnly. "It's a lot to take in." He suddenly grinned. "Figuratively *and* literally. Ha, nailed it." He clapped once, and it took Nick a moment to realize Dad had just high-fived himself.

"I've decided that I'm adopted," Nick announced. "That's the only thing that will get me through the next five minutes. I was adopted, and I want to go back to my real family."

"Anyway. If you're . . ." A complicated expression crossed Dad's face, forehead lined with deep canyons. "If you're going to . . . be the receiver, you need to learn about this stuff, kid."

Nick pushed himself up off the floor, glaring at his father. "Who said *I* was going to do anything like that? For all you know, I'm just learning about this stuff for *Seth*."

"Regardless, it's better to be prepared." He pulled a thin plastic vial of solution from the box. "Come here, I need your help."

"The fact that you think I'm going to help you with *anything* proves you've lost your damned mind."

"Oh, knock it off, Nicky. If you're able to look up this stuff online, then you can handle talking about it with me." He sobered slightly, forehead smoothing out. "I'm not making fun of you for this, kid. While I wish we wouldn't be having this talk for many, many years, I'd rather know you're being safe than make assumptions." He looked back down at the kit in his lap. "Pretty soon, you're going to be old enough that you won't care about what I think. I'll just be here, getting older, wishing my son would come visit me and—"

"This is blatant manipulation," Nick grumbled. "And you know it."

"It is," Dad agreed. "Working?"

Strangely, it was. Oh, Nick was never going to forgive his father for this, but how many queer kids had parents who'd go out and buy a freaking *enema kit,* of all things? Not many, Nick thought, and while he currently wished his father would spontaneously combust, he knew he was one of the lucky ones. Dad didn't have to do this—and honestly, Nick really, *really* wished he wouldn't—but he had, and Nick could almost picture him standing in a store, nodding along as the clerk explained enemas to him.

His father was ridiculous. Stupidly, wonderfully ridiculous, and Nick didn't know where he'd be without him.

So he steeled his nerves and pushed himself to his feet. Refusing to meet Dad's gaze, he stalked over to the bed, slumping down next to him. "Fine," he muttered, arms crossed. "Since you went to the trouble and all, might as well."

Dad bumped his shoulder against Nick's. "Might as well. Here." He handed over the solution and the plastic bottle. He left the nozzle on his lap. "You should do it since you're the one who'll be using it. Pour the solution in the bottle. See that line on the side? That'll tell you how much to use."

Nick nodded, setting the bottle between his knees and unscrewing the cap to the solution. Carefully, he poured it in, making sure to not go past the line to avoid saline squirting out his eyes and ears. This showed him he didn't really understand how anatomy worked, so perhaps that was something he needed to focus on ahead of his last year of high school.

"Good," Dad said. "That should be enough." He held out the nozzle. "Just screw that into the top, and you'll be good to go. According to the box, the nozzle has twenty-five percent more lubrication to make for easy insertion." He puffed out his chest. "I spared no expense, of course. Only the best for a Bell anus."

"*Dad,*" Nick said through gritted teeth.

Dad rolled his eyes. "What? I care."

"A little too much, if you ask me."

"Good thing no one did," Dad said cheerfully. "So, now that you have the solution and the nozzle attached, the instructions say you'll want to do this in the bathroom to avoid making a mess. Above the toilet or in the shower." He grimaced. "Just . . . make sure you clean up anything so I don't have to see it."

Nick turned over the bottle in his hand, the solution sloshing back and forth. "Seems easy enough." He squinted down at the nozzle. "What happens after I put it—"

"What are you guys talking about?"

When one is startled out of an enema-centric conversation with their father by their superhero boyfriend unexpectedly climbing in through an open window (and looking like a damned *snack,* what with his curls and his face and his entire existence), one tends to react involuntarily and without thinking. Case in point: Nick yelped, squeezing the bottle so hard that it went almost flat, causing saline to squirt into his eyes and face and open mouth. He screeched and hurled the bottle across the room, where it hit Seth's forehead and fell to the floor, bouncing, little arcs of saline flying through the air.

"My *eyes!*" Nick wailed, solution dripping from his mouth onto his lap. "The stuff that was made for anuses is in every place *but my anus!*"

"The what is *where?*" Seth asked, sounding as if someone had kicked him in the nuts, in that it came out as a squeak.

"Oh boy," Dad said, patting Nick on the back as his son continued screaming that he was *blind,* that his eyesight had been *destroyed,* and someone was going to need to ask the college admissions board for disability accommodations on his behalf. "I think if it's good enough to go inside you, it's fine that it's in your eyes. But just to be safe, let me read through the rest of the instructions. If anything, we can call poison control and ask them if solutions in enema kits are something that needs medical attention when used incorrectly."

"Enema kits," Seth repeated dubiously, taking a step back toward the window. "Oh no. I just realized that a supervillain is destroying Nova City and I need to go save everyone. What terrible timing. I'll—"

"Don't leave me," Nick pleaded, rubbing his eyes furiously, blinking against the burn. "My father is holding me captive and I demand that you save me!"

Dad said, "Says here that you should be fine, so long as you don't try and drink any more than you already have. But since there is a laxative component, you might experience some cramping." He smiled. "There. See? We're good."

"What about *any of this* is good?" Nick growled at him, more than a little Guardian filling his voice.

"Well," Dad said, "at least now you know how *not* to do an enema." He glanced at Seth, who was so pale, it looked as if he'd never met a color in his life. "Seth, I'm really happy you're here. Come on. Sit down. We can learn about enemas together. Nick is already practically an expert, so you're in good hands." He laughed. "That's *also* figurative and literal, if you think about it. Get it? Because—"

"Get *out*!" Nick shouted, rising from the bed and grabbing Dad by the arm, jerking him toward the door. "You've already made me enema my face, and now you want Seth to join in this travesty? I *refuse*. Leave this place and think about what you've done. We're going to have a long talk later about boundaries and the need you feel to educate me on how to have gay sex when you've never done it!"

And as if Dad's sole mission was to make the day even worse, he said, "How do you know I've never had sex with another guy? College, Nicky. I did things I haven't even told you—*wow*. You are a hell of a lot stronger than you look. Seth, he's ready for those fifteen-pound barbells."

Before Nick slammed the door in his face, he leaned forward, dropping his voice so that it was barely above a whisper.

"I will be your ending," he promised darkly. "You won't ever see it coming. But for the rest of your life, you'll have to watch over your shoulder, knowing that I will one day be there, ready to have my revenge." Then, because it needed to be said (even if it was just a *little* quieter), "Thank you for loving me too much."

Dad's expression softened. "That doesn't even begin to cover it, Nicky," he whispered back. "Anything for you."

Nick nodded and raised his voice. "And you will suffer!" *Then* he slammed the door in Dad's face, but not before Dad grinned at him. His footsteps faded as he went down the hall, the only sound coming from the open window.

Nick pressed his forehead against the door, not wanting to face Seth just yet.

"So," Seth said.

Nick sighed and turned around, wiping the rest of the saline off his face. Seth was standing near the bed, frowning down at the crumpled instructions Dad had left behind while holding the enema bottle. If Nick had been pyrokinetic like Seth was, he'd have lit the entire kit on fire. He considered using his own powers to fling everything out the window, but Seth's lips were moving silently as he read, and he didn't want to overreact just yet.

"So," Nick said nervously.

Seth lifted his head and looked at Nick. "This is for . . ." He swallowed thickly, pupils slightly dilated.

"Sex stuff," Nick said firmly, refusing to be embarrassed and partially succeeding. Dad was right; if he couldn't talk about it with someone he wanted to have sex with, he'd never be able to do it. No time like the present, right? "It helps to avoid fecal penis."

Apparently there was a bit of solution left in the bottle, because when Seth squeezed it, saline squirted out onto the floor, splashing on Nick's clothes from yesterday.

"Fecal penis," Seth said faintly, the bottle expanding as he loosened his grip.

"Exactly." Nick moved toward the bed slowly, not wanting

to spook Seth more than he already had. "No one likes fecal penis."

Seth nodded slowly, color filling his cheeks once more, red and splotchy. "I . . . can see the importance of avoiding that. And you want to use this on yourself?"

"Uh," Nick said, dizzy with the implication. "Ye-es? No. Wait. Yes." He nearly bit his tongue in two. "Just . . . you know. To be ready for anything. Like a prostate exam."

Seth looked down at the bottle in his hand thoughtfully before setting it on the bed. He took a deep breath, letting it out slowly. When his gaze met Nick's once more, his eyes were clear behind his glasses, and perhaps filled with a bit of heat. "I think proctology role-play is something we need to work up to rather than starting with it."

Sometimes, Seth could surprise the absolute *shit* out of Nick, and it never failed to knock him for a loop. He burst out laughing, sounding slightly hysterical, but unable to stop it. Seth began to laugh, too, and soon they had tears streaming down their faces. He recovered first and made his way over to Nick. They stood chest to chest, Seth's hands on Nick's hips, a quiet smile on his face. "This is what you want?"

"What?" Nick asked, distracted by the length of Seth's eyelashes.

Seth's grip tightened on him, fingers digging in. "Like. You know. Me . . . doing stuff to you."

Nick snorted, almost losing it again. "I think we'd be doing stuff to each other, but . . . uh. I get what you mean. Yes? I think I want to try it that way." Then, in a rush, "But not until you're ready for it. This isn't me pressuring you into—"

Seth kissed him, soft, sweet, before his tongue swiped Nick's lips, causing his mouth to open. Regardless of what else they were, they were absolute *champs* at the making-out thing. If Seth could get Nick this riled up from just kissing, he wondered what else Seth could do with his mouth. And his hands. And his . . . other appendages. Not feet, though. Nick was *not* into feet that way.

Seth pulled back, but only just, his forehead against Nick's. "I'm getting there," he whispered.

"Me, too," Nick whispered back.

Seth smiled nervously. "And I think I'd . . . like to do that with you. Scratch that. I *know* I want to do that with you."

"I don't know if I'm a power bottom," Nick said seriously. "But might as well give it a go and see what happens. Didn't know I had powers and look at me now. Bottoming might be something else I'm marginally good at. And at least then, I won't need a costume." He paused, considering. "Well, at least not for the first time. Remember what your aunt and uncle said? Your costume can probably be used as a dental dam if we need it."

Seth stepped back, coughing roughly. Amiably, Nick patted his back until he recovered.

"You just said that," Seth told him.

"I did," Nick agreed. "Don't tell me you haven't thought the same thing."

"I *haven't*." He blushed furiously as he looked away. "Okay, just once." He sighed. "Seven times."

Nick waggled his eyebrows. "Having a little alone time thinking about Guardian, huh?" He blew on his knuckles before rubbing them against his chest. "Yeah, don't blame you, dude. I've seen my butt in the mirror. I gots *cake*." Sure, it was like a grocery-store sheet cake, but still.

"That you do," Seth said, and decided that he needed a handful of Nick's cake. Nick, for his part, didn't mind in the slightest, especially when he had empirical evidence that Seth was as turned on as he was. "When?"

Nick blinked, mind a little fuzzy as Seth had big, big hands. "When what?"

Seth nipped Nick's bottom lip, stretching it out gently before letting go. "When do you want to do this?"

Oh. *Oh*. The *sex*. Nick's brain shorted out, the circuits fried and smoking. "Holy shit. Now? Should we do it right now? Now is good. Now is *really* good. Oh, crap. *Not* now. We need to wait until I've stuck that bottle up my butt before—"

Seth covered his mouth with his hand, eyes practically popping out of his head. "Maybe not now, then." He sighed and dropped his hands to Nick's shoulders. "We're probably going to be pretty bad at it. Neither of us have done anything like this, so it's going to be a lot of trial and error. But so long as we talk it through, we'll figure it out."

"I just want it to be good," Nick whispered, uncomfortable, but knowing this was a necessary conversation. "What if I'm bad at it?" So bad, in fact, that Seth would never want to do anything like that with him again. He might even reconsider their entire relationship. Why would Seth want to stay with someone who sucked at sucking?

Seth shrugged. "Then you are. I will be, too. But that's how we learn, remember? It's almost like training to be Guardian. You're getting the hang of that, right? Because of all the practice we've been doing. It'll be the same with this. Just have to learn the ins and outs." He narrowed his eyes. "And don't make that dirty."

"Too late," Nick said. "Because hopefully, there will be in. Then out. Then in. Then out again. Then *allll* the way back in—"

Seth jostled him slightly. "Nick. I'm being serious. If we're going to do this, I need you to promise me that if I do anything that you don't want, you'll tell me."

"I will," Nick promised. "If you do the same for me."

"Deal," Seth said, smacking a kiss on the tip of Nick's nose before taking a step back, dropping his arms. He glanced at the computer, the word *ENEMA* on full display. "Bottoming seems like a lot of work." He coughed, rubbing the back of his neck. "Guess I really hadn't thought about all that goes into it."

"I could've made that dirty, too," Nick said. "But I didn't. You're welcome."

"Thanks," Seth said dryly. "You're all heart, Nicky." He stepped around him and went to the bed, picking up the discarded instructions, frowning as he read, lips moving silently.

"Seems pretty straightforward," he said finally, looking up at Nick. A vein throbbed in his forehead. "Is this . . . something you want help with, or . . . ?"

"Oh god," Nick mumbled. "Dude, I love you, but I do *not* want you to see what comes out of me if I use that thing. It'll probably be some Lovecraftian horror better left vanquished down a drain." He slumped on the bed, laying on his back, staring up at the ceiling. "Gay sex is stupidly complicated. Damn heteros with their multiple options. I bet *they* don't have to worry about enemas and fecal penis."

"I don't think that's quite true," Seth said, dropping the instructions and crawling on the bed next to Nick. He mirrored Nick's pose, their faces inches apart as Seth clutched his hand tightly. "But just to be safe, let's not ask anyone because the only straight people we talk to are your parents and my aunt and uncle."

Nick shuddered. "Thank god we have the internet."

Seth laughed, the sound bouncing around the room. "I can't believe your dad bought you an enema kit."

"Right? I don't know what the hell he was—you know what? No. That's . . . actually pretty damn cool, if you think about it and are able to ignore how embarrassing it is that my *dad* tried to teach me how to give myself an enema. How many queer kids have a dad who'd do something like that for them?"

"Probably not many," Seth admitted. "He's a good guy."

He was. Even if it felt like torture to talk with Dad about sex, Dad only wanted him—and in turn, Seth—to be safe. He couldn't imagine a life where he didn't have Dad in his corner. Without Dad, Nick wouldn't have survived when Before became Af—

He frowned. Those words again. Shaking his head, he said, "What are you doing here? Not that I don't mind you popping in my window unannounced and causing me to squirt poop cleaner on my face, but—"

Seth groaned. "Why would you call it that?"

"That's what it *is*!"

"I know, but we don't have to keep saying it, Nick. Show some tact."

"Oh, I'm sorry. Did I offend your delicate sensibilities? Here, let me make it better." He rolled over on top of Seth, who settled his hands on Nick's sides. Nick swiveled his hips, and Seth's fingers dug in hard enough to leave bruises. "There. How's that?"

"Good," Seth said through gritted teeth, one of his curls bouncing on his forehead. "Jazz wanted help with her essay, and Gibby and I weren't getting much done." He huffed out an irritated breath. "*If* Owen is here, he's staying low. I don't like it. He's always been about the theatricality of it all. It makes me nervous that he hasn't showed his face yet."

"He did," Nick reminded him. "To Mom." A pause. "Or, at least that's what she said."

Seth eyed him for a moment. Then, carefully, as if he thought Nick would snap at him, "You think she's telling the truth?"

"I don't know. If she made a mistake, that's one thing."

"But if she didn't?"

"Then she lied about it." There it was, now out in the open.

"We'll tread carefully," Seth said. Seth was intuitive in ways that he would never be. "Keep our eyes and ears open."

"That can wait until later," Nick said, knowing he was deflecting but caring very little about it. Everything was too hazy, too wild, and the only thing that made sense was the guy underneath him. "We should probably take advantage of our current situation. I hope you're ready to swallow tongue, because I'm gonna stick it down your throat."

"Gross," Seth said with a grimace. "But let's do it anyway."

And so they did.

# 9

The following Friday morning, Nick went down the stairs, backpack slung over his shoulders, his Guardian costume stored safely inside. He was already running late. Jazz had decided they needed a day off from all the crap they'd been through, and had suggested a picnic in Metro Park, a long slash of green that cut through the heart of Nova City with winding paths surrounded by trees and seven different water features that would undoubtedly be filled with people trying to escape the summer heat.

Dad had already gone in to work with Cap, telling Nick he'd have his phone if he needed anything. Just as frustrated as the rest of them over the specter of Owen's shadow looming, he said that he'd ask his contacts within the NCPD if they'd come across anything that would lead to Owen. He didn't sound like he thought anything would come of it, but they had to use every option they had available to them.

"I still don't want you going anywhere alone," he'd said, leaning against Nick's doorway, smirking at the enema bottle sitting on top of the instructions on Nick's desk. "If you're going out, make sure you're with someone."

Nick promised he would, which was why he was hurrying down the steps toward the front door. Seth was waiting for him on the sidewalk outside the house, and Nick was itching to do something that didn't involve threats from a rich asshole or wondering if they were about to be attacked. A day off just to be stupid in the middle of their summer vacation was exactly what he needed.

He had almost made it to the door when he saw a figure standing in the living room in front of the window, peeking through the closed blinds.

Mom.

"What are you doing?" he asked.

Mom didn't look at him. "Watching."

"Uh. Okay? What're you watching?"

The slat on the blinds snapped as she let it go, turning to look at him. Her hair was wet and slicked back, as if she'd just come from the shower. She looked soft, face free of makeup, her eyes glittering as she saw Nick carried his backpack. "Where are you going?"

"Out. Meeting up with my friends. Seth's waiting for me."

"Saw that," she said, and Nick's skin crawled for reasons he couldn't explain. "He's a good boy. But are you sure that's the best idea? Maybe you should just stay home for now. You and me, what do you say? Feels like we haven't had mom-son time in quite a while."

She was right. He couldn't remember the last time it'd been just the two of them. Strangely, he felt the urge to agree with her, to tell her that he'd love to stay with her. A smile rose unbidden, and he almost said, "Yeah, sure, of course. That sounds good."

Almost.

But then he remembered how excited Jazz had seemed about the picnic, saying that they all needed a break from . . . well. Everything. Her eyes had lit up, and she'd made them all promise to let her handle all of it. It had been frankly rather adorable how much she'd taken charge over this, and Nick only wanted to see her happy. She'd earned it. They all had.

So he said, "Sorry. Already made plans. Maybe later? I'll be back before too late. Got my phone. Call if you need anything." He turned toward the door.

"Nick."

He stopped but didn't turn to look at her. The table next to the door rattled slightly. The air thickened, stagnant, heavy. The only sounds came from the clock.

He didn't hear her move, but when she spoke again, it sounded as if she was *right* behind him. The hairs on the back of his neck stood on end.

"I think you should stay home," she said again, and in his head, a voice whispered, *She sounds so worried. You should listen to her. It'll make her feel better. It'll make you feel better.*

He laughed. It sounded hollow. "Jazz put together a picnic. Don't want to disappoint her, you know?"

"Of course not," she said, close, so close. He thought he'd scream if she touched him, and he didn't know *why*. "But your friends aren't the be-all and end-all."

He tried to move toward the door, but his legs wouldn't work. "What is *that* supposed to mean?" he asked without turning around.

"They don't understand," Mom said, sounding melancholic. "Try as they might, Gibby and Jazz can never know what it's like to be us. Seth, too, if I'm being honest. I know he has his own powers, but it's not the same, is it? We're telekinetic. Powerful. More than he could ever be. I've often wondered if he's . . ."

Nick breathed through it, keeping his panic at bay. "If he's what?"

She laughed quietly. "It's silly, honestly. Probably just over-thinking things. You get that from me, after all." He felt her breath on the back of his neck. "Do you ever wonder if Seth is . . . I don't know. Jealous of you?"

Nick blinked, unable to turn around. "Jealous? Of *me*? That's ridiculous. Seth isn't the jealous type. He has no reason to be, at least not with this. He's been an Extraordinary a hell of a lot longer than I have."

"He has, hasn't he?" Mom said, and Nick flinched when her fingers trailed along his shoulders, rubbing over the bumps of his spine below his neck. "Doesn't mean much in the grand scheme of things, not with what you can do, but I suppose it doesn't matter, does it? Just . . . be careful, kid. And if you ever need to talk, I'm always here, ready to listen. You won't get any judgment from me. Do you want to do it right now?"

Cold, as if the temperature had dropped fifty degrees. "Yeah, that's . . . that sounds nice."

*Turn around,* the voice whispered. *Look at her. Listen to her. She's your mother. She loves you. She wants to protect you. She's right. You know she is.*

Nick started to turn, muscles stretching under flesh. But before he could look at her, he caught a glimpse of Seth through the glass of the door. He stood out on the sidewalk, looking down at his phone. The door solidified once more, and Nick felt sensation returning to his legs, as if they'd been frozen and were now free.

He said, "Why don't you have a job?"

The fingernails on the back of his neck stalled momentarily. "I wanted to stay home with you. Raise you. We've talked about this, Nicky. Are you sure you're all right? You sound confused."

He was. He wasn't. Fighting against the wave of calm washing over him, he said, "It won't be forever. I'm not going to be a kid for much longer. Pretty soon, I'll be gone and you'll have to decide what you want to do." He stepped away from her. He did not look back as his fingers circled the doorknob.

"Nick," she said, voice sharper. "I said I want you to stay home today."

*Step away from the door. Turn around. Look at her. See her. Love her.*

But Seth was there, Seth was *right there* on the other side of the door, and he couldn't keep him waiting, couldn't let him think Nick wasn't coming.

"Can't do that," he said, gripping the doorknob as if it was the only thing keeping him from doing what she asked. "Told you. Made plans. I'll be back later."

With that, he opened the door and moved quickly through it, slamming it behind him and hurrying down the walkway toward Seth.

"Hey," Seth said, grinning at him. It faded when he saw the look on Nick's face. "All right?"

"Yeah," Nick muttered. "Let's get out of here. Mom's acting weird."

"Weird how?" Seth asked, looking over Nick's shoulder at the house. "What'd she do?"

He couldn't explain it, but now that he was out of the house, if felt like he could breathe, like a weight had been taken off his chest. "She's . . ." He shook his head. "Forget it. Doesn't matter. Let's go. Don't want to be late."

And though the blinds were still shut when he looked back at the house one last time, he could feel her gaze boring into him.

The park was crowded, hundreds of people walking along the tree-lined paths or sitting on blankets and chairs in the grass, kids jumping and playing in the fountains that sprayed up from nozzles embedded into the ground. A group of people were doing yoga on a small field, backs arched, chins raised, hands firmly planted on brightly colored mats. A bigger group surrounded two men and a woman, clapping along as they beat the tops of trash cans and buckets with drumsticks, the sound bright and happy.

The sun was shining, not quite as hot as it'd been even the day before, fat, lazy clouds moving slowly across the sky. It was a perfect summer day.

Jazz and Gibby had staked a prime spot under a tall, leafy tree, blanket spread out underneath, dappled with shadows and sunlight filtering in through the thick branches. Jazz saw them first, waving her hand in greeting, Gibby's head in her lap. A large wicker basket sat in the grass next to the blanket, along with a cooler filled with ice and glass bottles.

Gibby lifted her head and nodded in greeting before settling back down on Jazz's lap. She had a yellow dandelion placed in the fold above her ear, the petals bent against her face.

"Hey," Jazz said as Nick collapsed dramatically on the blanket, Seth snorting above him. "You're right on time for once. Congratulations."

Nick lifted his arms as Seth removed his backpack for him, setting it off to the side. "I show up exactly when I'm meant to," Nick said. "And not a moment sooner."

"Sure," Gibby said as Seth sat down next to Nick, kicking off his shoes and curling his bare toes in the grass. "Let's go with that."

"Now that we're all here," Jazz said, touching the flower in Gibby's ear, "there are some rules that we are going to abide by."

Nick sighed, watching Seth smile at the grass between his toes. "I thought we were taking the day off from everything."

"Exactly," Jazz said primly. "Which is why my rules are this: No talking about Extraordinaries. No talking about people with the last name Burke. No powers, no villains, none of it. Today, we're going to have a picnic and the topics of discussion will be as follows: summer break, senior year, college applications, and how we're going to decorate our dorm rooms. Anything that's related will be acceptable, but that's it. If any of you try and break these rules, I'll stab you with one of the plastic forks I brought for the fruit salad. And before you say I'm threatening you, let me assure you: I am, and I'm very serious about it. Deal?"

"Deal," they all said, because Jazz was terrifying and awesome in equal measure.

"Good," Jazz said. She nodded at the basket and cooler. "Take whatever you want but leave the chicken-salad sandwich. That's Gibby's and I made it with love by ordering it and having someone else make it."

"Thanks, babe," Gibby said, closing her eyes and stretching out her legs.

Nick—always and forever Nick—immediately dug through the basket. Wrapped sandwiches from that deli he loved—they always put *way* too much meat on them—and plastic containers of fruit salad and potato salad, and individual bags of chips and cookies. "You went all out," he said. "I approve."

"Of course I did," Jazz said. "No point in having a picnic if you're not going to do it right."

Nick handed a sandwich over to Seth after checking it wasn't Gibby's. Seth took it with a quiet "Thank you" before setting it down at his side, lying on his back, arms folded behind his head. His shirt pulled up a little, revealing a pale, toned stomach with curly hairs around his belly button.

"Want," Nick whispered.

"What was that?" Jazz asked.

Nick startled, looking up guiltily. "Uh, nothing? Just thinking some thoughts that probably shouldn't be said out loud since we're in public."

"He's perving on his boyfriend," Gibby said without opening her eyes.

"I'm *allowed*," Nick said. "It's not my fault that Seth is freaking hot."

"I am," Seth said. "Not even going to apologize for it." Making sure Nick was watching, Seth trailed a hand over his stomach, and it was all Nick could do to avoid breaking public indecency laws like his father had warned him about.

"So unfair," Nick groused. Trying to get himself under control, he tore his gaze away and looked at Jazz. "How're the essays coming along?"

"Pretty good," Jazz said, reaching into the basket and pulling out a damp bag of grapes. She set it beside her before plucking one out and feeding it to Gibby, who nipped at her fingers playfully before chewing. "Gibby's helping."

"Could you help me, too?" Nick asked through a mouthful of roast beef and spicy mustard. "I thought I was getting the hang of it, but apparently, I'm too modest and don't know how to talk myself up."

"Yeah," Gibby said dryly, "I doubt that's the problem you're having. But sure, let me know when you want to work on it, and we can meet up."

Relieved, Nick said, "Are you excited about starting in the fall?"

Gibby opened her eyes, squinting against the sun in her face. She turned over in Jazz's lap so she faced Nick. "Honestly, I didn't think I would be, but I am. A little nervous." She paused. "Okay, maybe *more* than a little, but I can handle it."

"Why are you nervous?" Seth asked, turning around and facing them, shoes lying discarded in the grass.

She shrugged. "It's feels like a big step. And for one of the first times, I'll be answering only to myself."

"You don't have to," Nick said. "We're gonna be there. We'll always have your back."

"I know, but that's not what I'm talking about. I *want* to be responsible for myself. I want to make my own decisions, even if they don't work out like I hope. This isn't about Lighthouse or being an Extraordinary. It's about doing something for me, and what that means for my future."

"It can be whatever you want it to be," Jazz said, touching her forehead.

"Of course it can," Seth said, shooting Nick a warning look as if he thought Nick would push back at Gibby doing things on her own. Which, fair, because Nick was thinking *exactly* that, but he'd made a promise to listen to his friends, and he was going to keep it.

"Hell yeah, it can," Nick said. "Be nervous, Gibby. That's cool because you're right. It *is* a big step. You've got this. And if you need anything, all you need to do is ask."

Gibby smiled. "Thanks, guys. I knew you'd get it."

"How're your parents?" Seth asked. "They coming around?"

"Mostly. Mom got there first, but Dad's catching up. He still thought Howard was the best way to go, but after we toured the campus, he seems to be getting on board. He was more excited than I was. The tour guide couldn't keep up with all his questions." She hesitated. Then, "It probably helps that I told him I think I've decided what I want to do."

Nick swallowed, wiping the back of his hand across his mouth. "Really? Holy crap, Gibby. That's awesome. What did you decide?"

She said, "I think I want to go into civil-rights law. Maybe. Become an attorney. Help people whose voices need to be raised up. It's going to take a lot of work, but NCU has a great pre-law program and I'd be able to stay here."

"If there's anyone who can do it, it's you," Jazz said proudly, pressing her fingers to her lips before doing the same to Gibby.

"We're going to miss you," Seth said, unwrapping his own sandwich. "It's going to be weird without you next year." He frowned. "If I even get to go back, that is."

Close to breaking Jazz's rules, what with the reason Seth might not be at Centennial High for their senior year. But it was Jazz who said, "When are they supposed to decide?"

"There's supposed to be another board meeting in July or August. I'll know more then."

"And we'll be right there with you," Nick said. "We'll make signs and wear shirts with your face on them. I bet our parents will do the same."

Seth shrugged, setting his sandwich back down, half-unwrapped. "Maybe. But that probably won't do much to change their minds. They're all just . . ."

"Scared," Gibby said quietly. "Even though they shouldn't be. They're using you as an excuse."

"I know," Seth said. "But I don't know if I blame them for that." He looked off across the park. "I wonder, sometimes, what it'd be like if I didn't—if *we* didn't have all of this going on. If I wasn't who I was. Nick, too. If we were just kids who didn't have to worry about fighting to help others."

A low level of alarm pulsed in Nick's head, but he ignored it. This wasn't about him, and he refused to make it that way. Seth had always, *always* been supportive of Nick. It was only right that Nick should try to do the same with him. "It'd probably be a lot easier," he said.

Seth looked back at him with a half smile. "Yeah, it would be. But then nothing worth having is ever easy. It doesn't matter, though. We are who we are and we'll do what we have to."

"What do you want to do?" Nick asked him, thinking hard. "Not about the Extraordinary stuff. What do you want to go to school for?"

"I don't know yet." He cocked his head. "I haven't really thought that far ahead."

"We should," Jazz said, feeding Gibby another grape. "Let's pretend no one here can make fire or move things with their minds. The future is going to happen sooner rather than later. We're good at planning things, so we can do this."

"It's weird," Gibby said.

Jazz looked down at her. "What is?"

"You and me. Nick and Seth. Us. Making plans like this, like we think we'll always be together."

"Because we will be," Nick said firmly, not liking the implication.

"How many people can say that, though?" Gibby asked, almost sounding apologetic. "How many people can say they met the person or people they're going to spend the rest of their lives with in high school?"

"What if things change?" Nick whispered, suddenly no longer hungry. He set his own half-eaten sandwich back in the basket. "Paths diverge."

"Right," Gibby said. "I think about that a lot. I don't like it, but it feels important."

"It is," Seth said. "I think about that stuff, too. And not just—" He waved his hand, a little puff of smoke rising from his fingers. "We don't know who we'll be years from now."

Nick said, "Maybe we won't be together at some point. Maybe we'll want different things down the road. And like Jazz told me once, it won't make what we have now matter any less. I wouldn't be who I am without any of you."

Gibby snorted. "Oh, so you're blaming us for you? Not cool, Nicky."

He tapped his shoe against her ankle. "You know what I mean. We don't know what's going to happen tomorrow. Or the next day, or the day after that. We don't know where we'll be in a year, five years, ten years, but you know what? I love Seth. I love the both of you. And I will fight for each of you with everything I have. But *if* we end up going a different direction, I'll know it's not because you don't love me." He blinked against the burn in his eyes.

He was surprised when he was tackled, but it wasn't Seth. It wasn't Jazz. No, it was Gibby, launching herself at him and knocking him flat. She set her hands on either side of his head, looking down at him. "Nick," she said. "Remember when you wanted to put a cricket in the microwave because you thought it'd give you powers?"

"You mean last year?"

"I love that guy. And I love the guy he's turned into." She leaned down and kissed him, a peck on his lips. She tasted like the grapes Jazz had fed her, sticky, sweet. She squawked out a laugh when Nick reached up and tugged her down, hugging her tightly.

"I love us," Jazz said with a sniffle. "Nick's right. Maybe something will happen, but it won't be because we stopped caring about each other. Maybe people don't always meet the loves of their lives in high school, but we've always been the exception to everything we do. Why should this be any different?"

Gibby pushed herself off of Nick, settling on her knees. "Hands in the middle."

Jazz put her hand on top of Gibby's. Seth did the same on top of Jazz's. They looked at Nick, Seth arching his eyebrow, and Nick loved them. He loved them more than he could say. He put his hand on top of Seth's, and they looked at Gibby.

"Team Lighthouse," she said. "The four of us. No matter what happens, we'll always have today."

"Ditto," Jazz said.

"Ditto twice," Seth said.

"Ditto three times," Nick agreed, and for a minute, they just sat there, hands together, watching each other. Then the moment broke, and they ate, Nick trying to have Seth catch grapes in his mouth, Jazz finding another dandelion for Gibby's other ear. They laughed. They made fun of each other. Nick challenged Jazz to a wrestling match and lost almost immediately when Jazz knocked him flat on his back, Gibby and Seth cheering them on.

Later, as the sun crossed the sky, they ran through the fountains, clothes soaked, Seth shouting when they ganged up on him, dragging him toward one of the jets of water, watching him sputter his laughter as it sprayed him in the face.

By the time they got back to the blanket, they were exhausted, but the good kind of exhaustion that came from sitting in the sun and having at least a few hours without worrying about anything but each other.

For a long time to come, Nick would remember this moment as their last before everything changed. He would look back, years from now, and know that at the very least, they had this day, this afternoon where the sun was shining and nothing hurt. And he would smile, because regardless of what came next, he had the best friends a queer kid with an overactive brain could ask for.

But that was later.

This was now:

Seth said, "I think I swallowed fountain water. Ugh."

Jazz said, "It's in my damn *ears*."

Gibby said, "Did you hear how Seth screamed? Man, I thought someone was going to think we were kidnapping him."

Nick said, "We gotta do that again after I catch my breath. I—"

Someone sat down on the blanket next to them. Nick turned his head, a question on his lips, a look of confusion on his face.

But the only sound that came out of Nick's mouth was a sharp exhalation when he saw who was sitting next to him, resting back on his hands as if he'd always been there, just enjoying the day with the rest of them.

He looked different than when Nick had last seen him. Thinner. Paler, his blond hair shaggy. He wore shorts. Running shoes with no socks. A white shirt stretched over his strong chest. And that devastating smirk that drove Nick up the damn wall.

"Hey," Owen Burke said easily. "Long time no see. Missed you guys. What have *you* been up to?"

The effect was instantaneous. Jazz bared her teeth, grabbing a plastic fork and flipping it in her hand as if she was going to stab him in the face. Gibby stood swiftly, knocking over her bottle of sparkling water, the contents spilling onto the grass, hands curling into fists at her sides. Seth snarled, the temperature rising as a lick of fire burst from his hands.

Nick, though. Nick just sat there, dumbfounded, disbelieving what he was seeing. He couldn't move. He couldn't breathe. He couldn't do *anything* but stare at Owen, who turned his head toward him, winking in that way he did, inviting, dangerous. Nick's stomach twisted slickly, gorge rising in his throat, bitterness coating his tongue.

Seth raised his hand, eyes ablaze, and Owen said, "Ah, ah, ah. I wouldn't do that if I were you, Seth. There are so many *witnesses*. Have you thought this through? You look like you want to light me up in front of everyone." He pouted, bottom lip sticking out. "That doesn't seem very heroic of you."

"I don't care," Seth growled, more than a little Pyro Storm in his voice. "What the hell are you doing here?" He didn't lower his hand, the stench of smoke thick and pungent.

Owen tilted his head back and laughed, and Nick was reminded of when that sound thrilled him to no end. Owen had been Nick's first . . . well. Almost first everything. First kiss. First sort-of boyfriend. First breakup. First (and so far only) former flame who'd turned into a villain and had tried to kill them.

You never forgot your first.

"Calm down," Owen said, shaking his head as if disappointed. "I'm not here to hurt you. If anything, I want to help you." He stretched out his leg, tapping his shoe against Nick's leg. "Looking good, Nicky. Being an Extraordinary suits you." He grinned, all teeth. "Guess you didn't need those pills after all, huh?"

Nick crab-walked backward, hands squashing fruit and

half-eaten sandwiches. He yelped when his back collided with Seth's legs.

Never looking away from Owen, Jazz said, "Gibby, could you do me a favor? Move a little bit to the right. No, *my* right. There you go. Seth, to my left, please. Thank you. Nick, can you stand next to Seth?"

Nick nodded slowly, the roaring in his ears like a hurricane. He rose carefully, arm brushing against Seth's.

"Hooray," Jazz said, barely blinking, her big eyes wide and innocent. "Gibby, is anyone looking at us?"

"No."

"Perfect," Jazz said. "I've wanted to do this for a long time."

And then she lunged forward, stabbing Owen in the thigh with her plastic fork, twisting her wrist so the handle broke, leaving the prongs embedded in his leg. His face screwed up as if he were about to shout in pain but before he could, Jazz brought her arm back and then let it fly, fist colliding with Owen's mouth. His head snapped back, top lip splitting, an arc of blood falling onto his shirt, the red stark against the white.

"You goddamn—" Owen groaned, hands going to his face. "Shit, that *hurt*."

"Good," Jazz snapped, going for him again, only to have Gibby pull her back before she could do more damage. "You're lucky I'm not in heels because I'd have shoved one so far up your ass, you'd have been gargling the cow the leather came from."

Owen dropped his hand, staring at the blood on his fingers. Something dark crossed his face, and Nick was reminded of McManus Bridge, Shadow Star floating above him, Rebecca Firestone screaming. But the look disappeared, as if Owen had swallowed it back down. Cocking his head, he pinched the plastic jutting from his leg and pulled it out, grimacing. He stared at it for a moment before dropping it to his side. "That wasn't very nice," he said seriously. "Is that any way to greet an old friend? For shame, Jazz. Though, to be honest, I'm impressed. Wouldn't have figured *you* for the scary one."

"Oh," Jazz said, struggling against Gibby's hold on her. "I haven't even begun to show you scary."

Owen grinned at her, blood staining his teeth. "Promises, promises. Seth, who are you calling? The police? *Maybe* not the best idea, seeing as how dear old Dad has them all in his back pocket. You think they'd stop with just me? You can't possibly be *that* stupid." He sniffed. "Especially if I tell them you were working with me all along." He glanced at Nick, smile widening. "Guardian, too. Isn't that right, Nick? Man, that costume really works for you. Been working out? I can tell. Got some muscles in your arms now. Nice. Question. Do the cops know you're Guardian? Because I can tell them that, too."

Seth lowered his phone slowly, expression stormy. "What do you want?"

"That's better," Owen said. "And perfect question, Seth. What *do* I want? Many things, as you'd expect. World peace. A cure for cancer. A slice of pizza from that hole-in-the-wall off Nelson and Freeman. Remember that place, Nick? Took you there on our first date. You were so nervous it was positively adorable." He swiped his tongue over his lips, wincing when it touched the cut.

"You killed people." Nick said flatly. The sun was still beating down on them, but Nick had never felt colder in his life. He could hear the people in the park, but they all sounded far away.

"I guess nobody's perfect," Owen replied. "But then, I never claimed to be. I'm not as self-righteous as the four of you." His eyes narrowed. "Lighthouse. Like you're not a bunch of kids playing superhero. You have no idea what the real world is like."

"And you do?" Gibby said, the skin under her left eye twitching.

Owen shrugged. "Spend enough time in a padded room with the lights always on from all directions, it gives a man time to think, because sleeping is almost impossible. Have you ever been pumped full of drugs against your will? Because *I* have." His mouth dropped open as if something important had gone through his head. "You'd know all about that, wouldn't you, Nicky? Concentra. It'll help you concentrate!"

Now it was Seth's turn to hold someone back, as Nick tried to throw himself at Owen, to wrap his hands around the bastard's neck and squeeze and squeeze and *squeeze* until the light went out from Owen's eyes, until his breath rattled in his throat.

"Wow," Owen said, unperturbed. "Lotta anger issues. Must be a family trait. How's your dad, Nick? Hurt anyone else lately? Probably won't get away with it now, seeing as how he's not protected by his uniform anymore."

"I'll kill you," Nick snarled at him.

Owen laughed. "Where was *this* Nick back in the day?" He pressed a hand against his throat, voice mocking when he said, "But *Owen*, I don't know if I can take the pill. They're *scary*."

"You think we're going to sit here and listen to you?" Jazz asked.

Owen stopped laughing as he leaned forward. "I don't think you're going to listen to me. I *know* you will. Because I know things you don't, and oh man, I can't wait to see the looks on your faces when I tell you. I've been looking forward to this for a long time."

"We're not going to take your bullshit," Seth said. "Gibby, Jazz, let's go. Forget the blanket. We can replace it. Nick, we'll—"

"Before," Owen said, staring at Nick. "After."

Nick swayed, anger melting under a wave of unreality, dreamlike, hazy. His throat closed, and he struggled to breathe through it. Before. After. Before. After. There, on the tip of his tongue, dancing, a memory he couldn't quite grasp.

But it was Gibby who spoke, begrudging yet curious. "What does that mean? I've heard it before."

Owen couldn't cover up his surprise in time as he glanced at Gibby. "What? Really? *You* remember that?"

"No," Gibby spat, but she looked unsure. "I don't . . . I can't . . ."

"Huh," Owen said, tapping his chin. "I didn't think you'd be the one to almost break through first." He eyed her up and down. "I'm impressed. Her hold over you guys must not be as absolute as she thinks it is. Either that, or she underestimated

Gibby. Not surprised. She was never really able to see what was right in front of her."

"Who?" Gibby asked, taking a step toward him. "Who are you talking about? If your father is—"

Owen snorted. "I'm not talking about my dad, though he is part of it. No, this is someone else entirely." He looked at Nick once more. "How's your mom, Nicky? Good? Hope so. Do me a favor, will you? Next time you see her, would you tell her I said hi? I'd appreciate it."

"Why the hell would I do that?" Nick snapped.

Owen Burke grinned ferociously. "Because she's not your mom. She's mine."

# 10

Silence.

Then Gibby started chuckling. Jazz followed, and though she tried to cover it up, she failed spectacularly. That, of course, set off Nick, a wheezing laugh that sounded like he was screaming. Even Seth snorted, shaking his head as if disappointed.

That seemed to piss Owen off. His face twisted, and *there* was Shadow Star, lurking just underneath. For a moment, Nick's breath caught in his throat as he thought the shadows from the tree above them began to lengthen. Before he could warn the others, Owen relaxed, flexing his hands on his legs, fingers splayed over his kneecaps.

"What are you *talking* about?" Nick said, wiping his eyes. He was still furious, but he knew they could take Owen, if it came down to it. "What are you saying? That we're related?" Then, "Oh my god, please don't tell me we're related. Holy shit, I've made out with you! Oh, god, oh *god*. I made out with my half *brother*? I'm the bad fic tag! Why, *why*?"

"There's the Nick I know and tolerated," Owen said, sounding amused. "Good to know he still exists under all that misplaced bravado."

Nick gagged. "Incest is *bad*. Incest is so, so *bad*."

Seth rubbed his back, glaring at Owen. "Speak. Now."

"Ooh," Owen said, shivering. "I remember that voice."

"Hey, Owen?" Jazz asked. "Do you know what the uvula is?"

Owen blinked. "The little dangly thing that hangs at the back of the throat?"

"Yes," Jazz said sweetly. "If you don't tell us why you're here in the next five seconds, I'll show you yours."

"Okay, okay," Owen said, raising his hands as if to ward her off. "I get it. You're mad. Fair. But if I wanted to hurt any of you, I could've done it by now. I've found all of you alone at one point or another over the past few months. I didn't kill you then, and I'm not going to kill you now. Give me *some* credit."

Jazz lunged toward him again, and Owen blurted, "Jennifer Bell has been dead for over four years."

They all froze. Nick felt as if he were floating above his own body. *Before,* he thought. *After.*

When he saw Jazz wasn't going to shove her hand down his throat, Owen relaxed, though still wary. "The woman in your house, the Extraordinary known as TK, isn't Nick's mother. She's mine." He paused. Then, "Well, my stepmom."

"You really expect us to believe that?" Gibby asked. "We've seen your stepmother. They look nothing alike."

Gibby was right. Nick had vague memories of seeing her at the Burke home when he'd dated Owen. She was a severe woman with dark hair and an angular face. When he'd been introduced to her, he'd fumbled through it, disliking the way her knowing eyes had tracked his every movement, making his skin crawl for reasons he could never quite explain. And then after Owen, the only time Nick had seen her were the few times she'd stood at Burke's side in front of the cameras.

"Of course they don't," Owen said. He sighed, rubbing at the wound on his thigh. "We don't have a lot of time, so I'm just going to get right down to it. Patricia is an Extraordinary, but one unlike any other in the world. She can . . . alter her appearance. Anyone she's come into contact with, anyone one she *touches,* she can . . . well. Shift. To look like them."

"That's not possible," Seth said faintly. "We'd know if an Extraordinary could . . ."

A faint tug in the back of Nick's mind, insistent, pulling. Hadn't he read about an Extraordinary who could alter their appearance? But still, that couldn't be right. Owen was lying. His mother had always been there. She'd always . . .

*The bank*, he thought dully. *She went to the bank.*

"Would you?" Owen asked. "Because if she didn't want you to, believe me when I say you wouldn't." He glanced at Gibby curiously. "Most of you, anyway." He shook his head. "I'm getting ahead of myself. Let's back up a little because it's more complicated than just that. Not only can she change how she looks, she has an ability that I'm extremely jealous of. Think of it as an illusion, though perhaps a little more involved than that. She can create a . . . not reality, but an *un*reality. It's tenuous, and the more people she has to control, the harder it gets." He looked thoughtful when he added, "Which might explain why Gibby remembers something she shouldn't."

Gibby scowled at him, still holding on to Jazz's arm.

"She can make you believe anything she wants," Owen continued. "Plant memories in your head that aren't real."

"Yeah, no," Jazz said. "You really expect us to believe that? If Nick's mother died and Patricia took her place, don't you think everyone would question that? You say that it's hard for her. Then how would she be able to control *everyone*?"

"She can't," Owen said.

Hope rose in Nick, slight, but there all the same. "Then you're lying."

Owen rolled his eyes. "Nope. That's where another nifty little trick of hers comes into play. She has control over you and your immediate families, everyone Jennifer was close with before she died. Your parents. Seth's aunt and uncle. And even those who weren't, because that dumb cop and the drag queen are involved, too."

Nick laughed bitterly. "What about when she goes out in public, then? What happens when someone recognizes her?"

But Owen was ready for that. "She changes how she looks. Obviously. And when was the last time you saw her as your mother anywhere aside from in private? By the way, cool party, Jazz. Looked like fun. My invite must have gotten lost in the mail."

Nick paused, thinking as hard as he ever had. His mother didn't work. She was always at home, unless she was out as TK. And anytime she'd *said* she'd gone somewhere it'd always been alone. Though he didn't want to believe a word coming from Owen's mouth, part of him—a small, quiet part—doubted his own memories.

Before.

After.

Nick grasped the only thing he could. "What would stop any of us from talking about her? One of us *had* to have mentioned her to someone outside of our families."

"Yeah," Owen said. "That's where it gets *really* interesting. Watch." He looked around and brightened when he saw a man running toward them, arm stretched to catch a neon-green Frisbee spinning through the air. He jumped and his fingers closed around it. "Hey, man!" Owen called. "Great catch. Ask you something?"

The man eyed them curiously before nodding. He jogged over to them, gaze darting to the blood on Owen's shirt. He slowed, stopping a few feet away, looking unsure. "What's up?"

Owen looked back at Nick. "Tell him about her."

Good. Owen was wrong, and Nick would prove it. Then, after this farce was over, he'd smash Owen's face in for ruining their goddamn picnic with his idiocy. Nick said, "My mother's name is Jennifer Bell. She lives with us. I see her every day."

Or, at least, that's what he *tried* to say. What came out instead was, "My mother's name is Jennifer Bell. She . . ." But he could go no further. It felt as if his lips had been glued shut, and no matter what he did, he couldn't force the words out. He began to feel dizzy as he strained, and all that came from him was a low hum, as if he were exhaling through the tiniest of cracks.

"Nick?" Seth asked, sounding worried. "Are you okay?"

Nick shook his head. He tried again. "My *mother* is . . ." His mouth didn't work. His throat didn't work. His tongue was dead.

"Oh no," Jazz whispered, expression spooked as she turned

toward the man with the Frisbee, who looked like he wanted to be anywhere but where he was. "Jennifer Bell. She . . ." Her face turned bright red, the cords on her neck sticking out.

"Uh," the man said. "I don't do drugs unless they're prescribed by a doctor. No shame, but not for me." He backed slowly away from them before turning and running back toward his friends.

"You're under her control," Owen said. "You have been since just after Gibby's graduation. Which, congrats! Sucks you didn't get to be valedictorian. Though, you looked great walking across the stage."

He yelped when Gibby kicked his injured thigh, groaning and rocking back and forth. "*Goddammit*. Would you stop it?"

Gibby went back to Jazz, who high-fived her.

Owen glared at them but kept his distance as he sat back up. "Same thing happens with everyone else who knows she's here. Any of you try and say anything about her, you won't be able to. And usually, you won't even remember trying. Call them and ask if you don't believe me. Cap. Officer Rookie. Miss Conduct. Oh, *excuse me*. I mean Mateo."

That scared Nick more than he cared to admit. He thought they'd been careful, always aware of their surroundings. How much had Owen seen?

"Say that you're telling the truth," Seth said slowly. "Say that she's not who she says she is. That she's . . . your stepmother. I've seen her use her powers. She's telekinetic. We've all seen what she could do, and not just on prom night."

Savagely, Nick thought that'd be the end of it. That they'd cornered Owen and he had no way out.

Or so he thought.

Because Owen said, "Yeah, see, she isn't. Not really. And no, it's not *making* you believe she is, either. There were witnesses at the prom, right? They all saw TK coming through the ceiling."

"Then how does she do it?" Jazz asked.

"This is my favorite part," Owen said, eyes alight with excitement. "You know what my dad did to me, right? Gave me those pills. Made me who I am."

"Did to you," Gibby echoed, her scorn clear. "As if you didn't have a choice."

"I didn't," Owen snapped. "He . . ." His chest hitched, and Nick didn't think it was all for show. Or, if it was, Owen was a damn good actor. "He did things to me. Things you wouldn't even begin to understand." Nick was stunned when Owen wiped his wet eyes as he scowled. "I am who I am because of him. I trusted him. He was my father. I thought . . . if I did what he asked, he'd . . ." Owen looked away.

"Bullshit," Nick said, causing Owen to jerk his head toward him. "I don't give a damn about your daddy issues. *He* didn't make you try and kill us. *He* didn't make you kill anyone else. You did that all on your own."

"And that's your problem, *Nick*. It always has been. You've never been able to think of the bigger picture. Always about yourself. I've never met a more selfish person in my entire life. You want to know the truth? Fine. Those pills I showed you in my father's tower? How do you think he made those?" He raised his hand before Nick could speak. "That was rhetorical. You have no idea." He leaned forward, eyes glittering darkly. "He used her. Her powers. Her abilities. He used her blood, her DNA, and reverse-engineered Extraordinary abilities in pill form."

"He didn't do anything with them," Seth said grimly. "As far as we know, no one has taken them. If they had, Nova City would be *crawling* with Extraordinaries."

"Smoke and Ice," Nick whispered.

Owen startled. "No. They were just lackeys. They were born, not made. Don't you see? It's not about making Extraordinaries. It's always been about *un*making them."

Gooseflesh prickled along Nick's arms. "The cure."

Owen nodded. "That's what it started out as. Because while

he had the idea of building an army of Extraordinaries to be at his beck and call, he was always thinking ahead. What would be the point of having an army when there were others who could step in and try and stop them?"

Jazz scoffed derisively. "It's not like he can force that on anyone with powers. What's he going to do, shoot them with a dart filled with some kind of magical concoction? Honestly, Owen. You're good, I'll give you that. But there's too many holes in your story."

"Don't you get it yet?" Owen asked. "*She's the cure.* You want to know how she's telekinetic? How she can shape-shift? How she can alter memories? She *ate* those powers. That's her gift. That's her original ability. Dad experimented on her just as he did me, only with her, he got so much more than he bargained for. You thought I was the first?" He shook his head. "I wasn't. Patricia was his original test subject. There was a little girl. He found her. Promised her parents that he could help her. That he could *heal* her. She was telekinetic. He called her—"

"Eve," Nick breathed. The name rose in his mind like a shooting star, Burke's words ringing in his ears.

*A child was brought to us by their parents. This child, who we call Eve to protect their anonymity, exhibited signs of telekinesis. From a young age, Eve could move things around their house. The parents were frightened. At first, they thought their home was haunted. It wasn't until the child grew older that they realized Eve was the cause.*

"Eve," Owen said gleefully. "He said they found her after the whole Save the Children bullshit, but that was a lie. This was two years ago. The girl's parents brought her to the tower. Dad took her to the basement where Patricia was waiting. She stole Eve's powers, making them her own. That's how she became telekinetic." Owen glanced at Nick, and it took all Nick had to keep from screaming in Owen's face that he had to be lying, that none of it could be true. "She's a chimera, made up of all these different parts. And if she consumes a power, it becomes hers. Eve didn't remember what happened. Patricia made sure of that, and the parents thought she'd undergone a safe, noninvasive procedure. They didn't know what *really* happened. That way, Dad can test those specific powers without oversight or worrying about people asking questions. What she eats, he can study. She's the reason he has the pills."

The spark in Nick's head flared hotly. Above them, the tree branches rattled though there was no wind. "Did you know about all of this? You knew this entire time?"

"I didn't," Owen said bluntly. "What the hell do you think I've been doing since I escaped? I've been getting all the information I could. And no, before you ask, I haven't spoken to my father since I came back to Nova City. I don't want to say a goddamn word to that asshole unless it's telling him to beg for his life. The only reason he's not dead yet is because I couldn't figure out what his endgame is. It wasn't until I saw Jennifer Bell at Jazz's party that I started to figure it out. And I can prove it to you."

"How?" Seth demanded. "Give us one reason why we should trust anything you're saying."

Owen ignored him, eyes only for Nick. "You won't believe me, but I'm sorry for what's about to happen. Sometimes, brute force is necessary to get results. I don't even know if this is going to work, but I have to try. She underestimated the connection you have with Seth, and there's power in memory."

Sweat trickled down the back of Nick's neck, and when he spoke, it sounded as if it came from someone else. "What are you—"

Owen looked up at Seth. "Why did you become Pyro Storm?"

Seth blinked, mouth turning down as his forehead scrunched up. "What?"

"Pyro Storm," Owen said again. "You put on the costume for a very specific reason, ridiculous though it was. Do you know why?"

Seth paled, eyes unfocused. "I wanted to help . . . people."

Owen snorted. "That's some magnanimous bullshit, but sure, why not. You always were the Boy Scout, Seth. It got old so fast.

You don't know how many times I just wanted to reach across and slam your goddamn face into the lunch table at school. And sure, you *did* want to help people because you're so selfless." Mocking, angry. "But that's not why you became Pyro Storm. You did it for Nick."

"Why?" Jazz asked. "Why would he need to—"

Owen said, "Because my father had Jennifer Bell murdered when she wouldn't work with him. She walked into a bank and the people he sent after her made sure she never walked out. And you couldn't stand the thought of the boy you loved suffering, so you became Pyro Storm and—"

Nick jerked forward, quicker than he ever had before. Owen had no time to react, Nick sucker punching him in the stomach, breath exploding from his mouth. Before Owen could recover, Nick gripped the sides of his head, teeth bared, thumbs underneath his eyes and, oh, did he want to dig in. He wanted to make Owen hurt, wanted to tear out his throat so he couldn't speak anymore. "Shut up, shut up, *shut the fuck up*—"

He screamed when the worst pain he'd ever felt in his life bowled through his head. The illusion was gone and the only thing that remained was how much it hurt, how much *everything* hurt. It felt as if he were being turned inside out and Dad whispered, "Nicky, oh my god. *Nicky.* She's—"

Nick lifted his head and said—

Dad? What is it? What's wrong?"

Nicholas Bell was twelve years old. It was the last Friday of spring break and Nick was sitting on his bed, phone against his ear. Mom should've been back by now. She said she had to run to the bank and do a couple of other errands and then she'd be home. She was going to take him and Seth out for pizza. He'd cleaned his room.

Nick was twelve years old. Twenty-seven days before he'd officially become a teenager. *A man,* he sometimes whispered to himself. Laughable, this, but maybe if he became a man, he wouldn't have ADHD anymore. He'd be able to be normal. He could sit still for an entire class without causing a disruption where the teacher glared at him and the other students whispered about him behind their hands. He'd been told time and time again by the people who loved him that he was perfect, he was amazing, he was *exactly* the way he was supposed to be. But people lied to those they care for, lied to make them feel better. Little things, big things, but how many times had the school called his parents in for yet another meeting? How many times did Nick have to promise that he'd try to do better?

Later, he'd wonder why he didn't know the moment it happened. Wasn't that what he'd read online? Some people *knew*, a sort of precognition that couldn't be explained. A feeling, a sensation of *wrong wrong wrong* and *oh no* and *something happened something bad just happened*. Not déjà vu but *presque vu,* on the cusp of revelation.

But he didn't.

He didn't know what was coming when his phone rang. For a second, he thought it'd be Mom, telling him she was sorry she'd taken so long, Nick wouldn't believe how busy it was. "Everyone decided to run errands at the same time," she'd say in that grumpy voice she sometimes got, not angry, not exactly, because he'd be able to hear her smiling ruefully. "Didn't they know I had plans with my kid?"

It wasn't Mom. It was Dad.

He grinned as he answered the phone. "Hey, Pops. What's the—"

A sharp breath. An exhalation. Then, "Nicky. Oh my god, *Nicky.*"

*Hang up the phone,* a voice whispered, urgent, terrified. *Hang up the phone. Put it down. Ignore it. It's nothing. Everything is fine.*

"Dad? What is it? What's wrong?"

"Where are you?" Dad asked, shattered like so much glass. "Are you at home?"

"Yeah. I'm waiting for—are you *crying*?"

"I'm coming to you," Dad said, and voices were in the background, someone—Cap?—saying, "Aaron, Aaron, listen to me. We don't know what's—"

"Don't open the door," Dad said. "You hear me? You don't answer the door for *anyone* until I get home."

"O . . . kay?" Mind racing, a billion thoughts at once, but *none of them* were close to the truth. It was unfathomable. It was impossible. He was twelve years old—not yet teenager, not yet a man—and he didn't yet understand that no matter how much he loved someone, it wasn't enough to save them. "Have you talked to Mom? She was supposed to be back by now. I tried calling her, but she didn't—"

"I'm coming," Dad said again. "I love you, kid. I love you so much."

Alarm bells began to ring deep in Nick's head.

Then everything stuttered, the frame rate skipping, jumping, and he was pacing downstairs in front of the door, phone gripped in his hand. He tried to call Mom again. No answer. Again. No answer. Again, and then Dad burst through the door, face wet, eyes swollen, mouth twisted down. Suit wrinkled, tie lopsided, hair sticking up. He looked old. So old, as if decades had passed since Nick had seen him that morning when Dad had popped his head into Nick's room, telling him that just because it was summer didn't mean that he could stay in bed all day.

And just like that, he knew.

He *knew*.

"No," he said, taking a step back and shaking his head, heart in his throat. "No. I don't want—"

Dad reached for him, hands shaking, and though Nick tried to fight him off, tried to shove him away, Dad was bigger than him. Stronger, and he crushed Nick against his chest, entire body quivering like he was being electrocuted.

Nick breathed him in and Dad was crying, he was *sobbing* when he choked out, "She's gone, kid. Oh my god, she's gone, she's gone. I'm sorry. I'm so sorry. I—"

Nick screamed, then. He screamed and screamed until his throat was raw, and for days after, when he spoke—rarely, and only when asked a direct question—his voice was hoarse, gravelly, barely above a whisper.

Skip, jump.

Seth. Bob. Martha. Gibby. Jazz, all hugging him, all telling him they were here, they were with him, they would never leave him.

Skip, jump.

An urn. A funny little thing. He didn't know what it was made of. Metal. It felt like metal, cold and impersonal. Her name carved into the surface: JENNIFER MARIE BELL. Everything she was reduced to ashes, and Nick *hated* her, hated her for leaving them, for leaving *him*. She was supposed to come home because they were going to get pizza. She was supposed to be there when he woke up, when he went to bed, when he came home from school, when he figured out that he was queer, when he realized he loved Seth as more than his best friend. When he graduated. When he went to college. She was supposed to be there for all of it, to help him make sense of the world, and he *hated* her for taking herself away.

Another skip, another jump, and he was cold, a mist of salt water spraying on his face, the sky gunmetal gray, the lighthouse in the distance, dark and looming over them. Dad held the urn and pulled out the plastic bag that held her remains, a pile of ash that looked like what Dad scooped out from the fireplace.

No one was with them. There'd been offers, many offers, and they'd had a service for her, agnostic, calling it a celebration rather than what it really was. No one used the word *funeral*, and Nick was absurdly grateful for it, even if he thought a celebration was the last thing he wanted.

Dad had dark circles under his eyes, deep bruises that would take years to fade, if they ever did. Nick knew he looked no better, but he couldn't worry about that now. Dad needed him to be strong, needed him to be a man. Dad, who was clutching the urn to his chest with one arm, stupidly looking down at the bag in his other hand as if he thought he was dreaming, that none of this could be real.

They stood there, staring at it, shivering as the wind whipped over them. For the longest time, neither of them spoke because they both knew the moment they did, it was over. Done. Finished. The end.

It was Nick who spoke first, Nick who never met a silence he couldn't fill. He said, "You and me. No matter what. You and me."

"A team," Dad whispered, coming out of his stupor. "We stand together so we don't struggle apart."

They held the plastic bag together, Dad untying the offensively festive ribbon holding the bag shut—red with a glittering gold trim. It opened, and as one, they turned the bag over, spilling out the contents into the sea, the same place they'd come to because it made her happy, it made her smile. Nick had proof of this in a photograph on his desk.

She was gone in seconds, bits of ash fluttering in the wind, heavier pieces falling into the water, ripples forming, small splashes.

Before she died.

After she died.

They stayed there for a long time, clutching each other.

Years, then. Years passing by in between heartbeats, years where they grieved and fought and loved each other with everything they had. Good days, bad days, days when Nick felt like he was crawling out of his skin, days when it didn't hurt as much as it had before.

The tapes. The pills. The power hidden deep within him, waiting, waiting until the day it would rise and rise and *rise*.

The bridge.

The prom.

Pyro Storm.

Shadow Star.

Smoke and Ice and Miss Conduct and Burke, Simon goddamn

*Burke,* smirking in his limousine, picking up a piece of plastic that had chipped off the light above them, saying, "You remind me of your mother. I see her in you."

He was right. As much as Nick hated him, he was right. He saw her when he looked at his reflection, saw her when he put on Miss Conduct's gift the first time, saw her when he opened his eyes, when he closed them. He saw her in their house, in his head, in everything he did.

Twenty-seven days before Nicholas Bell turned thirteen years old, his mother walked into a bank. She did not walk out.

Skip. Jump, the final, the last, the end, and Nick was seventeen, not yet a man, but close. Summer starting, the future brimming with possibility. He knew what he was capable of, now. He knew what he could do, and it wasn't *about* being a hero. It wasn't *about* the accolades, the praise, the gratitude. It was about helping people, protecting them, just like his mother had. He had taken her name not because it was known, but because it was *her.* He was Guardian because *she* had been Guardian.

He was at home. Texting with Seth about the future. What they wanted. What lay ahead. What they'd do together, because Nick had already lost too much to ever want that to happen again.

Then Dad came home.

Nick tilted his head back on the couch. "Hey, Pops. How'd it go with Cap? Did you guys figure out what it'd take to get licensed for the—"

Dad said, "Nick. It's a miracle. It's a *miracle.*"

"What is?" Nick asked, twisting around, phone forgotten in his lap. He frowned at the look on Dad's face. Eyes glazed over, mouth slack. If he didn't know his father as well as he did, he'd have thought Dad was . . . high. Like he'd taken something. But that was ridiculous. Dad would *never.* "What are you—"

Then a woman stepped through the open front door. Short blond hair. Tan skin. Jeans. A loose shirt. Jennifer Bell smiled and said, "Hey, kid."

He wanted to scream, then, just like he had before. It wasn't possible. This was not his mother. Jennifer Bell was four years gone, and *this wasn't her.*

The spark in his head flared to life brighter than it ever had before. Not a star. *The* star. The sun, light blasting through him, and he raised his hand toward her, raised his hand to knock her through the goddamn *door,* but she was on him, she moved so *fast,* a blur of movement, her hands on the sides of her head, Dad just standing there, swaying, eyes distant, and Nick cried out for him as he struggled, yelling at Dad to help him, please help me.

But it was too late.

A tsunami crashed into him, obliterating the past, the truth, words whispered in his ears, saying, "I am Jennifer Bell. I am your mother. I'm here. I've always been here. Remember me. Love me. Everything is fine."

When she stepped back, hands trailing along his cheeks before falling away, Nick grinned up at her and said, "Hey, Mom. I didn't know you were out with Dad." For some reason, he thought she'd been . . . well. He didn't know where. Upstairs, maybe.

She ruffled his hair. "Doing patrols. Gotta keep the streets safe. I can't wait until you're able to join me. You and Seth. Team Lighthouse."

Dad groaned as he came over to the couch, kissing his wife on the cheek. "You're both going to be the death of me."

Nick rolled his eyes. "Drama queen."

Mom winked at him. "He's just jealous that we have powers and he doesn't."

That night, she came into his room, sitting on the edge of his bed. He smiled sleepily at her, and she brushed his hair off his brow. He flinched when she did, but she didn't move her hand. "Hey," she said. "I was thinking. Why don't you invite Seth and Gibby and Jazz over tomorrow? I'll make lunch. It's been a long time since I've been able to talk to them without having to punch some jerk in the face for trying to hurt you all."

"Your hair," he said, feeling like a bug caught in a web, the spider coming closer and closer. "Why . . . why did you cut your hair?"

Her hand stilled on his forehead. "Don't you worry about that, kid. It doesn't matter. There are bigger things to focus on."

He closed his eyes, and the last thing he heard before drifting off to sleep was when she whispered, "Everything is fine."

He believed her.

don't remember," Seth admitted, arm wrapped around Nick's shoulders. Nick, who had woken up in the park, surrounded by his worried friends. He'd rolled over and vomited on the grass, Jazz's hand rubbing his back, Gibby holding Owen against the tree. Seth had given Nick a bottle of water to rinse his mouth out once he'd finished. He'd taken the bottle gratefully, swishing water around his mouth before spitting.

He remembered. All if it. Shards of glass just underneath his skin, embedded, working their way out. It felt as if he'd woken from a long sleep, the kind that left him more exhausted then when he'd closed his eyes.

"I don't remember either," Jazz said, face pale. She sat at Nick's feet, hands on his ankles in a loose grip. He didn't know if it was for him, or if she was trying to ground herself. Either way, he loved her for it. "She's always been there. Anytime I think about the last four years, she's always been part of it."

"That's how she wants it to be," Owen said, hugging his knees against his chest, looking impossibly young. "Makes you think things that aren't real. She's doing what she's doing because my father told her to."

Gibby shook her head. "But why? If Burke wanted to take out Nick and Seth, why not just have her take their powers away? Why string us all along like this?" Then, "Before. After. I can't get those two words out of my head. What does that mean?"

"You heard it from me," Nick said roughly, Seth making a wounded noise behind him. "That's what I called it. Before she died. After she died. A division between the two." He glanced at Gibby before looking at Owen with narrowed eyes. "But Gibby's right. If what you're saying is true, why do it this way? It doesn't make sense."

"Because he has a campaign to win," Owen said. "Why take your powers away when he can just control you to turn public opinion away from the Extraordinaries? And he wants you to suffer."

Nick rested the back of his head against Seth's shoulder. He wanted nothing more than to sleep for a week. "I told you she was acting weird this morning." He laughed, though he found nothing even remotely amusing. "I don't know, man. As much as I hate Owen—and I mean really, *really* hate him—"

"Gee, thanks, Nicky."

"—it sounds exactly like something Burke would do." He scrubbed a hand over his face. "You want it to hurt, you don't attack head-on. You try and worm your way in and destroy it from the inside out. At least, that's what I'd do if I was the bad guy."

"And we're thankful every day you're not," Jazz told him, patting his knee. "You'd make the best villain, Nick. And no, that wasn't a compliment."

"You're welcome, by the way," Owen said. "Bet you never expected me to be the one to help you. Maybe there's something to being one of the good guys after all." He sounded way too pleased with himself.

"If you're waiting for us to thank you," Seth muttered, "you're going to be disappointed."

"Yeah, yeah," Owen said. He leaned his head back against the tree trunk. "At least I got through to you. I wasn't sure if it'd work." He closed his eyes. "Pretty ridiculous that something like *love* can break through the hold she had over Nick."

Nick sat up away from Seth, though he stayed between his legs. He motioned for Gibby to step out of the way. She hesitated but did as asked. Owen opened his eyes and watched him warily. "Why the hell would your father want my mother dead?" The lump in his throat thickened, but he forced his way through it. "They were friends once."

Owen sighed. "My father doesn't see people like you do. Not what they can do for each other, but what they can do for *him*. He wanted her to help him make other Extraordinaries, to figure out how to weaponize them. She refused. He threatened her. Said if she wouldn't help him, she'd regret it. She still said no. And if she wasn't going to help him, then she was in his way. So he—"

"Why should we believe you?" Jazz asked. "For all we know, you're working with your dad."

"Maybe I am," Owen said. "Maybe all of this is part of the plan to make you doubt yourselves and each other." He laughed bitterly. "It'd be what *I'd* do if I wanted to hurt you the most. But you know I'm right. Whether or not you can admit it to yourselves, some part of you knows I'm telling the truth. Isn't that right, Nicky?"

But before Nick could say anything, Seth said, "Why are you telling us any of this? You just said yourself this is something you'd do. You hate us as much as we hate you. Why not just let your father get away with all of this?"

"It's so easy for you," Owen snapped. "Black-and-white. The good guys and the villains. Nothing in between. It's always been your problem, Seth. You'd think after all you've been through with the NCPD, you'd realize it's vastly more complicated than you're making it out to be."

"That's because we *are* the good guys," Seth said coldly. "And you're not. It doesn't get much clearer than that."

Owen flipped him off, and Nick had to stop himself from reaching out and breaking his finger. "Whatever helps you sleep at night, Gray. You're so hyperfocused on doing the right thing that you miss what's right in front of you. It always comes back to Nick with you. He's the reason you became Pyro Storm." He rolled his eyes. "And I would bet my life that the reason you took off your helmet on prom night was because of Nick, too. No one deserves that kind of devotion, because it will blow up in your face when you least expect it."

"If you're expecting us to feel sorry for you," Gibby said, "then you don't know us as well as you seem to think."

Owen scowled at her. "Like I give a shit about that. I'm not . . ." He looked down at his hands. "Whatever Dad did to me, it changed me. Altered my DNA. I wasn't an Extraordinary before. I wasn't born with powers. I took those pills and it gave me the ability to control shadows. And once I couldn't get them anymore, I thought that was it." He scrunched up his face, and the shadow of the tree on the grass began to tremble. "But it wasn't. I can still control shadows." He raised his hand, and Gibby stumbled back when a shadow lifted *off the ground,* a slim black tendril that shuddered before it collapsed back into the grass and became the shape of the leaves, the branches above them. "I'm not as strong as I used to be. I can't stop my father on my own."

"So you want us to help *you*?" Nick asked incredulously. "Why the hell would we do that?"

Owen leaned forward, a glint in his eyes Nick didn't like. "You know why, Nicky. Separately, we stand no chance against him. But together, we might just be able to stop him. You know what I'm talking about. How does it go? It's easier to stand together than it—"

"Yeah," Jazz said, a plastic fork appearing in her hand as if by magic. "I wouldn't finish that if I were you. I've gotten a taste of your blood, and it's made me hungry for more."

"The note," Nick said suddenly. *"See you soon."*

Owen grinned, and for a moment, Nick could see the boy he'd once been, the one who'd sat with them at lunch for reasons they hadn't quite understood. If only he'd known then what he knew now. "You got that, huh? Wasn't sure if you did. Thought Patricia might have intercepted it."

"Seemed liked a pretty clear threat," Seth muttered.

"Well, *yeah*. It was supposed to. I wanted to kill you all. Still do, at least a little bit. But dealing with my father comes first." Owen puffed out his chest. "Priorities, wouldn't you know.

You're not the only one who's learned things since we last saw each other."

"And you're expecting us to trust you?" Nick asked incredulously.

Jazz scoffed as she flipped the fork and caught it without looking at it. "You must think we're pretty stupid."

Owen burst out laughing. "Oh, absolutely. You guys are the worst. And trust, Nick? *Trust?* Why the hell would you trust me? That's dumb." He wiped his eyes. "No offense, of course. It's part of your . . . charm."

"Not helping your case," Gibby muttered.

Owen made a face. "What can I say? Old habits die hard."

"It sounds like a trap," Seth said. "Like you're manipulating us just as much as you claim Burke and your stepmother are."

"Does it?" Owen asked. "Maybe there's something to the whole trust thing after all. You'll have to trust me not to kill you." He grew solemn, raising his hand to his chest above his heart. "You have my word that I won't hurt the pretty little hairs on any of your heads. Gibby, that includes you, too, even though you don't have hair."

"Because *that* counts for anything," Jazz said.

Seth pushed Nick forward, standing behind him, knees popping loudly. He held out a hand for Nick and lifted him up. He squeezed Nick's hand before looking back at Owen, who watched them curiously. "How many others?"

Owen blinked. "What do you mean?"

"If she is who she says she is, and if she can do what you claim, how many others has she cured? Aside from the shape-shifting. And the telekinesis. And the memory alteration. Oh man, are we screwed? Because it sounds like we're screwed."

Owen nodded slowly, eyes narrowing. "You're smarter than I remember. I'm not sure if I like that or not." Then, without waiting for a retort, he said, "Three more, or at least as far as I know. You know two of them." He paused for dramatic effect. "Christian and Christina Lewis."

Gibby frowned at him. "Smoke and Ice?"

"Yep," Owen said. "Dad has connections. Got Mom in to see them without anyone watching. Mom did the same thing to them that she did to Eve. And now she can manipulate ice and smoke, but if you ask me, smoke is nowhere near as cool as shadows. What a goddamn rip-off."

"She has their powers now?" Nick whispered, feeling as if the ground was shaking beneath his feet.

"Think so," Owen said. "I don't have proof of it, but why else would she have met with them?"

"Who's the third?" Seth asked.

"I don't know," Owen admitted, looking almost sheepish. "All I have is a first name. Martin. Remember the interview where Dad talked about Eve? He mentioned someone else. A man in his fifties. Since Dad lied about when he found Eve, he probably lied about the timing of the man, too. Why mention him if—"

"If she already hadn't taken his powers, too," Jazz whispered.

"Exactly," Owen said. "But I don't know what those powers are, or what she can do with them."

"Why stop there?" Gibby asked. "Why not do the same to Seth? Miss Conduct? Nick, even if she's already telekinetic? Why hasn't she taken their powers, too? Make them think they never had any to begin with?"

Owen stared at her. "Don't you know anything about the strategies of war?"

"Must have missed that class," Jazz said. "It is an elective?"

Owen rolled his eyes. "Why would he have her take those powers when everyone knows who Pyro Storm is? Don't you think it'd be weird if one day, Seth suddenly wasn't pyrokinetic anymore? Even people who hate Extraordinaries would ask questions that could lead back to my father. He wouldn't take that chance. Why run the risk when he can draw you out and make you look like a threat?" He grinned. "Which you fell for. You did more for his campaign in ten minutes when you crashed his rally than six months of politicking. So, if that's what you were going for, good job."

"Still doesn't explain why your mother didn't try and make things easier for herself," Gibby said.

"I don't think she can," Owen said. "It's like . . . okay. So, you know when lightning strikes a power line? It sends a charge through wherever the line goes. Sometimes, it'll knock out power all over. But most places are outfitted with surge protectors. I think she's like that. A limit to how much she can take in. Regardless of what else Extraordinaries are, we're still human. Our bodies can't handle that much energy." He raised his hands, bringing them close, the tips of his fingers pressed together. "I think if she tried to take any more she'd . . ." He made a noise as he spread his hands quickly.

"Boom," Nick whispered.

"Boom," Owen agreed. "It'd overload her."

"How do you know?" Gibby asked. "You have any evidence?"

Owen blinked innocently. "My word isn't enough for you? How rude."

"I bet your uvula is so precious," Jazz whispered. "I can't wait to tear it out and see it for myself."

"Cheerleaders," Owen muttered. "Yes, I have evidence. Heard it directly from the source when I was following her right after Gibby's graduation. She was on the phone with my father and didn't know I was listening in. After she ate Ice and Smoke's powers, it nearly killed her. Too much all at once. Dad was trying to convince her it was just a fluke, but she said that to do more, she'd have to give up something she'd already taken. Dad wasn't too happy about it, but from what I could gather, he seemed to listen. Why would he do that if she wasn't telling the truth?"

"Then why don't you do us all a favor and let her take yours?" Jazz asked. "Then we'd be rid of her *and* you."

"Aw, Jazz," Owen simpered. "I didn't know you cared."

"I don't," Jazz retorted. "Stay there. If you move even a muscle,

I'm going to make you regret ever being born." She stood, motioning for the others to follow. Nick leaned heavily against Seth as they walked away from the tree, Gibby bringing up the rear.

Once they were out of earshot, they stopped, forming a small circle, heads bowed close together, shoulders touching. Nick took solace that—even in the face of this fresh wave of bullshit—his friends were with him.

Which was why he said, "I don't trust him. None of us should. But I need you to trust me." He sucked in a breath, closing his eyes. "He's telling the truth, at least about my mother. I don't know about all the rest, but I remember. Please believe me."

He opened his eyes when he felt them grab his hands. Jazz to his right. Seth on his left. Gibby wrapped her hand around the back of his neck. "We do," she said quietly. "We may not remember like you can, but we trust you, Nicky. Always have. We don't need to believe him because we believe in *you*."

Nick shuddered and did nothing to stop the tear that fell onto his cheek. "She's gone," he whispered. "I . . . it hurts so bad. It's like I just lost her all over again."

Jazz sniffled. "You have. And you need to allow yourself to grieve." She shook her head. "I can't believe Burke would . . . okay, so I *can* believe he'd do something like this. I just didn't expect it. And that somehow makes it worse."

"We need to stay away from her," Seth said, obviously troubled. "We can't take the chance she'd mess with our heads even more than she already has."

Gibby sighed as she let Nick go, taking a step back. "It's like Nick said after graduation, remember? We're alone. We don't have our parents. We don't have Miss Conduct. Chris. Anyone. What're we supposed to do now?"

"Exactly the opposite of whatever Owen says we should do," Jazz said. "He wants our help, but it sounds like he only wants revenge. That's not who we are. We don't hurt people, even if they deserve it."

For a moment, Nick wanted to snap at her, tell her she was wrong. He *wanted* to hurt people. He wanted to hurt the woman pretending to be his mother. He wanted to whirl around and make Owen suffer. And once they were done, he'd find Simon Burke and make him pay for everything he'd done.

The idea of revenge was seductive, and if he didn't have his friends by his side, Nick wondered how quickly he'd give into it. The spark throbbed, but Nick rose above it. It didn't control him. He controlled it.

"We might have to," he said begrudgingly. "I don't see how we can stop them without *someone* getting hurt. And I'd rather it be them than us." He thought hard. "If Owen's right, then we might have the upper hand."

"What do you mean?" Seth asked.

"My mot—" *(No.)* "Patricia Burke is stretched too thin as it is. She doesn't have the level of control she thinks she does. Gibby's proven that." He looked at her proudly. "I don't know why you can remember some stuff, but you're badass, dude."

"Damn right I am," she said. "That's why they call me Butch Fatale."

"Oh my god," Jazz whispered. "I know things are superserious right now, but that's the hottest thing I've ever heard. You should get a costume and say that to me again."

Gibby winked at her. "Rain check, babe. But yeah, I've got some ideas. How do you feel about—"

"Focus," Nick said, and Gibby nodded. He glanced back at Owen, who watched them, obviously amused. Owen gave a little wave, and Nick drew his finger across his neck pointedly before turning back around to his friends. "We don't trust him. We don't trust the woman pretending to be my mother. The cops are in Burke's pocket, so it's not like we can go to them."

"What about your dad?" Seth asked. "Maybe he'd believe you if you told him."

Nick wished that were true. He wanted nothing more than to go running to Dad to make everything better. It hurt to think Dad might not listen to him. And could he blame him for that? In Nick's own head, memories warred with one another.

"I don't know," Nick admitted. "Do you think your aunt and uncle would listen? Or Jazz's and Gibby's parents? What if she finds out and tries to use them against us?" He trembled at the thought. "It'd be the four of us against all of them. We have to protect them as much as we protect ourselves." He laughed bitterly. "Which means we'll be doing the exact thing we've been wrestling with for a year: keeping secrets. God, I'm such a hypocrite."

"What choice do we have?" Jazz asked, worry etched across her face.

"We can't go on like this forever," Gibby said. "Something has to break. We need to figure out a way to get through to them." Her forehead furrowed. "It all comes back to Patricia Burke. She's the one who has a hold over them."

"And us, too," Jazz said. "Because even though I believe she's not Nick's mom, my mind is telling me she is."

"So, what?" Seth said. "We confront her? She's strong, guys. If what Owen said is true, she's telekinetic in addition to being able to manipulate smoke and ice. Change her appearance, too."

"And maybe another power we don't know about yet," Nick said, thinking back to what Owen had told them. "We need to find out what that is. *Who* that is."

"How?" Gibby asked. "Owen said he couldn't find him."

"Right," Nick said. "But we have something Owen doesn't: your brain. You practically built the systems we use on your own. If anyone can do it, it's you."

Gibby looked away, obviously pleased with the praise. "We need to get to the secret lair. I'd do it on my phone, but I don't want to take the chance that someone's tracking us like Burke did with Nick. The Lighthouse app is encrypted, so we'll have that if we need to communicate."

Speaking of, Nick pulled out his phone and opened the app. He clicked on the eight-bit icon of TK, and a map appeared, zooming in to show she was at their house. He gripped his phone so hard he thought the screen would crack.

He looked back up at his friends. "We need to split up." Seth started shaking his head, but Nick expected that. "No, listen. I know it's dangerous, but if we're going to do this, we need to be smart about it. We need eyes on her so we know where she is in case she decides to leave. I'll go with Gibby to the secret lair. Jazz, Seth, go to my house but *don't go inside*. Stay the hell away from her. We'll meet back up once Gibby and I are done and go from there."

"I don't like this," Seth said.

"I know," Nick said quietly. "But what choice do we have?"

To that, Seth had no answer.

"What are we going to do with Owen?" Gibby asked, and they all turned to look at him. He grinned at them, and Nick gave brief thought to making the tree fall on top of him. It'd certainly make things easier. "We can't just let him go. And where's he staying, anyway? I almost want him to be homeless, but I'm not *that* big of a dick."

"I have an idea," Jazz said, her own smile growing, causing Owen's to fade. "It's time to bring on a new member to Team Lighthouse."

They didn't have to wait long. Owen asked what they were doing, but they ignored him, marching him toward the busy street that ran along the side of the park. They stopped on the sidewalk, Gibby and Seth on either side of Owen, gripping his arms tightly to keep him from trying to run away. As much as the sight of Owen fleeing in terror from them made Nick giddy, Jazz's idea was better.

"Are you just going to throw me into traffic?" Owen asked, sounding uncharacteristically nervous. "That's a little much, even for you guys."

"Dammit," Nick muttered. "That's even better. Maybe we could do that instead."

Seth coughed pointedly, even as he tried to cover up his smile by looking away.

Nick sighed. "Yeah, yeah. We don't kill."

"You should try it," Owen said. "You might like it more than you—what the hell is *that*?"

"That," Nick said excitedly, "is Matilda."

The van screeched to a stop in front of them, the woman painted on the side still riding the ridiculous seahorse. A moment later, the driver's window rolled down and Burrito Jerry leaned out, arm resting on the door, his eyes glittering. "You guys call for a ride?" He squinted down at his phone before looking back at them, gaze resting on Gibby. "Jasmine Kensington? Heard that name before. Recognize you, too, miss. Given you a ride, yeah?"

"Hey, Burrito Jerry," Gibby said with a little wave. "Good to see you again."

Nick stepped forward, leaving Owen with the others. "Burrito Jerry, my name is Nicholas Bell. The last time you saw me, I was in costume."

Burrito Jerry brightened. "That's right! You looked wicked cool. Took you to that rally so you could save the day. How'd that go?"

"Bad," Nick said immediately. "And it's only going to get worse." He took a deep breath. "I have something to tell you, something I've only told people close to me."

"Nick," Seth said from behind him. "You don't have to do this. Especially if you're not ready."

Nick looked over his shoulder. "I know. But if we're going to be the heroes the people of Nova City trust, then we need to trust them first. I'm tired of secrets."

"Got your back, Nicky," Jazz said.

"Whatever you need," Gibby agreed.

Seth moved to Nick's side, taking his hand, fingers intertwined. He must have found what he was looking for on Nick's face, because he nodded. "Just like coming out. You did that once. You can do this, too."

"Ooh," Burrito Jerry said. "This sounds serious. Lay it on me,

Nicholas Bell. I promise I won't judge. Not really who I am. Live and let live, you know? So long as you're not hurting yourself or others who don't deserve it, it's all good to me."

Nick took a deep breath as he looked back at Burrito Jerry. "I was in costume because I'm an Extraordinary. I'm telekinetic and I go by the name Guardian. And it scares the hell out of me to tell you this, but if I'm going to ask for your help, you deserve to know who's asking."

Burrito Jerry nodded slowly before motioning for Seth and Nick to step back from the van. They did, and he opened the door, climbing out with a groan, wrappers falling onto the ground. He was a big man, legs strong, the slope of his stomach straining against his shirt. Once standing, he looked Nick up and down before holding out his hand.

Confused, Nick stared at it.

"Come on," Burrito Jerry said, wiggling his fingers. "Always wanted to shake hands with a real live superhero."

Nick took the hand that dwarfed his own, and Burrito Jerry jerked it up and down. Once done, he let Nick go and said, "Heard about you, Guardian. You hang out with the fire guy, yeah?"

"That's me," Seth said. "Pyro Storm."

"Whoa," Burrito Jerry breathed. "*The* Pyro Storm? It was because of you I get free burritos for life! Put 'er there, pal." He shook Seth's hand just as hard. "I can't believe I just met two Extraordinaries. Holy cow, that's crazy. And you want *me* to help you? Man oh man, when I woke up this morning, I had a feeling today was going to be different. What do you need me to do?"

That . . . was easier than he expected it to be. "You believe me?"

Burrito Jerry laughed. "Well, yeah. Why wouldn't I? Doesn't seem like something you'd lie about."

Nick blinked against the burn in his eyes. "I . . ."

"Oh, hey, you're all right," Burrito Jerry said as his expression softened. "Thank you for telling me. I can't imagine how scary that must have been. That takes guts, Guardian. I promise I won't let you down. You can count on me."

Nick sniffled as Seth squeezed his hand. "You're pretty much the best, Burrito Jerry."

He puffed out his chest. "Yeah? Coming from someone like you, that means something." He looked beyond them. "They Extraordinaries, too? Oh, shoot. Don't know if that's something I can ask. Sorry, friends. Just a little excited. You know how it is."

"They are," Nick said. "In their own way. That's Gibby." She waved. "And Jazz." She smiled. "They're with us. They always have our backs."

Burrito Jerry nodded in greeting before looking at Owen. "What about that one?" he asked out of the corner of his mouth, going for subtle and missing by a mile. "Don't know if I like the looks of that one."

"Screw you, too," Owen retorted. "I don't know what you think you're doing, but—"

"That's an asshole," Nick said. "Owen tried to kill me and my friends."

Burrito Jerry glared at him. "Not cool. Why try and kill people when you could do other things like read a book or go to a museum?"

"Where did you *find* this guy?" Owen groused.

"Need you to give him a tour of Nova City," Nick said. "As in-depth as possible. You still got the ropes and bungie cords?"

"Yep," Burrito Jerry said. "Safety first!"

Nick grinned.


Owen, as it turned out, was *not* a fan of being tied up and thrown in a windowless van called Matilda. He struggled, but Nick and Seth held him down while Gibby and Jazz hogtied him, feet attached to his hands, forcing him to lie on his stomach on the bench seat. A few people stopped and asked what they were doing, and Burrito Jerry told them they were making a student film about something near and dear to his heart: stranger danger. "It'll help keep the kids safe from people who want them to get into a windowless van," Burrito Jerry explained to a group of tourists who said they were from the Midwest. They nodded, took a couple of pictures, then moved on.

"You think this can hold me?" Owen snarled, outraged. "It *won't*."

Nick bent over, face inches from Owen's. "If you do *anything* to Burrito Jerry or Matilda, I'll deal with you myself. You think you know me, Owen. But trust me when I say you haven't even begun to see what I'm capable of. If you want us to believe you, if you want us to help you, then you will do *exactly* what Burrito Jerry tells you to."

"I'll make you pay for this," Owen muttered darkly. "Don't think I won't."

"Promises, promises." He stepped back and slid the door shut as hard as he could.

Burrito Jerry climbed back inside the van, looking back at Owen. "I hope you like ASMR and explanations of the history of every city block. No one knows this town better than I do. But before we begin Burrito Jerry's Magical Tour of Nova City, can I get your pronouns? I use he/him."

Owen groaned loudly.

"We'll let you know where to drop him off," Jazz said. "Charge us whatever you want, and then add another zero. And if he tries anything, feel free to call us. Especially if you see shadows start to move."

"I have pepper spray, access to multiple marsupials, and snacks," Burrito Jerry said, patting the door below the open window. "I think we'll be all right. Later, gator. Oh. Wait. Later, *Guardian*."

He gunned the engine and peeled away from the curb, narrowly missing a cab.

# 12

They reached the Gray brownstone without incident, Martha seeming surprised to see them. They told her they needed to update something on the computer in the secret lair before meeting up with Jazz and Seth. She didn't question them, letting them in before going back to the kitchen

When they reached the basement, Nick hurried to the pocket door, sliding it open and dropping his backpack next to it. Seth's old Pyro Storm costume—the one with the cape—hung on a rack beside a shelf of gadgets Jazz and Gibby had bought last spring. Night-vision goggles, a Geiger counter, high-powered binoculars, all things Gibby had taken apart and rebuilt, incorporating what she'd learned into Nick's and Seth's costumes.

Gibby sat in front of the computer, fingers flying along the keys as Nick stood over her shoulder. The Systemax was long gone, replaced by a machine far more powerful, with three separate screens, the middle one almost as big as Nick's television. The word LIGHTHOUSE appeared, along with a box to enter the password. As Gibby typed, she explained she was checking to make sure no one had tried to piggyback off their systems, tracking whatever they did like Burke had done to Nick's phone. Nick hadn't even thought of that. Nervously, he waited.

"I think we're all right," she said after a time. "But I'm going to use a Tor browser, just to be safe. Makes it harder to track." She pulled it up, a light green screen with the picture of an onion next to a search box under the words CONGRATULATIONS! THIS BROWSER IS CONFIGURED TO USE TOR. YOU ARE FREE TO BROWSE THE INTERNET ANONYMOUSLY.

"Directory, right?" she asked. "That's what you're thinking?"

Nick nodded as he looked over her shoulder. "Seems simple enough. May not work, but at least it's a start."

"He might have wiped any mention of Martin," Gibby warned him. "He did the same with Smoke and Ice, remember? We couldn't find any trace of them after prom."

"I know. But maybe we'll get lucky. We deserve a break."

She went to the website for Burke Tower. Across the top, a brightly colored banner with the Stars and Stripes waving next to a picture of Simon Burke, looking dangerously handsome in a black suit with a red tie. Underneath him, the words FOURTH OF JULY SPECTACULAR! JOIN US AS WE CELEBRATE AMERICA AND THE FUTURE OF NOVA CITY!

"Ugh," Nick muttered. "With everything going on, I forgot about the holiday."

Gibby clicked on the banner, bringing up another screen. Simon Burke would be speaking at sunset in front of Burke Tower as part of his mayoral campaign, to be followed by what was proclaimed to be the largest fireworks display in the city.

"Could be useful," Gibby said. "At least we'll know where he'll be." She clicked off the screen and scrolled down the first page until she got to the bottom. "Burke Pharmaceuticals," she said, clicking on a link, bringing up another website with an obvious stock photo of two people wearing white lab coats and goggles. One held up a beaker filled with blue liquid, the other looking as if it was the greatest invention mankind had ever come up with. Farther down, another link that read ABOUT US.

Gibby clicked on it as their phones chimed at the same time. "I got it," Nick said, pulling out his phone. He clicked on the notification and pulled up the Lighthouse app. "Seth? Jazz? You there?"

"Yeah," Seth said, and Nick clicked the speaker button, setting the phone down next to Gibby. "We're at your house. Can't tell if anyone's home. Blinds shut. Can't see inside."

"App says she's here," Jazz said, voice crackling. "Anything on your end?"

"Not yet," Gibby said. On the screen, a long directory had been pulled up, a list of names next to credentials. Scientists, doctors, lab techs. "Doing name search. Hold on."

Nick held his breath.

A moment later, Gibby shook her head. "No Martin listed with Burke Pharmaceuticals."

"Check the support staff," Seth said. "In the building. A guard. A janitor. HR, something like that."

"On it," Gibby said, switching screens and scrolling more until she found another directory. It took another five minutes before she sat back with a sigh. "Nothing there, either."

"Shit," Nick muttered. "It was a long shot, but . . ."

"I really thought we'd find something," Gibby finished for him.

"Why not just search *Simon Burke* and the name *Martin*?" Jazz asked. "If there's any connection, it might show up somewhere else."

Gibby and Nick stared down at the phone, dumbfounded. Then Gibby snorted and shook her head ruefully. "Jazz, you're amazing."

"I know," Jazz said. "But thank you for telling me."

Gibby leaned forward and pulled up the browser once more, typing in SIMON BURKE MARTIN.

A dozen links popped up, but before Nick could get too excited, Gibby pointed out they were nothing more than the gossip pages in tabloids showing Burke out on the town, drinking martinis. She scrolled down farther, and Nick started to deflate. Nothing. Maybe Owen got the name wrong. Or worse, he was messing with them, sending them chasing after something that didn't exist. He was about to admit defeat when Gibby said, "Wait. Hold on. I think I found something." She frowned as she clicked on a link. "It's a story from . . . twelve years ago. From a defunct Nova City blog. They haven't updated anything in almost a decade." She began to read. "'Attorneys announced today that Burke Pharmaceuticals had reached a settlement agreement with Martin Underwood. Underwood, a security guard at Burke Tower, sued Simon Burke last year, claiming wrongful termination. While the details of the settlement are sealed, word on the street is that Burke paid well into six figures rather than proceeding to arbitration or a trial. Seems as if someone is keeping secrets. What does Simon Burke want to hide? What does Martin Underwood know about the goings-on in Burke Tower?'"

"That has to be him," Nick breathed. "Right?"

"Maybe," Gibby murmured, silently reading the rest of the article. "He . . . okay. It doesn't say *why* he was fired, or what happened to him after. Hold on. Let's see if we can find Underwood somewhere else. If this is the right person, and he's still in Nova City, we might be able to see where he lives."

"Good work," Seth said. "Nick, do you think we could see any better through the back of the house?"

"Only through the window on the back door. It doesn't have a blind on it. The other windows do."

"Hold on," Gibby said grimly. "I found him. He's dead."

"*What?*" Nick demanded. "When?" He looked back at the screen to see she'd pulled up an obituary. Next to the words was a picture of Martin Underwood, an older white man with a solemn smile and cavernous wrinkles on his kind face. The obituary was short, giving few details aside from his place of birth and the date of his death, which happened almost five years before. The only hint of the manner of death was the phrase *Underwood passed away unexpectedly.* The last line of the obituary read: *Mr. Underwood is survived by his only daughter.*

"Maybe we can find her," Nick said. "See if she knows anything. Long shot, but I don't know what else to do. We don't even know how he died." He glanced down at the phone. "Guys, you hearing this?"

No response.

"Seth?" Nick asked. "Jazz?"

Nothing.

"Nick," Gibby said urgently. "Look at this."

On the screen, a news story. Not from Action News, but another site. A short article, saying that police were baffled by the death of Martin Underwood, who was found in his East Side apartment deceased after neighbors complained of a foul smell in the hallway. According to the coroner, it appeared Martin Underwood had been dead for a least a week before he was discovered.

But it wasn't the length of time it took to find him that baffled investigators.

It was the fact that he'd *drowned*. His lungs were filled with water, but there was no other physical evidence to show his body had ever been in water. Police were continuing to investigate.

"Water," Nick whispered. "Jesus, Gibby. What if he could manipulate water? What if that was his power?"

"And Patricia Burke took it from him," Gibby said. "Then . . . what. Turned it on him? Drowned him with his own powers? Nick, that means she can—"

*So this is what it's led to,* a voice whispered in Nick's head, foreign, intrusive. He blinked slowly, as if caught in a dream. *We underestimated you. We won't do that again. Stop him. Stop him* now.

"Gibby," Nick said, sounding far, far away. "Did . . . did you hear that?"

No answer.

He looked down at her.

Sweat sluiced down the sides of her face as she gripped the table, knuckles bloodless. Through gritted teeth, she bit out, "I . . . can't. Stop. It. It's so . . . *loud*." She turned her head toward him, eyes wide, frightened. "She's . . ."

*Do it. Stop him by whatever means necessary.*

The door to the basement opened above. Steps creaked. "Nick? Gibby? I have cookies. So many cookies."

Martha.

Gibby hunched over the desk, head in her hands. Nick rushed to the entrance of the secret lair. "Martha! Something's wrong with Gibby! I need your . . ."

*Help,* was how he meant to finish. But his voice was stolen from him when he saw Martha Gray descending the stairs holding a large kitchen knife, the blade glinting in the light from the bare bulb above the stairs.

"Cookies," Martha singsonged. "So many cookies."

"Uh," Nick said, taking a step back as she reached the bottom of the stairs, her eyes vacant, expression slack. "That doesn't look like cookies."

He stumbled back when Martha hurtled toward him, knife raised above her head. Managing to stay upright, he slammed the pocket door, screaming when the knife went through it, the tip of the blade inches from his right eye.

"Martha!" he bellowed through the door. "What the hell?"

"It's *her*," Gibby wheezed behind him. "Nick, it's Patricia Burke. She knows. *She knows.*"

"I'm supposed to be in a romantic comedy, not a horror movie!" Nick cried as the blade wiggled from side to side as if it was stuck, Martha trying to pull it free. With all his might, he jerked the door open again, causing Martha to lose her grip on the knife. It bounced off the cement floor, sliding underneath the washing machine.

"Ha!" Nick crowed. "See that? That's how I get things *done*—"

For an older woman, Martha Gray certainly knew how to throw a punch. Nick learned this firsthand, her fist colliding with his cheek, knocking him back as his vision exploded in stars. Before he could recover, Martha's hands were around his throat, grip tight, cutting off his air.

He struggled against her, but he couldn't hurt her. This was *Martha*, the woman loved him almost as much as she loved Seth.

The spark in his head pulsed, and he managed to say "Please don't hate me for this!" before he *pushed*. The air around him grew thick, and then Martha flew back, hitting the wall near the door and slumping to the floor in a heap, head lolling to the side as she blinked rapidly. "Nick?" she asked, voice faint. "What . . . how did I get down here? I . . ." Her vision began to cloud over. "Cookies. I brought you cookies." She rose slowly, using the wall to push herself up. "Also, I want to see what your *insides look like*." Fingers hooked like claws, she began to advance toward them.

Gibby grabbed Nick's hand, pulling him around the desk, keeping it between them and Martha.

"We gotta get out of here," Gibby said, pulling Nick back as Martha tried to reach them across the table. "I can hear her. In my head."

Nick ducked as Martha swiped at him. "We can't hurt her."

"I know," Gibby ground out. "Good thing my girlfriend is rich." With that, she let Nick go before upending the table toward Martha as hard as she could. The table flew up, the monitors and keyboards crashing against Martha, the impact forcing her to her knees. "Go!"

They went, both of them leaping over Martha as she tried to stand again. Nick leaned down and grabbed his backpack by the strap, never slowing. They hit the stairs, thundering upward, Martha shouting after them. They reached the first floor, slamming the door shut and locking the knob, followed by the dead bolt.

"In case I haven't said it today," Nick said, "I really hate the Burkes."

"Ditto," Gibby said. "Come on. I don't know how long that'll hold her. We need to get out of here before Bob comes home." They headed for the front door, Gibby pulling out her phone and opening the app.

"Anything?" Nick asked, stopping at the front door, peering out the glass to make sure no one they loved was waiting outside to try to kill them.

"No," Gibby said, shoving her phone back in her pocket. "Nothing. This isn't good, Nick. I can still feel her in my head."

Nick no longer could. Whatever hold she had over him was gone, or she'd given up trying to control him. "Can you handle it? If you can't, you have to stay here. It'd be safer for both of us." He shuddered at the idea of Gibby turning on him. Even with powers, he'd probably get his ass kicked.

Gibby shook her head. "I'm good. I know it's there, that *she's* there, but I've got it. If that changes, I'll let you know."

"You better," Nick told her, looking out the window again. Nothing. No one waiting. Thinking fast, Nick dropped his backpack, ripping it open and pulling out the Guardian costume. He handed the bundle over to Gibby before kicking off his shoes. "You don't get to make fun of my underwear."

She rolled her eyes. "We don't have t—nope, we have time. Nick, honestly. You are seventeen years old. You need underwear that doesn't have cartoons on it."

"Cartoons? How very *dare you*. These are comic-book symbols! See? *Blam! Pow!*" He turned to show her.

"I can see your ass crack."

"We don't have time!" he cried, kicking off his shorts as he pulled his shirt up and over his head.

"Thank you, though," Gibby said, handing over his costume.

"For what? Rescuing you? Dude, I think you saved me, so—"

"Not that," she said, eyeing him up and down as he shoved one leg inside his costume. "I can see the outline of your testicles, and it reminded me why I'm a lesbian."

"Gibby!"

"Don't yell at me. I'm not the one who brought them out."

"It's not my fault they're so big!"

She turned her face toward the ceiling. "How is today not over yet?"

Costume on, Nick picked up his helmet off the floor. He slid it over his head, and the screen inside burst to life. WELCOME, GUARDIAN.

"Let's go," Guardian said. "It's time to take out the trash."


They stepped outside, and Guardian groaned. "Goddammit. I forgot I don't know how to fly. What the hell. How is today not *over* yet?"

"Burrito Jerry is forty minutes away," Gibby said, glancing

down at her phone. "No help there. If we start running now, we can make it in fifteen minutes."

"Like I'm going to be caught dead running in public again. Trust me. I've got this. Watch and learn. You there, sir! Yes, you, the one climbing into the sedan. This is an emergency. We need to commandeer your vehicle in order to save—why are you screaming? I'm not trying to carjack you! Sir. *Sir.* Put the pepper spray away! Don't you point that thing at me! Do you have any idea who I am? If not, that's okay because that sounded really conceited. That's right, drive away! Yep! Don't even look back!"

Guardian turned back around.

Gibby arched an eyebrow.

"Yeah, yeah," Guardian muttered. "Shut up. Now what?"

She reached into her pocket and pulled out a familiar bandana, now wrinkled. She tied it around her face before twirling her finger, motioning for Guardian to turn around.

"I don't get what I'm supposed to—*oof.*" He grunted when Gibby jumped on his back, wrapping her legs around his waist. He put his hands under her legs to keep her from falling. "What are you *doing*?" he hissed at her. "You want me to run *and* carry you? Screw that. Burke wins. I give up."

"You're a goddamn Extraordinary," she snapped, her chin digging into his shoulder. "It's time you started acting like one. Your boyfriend and my girlfriend are in danger. The people we love are being mind-controlled by a bitch and a bastard, and the only people we can trust are the man who gets free burritos and maybe your psycho ex-boyfriend. Are you just going to stand there and let the bad guys win?"

Gibby was right, as usual. "Hell no."

"What are we gonna do about it?"

"Kick names and take ass," he growled dangerously. Then, "Wait, shit. I screwed that up. Let me—"

"Run," Gibby said. "Up the front of Seth's house. Get to the roof, and then you jump from building to building like a superhero."

"Uh, I think you're overestimating my ability to—"

"*Do it!*" she bellowed, squeezing her thighs against his sides, as if he were her horse.

He turned around, heart thundering against his rib cage. Unexpectedly, his mind was his own, clear, free from muddled, racing thoughts spinning in never-ending circles. All he could hear was Gibby's breaths against the side of his helmet. All he could feel was her weight on his back, tethering him, refusing to let him spiral off into indecision.

The spark bloomed in his head, and he welcomed its warmth, holding it close.

He moved without thought, the thin muscles in his legs coiling, lips pulled back against his teeth. Everything melted away, and there was only Gibby, only Guardian, and as he sprinted toward the house, he thought, *Oh, please, let this work.*

Six feet away from crashing into the house, he jumped.

But this time, he didn't kick his feet out. Instead, he imagined the air around him solidifying, becoming a tangible thing that he could control. As he started to fall toward the house, he *pushed,* and that old familiar feeling—pain, slight yet delicious—lanced through his head as the spark burst in a furious flash.

Beneath his right foot, the air hardened with a crackling *snap,* wavering, but holding as he landed on it. He said, "Hold on. This is probably going to be a little weird."

"Great," Gibby muttered weakly in his ear. "Just what I was hoping f—*Nick!*" She screamed in his ear as the solidified air beneath his feet began to *rise,* lifting them up toward the roof. The air rushed over them, the façade of sandstone a blur in front of his face. Right when the air became level with the roof, he jumped. They landed on the slanted roof, Guardian's toes curling in his boots as if he thought that'd give him any purchase. It didn't, and they immediately began to slide toward the edge.

"*Jump!*" Gibby screamed in his ear right before they ran out of room. "Oh my god, *jump!*"

He did, right before they slipped off the edge. It felt as if he had launched himself from a springboard, hurtling through the air toward the roof of the house next to the Grays'. He began to cackle loudly as he looked down, their lumpy shadow racing across the ground below them. They landed on the peak of the next roof, and with his momentum carrying him forward he ran, finally trusting his own abilities.

Alive, he felt so *alive,* and he jumped again and again, hitting each roof, the buildings growing in height, but that didn't stop him. If anything, it pushed him further, to do more, to be *better.* He wished his father could see him now. He wished all their enemies could witness what he was becoming.

He was the Extraordinary known as Guardian, and it was time to show everyone why messing with his family was a terrible mistake.

They hit the ground just outside of his neighborhood, people in front of a coffee shop gaping at him as he rose from a crouch, Gibby sliding off his back on shaky legs.

He whirled around. "Did you *see* that?"

"I did," she said evenly. "Can you stand between me and the people looking at us so I can do something real quick?"

"Uh, sure?" Nick moved between her and the people staring at them. "Like this?"

"Take a step back."

He did. "Better?"

"Much. Thank you." Then Gibby lifted the lower half of her bandana and vomited on his feet.

"Oh my *god!*" he screeched, stumbling back, trying to shake off the string of bile that hung off his boot. "Why? *Why?*"

"Heights," Gibby said weakly, grimacing as she wiped her mouth with the back of her hand. "I hate heights so much."

"That explains all the screaming. My bad, dude. Hold your breath and lower the bandana real quick." He turned toward the people sitting outside the coffee shop and saluted them. "Citizens,

I need water for my friend. Consider it a good deed in service of the city."

A woman rose from her chair, grabbing her sweating glass of ice water and handing it over, hand shaking. "Thank you," Guardian said. "I won't forget this." He gave it to Gibby, who drank the entire thing in one go. After she finished, she lowered the bandana and handed the glass to Guardian, who set it back down on the table.

"Let's go," she said, and they hurried around the corner, down the familiar street. He faltered when he saw people gathering on the opposite side of the street from his house, pointing at something blocked by parked cars and thick trees. Because he could, he jumped *over* a car rather than running around it, the spark barely pulsing as he did so. It was easier, now. Somehow, it was easier, his to harness, his to control.

As soon as he jumped across the street, landing on the opposite sidewalk, he saw what everyone was looking at.

People, standing stock-still in front of the Bell home, gathered on the walkway, backs stiff, arms hanging at their sides, eyes clouded over.

Cap. Mary. Bob. Trey. Aysha. Jo. Miles. Chris. Mateo. Jazz.

All of them, watching, waiting without a trace of recognition, blocking the way forward. But where was Dad?

Guardian skidded to a stop, Gibby crossing the street off to his right. She reached him and said, "Why are you—Mom? Dad? What are you doing here? Jazz?"

No response. Dead-eyed, staring forward but unseeing. Trey twitched at the sound of his daughter's voice, but that was all. Gibby started forward, but Guardian grabbed her by the arm, pulling her back. "No," he told her. "She's controlling them. They're not—"

"What are you—*look out!*" Gibby shoved him hard as a snarl of electricity ripped through the air, an arc of lightning slamming into the sidewalk where Guardian had been standing, causing it to crack. He hit the ground hard, rolling once, twice before he shot back up to his feet in time to see Mateo lowering his hand, electricity crackling around his fingertips.

"No," they all said as one, their voices lifeless, the sound like wind through a graveyard. "You can't stop this. It's already too late."

Behind them, the windows of the house lit up in a fiery, blinding light, and someone screamed inside as if they were being torn apart. It shook Guardian to his core, because he *recognized* that voice.

Seth. It was Seth screaming. The boy from the swings, the boy who loved Nick despite his faults—and, perhaps, because of them. The most selfless boy, who only wanted to keep people safe.

"You fucked with the wrong family," Guardian snapped, and as Gibby shouted his name, he ran full tilt toward the house.

Bob was in the front, and he moved stiffly, hands coming up as Guardian rushed toward him. Guardian quickly ducked underneath them. It was as if they were all underwater and he wasn't. He rose up from his crouch and shot his leg back, foot hitting Bob in the ass, knocking him forward. Without stopping, Guardian dodged Mary Caplan's fist as it flew toward his head. The momentum spun her around, knocking her off-balance. Guardian dropped his hand to his side and jerked it up, fingers crooked. Mary lifted up off the ground, feet kicking into nothing, one of her sandals falling to the ground.

Someone grabbed his shoulders, and Guardian remembered what Seth had taught him. "Backflip of Chaos!" he bellowed, grabbing the hands and pulling them as hard as he could. He bent over, and Miles Kensington flew over him, crashing into Mary, still suspended in air. They landed in a heap off the walkway, knocking against Chris's legs, causing him to fall on top of them, but he quickly pushed himself up.

"Behind you!" Gibby shouted.

Guardian turned and saw Jo and Mateo stalking toward him, and he clapped his hands together before spreading them apart.

Both Jo and Mateo spun away, almost like they were dancing, spinning so quickly their faces became blurred. Jazz came after him next, and he said, "Please don't stab me with a fork or your shoe when you remember this." He brought his hands to his chest before pushing them out toward her. A wave of air slammed against her, hair billowing as she fell back.

A hand closed around his neck, and Guardian twisted around, fist raised.

Rodney Caplan. Cap.

*And Guardian hesitated.*

"Cap," he said as the hand wrapped around his throat. "Cap, *don't*!"

But Cap was gone, gone, gone, and Guardian's breath rattled in his throat as the grip around him tightened painfully. Then other hands were on him, so many others, pulling him down, covering him, the sky blotting out as they loomed above him. The edges of his vision began to darken. Slack faces stared down at him, their hands digging into him. Distantly, he heard Gibby screaming, begging for them to let him go. Beyond her, the sound of an overtaxed engine and the screeching of tires.

But the spark was still there in his head, shifting, growing bigger, gaining mass. He reached for it once more, and when his hand closed over it, his body began to thrum.

And then Guardian exploded.

The hands holding him down fell away as everyone in front of the Bell house flew upward, legs and arms flailing. Then they *stopped*, hanging suspended in air, their shadows crawling along the ground. Guardian rose in time to see Mateo lifting his hand toward him, electricity rolling down his arm, coalescing into a ball of blue light in his hand.

It shot toward him.

But before it hit, the shadows on the ground burst up in front of Guardian, black and semitransparent as they joined together, creating a wall of darkness that towered above him.

The ball of electricity struck the shadow wall, causing it to shudder as the ball shattered, lines of blue shooting off and striking the house, scorching the wood paneling, lines of black like smoldering veins etching up the front.

Guardian turned his head toward the street and saw Owen Burke, hand raised, face twisted in concentration and drenched in sweat, the blood from earlier now brown on his shirt. Behind him Burrito Jerry stood next to Gibby, Matilda sitting half on the sidewalk with her doors hanging open, engine idling.

"Get inside," Owen told him through gritted teeth. "I can't hold them for long."

Guardian nodded and turned toward the house. He hit the steps, lenses on his helmet narrowing against the bright lights flashing through the window. He could hear his ragged breath echoing around him, and he was tired, so damn tired. He pushed through it, but barely, his exhaustion clinging to him, threatening to pull him back down. He'd never used so much of his telekinesis all at once, at least not since prom night.

The door was unlocked, and as he pushed it open, he heard a voice crooning, "It'll be over soon. I've seen what's inside your head. You want to give it to me. Everything is fine."

He stepped into the house.

The kitchen entryway, off to his right.

The living room, off to his left, looking as if a bomb had gone off. The couch was upended, lying on its side. Dad's armchair ripped apart, springs and wool poking through ragged tears. The bricks of the fireplace looked scorched, black soot thick and peeling. The television lay flat on the floor, surrounded by shards of glass.

And there, sitting on top of Seth Gray, holding him down, was his father, eyes blank, lips slack. His suit had been torn, a split down the middle of his back. Seth struggled feebly, frightened, pained sounds falling from his open mouth as little licks of fire crackled between his lips.

A woman sat on her knees above his head, hanging over him. She gripped the sides of Seth's head to keep him from moving. Her gaping maw was a foot above Seth's mouth, and she was *inhaling,* as if trying to suck up the fire that came from Seth.

She was Jennifer Bell. Then the frame rate stuttered, and her face changed, features melting into someone older, hair lengthening and turning black. Tan fading, changing into pale, milky skin. The tip of her nose turned upward as her eyebrows thickened, her mouth wide open, thin lips pulled back against small teeth.

Patricia Burke.

"Get off of him," Guardian snarled, and Patricia snapped her mouth closed, eyes narrowed as she lifted her head toward him.

And for a moment, didn't she look scared?

Brief, sure, but he saw it. *He saw it*.

"Aaron," she said, and it wasn't her own voice that came out, but that of his mother. "Deal with him. He wants to hurt me. Don't let him."

Seth moaned, eyes rolling back in his head as her fingernails dimpled his cheeks.

Dad rose stiffly.

He turned toward his son.

Guardian lifted his hands to the sides of his helmet, pulling it off and letting it fall to the floor. "Dad," Nick begged, taking a step toward him. "Please don't do this. You're in there. I know you are."

Dad paused, a flicker of confusion crossing his face. It was only then that Nick saw the stun gun in his right hand, compact and black with bright-yellow accents. Two metal probes stuck out from the barrel, and Nick watched as his father raised the stun gun and pointed it at him. It wavered. Dad's finger slid to the trigger.

Nick rushed toward him, reaching out and grabbing his wrists, the stun gun inches from his face. "Don't do this," he begged. "You and me. It's always been you and me. She's not real. Mom is *gone*. It's not her. It never was. She wouldn't do this to us. You know she wouldn't."

Seth moaned again, but Nick never looked away from Dad. The cloudiness in his eyes shifted, and Nick reached up, closing his hands around Dad's wrist. "Dad, *no*."

"Dad, *yes*," his father said automatically, and then clarity returned to his eyes, expression stuttering, collapsing. He inhaled sharply, jaw tensing as he ground his teeth together. "Kid?" he said, voice hoarse. "*Nicky?*"

Nick nodded, hoping against hope. "Yes. *Yes.* It's me. Dad, she's controlling you. She's been controlling you this entire time. All of us. None of it has been real."

"Do it," Patricia Burke snarled. "Shut him up *now*."

For a moment, Nick thought his father would do just that. In the back of his mind, he heard Trey whispering that this was some Shakespearean shit right here. But then Dad blinked rapidly, the cloudiness over his eyes disintegrating. He said, "Nicky, oh my god. *Nicky*," and Nick was thrown back years and years, to the day in the spring where everything fell apart around them, leaving them sifting through the wreckage. They had come through the other side because they'd had each other to lean on, their grief shared as much as their strength.

Dad gasped, jerking his hand from Nick's grasp, wrapping an arm around his son's shoulders and spinning them both around toward Patricia Burke as she tried to suck up Seth's fire. "I got you, kid," Dad said, raising the stun gun once more and firing without hesitation.

The aim was true, but the probes stopped inches from her chest, wires suspended in midair. Patricia lifted her head and grinned at them. "Almost." The probes snapped and snarled as they spun slowly back toward Nick and his father.

"Drop it!" Nick shouted. "Dad, drop the—"

Seth's eyes snapped open, and he growled, "Not today," as his right hand curled into a fist, fire blooming around his fingers. Moving almost quicker than Nick could follow, Seth punched Patricia under her chin, fire exploding in her face, a blast of heat slamming Nick and his father. The taser probes fell to the floor as Patricia flew back against the fireplace, the scorched brickwork cracking under the impact.

But as soon as she hit the floor, she was up and moving, spinning around and raising her hands toward a wall. Nick felt the familiar thickening of the air as the wall began to crack and break apart, but it felt bigger, more focused. *Oh shit,* he thought wildly as Seth shot to his feet, grabbing Nick and Dad to shield them. *She's stronger than I am.*

The house shook as Patricia Burke burst through the wall, a plume of plaster and dust billowing as sunlight poured in through the opening, and then she was gone.

Noise from outside, people screaming as the house settled and groaned. Nick coughed roughly, bending over and choking on the thick dust that coated his throat. He felt someone grab his hand and he was pulled outside. He blinked against the brightness as he hit the porch, falling to his knees and gagging, spitting, a thin string of drool hanging from his bottom lip. Before he could react, something heavy pressed against the top of his head, and he began to panic.

"No," Dad whispered in his ear. "Just me. Helmet, Nicky. Put your helmet back on." Nick stopped fighting as Dad pushed the helmet firmly on his head, the lenses inside the mask flashing. Strong arms wrapped around him. Out of the corner of his eye, he saw Seth slump down next to him, face covered with splotches of white, sucking in air.

Others, then. So many others who helped Nick and Seth up, away from the house, leading them down the steps to the walkway. Jazz. Gibby. Their parents. Mary and Cap. Bob. Chris. Mateo, apologizing profusely with a look of horror on his face. Sirens, in the distance, growing louder the closer they got.

And Dad. Dad, clutching Nick tightly, never letting him go. Dad, his chin on the top of his son's head, rocking him back and forth, whispering in a choked voice that they were all right, they were good, they were safe, *Nicky, I love you, kid, I love you so much.*

He held on just as tight. Beyond his father, he saw people gathering on the street. Most looked scared, but more than a few started filming them and the house. If Dad hadn't remembered the helmet . . .

*Would it be so bad?* he thought as Dad pulled Seth into the hug. Later. He'd worry about it later. Nothing else mattered because his people were safe.

For now.

"Uh," someone said, and they all looked over to see Burrito Jerry standing nervously at the end of the walkway, the crowd behind him growing bigger. "So, the guy I kidnapped for you is gone. Tried to stop him, but then he made my shadow move on its own, so I made the executive decision to nope outta that. My bad. I hope you'll still give me a good rating. But there's good news! Matilda didn't get a scratch on her."

# 13

. . . the home, owned by former Nova City police detective Aaron Bell, sustained damage from what sources within the NCPD—speaking anonymously—are calling an "event involving Extraordinaries." Though the names of those involved have yet to be released, viral videos captured Friday by witnesses at the scene showed a group of people standing outside the home, facing off against an Extraordinary in a blue-and-white costume, the same Extraordinary who interrupted mayoral candidate Simon Burke's speech last week. This Extraordinary appears to be operating under the code name Guardian, the same name used by a costumed vigilante who haunted the streets of Nova City in the early 2000s, though it is unclear if this is the same individual.

Former Nova City police chief Rodney Caplan—who resigned his position this spring—was one of the people present. Speaking with reporters following the event, Mr. Caplan cautioned against speculation, saying appearances can be deceiving. "If you want to know the truth about who attacked the Bell household, I'd suggest speaking with Simon and Patricia Burke. Good day."

Witnesses also claim that Owen Burke—the son of Simon and Patricia Burke—was present, though no video captured him. Owen Burke was the Extraordinary known as Shadow Star and was responsible for the deaths of three people.

Initially, Rebecca Firestone—press secretary for Simon Burke's mayoral campaign—released a statement that said, in part, "While Mr. and Mrs. Burke are relieved that no one was injured during the attack, they are disappointed in Rodney Caplan's disparaging remarks. The Burkes were not involved in what transpired, and as always, they are urging their son to do the right thing and turn himself in. There will be no further comment at this time."

However, Simon and Patricia Burke spoke to a group of reporters in front of Burke Tower this Sunday morning before heading to church. Patricia Burke, speaking publicly for the first time since Mr. Burke announced his candidacy, said, "The fact that we are being blamed yet again is a sign that Simon's message to the people of Nova City is working. The very idea that we—I—would be involved is a sorry attempt to slander our good name, and the work my husband has done for this city. My heart is heavy for all those Owen has hurt. I grieve with those affected by his and every other Extraordinary's actions."

Mr. Burke added, "This is nothing but an attempt to smear me and to derail my campaign. I will not stand for it. The attention should be on how yet another event occurred where Extraordinaries could have hurt innocent bystanders. You have my solemn promise that if elected, I will do everything in my power to make sure you and your children are safe. As a show of good faith, I am offering to pay for the damages to the residence. As an old friend of mine once said, it's easier to stand together than it is to struggle apart."

A new poll released late Saturday night shows incumbent Stephanie Carlson narrowing the gap, trailing Mr. Burke by three points, the closest margin since he announced his candidacy. When asked for comment, the office of the mayor said only, "Mayor Carlson is being apprised of the situation by the NCPD and will continue to monitor the events."

There has been no response to repeated attempts to contact any of the individuals identified in the Extraordinary event. Knocks at the damaged Bell home went unanswered through the weekend.

* * *

Early Monday morning, Nick blinked up at the ceiling in a spare room at the Kensington home. Jazz and her parents had told him and Dad in no uncertain terms that they could stay as long as they needed while their house was being repaired. They had enough room, after all. Nick knew they were being good friends, but he also knew that part of it had to do with their guilt over what had transpired, misplaced though it was.

Rolling over in the bed, Nick sighed, burying his face in the pillow. He wanted nothing more than to try to go back to sleep, but his brain was already kicking into gear, a billion thoughts running through his head all at once. He'd expected to feel like he'd been torn apart, losing her again. But then, she'd never *really* been here, had she? No. She hadn't. Jennifer Bell was dead and gone, nothing but ashes in a cold, salty ocean breeze.

He grieved. Of course he did. But it wasn't nearly as bad as when Before had become After.

He was drifting off again when someone knocked on the door. Lifting his head, he called out, "Yeah, come in."

The door swung open slowly. Dad stood on the other side, looking as haggard as Nick felt in rumpled jeans and an NCU shirt, the dark circles under his eyes and pale skin evidence of his lack of sleep. Nick hadn't seen his father for any length of time in the last couple of days. Dad had been with Cap, or at the house, reviewing the damage with a contractor that Burke was *not* paying for, no matter what bullshit offer he extended. Nick understood his Dad needed to process things his own way, and that eventually he'd seek Nick out.

Which seemed to be now, given the hangdog expression he wore. Nick's heart squeezed painfully, and he pulled back the comforter in invitation, patting the empty space in the bed next to him. Dad sighed, kicking off his shoes as he closed the door behind him. He crossed the room toward the bed, climbing onto it next to Nick, who pulled the comforter over them both, Dad's head resting on the pillow next to his.

Nick waited, hard though it was. A thousand words threatened to burst through his lips, but he swallowed them all down. He knew his father better than anyone. Dad was working himself up toward something, and interrupting him wouldn't help.

So Nick counted in his head. He reached fifty-two before Dad spoke.

He stared at the ceiling, rubbing a hand over his face as he said, "This is my fault."

"That's not—"

"Kid," Dad said tiredly. "Let me get this out. I'm not shutting you down, but I need you to listen to me, okay?"

"Okay," Nick whispered, turning on his side and looking at Dad's profile, hands twitching to reach out and provide some form of comfort.

Dad nodded, licking his cracked, dry lips. "I should've . . ." He closed his eyes. "I should've known. That something wasn't right. That she wasn't who she said she was. I brought her into our home and she . . ." He cleared his throat, and when he opened his eyes, Nick saw how wet they were.

"You couldn't have known," Nick said fiercely, the anger in his voice causing Dad to look over at him, a single tear spilling over and dripping down the side of his face. "It wasn't just you. She did this to all of us. No one blames you."

Dad laughed bitterly. "They should. All of you should. If I hadn't—"

"You didn't do it on purpose," Nick said, and he believed it down to his bones. "She used you. She used every single one of us. She used our memories against us. She twisted them and made us believe something that wasn't real."

"I wanted it," Dad whispered. "I wanted it so bad." His chest hitched. "I wanted it to be real. I wanted her to be here, with me. With you. What does that make me?"

"Human," Nick said promptly. "It makes you human."

"Don't feel like it much right now."

"I know. And I wish I could fix it for you, but I can't." Frustrated, Nick rolled onto his back, hands in fists at his sides. Then, because this was his father, he admitted, "I want to hurt them. I want to make them suffer. What does that make *me*?"

"Human," Dad said, taking Nick's hand in his, unfurling his fingers. "It makes you human."

"Don't feel like it much right now."

Dad laughed again, but this time, it seemed to be more genuine. "Quite the pair, aren't we?"

"We are," Nick agreed. "You believed me. In the house."

"It was hard," Dad said quietly. "All I could hear in my head was her voice, telling me that you were coming to hurt her. I was in there screaming for myself to wake up. I couldn't do it."

"You did, though."

"Because of you, kid." Dad gripped his hand tightly. "I heard your voice through the hurricane. It was like . . ."

"A lighthouse."

Dad nodded. "Yeah. You were the only thing that made sense. I latched on to it, and I felt myself waking up. Like I'd been trapped in a nightmare and . . . I'd never been so scared in my life." His lips quirked slightly. "You saved me. Again. Just like you always do."

Nick blinked. "I don't—"

"You do. I don't know where I'd be without you, Nicky. When she . . . died, it felt like it was the end of the world. And it was, in a way. Catastrophic. Apocalyptic. And I almost lost myself in it. But I didn't, and it was because of you." He sniffled, and Nick felt his own eyes start to burn. "I don't know how I got so lucky to have you as my kid, but I'm thankful every day that you exist."

"Dad," Nick whispered.

Dad tugged him over, wrapping his left arm around Nick's back as he laid his head on his father's shoulder. Dad hesitated. Then, "I talked with Seth. Told him I was sorry for what happened. That I'd understand if he didn't want to be around me, but to not let that affect how he saw you."

"What did he say?" Nick asked. He already knew. Seth had told him, but he wanted to hear it from Dad.

"He said he didn't blame me for what happened at the house. And that he knew we were a package deal."

"He's a good guy," Nick said, rubbing his own tears away on Dad's shirt.

"He is. You both remind me of . . . how it was for me and your mother. And I hope you get to experience what we had because no matter how it ended, it was good. So damn good. Maybe that'll be with Seth. Maybe it'll be with someone else, but I want that for you."

"Me, too. I think it'll be with Seth, though."

"Yeah?"

"Yeah. If you didn't scare him away with the banana on the condom or the dental dams or the unfortunate enema demonstration, I have a feeling he'll stick around." He glared at his father. "Which, you know. What in the absolute hell is *wrong* with you?"

"So many things," Dad said. "But I have no regrets; the look on your face each time was worth it." He twisted his mouth, eyes bulging comically from his head as he pitched his voice high and said, "But, *Dad*. You're embarrassing me in front of everyone!"

Nick scowled at him. "I don't sound anything like that!"

"You do," Dad assured him. "It's adorable." His expression collapsed, bottom lip starting to tremble. "Hey, kid?"

"Yeah?"

"I think I'm going to cry right now. Just for a little bit. Need to get it out. Is that okay?"

"It is," Nick said, and as they held each other, the morning sun spilling into the room through the window, they cried. For what they had lost. For what they had found. For Before and for After, for a woman who had been their everything. They cried for her, and themselves.

But they did not cry alone.

Later that day, Nick went to the only other place he felt safe. He kept his head down, a baseball cap tugged low on his head and a pair of Jazz's oversized pink, glittery sunglasses covering his face. He managed to avoid the reporters camped out in front of the house by going through a side gate. In the backpack slung over his shoulder he had his costume.

He hurried, and by the time he reached his destination sweat was dripping down his face and his shirt felt gross under the straps of his backpack.

He cut through the space between the houses, hopping over a small chain-link fence that led to the postage stamp of a backyard behind the Gray brownstone.

He took a deep breath and knocked on the door.

He didn't have to wait long before the blinds parted a bit, Martha's familiar eyes looking out at him. The door opened, and she pulled him inside quickly, shutting and locking the door behind him. He didn't have a chance to speak before Martha wrapped him in a crushing hug. "I'm so sorry," she whispered into his shoulder.

Nick patted her back. "It wasn't you. You didn't know what you were doing."

"Still. That was a pretty big knife."

"It was," Nick agreed as she pulled away, looking him up and down as if checking for injuries.

"I'm so relieved I didn't stab you," Martha said seriously, which, to be fair, wasn't something Nick ever expected to hear her say. These were strange days. "I'd have never forgiven myself."

Nick shrugged. "You tried, but then I respectfully kicked your ass, so." He winced. "Uh, sorry about that, by the way. I hope you're all right."

"I'm fine," she said. She stepped around him, going to the sink where a pile of dirty dishes sat stacked, the remains of their breakfast. "Bob thinks people would believe us if we told them what happened. I wish I could think the same, but I saw how everyone reacted when Seth spoke his truth." She angrily scrubbed a sponge against a plate. "They think he's dangerous."

"He's the best of us," Nick said firmly. He glanced toward the kitchen entrance. "Is he okay?"

Martha sighed as she flipped on the faucet, washing the dish soap away. "I don't know. He's been down in the basement, punching that bag. You know how he gets. He says he's all right, but he's been . . . quiet, the last couple of days. I don't know what's going on in that head of his."

Nick didn't either, not really. He hadn't seen much of Seth since Friday, their only contact through texts. Jazz had spoken to him once, but Gibby hadn't, dealing with her parents' anger over what had happened. Trey and Aysha were furious, and rightly so. But not at them, Gibby had reassured him. At the Burkes, and at the police who had tried to arrest them all in front of the house. It was only because of Cap that it hadn't happened, Cap who had stepped in and demanded to speak with the interim chief.

"I'll find out," Nick promised. "Make sure he's good."

"Thank you." Without turning around, she asked, "How's your dad?"

He'd left Dad sleeping in the bed, with a note on his chest telling him where he'd gone. Dad needed sleep, and Nick hadn't wanted to wake him. By the time they'd finished the Bell Cryfest for Reasons, Dad had smiled a bit, laughing at Nick's usual idiocy. Then his eyes had grown heavy and a moment later, he'd started snoring.

"He'll be all right," Nick said. "It may take time to get there, but he's done it before. He can do it again. He has me."

"He does, doesn't he?" She paused, looking down at the soap on her hands. "Go. Talk to Seth and see if you can get him to stop hitting things. I'm sure he'll be happy to see you. I made Bob an appointment with his doctor. His blood pressure is already high enough, and he's not getting any younger. Better to be safe than sorry."

"You need help going out front?" Nick asked, itching to head to the basement.

Martha shook her head. "We'll go out through the back. I'll call if it takes longer than I think it will."

Nick nodded. He started toward the entryway and stopped

before passing through. He looked back at Martha in front of the sink, her shoulders squared, hands scrubbing the rest of the dishes. "Martha?"

She looked back at him.

"I love you."

And oh, how she smiled. "I love you, too, Nicky. Now get out of my kitchen."

"Yes, ma'am," he said, and left her behind.

He could hear Seth going hard at the punching bag as soon as he opened the basement door, meaty thuds punctuated by heavy grunts. He'd probably been going at it for a long time, and Nick started to doubt his welcome. Sometimes, Seth needed to work through things on his own.

But then, Seth had told him to come over when Nick had offered, so it wasn't like it was going to be a surprise.

He reached the bottom of the steps, greeting on the tip of his tongue. But it died a strangled death when he saw what was waiting for him in the basement.

Seth wore nothing but black mesh shorts, back muscles shifting under a sheen of sweat as he punched the bag, left, right, right, left, left, the thick veins on his forearms bulging. The curls of his hair bounced wetly with every movement, and Nick feared if he spoke first, it was going to come out exceedingly dirty, given how appreciative he was of the sight before him.

He made as much noise as possible to let Seth know he was there, dropping his backpack on the cracked cement floor, jumping up on the dryer against the wall, letting his feet bounce against the metal side as he touched the towel and bottle of water Seth had brought down with him. Seth didn't look at him, stepping back and swinging his leg out in a flat arc, bare foot striking the punching bag, causing it to fly to the side.

It went on for a few more minutes before Seth stopped, moving away from the bag, shaking his arms and legs out. Nick held up the towel for him, which he took with a nod, wiping it over his face and chest, under his arms, across his back. It was positively obscene, and Nick was trying his level best to ignore the display.

He cleared his throat and asked, "Feel better?"

"I don't know."

"Want to talk about it?" Ever magnanimous, Nick was. He knew of many things he'd rather do than talking, but that was part and parcel of being a hormonal teenager. Almost everything threatened to turn him on. Seth. Dudes in briefs on underwear packaging. Bigfoot (long story, and the less said about it, the better).

"It's funny," Seth said, the towel around the back of his neck, the ends hanging over his shoulders. He looked down between them, frowning. "I thought . . . I wondered what it would be like if I wasn't who I was. If I didn't have powers. If I wasn't Pyro Storm. If I was just like everyone else."

"Okay," Nick said slowly. "You've said that before."

"I have," Seth agreed. "And there was a time when I wasn't sure if I wanted to be Pyro Storm anymore. Maybe I still think that, every now and then. Hanging up the costume. Ignoring all the calls for help that came in. Why is it *my* responsibility to help everyone? So many of them don't ask for it, so why is it up to me to help them?"

"Because someone has to?" They'd been here before, but this felt different, somehow.

Seth startled, jerking his head up and looking at Nick for the first time since he came downstairs. "Yeah, I know. But why *me*? Why us? Everything we've been through, everything we've done, and for what? To get it thrown back in our faces? To be treated like *we're* the enemy?" He shook his head. "I hate it. I don't want to, but I do. I hate that people treat us like crap. That no matter what we do, no matter how many people we help, they still find some way to blame us."

Nick reached out and tugged on the towel, pulling Seth closer. He came willingly enough, stepping between Nick's legs, hands resting on his thighs, pinkie finger brushing against the skin just below Nick's shorts, sending a hot jolt through him. He ignored it, at least for the moment. Seth needed his undivided attention. Granted, it'd probably help if he put on a shirt (or a snowsuit, just to be safe), but Nick didn't let himself get distracted. Mostly.

"Would you change anything if you could?" Nick asked.

Seth hesitated a moment. Then, "No. Not anymore. When she was . . . when she was trying to take my powers from me, I was in this . . . fog. I felt myself wanting to give in, to let her have it, and part of that had nothing to do with what she was doing to me. It was *mine,* and there was a split second when I thought I could give it to her. Let her have it. Let her deal with all of it and leave me ordinary."

A chill ran down Nick's spine. "But you didn't. You fought it."

"I did," Seth said. "Maybe if you hadn't shown up, it wouldn't have been enough, but you did, and I heard you through the fog. It helped to remind me of what's important. And not just you. I thought about my aunt. My uncle. All they'd done for me. Everything they did to help me be . . . me. I think I forget sometimes that I'm not the only one who lost someone when my parents died. They did, too. They took me in. Gave me a home. Loved me. And this is how they're repaid for all they've done?" He laughed ruefully and stepped away from Nick, spreading his hands. "In a way, Patricia Burke did me a favor, even though she didn't know it." Fire bloomed in his palms, twin balls that flickered and snapped, the heat unpleasant in the stuffiness of the basement, but not yet uncomfortable. He rolled the balls in his hands, up his arms, behind his neck and back down to his hands. When they reached his palms, he closed his fingers, snuffing them out, leaving wisps of curling gray smoke. "She and Burke think anything is theirs for the taking. It's not."

"You sound like you're sure." He didn't know if that was a good thing or not, but he trusted Seth to know what was right for himself.

"I am," Seth said. "More than I've been in a long time." He

shook his head. "We can't make everyone happy, and there are people actively fighting against our rights to just *be*. But I would still keep them safe if called to do so."

"That makes you a better person than me," Nick admitted.

"I get that. I wish I had the right answer—*any* answer—but I don't. The best I—*we* can do is try our hardest to make sure no one has to suffer like we have."

"That's not possible. Someone's always going to get hurt, no matter what."

Seth blinked. "That's . . . huh. Yeah, I guess you're right. Collateral damage." Then, "I'm sorry."

"For what?"

He stepped back between Nick's legs, hands on his hips. "Your mom, Nicky. I'm so sorry you had to go through that."

Nick swallowed past the lump in his throat, looking away. "It sucked." Understatement, that, but it encompassed all he was feeling. Words were never Nick's problem—his mouth, like his brain, never stopped moving. But now? Now words failed him, and all he could do was repeat "It sucked."

"How's your dad?"

Nick laughed wetly, rubbing the back of his hand over his eyes. "He's . . . sad, you know? Not like he used to be after she . . . After. But this wasn't just a bad guy wanting to kill us like others have. This was more than that."

"It was cruel," Seth said quietly.

"It was. It is. But then I'm starting to figure out that cruelty is the point. Owen said that Burke . . . my mom . . ." His chest hitched painfully as he ground his teeth together, jaw tense.

"I know, Nicky," Seth said, hands leaving his knees as he cupped Nick's face, thumbs brushing his cheeks. "Did you talk to your dad about it?"

"No," Nick said hoarsely. "And I hate how it's making me feel. I want to kill him, Seth. I want to find Burke and make him feel every ounce of pain he's inflicted on us. More, even." He rolled his eyes at his own ridiculousness.

"Would you feel better?"

He hesitated. "For a little bit. But I know that once it faded, that anger would still be there."

"That's the difference," Seth said, "between us and them. That's the reason we do what we do. We're not out for revenge, because revenge can only sustain a person for so long. When you don't have anyone else to burn, what remains?"

"Ashes," Nick whispered, thinking of the sea, of a lighthouse in the distance. Of two heartbroken people standing at a railing, clutching a dirty plastic bag that had held a woman so filled with light, she blazed like the sun.

"And that's not who we are. That's why we'll always be better than people like Burke. Like Patricia. Like Owen."

Nick looked down at Seth's hands on his legs. "I want . . ." What did he want? He didn't know what tomorrow would bring, but he was here, now, in this moment, and he was alive, Seth was alive, and he was tired of waiting. He wanted to feel safe, loved, even if just for a moment. Which was why he whispered, "I want you."

Seth tensed, but only for a split second. He studied Nick thoughtfully, and he thought he saw a flash of something like fire in Seth's eyes. It chased away the cold. "Are you asking what I think you're asking?"

Instant flop sweat. "Ye-es?"

"You need to be sure, Nick."

"I don't have dental dams," Nick blurted, starting to panic. "And I didn't use the enema. What if you get fecal penis?"

Seth grimaced. "Your seduction technique needs work."

"I have *seduction technique*? *Cosmo* said I wasn't ready for that yet! What else have they lied to me about?"

"Oh boy," Seth said, lips quirking. "I'm not even going to touch that."

"You can touch me," Nick said quickly. "If . . . if you want. But only if you want. Just because I'm ready doesn't mean you have to be. Consent is important, but just because you give it at first doesn't mean you can't take it back. You know what? Why don't we just—"

"Nick."

He sagged in relief. "Oh my god, what is *wrong* with me? I'm trying to get laid while also trying to talk you out of it? No wonder I'm a virgin."

"Hey, Nicky? What do queer men call hemorrhoids?"

Nick gaped at him.

"Speed bumps."

Nick burst out laughing, the sound tearing from his throat, half-hysterical, almost like he was screaming. But it worked, knocking him out of his head, cementing him firmly in the present. He laughed and laughed, Seth joining in. They were laughing, and then they were kissing, still smiling, somehow. It was chaotic, messy, and then Seth bit his bottom lip, stretching it, letting it fall back.

He shook when Seth kissed him again, humor gone, replaced by something heavier, something that felt like fire burning him up from the inside out. He gasped when Seth broke the kiss, tilting his head to the side and sucking on his neck, teeth scraping against sensitive skin, the negligible pain chased away by the swipe of his tongue. His hands were in Seth's curls, tugging, tugging his face upward, and Nick kissed him for all he was worth. Sloppy and artless, but real.

Hands under his shirt, those same hands that Nick had dreamed about, trailing along his chest, tweaking his nipple, causing him to gasp and arch his back. Struggling against his shirt, he lifted it over his head and got stuck, arms above his head, the top half of his face covered in cotton, and Seth kissed him again, slow, sure hands rising up Nick's side to help him escape from his shirt, letting it fall to the floor.

It was the first time they'd been shirtless like this, when it wasn't changing clothes or going swimming. He sucked in his stomach a little but Seth kissed his mouth, his chin, the sharp bones of his clavicle, his hair tickling the underside of Nick's jaw. Seth's hands went to the zipper of his shorts, and Nick's eyes bulged. This was happening. This was definitely happening.

Seth paused, bent slightly at the knees, looking up at Nick with hooded eyes. "Are you good?"

"So good," Nick breathed. "What are you going to do?"

Seth grinned at him, all teeth. "I was thinking about trying out a blow job. See what all the fuss is about. That all right with you?"

Nick's brain shorted out as he squeaked, "Yes. That. Do that. You have consent. All the consent. There has never been anything more consensual than right at this moment."

Seth nodded, and with shaky hands, unbuttoned Nick's shorts, pulling the zipper down, the sound so loud Nick thought it could probably be heard in space. Seth motioned for him to raise up a little and he did.

Nick had often lamented that he was . . . well. *Average* was probably the best way to put it. His dick wasn't big. It wasn't thick. He'd never look at it and think *Holy shit, that's a god-damn monster right there*. And if he was being honest with himself, having someone *else* come to the same realization wasn't exactly the sexiest thing he could think of.

But Seth didn't seem to mind, pulling Nick out of his underwear, the metal of the dryer cold against his butt. Nick shivered, but then Seth's hand wrapped around him, and all rational thought left his head, leaving nothing but static in its wake. He didn't know it could feel like this, having someone else touch him in such a way. The callouses on Seth's palm. The way his fingers trembled as if he were as nervous as Nick was. Seth seemed unsure of himself, and Nick couldn't have that. He choked out, "That's good" as Seth *squeezed* him, moving his hand up and down.

"It is?" Seth asked quietly.

"Yeah. Little tighter. Oh my *god,* that's awesome."

Seth chuckled. "Good to know. I . . ." He swallowed thickly. "Could I . . . ?"

"What?"

"Try something."

"Uh, sure? What did you have in—and now you're bending

over. Why are you—oh. *Oh.* Holy crap, dude. Are you going to . . . ?"

"I think so," Seth said, looking up at him. "That all right?"

"Yes," Nick said quickly. "That sure sounds swell." He cringed inwardly. *Swell?* His boyfriend was literally asking to fellate him and he said it sounded *swell?* He did not deserve oral sex.

But Seth didn't seem to think the same (quite the opposite, apparently) because he tried to take too much at once, gagging, eyes watering as he pulled off, lips shiny with spit. "Crap," he muttered, cheeks darkening. "Sorry."

"Nope," Nick said. "No apologies. We're figuring it out, yeah? You can do it again, if you want. Maybe just go a little slower?"

Seth did, and when it came down to it, it probably wouldn't be considered the best blow job in history. Too much spit, too many teeth (Nick hissing, Seth apologizing), Seth's gag reflex kicking in. But it didn't matter. It didn't matter if it wasn't the best because it was *Seth.* It was Seth Gray, and Nick loved him.

They were in love and Seth was *actually blowing him.* Nick's imagination—a wondrous, terrifying thing—had done nothing to prepare him for how real this felt. It was in the way Seth looked up at him. It was in the way he licked. It was in the way he held Nick as if he were something precious, something important, Nick's hand in his hair, not pushing, but encouraging him on.

To a point, at least, because even if Seth hadn't done this before, Nick was on a hair trigger, and he didn't want it to be over just yet. He pulled Seth off him, hands under his arms, lifting him up. He kissed Seth, tongues brushing together. Against Seth's mouth, he said, "I want to try. Is that okay?"

Seth froze. Then, "Yeah. That's okay. I want that, too."

"I'm not going to be good at it," Nick warned, embarrassed, but knowing it needed to be said. "Just so you know."

Seth chuckled, shaking his head. "I wasn't either. But that's where practice comes in. We'll do it again and again until we get it right."

"You have the best ideas."

Never looking away from Nick, Seth stepped back from the dryer, stopping a few feet away. His hands went to the top of his shorts, and he pushed them down slowly. The skin of his hips and groin was paler than the rest of him, the patch of wiry dark hair almost shocking. And then lower and lower. Nick had felt Seth before. Grinding against him when they were making out. But nothing prepared him for the sight of his boyfriend stepping out of his shorts, letting them fall to the floor, standing nude in the basement. Seth was strong; Nick knew this. But having incontrovertible evidence in front of him was something else entirely.

It wasn't Seth's dick. Okay, wait: it wasn't *just* Seth's dick, though Nick could barely look away from it.

It was more than that.

It was the scar on his hip, the one he'd gotten when they were eleven years old, trying to climb a fence at the park, Seth cutting his side as he climbed over the top.

It was the small freckle just above his groin, like a misshapen heart.

It was the look on Seth's face, nervous, but sure, filled with so much trust it threatened to send Nick reeling.

And, of course, Seth's dick. Obviously. It wasn't a monster. It wasn't like porn. It was longer than Nick's, but a little thinner, the flared head reddened. As if moving in a dream, Nick practically floated off the dryer, kicking off his shoes, his socks, and Seth was waiting for him, hand outstretched. Nick took what was offered, and for the first time in his life, touched a dick that wasn't his. Seth's eyes fluttered shut as he panted against Nick's throat, and the *power* he felt then was enormous, life-altering. It had nothing to do with being Extraordinary.

It had to do with Seth. With his bow ties. With his loafers. With his ridiculous idea that Nick was someone important, someone worthy.

"I'm going to suck your penis now," Nick said, nipping at Seth's ear. "Is that okay?"

"All the consent," he ground out as Nick flicked his wrist, the heat of Seth like a brand against Nick's palm.

He was *not* great at it, far from it. He tried, he did, but he kept forgetting to cover his teeth with his lips, tried to take in more than he was able to. His own gag reflex kicked in, the taste of clean sweat on his tongue, the scent of *SethSethSeth* filling his nose. He tried again, relaxing his throat, crowing inwardly when Seth said, "Like that, just like that," and yes, he felt powerful. Yes, he felt strong. Yes, he felt loved when Seth touched the top of his head, tugging gently on his hair, urging him on, telling him it was good, *You're doing so good, Nicky,* his words whispered in reverence. Maybe he wasn't great at it, but his enthusiasm more than made up for it. He wanted more, wanted to go as far as they could. He was practically vibrating out of his skin, but they hadn't prepared for this. Later. It would have to come later.

Eventually, Seth pulled him off, panting, face flushed, lifting him up and kissing his swollen lips. They took each other in hand, and Seth leaned his forehead against Nick's, exhaling as Nick inhaled, and then Seth *groaned*, a low, deep sound that Nick had never heard him make before, at least outside of his dreams. He spilled first, hips stuttering. Nick wasn't long to follow, feeling a heated coil unfurling in his stomach as his toes flexed, his back ramrod straight. He grunted and then cried out when Seth continued stroking him through it, his skin too sensitive.

Knees weak, they leaned together, holding each other up. Neither spoke. They breathed through it, knowing everything had irrevocably changed, but happy about it, if the way they grinned at each other was any indication.

And Nick—always and forever Nick—said, "Why the hell haven't we done *that* before? And when are we going to do it again?"

Seth rolled his eyes fondly, curls damp with sweat hanging down on his forehead. "I take it you enjoyed yourself?"

"That might be an understatement," Nick said, grimacing

down at the evidence splashed on the cement floor. He laughed as he looked back up at Seth. "We just did *sex* stuff. I'm only half a virgin now."

"I don't think that's how it works."

"It does," Nick assured him. And because he could, he kissed Seth all over his face, loud, obnoxious smacks that echoed flatly through the basement. Seth, for his part, gave as good as he got, holding Nick close.

He closed his eyes, laying his head on Seth's shoulders. He knew everything was still waiting for them outside of the basement, but for a moment—perhaps a little longer—he ignored it. All that mattered was Seth's hand rubbing his lower back, his other hand on the back of Nick's head.

"Thank you," he whispered. "That was frickin' rad."

Seth snorted before kissing the side of his head. "I think so, too."

He was about to suggest another round—short recovery time, hell *yes*—but before he could, the basement door opened and an amused voice called down, "Are you guys done? Yay for you and congrats on the sex, but Gibby says she could have gone the rest of her life without knowing Seth was a screamer."

"Oh my god," Nick blurted, starting to panic all over again. "Jazz? Don't come down here! Our penises are out!"

Seth sighed deeply.

"Ew," Jazz said. "But also, aw. And don't worry. I wouldn't dream of coming down there. I bet it smells weird, like SeaWorld in August."

"Why is she so *descriptive*?" Nick lamented. Then, louder, "Stop ruining our special moment!"

"Our special moment," Seth repeated. "Really. That's what you're going with."

"Sorry about this," Nick said, and picked up the towel that had fallen to the ground, dropping it on top of the evidence splattered on the floor. He shuffled his feet back and forth and looked up when he felt Seth watching him with a half smile. "What?"

Seth shrugged. "I love you."

When faced with an admission of love after coupling, there was only one appropriate response. Nick flung himself at Seth, tackling him to the floor and kissing him within an inch of his life. "I know," he whispered against Seth's mouth. "I love you, too."

# 14

They dressed and walked up the stairs, hands joined between them, Nick giddy but trying to tamp it down as best he could. Everything seemed different, funnier. Lighter, somehow. He marveled at Seth's fingers between his own, the way Seth kept glancing at him out of the corner of his eye, blushing but doing nothing to hide it. He had to stop himself from rushing up the stairs and going outside, shouting to the world that he'd gotten *laid*.

He wasn't stupid. He knew what still lay ahead, but he allowed himself this brief moment in time where he felt happy. Whole. Powerful. And Seth seemed to feel the same, holding the basement door open for Nick, bowing low to let him walk through first. "After you."

"My hero," Nick said, batting his eyes.

Seth swatted his ass, a quick slap before squeezing. Later, Nick reminded himself. There was so much more that they could do, and he was going to make sure they did all of it.

Thankfully, he managed to keep this to himself, especially when he saw Gibby and Jazz in the kitchen, seated at the table, both of them with shit-eating grins on their faces.

He waited until Seth had sat down on an empty chair, pulling Nick down onto his lap. It was a little awkward, but Nick didn't want to be anywhere else. Once settled, he set his backpack on the table as he glared at Gibby and Jazz. "Not a word," he warned them. "What just happened was a beautiful thing, and I won't have you ruining it by asking for details."

"We won't," Gibby assured him. "There nothing I want to know less than what you—"

"I can do blow jobs!" Nick said, pumping his fists in the air.

Seth groaned, burying his face in Nick's side.

Nick blanched. "Oh, my bad. Don't want to hog all the credit. Seth can do blow jobs, too. But! There's no need to be jealous. I know you don't like penises, so I don't want you to think you're missing out on anything."

Gibby got that look on her face, the evil one where Nick knew she was going to say something that would devastate him physically and emotionally. "Go down on a girl, and then get back to me. We'll see who's really missing out." She high-fived Jazz without looking at her.

"Oh no," Nick whispered fervently. "My good feelings."

"You earned that," Seth said, hooking his chin over Nick's shoulder and looking at their girls. "Ignore him. You know how he gets."

Nick scoffed. "What? It's *true*." Then, because he wasn't a complete asshole, he added, "I'm sure going down on a girl is . . . not for me, but you do you."

"Gee, thanks," Jazz said. "It's good to have your support, especially since Gibby is a pro with her mouth and fingers. Can't let talent like that go to waste."

Yeah, he was going to leave that one alone. "What are you guys doing here?" Nick looked around, nerves prickling. "Are Martha and Bob gone? Oh shit. Please tell me they left before . . ."

Seth choked and started coughing.

"They did," Gibby said. "They let us in through the back before they left. Told us you two were talking and that you'd be up when you were done."

"Talking," Nick said. "With our *penises*. Okay. I've gotten it all out of my system now."

"Finally," Gibby muttered. "Jazz said you were coming over here. We texted but didn't hear back, so we wanted to make sure you guys were good." She made a face. "If I'd known what you were doing, I'd have stayed far, far away."

"Sorry," Seth said. "Phone's upstairs. Didn't think to bring it down to the basement with me."

* 243 *

Nick glanced at his backpack, feeling a little guilty. "We didn't mean to worry you."

Gibby nodded. "It's all right. With everything that's happened, it scared me a little when we didn't hear back." She eyed Nick up and down. "You okay? And I'm not asking about anything you just did with Seth, so get that out of your head right now, Nick. We haven't had a chance to really talk in the last couple of days."

"I don't know," Nick admitted. "I talked with Dad. He's . . . dealing with it as best he can."

Jazz reached over and patted his shin. "And what about you?"

He leaned against Seth, grateful when he wrapped his arms around Nick's stomach, grounding him. "I'm pissed off. And sad. And a bunch of other things all at once. I don't know that I've processed any of it yet." He looked down at Seth's hands. "I don't even know how to start."

Gibby and Jazz exchanged a glance before looking at him again. "We can't imagine what that's like," Gibby said quietly. "Mom and Dad are furious. I am, too, but that doesn't compare to what you and your dad must be feeling right now."

"Same with mine," Jazz said. "Mom had to stop Dad from marching down to Burke Tower and confronting him head-on."

"You saw the interview they did?" Nick asked bitterly. They nodded. "Always spinning things in their favor, and everyone falls for it again and again. How the hell are we supposed to stop them if no one will believe us?"

"I don't know," Jazz said. "Maybe we won't be able to." She raised her hand toward Nick when he started to retort. "I know how that sounds, but I've been trying to think of where we go from here. What can we do? We can't kill them."

"What about Chris and Mateo?" Seth asked. "You hear from them?"

"I called Mateo," Gibby said. "Yesterday. He . . . well. He yelled a lot. Not at me, but man, I don't know what Burke was thinking pissing off a drag queen. It won't end well for him.

Mateo said Chris is just as angry, but he's at a loss of where to go from here." She paused. "He wants to quit the force. At least that's what Mateo told me."

"Good," Nick said savagely. "They don't deserve him. He's better than all of them put together."

"We'd lose the only contact we have with the NCPD," Jazz said. "But he needs to do what's right for him."

Nick's phone began to vibrate in the front pocket of his bag. "And if it gets out he was part of this, he might have a target on his back. He's gotta be careful." He dug through his bag until he found his phone. A few notifications. Jazz. Gibby. Dad, saying he'd gotten Nick's note and admonishing him for going out alone. Nick typed back a quick reply, letting him know he was with his friends.

The other notification, though. The one that had caused his phone to vibrate. Nick frowned at the screen. A missed call listed as private. No way to call it back. No voicemail left, either. He set the phone on the table and said, "And then there's Owen. I don't know where he is, and I know he helped us, but that doesn't mean he's on our side. We can't trust—"

His phone began to buzz again, rattling on the table. The screen lit up. Private number.

"Who is it?" Seth asked, looking over Nick's shoulder.

Nick gnawed on his bottom lip. "Don't know. Blocked number." He showed Seth the screen. "Should I answer it?"

But the call dropped before he could answer.

Only to have another notification come through in the form of a text.

ANSWER YOUR PHONE.

"Is it your dad?" Jazz asked. "Cap, maybe?"

Nick shook his head. "I've got their numbers saved. They know I wouldn't answer if I didn't recognize who was calling."

The phone vibrated once more with another incoming call. Private number.

"Answer it," Seth said. "Put it on speaker so we can all hear. Whoever it is, don't tell them anything. Listen. Wait."

Nick nodded, heart thudding. He swiped the screen, connecting the call before hitting the speaker button and laying the phone flat on the table. "Who is this?"

A heavily modulated voice said, "Shut up and listen. I don't have time to—"

"Uh, rude," Nick said. "Do you know how phone calls work? Like, you called me and so I should probably talk, at least a little bit."

A pause. Sounds of traffic and people, a low rumble in the background. Somewhere in public? Then, angrier, "Nick, I said to shut. *Up.*"

"How do you know my name?" Nick demanded. "Are you stalking me? That's illegal!"

More silence. All the silence.

"Hello?" Nick asked. "Did you get that? About the stalking thing? Honestly, I'm not sure of the etiquette when speaking to a stalker—"

"What is *wrong* with you?"

"Many things," Nick said promptly. "Some are diagnosed, but others are still a mystery. I probably won't find out what those are until I'm twenty-five and working a dead-end job that's sucking out my soul."

"Who are you?" Seth asked, leaning over the table and glaring down at the phone.

A longer pause. Then, "How many people are listening to this?"

"Just me," Nick said. "But also Seth. And Jazz. And Gibby."

"'Sup," Gibby said.

"Hello," Jazz said.

The voice groaned. "Of course. You idiots can't do anything on your own. Of *course* you're together."

"You're the one who called us," Nick reminded them. "Also, who calls people anymore? You know how to text, right?"

"I know how to text!" the voice shouted. "I literally just sent you a text!"

"Yikes," Jazz said. "If you're a telemarketer, you're not doing a very good job. You need to be friendlier when you're trying to sell us something."

"Oh my god," Nick breathed. "What if I won a cruise? I wouldn't go because I read that we haven't mapped much of the ocean and that means there might be sea monsters that we haven't discovered yet, but *still*. I never win anything."

A muffled banging sound, as if the person on the other end of the line was hitting something, either with their fist or their head.

"You still haven't answered my question," Seth said. "Who is this?"

"This is . . . Armenian . . . Laundromat."

"Wow," Nick said, impressed. "That's a rad name. I respect your storied culture, whatever it may be."

Gibby sighed. "Nick, they're obviously outside and just looking at businesses around them."

"If you knew what I was risking here," Armenian Laundromat snapped, "you little shits would be on your knees *thanking me*."

And just like that, Nick knew. No one threw out *little shits* like the one person he despised almost above all others. His nemesis. The dark to his light. The unfinished fanfiction to his completed work.

"Rebecca Firestone," Nick snarled at the phone.

The longest pause. Then, "What? Noooo. That's not who I am. I'm . . . Lexington . . . CVS. *Dammit*."

"She's at Lexington and Bennett Ave," Gibby said. "There's a CVS right on the corner next to an Armenian deli and that laundromat that went out of business when the owner was arrested for working for the mob."

Jazz nodded sagely. "Laundering money at a laundromat. Of course. It makes perfect sense."

"Would you *listen to me*? I'm trying to help you!"

"Really," Seth said flatly. "You've never helped anyone but yourself. The bridge. The prom. All the news reports. And that doesn't even begin to cover how you're working with Simon Burke."

"That's not who I am! I'm a concerned citizen who . . . happened upon information that could—"

"Rebecca Firestone?" Nick asked.

"What?"

"Ha!" he crowed. "It *is* you! Why do you have my phone number, you psycho?" A thought struck him, terrible yet obvious. "You're trying to get to Owen through me because you still have feelings for him! For *shame*, Rebecca Firestone. He's eighteen. You're middle-aged! Also, he's, like, a murderer." He grimaced. "Unless that's what you're into. If so, I'd suggest checking yourself in to a hospital for a mental evaluation. Society's glamorization of murderers is not only a slap in the face to victims, but also—"

"I am *not* middle-aged," she hissed at him. "And I don't have *feelings* for anyone!"

"Well, yeah," Nick said. "You're a lizard monster incapable of love, so. You know. Tell us something we don't know."

"Burke is planning an attack at his Fourth of July celebration," Rebecca Firestone said. "Patricia Burke is going to pose as Guardian and attempt to assassinate her husband. He's going to put the blame all on you. Everyone will believe Guardian tried to kill him, and you'll become the most wanted fugitive in the city. You want to know why you didn't find Owen at the rally you interrupted? It's because he wasn't *there*. The man in the hoodie was Patricia Burke."

It was their turn to be silent.

Then, Gibby said, "Hold, please," and muted the call with a flick of her finger. She looked up at them. "Code word. Now."

Right after the attack on the Bell house when Patricia Burke showed her true face, they'd decided each of them needed a code word to prove they were who they said they were. Nick had come up with all of them for their friends and family, tailored specifically to the individual.

"Princess Amazing," Jazz said.

"Butch Fatale," Gibby said.

"God of Wikipedia and Most Other Things," Nick said.

They all looked at Seth, who folded his arms with a grumpy expression on his face.

"Say it," Gibby told him.

"No. It's stupid."

"Oh no," Nick whispered. "Are you Patricia Burke? Did I give Patricia Burke a *blow job*? My innocence! Ack! Gross! I trusted you! How dare you seduce me posing as my boyfriend!"

Seth sighed and mumbled something under his breath.

"Louder," Jazz said. "Don't make me get a spork. It's for stabbing *and* scooping out your eyes."

Seth said, "Sexy Sex Beast Who Looks Good in Pretty Much Everything."

"Oh, thank god," Nick said, relieved. "Our special moment in the basement means something again. I love you, dude."

"Yeah, yeah," Seth muttered, though he was smiling.

"Guys," Gibby said. "Maybe we should focus on the fact that Rebecca Firestone told us Nick is about to be blamed for attempted murder? Seems important." Then, almost as an afterthought, "Also, she said she knew Nick was Guardian."

Nick startled out of a daydream where he was objectifying Seth's ass. "Crap. You're right. We can't trust anything she says. For all we know, it's part of Burke's plan to bring us out of hiding."

"We're sitting in a kitchen," Jazz said. "I don't think we're very good at hiding."

"Listen to her," Seth said. "But take everything she says with a grain of salt."

Nick nodded and unmuted the phone. "You still there, bane of my existence?"

"Screw you!"

"Back at you, dumbass. What's this about Guardian? Why, I've never heard such a name before." There. That should do it.

That did not do it. "You can't be serious. You're Guardian. That everyone hasn't figured it out is ridiculous. The people of this city are morons who— *Stop distracting me*." Her voice crackled through whatever she was using to modify it. "Did you hear what I said? Burke is going to—"

"Yeah, we got that," Seth said. "But that doesn't explain why you're telling us. You work for him. Everything you've done has been to help him or yourself. Why should we trust you or anything you're saying?"

"Because it's the truth!" she shouted. "Don't you get it? He plans for *everything*. If Patricia Burke as Jennifer Bell failed, he already had a backup plan in the works. If he couldn't tear you apart from the inside, then he's going to make sure you're persona non grata."

"We don't speak Italian," Nick said.

"Jesus, Nicky," Gibby said. "It's not Italian. It's Latin. It means people will be gunning for you."

"And not *just* you, Bell," Rebecca Firestone said. "Your stupid little team, including that drag queen. Your parents. The Grays. Hell, even Officer Morton. He's going to say all of you conspired against him, and that you were working together with Owen Burke in order to kill him. Every cop in the city will be coming for you."

Nick's spine turned to ice. "What?" he whispered.

"Oh, now I've got your attention? No pithy retorts?"

"Not helping, Firestone," Seth warned her. "Why should we believe this?" He looked thoughtfully at the phone. "What changed?"

"Nothing," she said. "Everything. I work for him, yes. And *yes*, I hate you just as much as you hate me, but . . ." She huffed out a breath. "I have my reasons. You don't get to ask what those are."

"Bullshit," Gibby snapped. "If you expect us to believe you,

you gotta give us more. We're not stupid enough to just take you at your word after everything you've done."

"No," she said.

Gibby shrugged. "Then go to hell." She slapped her hand against the phone, disconnecting the call.

They stared at her.

She arched an eyebrow. "What? She'll call back. Three. Two. One."

The phone started to vibrate from an incoming call.

"Told you," Gibby said smugly.

"You're scary cool," Nick said. "I'm so glad you're on our side." He pressed the answer button. "Hello?"

"You goddamn—"

Nick hung up on her.

They stared at him.

"What?" he asked. "She'll call back. Three. Two. One."

The phone did not vibrate.

"Well, that's disappointing," Nick said. "Having evidence that I'm not scary cool sucks balls."

The phone vibrated once more. "Validation is the best!" Nick said, connecting the call. "Are you done?"

For a long moment, Nick thought she wouldn't answer. He could still hear the sounds of the city in the background, so he knew she was still there. *Wait,* Seth mouthed at them, nodding toward the phone.

They didn't have to wait for long. "Fine," she muttered, whatever she'd been using to modify her voice gone. "I can't believe I'm telling you this, but I can see I don't have any other choice."

"We're listening," Seth said, leaning forward, eyes narrowed.

"I've been investigating Simon Burke for the last four years. And before you ask, I'm not affiliated with any news organization or law enforcement. I've been doing it on my own."

Nick blinked. That wasn't what he expected to hear. "For someone who claims to be investigating Burke, you sure seem happy being his personal bootlicker."

"I needed him to trust me," she retorted. "To believe I was on his side. To work my way into his inner circle."

"Why not just go to the police, then?" Jazz asked. "If you've found anything, why come to us?"

Rebecca Firestone laughed. "Are you out of your mind? You know he's got the NCPD in his pocket. Aaron Bell and Rodney Caplan resigning was the best thing that could've happened to him. With them out of the way, it leaves his sycophants to step up and take over. After he's elected, he'll appoint a new police chief, one who backs his anti-Extraordinary agenda. That, coupled with putting the blame of an attack on him squarely on your shoulders, will mean no Extraordinary will be safe."

Nick scoffed, a swell of anger coursing through him. Listening to her attempt to rewrite history made him want to scream. "As if you care about Extraordinaries. You're one of the big reasons people are scared of us."

"Fair," she allowed. "But there's a reason for everything." She hesitated, and Nick was about to snark at her, but he didn't get the chance. She said, "My name wasn't always Rebecca Firestone. I changed it when I became a reporter. My name used to be—"

L auren Underwood," Nick said, still reeling even hours later. All attention was on him and Gibby, who stood next to him in the Kensington backyard as the sun set, a tablet in her hands, pointed toward their rapt audience. On the screen of the tablet, a picture of a girl at age eighteen, mousy brown hair, her front two teeth crooked, wearing a blue cap and gown and holding her high-school diploma tightly in one hand. Next to her, his arm wrapped around her shoulders, was a heavyset man beaming with pride. They looked so much like each other, they had to be related.

"The daughter of Martin Underwood," Gibby said. "Who we think was murdered by Patricia Burke four years ago. She consumed his abilities to manipulate water, and then used them on him. She drowned him in his apartment."

Trey said, "Hold up, Gibster. You're saying Rebecca Firestone is Lauren Underwood?" The adults sitting in folding chairs around him on the patio looked just as confused. "How does *that* work? Someone like Burke would vet the hell out of anyone who came to work for him, especially a former reporter."

"He did," Jazz said, standing up from her chair and joining Gibby and Nick. "May I?" Gibby handed over the tablet, and Jazz swiped along the screen. "If you look up *Lauren Underwood Nova City,* you won't find much. She paid to have her entire online footprint wiped out. No photos. No announcements. No mentions of her in any articles. Nothing. As far as the internet is concerned, this Lauren Underwood never existed. But if you look up Rebecca Firestone, you get years of hits that pertain to her reporting along with a manufactured backstory that's vague enough not to have holes poked through it." She shook her head. "It's really clever, if you think about it. It must have cost a fortune."

"Underwood's obituary mentioned he was survived by his daughter," Seth said, leaning forward on his own chair, elbows on his knees. "Firestone sent us the graduation photo as proof. Gibby says that as best she can tell, it hasn't been altered. That's Martin Underwood with her, the same Martin Underwood who worked for Burke."

"I knew that hair wasn't her real color," Mateo said as Chris chuckled next to him.

"Okay," Cap said slowly, hands folded over the swell of his stomach. "So she went by a different name. Still doesn't mean we can trust anything she's saying. Why the sudden conscience? She's done everything she can to hurt you kids and other Extraordinaries."

"That's what I said," Nick muttered. "But she claims it's because she's undercover, gathering all she can about what Burke's doing. She tried to stick it out with Action News as long as she could, but she hit a wall. The only way she could get further was to join his campaign."

Dad spoke for the first time. He'd been eerily quiet since coming to the backyard, face pinched. He'd taken a seat next to Cap and Mary, listening intently, but not saying a word. At least until it was time to ask the one question Nick knew was coming but didn't know how to answer. "Do you believe her?"

"We don't want to," Seth said slowly. He glanced at the tablet Jazz held, the photo of Lauren and her father on the screen. Then he looked at Nick, silently asking for permission. Gnawing on his bottom lip, Nick nodded. "But she confirmed something that we'd heard from Owen and it makes us believe most of what she said."

"What was that?" Chris asked.

Nick didn't look at him. He only had eyes for Dad, going over to him and crouching down before him, taking his father's hands in his own. Dad gripped him tightly. "I'm sorry."

"For what?" Dad asked gruffly.

"I don't want to hurt you," Nick whispered. "But no more secrets, yeah?"

Dad pulled his right hand free, wrapping it around the back of Nick's neck. "No more secrets, kid. I can handle it."

Nick nodded. He took a deep breath, knowing he was about to break Dad's heart even more, but powerless to do anything to stop it. "She . . . the bank. The robbery. It was all a ruse. Burke ordered those men there. She—*Mom* wouldn't help him. He wanted to use her. She refused." He swallowed thickly. "So he had her killed. It was Burke, Dad. He might not have pulled the trigger, but it was on his orders that she died."

People began to mutter around them, but Nick didn't look away from Dad, who exhaled explosively as if the breath had been knocked from his chest. He squeezed his eyes shut, fingers on Nick's neck digging in. When he opened his eyes again, they were wet, pained, but clear. "I . . . okay." He gritted his teeth together. "I always thought there was more to it than we found out."

"I'm sorry," Nick said again.

Dad shook his head. "You have nothing to apologize for, kid. If anyone needs to apologize, it's me. I was the one who brought Burke into our lives. I was the one who thought he could help us. Help you. If I hadn't . . ." He made a strangled noise, whatever else he wanted to say lost.

"It's not your fault," Martha said, causing both Nick and Dad to look at her. She smiled sadly, Bob nodding in his seat next to hers. "Not you. Not Nick. Not anyone here. It's all on Burke, and we'll remind you of that as long as you need us to." Her smile faded slightly. "But that does raise some concerns."

"About what?" Seth asked.

"Whether we're thinking with our heads, and not our hearts," Bob said, and Nick loved him for making it about all of them, not just Nick and Dad. "Stopping him is one thing, especially if it's for the greater good. But if this is revenge, we're going to fail before we begin. Anger changes a person. Blinds them, leading to mistakes. And the stakes are too high for that. I trust you, Nick. I won't pretend to know what you and Aaron must be feeling right now, but I know what grief does to a person."

"Jazz asked the same thing," Nick said, glancing at his friend, who nodded at him, encouraging him on. "If I'd answered right away, I'd have said hell yes, it was about revenge. And I'd have meant it."

"But," Dad said.

"But then I remembered what someone did for me once, even though I didn't know it at the time. I needed something to believe in. I needed a hero. And Seth knew that. He became Pyro Storm because he saw how much losing Mom destroyed me. It wasn't about revenge for him. It was about trying to stop the same thing from happening to anyone else."

Martha wiped her eyes. "He's a good boy. The best, really."

Seth blushed, but looked determined. "If we can stop Burke from hurting anyone else, then we owe it to them and ourselves to try. It's not just about us, or what he's done *to* us. It's about protecting people, even if they hate us. It's about making sure anyone who comes after us—anyone who can do what we can but are scared because of the rhetoric—gets to feel safe. Gets to be free to be who they are without fear. That's why we're doing this. That's why we're Lighthouse."

"Spoken like a true hero," Jo Kensington said. "I'm proud of you kids. I wish more than anything it didn't have to be this way, but it is, and so long as you remember that you're not alone, I know you'll do the right thing. With our help, of course."

"Damn right," Miles agreed. "Lighthouse, with support from the Dad Squad."

Aysha laughed. "I'm going to bedazzle the hell out of your shirts. A good team looks uniform, so no one gets to argue."

"Hell yes," Trey breathed. "We are going to look so badass." He frowned. "Wait, back up. What are we saying here? We're going to . . . what. Attack them head-on? Who's going to believe us when Patricia Burke can change the way she looks? Or manipulate people and make them believe things that aren't real?" He folded his arms. "If you think I'm going to let my daughter walk into a trap, you're out of your damned minds."

"*Dad,*" Gibby said. "I can handle myself. And even if you think I can't, I'm eighteen now, which means I get to make my own decisions."

"No one's saying you can't," Aysha told her. "But this is different, Lola. This isn't Smoke and Ice at your prom, though that was scary enough. This is Burke. We know what he's capable of. And you do, too."

"They're right," Miles said, and Jazz glared at him. "I can't speak for Seth and Nick, but there are limitations to what the rest of us can do. The rest of us don't have powers. Patricia Burke already got ahold of us once. What if she does it again, only this time, she makes you or all of us forget everything? You really think we're going to put our daughter in that position?" He exchanged a glance with Jo, who nodded. "We can't take that chance."

"*If* we're going to do something," Jo said, "and I'm not agreeing to anything yet, why couldn't Jazz and Gibby run comms in the secret lair like they always do?" She blanched. "Not that I want Seth and Nick in danger, but . . ."

Gibby and Jazz began to sputter angrily, and everyone else seemed to have an opinion on the matter, voices raised, talking over each other. It wasn't until someone cleared their throat quite loudly that they all fell silent, looking at him. He had his legs crossed, fingers tapping on his thigh. "Hey," he said. "Thanks for including me. I have no idea what's going on, and this is some crazy-ass shit, but I like being part of things."

"I don't think I know who you are," Mateo said, squinting at him.

He stood abruptly, going around and shaking hands, starting with Mateo and Chris. "Hi. Hello. Hi. You look lovely. Nice to meet ya. Dig the shaved look, my man. See where Gibby got the shape of her head from. Hello. Hello. Pleasure to meet you. They call me Burrito Jerry. You might've seen my ride Matilda in the driveway." He puffed out his chest in pride. "Painted her myself."

"He helped us," Seth said. "Jazz brought him on." It was a little more complicated than that but everyone seemed to take it in stride, much to Nick's relief.

"And I have questions," Burrito Jerry said, returning to his seat. "Like, a billion questions, however I think those can wait for now. I can't move stuff with my mind or set things on fire, but I think I've got a way to help, if Jazz and Gibby are up for it." He looked sternly at the girls. "Only if your parents agree, that is."

"How?" Miles asked.

"Matilda," Burrito Jerry said. "I don't know about secret lairs or villains who can change shape and wipe minds, but I know my lady. She's sturdy. Plenty of room. Jasmine and Gibby could get whatever they need, and we can park her as close to Burke Tower as possible. Out of the way, but still there in case backup is needed."

"Mobile Lighthouse," Nick said, trying to temper his excitement as he stood in front of his father. "Dude, that's *awesome*."

"It could work," Gibby said thoughtfully. "Might take a bit

to retrofit Matilda, but the Fourth is still a few days away. We have time."

"We do," Burrito Jerry said. "But again, only if your parents give the okay; they get the final word."

"Damn right," Trey said. "And since my daughter pointed out that we have time, we're not going to make any decisions right this second." He held up his hand as Gibby opened her mouth to argue. "Honey, I'll listen to you. I always have, and you know that. But your mom and I need to think about this, okay?"

"Same," Miles said. "We get you want to help, Jasmine. And Nick and Seth have said repeatedly they couldn't have gotten as far as they have without either you or Gibby, but we want to make sure we're going about this the right way with as little risk as possible."

Jazz whispered something in her ear, and Gibby sighed. "Fine. So long as you remember what we're capable of."

Aysha chuckled. "Trust me when I say we know that very well."

"That still doesn't explain how we're going to stop Burke," Chris said, Mateo's hand resting on his thigh. "If Firestone is right and he's going to have Patricia Burke impersonate Guardian, who's going to believe us? The permit they requested for the celebration said they expect a crowd of at least ten thousand people. The NCPD is giving him as many cops they can without stretching the force too thin. The Fourth of July is busy across the city. Burke's fireworks display won't be the only one."

"Not to mention counterprotestors," Trey said. "And probably every news outlet in the city. Everyone's eyes are going to be on Burke, just like he wants. You have the attention of Nova City, you can do anything you want with it."

"If we can't have him arrested, what's the alternative?" Mary asked. "Killing him? Even *if* that was on the table, what would it solve? It'd only make him a martyr for his cause."

Nick and Seth went to their friends, standing on either side of them. A team, united. "Tell them," Seth said, nudging Gibby's shoulder. "It was your idea."

"Yours, too, Jazz," Nick said. "And I know it's going to work."

Gibby took Jazz's hand and said, "You're right. Killing him wouldn't solve anything, and that's not who we are. But there's a reason Jazz and I want to be there, and not because we want to get in the middle of a fight."

"Instead," Jazz said, "we're going to make him wish he'd never been born. If all goes well, he won't even know we're there. We don't need to destroy Burke, because he's going to do it himself. And by the time we're done, no one will believe him ever again. Burrito Jerry, I hope you were serious about letting us use Matilda, because we're going to need her."

He nodded. "What's mine is yours. I got you, girl."

"Good," Gibby said. She grinned, razor-sharp. "You ready for this? It has a lot of moving parts, and we'll need more than a little luck on our side, but Burke has proven he likes to be the center of attention. Might as well give him what he wants."

Everyone leaned forward. "Tell us," Trey said, eyes glittering in the encroaching dark.

And so they did.

# 15

In the days that followed, the heat wave that had held Nova City in its grasp for weeks loosened slightly, the humidity dropping to more tolerable levels, a bit of rain falling and breathing new life into the stagnant, heavy air. Forecasters warned it wouldn't last, saying the Fourth of July promised to be clear and hot with little chance of the fireworks celebrations across the city being rained out.

Nick and Dad went back to the house midweek, looking at the damage. Repairs were already underway, but it'd be at least another week before they'd be able to move back in. He was surprised to find that it still *felt* like his home, even with all that had happened. Patricia Burke had violated their sense of security, but that singular event was no match against the history of this house, the memories embedded in every inch of the floors and walls. This was where they'd lived with her. This was where they'd laughed and cried, where they'd argued and then forgiven.

"It's coming together," Nick said, watching construction workers rebuild the living room wall, the hole covered in plastic sheeting, the air thick with dust and plaster, so much so it caused him to sneeze.

"It is," Dad said. He looked a little lost standing in the living room and startled when Nick bumped their shoulders together. "It may not be like it was, but maybe . . ."

"It doesn't have to be," Nick finished for him. "It might even be better. Fair warning: Jazz wants to handle the decorating once they finish. She says she hopes we like frilly pillows."

Dad sighed. "It's not like we can tell her no. I don't want to get stabbed with a fork."

Speaking of.

Owen Burke had disappeared but Nick didn't believe he'd left Nova City. He was biding his time, just like the rest of them.

But for what, Nick didn't know. He didn't believe for a moment that Owen was on their side, or that they'd seen the last of him.

Dad wrapped an arm around his shoulders. "We'll be all right."


The days leading up to the Fourth were busy. Nick went to bed each night in the spare room at the Kensington house exhausted, mind unusually sluggish, body complaining about everything he'd put it through. While Jazz, Gibby, and Miles had worked on Matilda with Burrito Jerry—gutting the back of the van, installing shelving and power sources to keep the electronics running while Jo went through the secret lair, making a list of everything they needed—Mateo and Seth had worked Nick to the bone under the watchful eyes of Mary Caplan and Trey. Dad and Cap had a client list they needed to keep up with, Dad up and gone early in the morning so he and Cap could finish sooner and return to the Kensington home.

"You have powers," Mateo snapped at Nick after he failed to block an incoming punch for the third time, sweat dripping down the sides of his face. "Why are you acting like you don't?"

"I don't want to hurt you," Nick panted, bent over, hands on his knees. Out of the corner of his eye, he saw Seth circling him slowly, waiting for Mateo's signal to go again.

"I'm not telling you to hurt me," Mateo said, eyes narrowed. "I'm telling you to protect yourself. Again. Seth."

Nick managed to move in time when Seth hurtled toward him, ducking as his arm swung out in a flat arc. Seth didn't wait for him to recover, jumping on his back, arms wrapped around Nick's neck, knees clamped against his hips.

"What do you do now?" Seth whispered in his ear.

"Hope the others will leave so I can take off your pants and mine?"

Trey snorted. "I don't think that'll stop Burke, but for all I know, his one weakness is skinny white-boy legs. It might be his kryptonite."

"Gross," Nick muttered, and then Seth used his weight to pull them both backward, flipping Nick over him, causing him to land on his back, blinking up at fat clouds hanging suspended above him in a deep blue sky. "Oh my god, *ow*. Why would you do something so awesome, and why did it have to be to me?"

Before Nick could recover, he heard a familiar crackling, and rolled quickly to the side as a bolt of electricity struck the ground where he'd been, singeing the grass. He lifted his head to see Mateo standing, hand outstretched toward him, bright-blue lines crawling along his fingers. It wasn't a high voltage— Mateo had an envious amount of control—but Nick did *not* like getting electrocuted.

"Get up," Mateo said. "We've still got work to do. If you're going to claim to be an Extraordinary, it's time you start acting like one."

This was the third day of practice, and Nick had had enough. Muscles he didn't even know he had protested angrily as he pushed himself off the ground. The spark in his head flared brightly, and as he pulled himself to his full height, he said, "I *am* an Extraordinary."

Mateo scoffed. "Really. Prove it." He pulled his arm back and thrust it forward without warning, a bright-blue ball rocketing toward Nick.

A split-second decision—a single thought: *Stop running, face it head-on, I can do this*—and the spark in his head burst in a furious explosion. Without thinking Nick raised his own hands and thought of a stone wall, thick and unmoving. The air in front of his palms wavered, then solidified as the electricity struck it. The ball exploded a foot away from his chest as if striking something corporeal. As it began to break apart, Nick *pushed* with all his might. In wonder, he watched as the electricity—crawling up and down the invisible wall, illuminating his face—seemed to *pause,* reaching a limit as to how far it could expand. He closed his hands into fists, and the ball reformed, floating in front of him. No pain. Without hesitating, he hurled it back toward Mateo, who caught it, even as it sent him sliding back through the grass, leaving divots in his wake.

"My word," Mary breathed as Trey's jaw dropped.

"Hell *yes*!" Nick crowed, pumping his fists into the air. "Did you see that? Holy shit, I *caught electricity.* I am the best—*oh my god.*"

A tornado of fire rose up and around him, Nick in the eye of the storm. The flames were hot, spinning in red and orange, snapping, crackling. He panicked, but just when he thought it would overtake him, a wave of calm washed over him. "I can do this," he whispered to himself. "I can do this."

Around him, he imagined another tornado, only this one made of air. Wind began to spin around his feet, crawling up his legs, his hips, his torso, until it roared in his ears, hair whipping back and forth. He pushed again, harder this time, and his tornado *expanded*, hitting the flames, tearing them apart. The windows of the house rattled, and Trey and Mary fell back in their chairs, tipping over, legs and arms flailing. Mateo hit a pillar on the porch as Seth was knocked off his feet and thrown into a green hedge near the back of the yard.

The fire dissipated, leaving only the smell of smoke.

Nick took a deep breath, pulling his powers back. The spark dimmed slightly, but it did not go out.

Seth sat up in the bush, leaves in his hair. "What was *that*?"

"That," Mateo said, grimacing as he pushed himself off the pillar, "was exactly what I asked for, but now immediately regret. Damn, Nick. You've been holding back. Good to know."

Nick grinned even as he helped Mary and Trey to their feet, apologizing profusely. Seth crawled out of the bush, and they began again.

They did their best. They knew the stakes, that they'd only get one shot to get this right. So many moving parts, and if one failed, the rest was sure to follow. Nick knew his weaknesses. Obstinate. Loud. Opinionated. Never met a word he didn't like. Chaos personified.

But he also knew his strengths. Brave, even though a little voice still sometimes whispered that he was a coward. Strong, and only getting stronger. Smart, sometimes. Did he make mistakes? Hell yes, but he still tried to right his wrongs as best he could, and learn from the experience.

It was these thoughts Nick had that last night before the end. A Thursday evening, the moon growing fatter, faint stars blinking across a black sky. The lights around the Kensington backyard had been dimmed to a faint glow. It was warm, but nowhere near as stifling as it'd been. It could have been any day in the middle of summer.

Gibby, Jazz, and Seth sat on the edge of the pool, their legs and feet in the water. They'd been talking about tomorrow, going through their plan again and again until they were sick of it. But that had faded after a time, all of them falling quiet, lost in their own thoughts.

Nick lay on his back behind them, hands on his chest as he looked up at the sky. He wondered, as he sometimes did, what she would think of them if she could see them now.

He looked at his friends, their backs to him. Seth's head lay against Gibby's shoulder, his curls bunched up against her cheek, her ear. Jazz kicked her feet in the water, causing ripples to spread throughout the pool.

"What are we going to do this weekend?" Seth suddenly asked.

Nick and Jazz looked at him as he lifted his head from Gibby's shoulder. He moved his legs, water splashing. From somewhere in the city, the sound of sirens, distant. Someone in the house laughed.

"This weekend," Gibby repeated. "You mean . . ."

Seth shrugged. "After tomorrow. What are we going to do? What if we went to the movies? Or we could have another picnic in the park. And maybe this time we'll be able to finish without anyone needing to be stabbed with a fork." He rose from the ledge of the pool, coming over to Nick, bare legs dripping water. He sat down next to Nick, leaning back on his hands.

Jazz came next, Gibby trailing after. Jazz lay down on the other side of Nick, her hair brushing against his face. "Picnic sounds good. Movies, too. We could make a day of it. M&M's in the popcorn. Sodas. Nachos with that gross movie-theater cheese."

Gibby settled against Seth, her head in his lap. He looked up at the sky. "Or maybe we could go to a museum. See old dinosaur bones. I haven't been since . . . wow. Since Nick's mom took us when we were . . . what. Ten. Eleven?"

"Eleven," Nick said. "For your birthday, remember? You wanted to be an archeologist after we watched those old Indiana Jones movies a billion times that fall."

Seth chuckled, cheeks darkening. "I remember. But . . . uh. It wasn't just that."

Gibby grinned up at him. "You had a crush on him, didn't you?"

"A little," Seth admitted. "Okay, maybe more than a little. Didn't know really what it meant, but when he cracked that whip . . ."

"Hell yes," Nick said. "Good taste, man. Tell you a secret?"

They looked at him.

"I used to have this dream. Of the *sexy* variety. Me and Han Solo in a hot tub."

Seth gaped at him. "You had sex dreams about Han Solo?"

"Yep," Nick said. "And I don't even feel bad about it. Believe me when I say that Han shot first."

Jazz began to giggle, Gibby following soon after, arms wrapped around her stomach as she rolled back and forth. Seth snorted, shaking his head. "I'll give you that, Nicky. I'm not even jealous."

"You shouldn't be," Nick told him. "You're better."

"Aw," Jazz said, wiping her eyes as Seth spluttered. "Hear that, Seth? You're better than Indiana Jones and Han Solo."

Seth rolled his eyes fondly. "That's a lot to live up to, but I'll take it, I guess."

Jazz shifted until she curled against Nick's side, her head on his chest. He put his face in her hair, breathing her in. "Maybe it's unrealistic. Maybe we won't always be like this." She sniffled. "I worry about it. Not all the time, but some."

"You do?" Gibby asked, sitting up from Seth's lap and looking over at Jazz.

"Yeah," Jazz said. "Doesn't everyone?"

"I think so," Seth said. "The future is scary because it's unknown. But look at us now. Look at all we've done."

"Ooh, I have an idea," Jazz breathed. "Maybe one of us should run for office one day. Change stuff from the inside. Be the anti–Simon Burke."

Seth said, "What about you? You could do it, Gibby."

"Whoa," Nick said. "Yeah. That could work." He looked at Gibby. "Would that be something you'd want?"

Gibby seemed a little flustered, picking at blades of grass, brow furrowed. "Maybe." She smiled. "Could start small. Maybe a seat on a council somewhere."

"And from there, a congresswoman," Jazz said, eyes alight. "Then, twenty years from now, President Lola Gibson, the youngest president ever elected."

Gibby laughed. "Think we might be getting ahead of ourselves, at least a little bit."

Jazz scoffed. "People would be people and underestimate

you, but you'd prove them wrong every single time. And you wouldn't be doing it alone. I could be your press secretary."

"And Nick and I could campaign for you," Seth said. "You'd be the boss, telling us what to do, where to go."

"That's pretty much how it is already," Nick said, brushing a lock of Jazz's hair off her forehead. "Because Gibby's smarter than the rest of us combined. She could be president. Jazz could work for her. I'll join Dad and Cap at their PI agency, and Seth can . . ." He frowned. "What do you want to do, Seth?"

They all looked at him, but Seth had tilted his head back, looking up at the sky. Pitch-black now, with lights from the city casting an ethereal glow around the edges. "I don't know," Seth said after a time. "Maybe helping people, somehow. Those like us. Extraordinaries. Make sure they know they're not alone."

"That sounds perfect," Nick said. "They'll come to you, looking for guidance and you'll give them direction. A point. Purpose."

"You really think I could do something like that?"

"Yeah," Gibby said. "There'd be no one better."

"But you don't have to decide now," Jazz said. "None of us do. We have time."

It all felt real, like it was within their grasp, if only they were brave enough to reach for it. It was vast and wild, a shining future where they were still together and no one could tear them apart. Nick startled when a tear slipped down his cheek. "The weekend," he said hoarsely. "What should we do this weekend?"

"Movies sound good," Gibby said without missing a beat. "I like that. Though, it can't be some overdone superhero sequel. I've had enough of that to last me a lifetime. A French period piece in black-and-white with subtitles and lesbians."

"Subtitles and lesbians," Seth said. "Can't argue against that."

"And when the movie's over, we'll get Gibby to help us finish out our college essays," Jazz said. "Then she'll go to NCU while the rest of us finish out our senior year. We'll graduate. We'll go on adventures. Here, in the city, or all over the world.

And when we come back, we'll begin the rest of our lives. Together."

"Together," Gibby said.

"Together," Seth said.

Nick watched each of them in turn, marveling that a loud,
obnoxious kid with ADHD and telekinesis could have found
kindred spirits in the three of them. It'd been a long road.

"Together," Nick said. He meant it down to his bones.

# 16

Friday morning—the Fourth of July—Nick opened his eyes in the Kensingtons' spare room. Next to him, Seth was snoring in his ear, arm slung over Nick's side. Next to them, Jazz and Gibby were spooning, eyes closed, breathing deeply, strands of Jazz's hair on Seth's shoulder. Nick felt warm. Safe. He wanted to drift back off to sleep, but knew that wouldn't be possible. His brain was already kicking into gear, mind flooded with racing thoughts about what this day would bring.

He lifted his head when a quiet knock came at the door. It opened slowly, and Dad stepped in. He wore jeans and a thin coat, zipper all the way up under his chin. He looked exhausted as he nodded at Nick, closing the door behind him and moving toward a high-backed chair that sat near the window, morning sunlight filtering in. He sat down, hands gripping his knees.

"Hey," Nick said, voice hoarse with sleep. "Time is it?"

"Early," Dad said.

"Couldn't sleep?"

Dad shrugged. "A few hours."

Nick extricated himself from his friends carefully. Seth smacked his lips as Nick pulled away, muttering something unintelligible before burying his face in the pillow.

He stood, stretching, and went to the window where Dad sat, looking out onto the side yard. Beyond the bushes, beyond the trees, metal and glass of Nova City in the distance, skyscrapers reaching toward a cloudless blue.

He said, "I was scared, yesterday. And I still am, but it's not like it was." He glanced over at Dad, who watched him with an expression Nick couldn't make heads or tails of. Faith, Nick thought.

"What is it now?" Dad asked quietly.

Nick thought for a moment. "Resolve. I know what we have to do. And beyond that, I know it's the *right* thing to do." He looked away. "When this is over with, I want to go back to the coast. To the lighthouse. Talk to her. Will you go with me?"

Dad pushed himself up from the chair, wrapping Nick in a hug. "I'd like that, kid."


They descended the stairs, the five of them, Dad leading the way.

As they stepped off the stairs into the foyer, faces turned toward them from the living room. Parents. An aunt and uncle. Friends in Mateo and Chris. In Mary and Rodney Caplan. In the amazing Burrito Jerry, who, as his name suggested, was munching on a breakfast burrito, cheeks stuffed with cheesy eggs and potatoes.

Seth said, "Nick's got a new catchphrase he's been working on." He nudged Nick's shoulder. "Tell them. It's a pretty good one.

"Yeah, yeah," Nick said, distracted. "It's awesome. 'Let's fucking ruin Simon Burke's entire life.' That's it. Now, new point of order: Trey, you seem to be wearing a coat indoors in the middle of summer. Miles and Bob, too." He frowned. "And my dad. Why are you—"

Miles stood from his chair. "You call that a catchphrase? Bah. Kids these days. You think once you've saved the city a time or two, you know everything. You want to hear a *real* catchphrase? Watch and learn, children."

Nick blinked when Trey stood up, followed by Bob. Dad joined them in the center of the living room, motioning for Nick to take a step back. Muttering under his breath about parents who decide to steal the spotlight, Nick moved back with his friends, wondering what fresh hell was about to befall them.

It was both better and worse than he expected. Miles nodded at the other men, receiving three nods in response. And they showed why parents were the most embarrassing people in the history of anything ever.

Miles said, "We are the protectors."

Trey said, "We are the fighters."

Bob said, "We are strength."

Dad winked at Nick and said, "We are unstoppable."

Then, all as one, they turned away and said, "We are . . ."

They all unzipped their coats at the same time before spinning around and shouting, "*The Dad Squad!*"

Each of them wore a white shirt with glittering pink-and-red letters that spelled out DAD SQUAD. Underneath the words were pictures that looked as if they'd been ironed onto the shirts. On Miles, a young Jazz, her two front teeth missing. On Trey, a photo of Gibby, head half-shaved, Trey standing behind her, clippers in his hand. On Bob, Seth curled up in a chair, a book in his hands, glasses hanging off the tip of his nose. And Dad's had a picture of Nick as a toddler, chubby arms and dimpled knees, sitting in front of the television with a gigantic block of orange cheese between his legs. The cheese looked like it'd been gnawed on, Nick's cheeks puffed out, the picture capturing him midchew.

"Oh my god," Nick breathed. "Why? *Why?*"

"Because we could," Miles said.

"This is the daddest thing I've ever seen in my life," Mateo said, though his phone was raised toward them, recording it for posterity.

"Sweet threads," Burrito Jerry said, eyeing the men up and down. "I wore glitter once during Pride Week when I was driving people around. I got hit on by a guy who called himself Tank, and it made me question my sexuality. Figured out I'm a bit more fluid than I thought. Good guy, Tank."

They all turned slowly to look at him.

He shrugged. "Haven't really done much with it yet." He glanced at Mateo. "You're cute. What's up? You got a boyfriend?"

"He does," Chris said, sounding amused and horrified in equal measure. He dropped his hand on Mateo's leg pointedly.

"Cool, cool," Burrito Jerry said easily. "Congrats or whatever. Looks like Aaron and I are the only single people here. Whaddya say, my guy? Wanna see if there's any magic between us? I know the past few weeks have been difficult with the weird lady pretending to be someone she wasn't, so if you need time, I understand. I can wait."

"Sure," Dad said. "I bet Nick would like a new stepdad to— Nick. *Nick.* Would you stop screaming?"

Nick did not stop screaming until Seth clamped a hand over his mouth. Even then, he continued, though it was muffled, eyes bulging, horrible visions of a fall wedding between Dad and Burrito Jerry, both of them leaving in Matilda with cans on strings fixed to the back bumper. Suffice to say, Nick was not a fan.

Or was he? Nick *did* love burritos, and if Burrito Jerry got them for life, then wouldn't that mean Nick could partake? Wouldn't that be worth possibly considering the idea of Dad and Burrito Jerry . . . if they were, like . . .

Nope. Nope, nope, nope.

"You good?" Seth asked him, sounding like he was trying not to laugh. "Or do you need to scream some more?"

Nick nodded, showing he was good. As soon as Seth dropped his hand, Nick blurted, "If Burrito Jerry *ever* comes to our house, you guys have to keep the bedroom door open, you hear me? And I will count every plastic baggie in the damn house, so if any go missing, I'll know what you're doing and we'll have words! So many words!"

"Where would the plastic baggies go?" Burrito Jerry asked Martha, brow furrowed.

"Oh," she said. "I'm so glad you asked. It's really rather clever. When you perform—"

"Enemas!" Nick bellowed. "You have to have *enemas* to avoid fecal penis—"

"I might have made a mistake," Dad said, blood draining from his face.

"Nah," Miles said. "If we can't have fun watching Nick melt down over the idea of you and Burrito Jerry getting down to bidness, we're doing it wrong."

"Daddy," Jazz said with a pout, her bottom lick stuck out, princess eyes wide. "We talked about this. You can't say *bidness* because you're old and it's gross. You're embarrassing me in front of my friends."

Trey snorted. "Oh, please, Jasmine. As if we didn't talk to you and Gibby about—"

"Nothing!" Gibby cried. "He didn't talk to us about *anything that needs to be brought up right this second.*"

And not to be outdone, Nick exclaimed, "Don't listen to them! I know for a fact dads are liars because I have incontrovertible proof that Seth doesn't orgasm fire!"

Silence, only interrupted by Seth banging his head against the nearest wall over and over, each hit punctuated by the word *why*.

"Uh," Nick said hastily. "Ignore what I just said. Dad Squad! Hooray! I have notes."

All was right in the world.

The plan was this:

Mary, Jo, and Martha would head to the secret lair in the Gray brownstone, running comms, Martha in charge since she knew the programs almost as well as Gibby.

Burrito Jerry, Gibby, and Jazz would handle Mobile Lighthouse, the van outfitted with all the tech Gibby thought they'd need to see their operation through. Aysha would be there, ready to assist as needed. Jazz told Nick and Seth that she had the night-vision goggles stored in Matilda, just to be safe. "I'm disappointed in all of you that we haven't used them yet," she told them. "I didn't buy them to let them sit on a shelf." Mateo—now Miss Conduct with her sparkly leotard, blue curly wig, and bangles that only a queen of her caliber could pull off—would act as the first line of defense. Burrito Jerry said that if push came to shove, Matilda could get up to at *least* sixty miles an hour before she started shaking and groaning. This did not help as much as he seemed to think it did.

Chris was on duty that night, assigned with a contingent of cops to patrol the crowd in front of Burke Tower to help keep the peace. He showed them a memo that had come from the brass at the NCPD, stating that while they'd received no credible threats, they were all to be on guard.

Which left Seth, Nick, Cap, and the Dad Squad. They'd be in the Kensingtons' black SUV, a tank of a vehicle with three rows of seating in the back. They'd follow Matilda into the city, parking in a garage a few blocks away from Burke Tower, since the streets would be blocked off by cops. No vehicles, aside from those belonging to the police, would be permitted to pass through. After parking the SUV, they'd be on foot along with thousands of others.

Nick stepped away from the others at the Kensington house as Gibby outfitted the Dad Squad with buttons that read DAD POWER, each with a high-definition camera hidden inside for video and audio that would feed back to Matilda. Nick pulled out burner phones Bob had bought for each of them. Though Gibby had wiped all their phones, they couldn't be too careful in case Burke was still somehow tracking them. Their usual phones were all inside the house so *if* Burke had a bead on them, it would seem they were far away from Burke Tower. By the time he realized that wasn't the case, it'd already be too late, or so Nick hoped.

He sent a text to an unsaved number. We're ready. R u?

The reply only took seconds. Yes. It's where we discussed. Swipe, followed by the numeric code in the keypad next to the door.

Anything changed?

The reply took a little longer. Nick began to sweat, glaring at his phone. Finally, No. He doesn't know.

R u sure?

YES. I'M SURE. STOP ASKING QUESTIONS. YOU ONLY GET ONE SHOT AT THIS!!!!

"Hate you, too," Nick muttered. Then, just because he knew it'd piss Rebecca Firestone off, he sent back a dozen kissing emojis, followed by ten emojis flipping her off. He immediately felt better, imagining her outrage.

A hand fell on his shoulder. "All right?" Dad asked.

Nick nodded, shoving his phone back in his pocket. "She says she did what she promised."

"Do you trust her?"

"No," Nick said honestly. "But I believe her."

They went back to their family, and for a moment, no one spoke. They stood there, watching each other, eyes alight. Excited. Nervous. Proud. Determined. Gibby acted for all of them when she held out her hand, palm toward the ground. "Bring it in," she said. It was difficult—so many people crowding together—but they did as she told them, a sloppy pile of hands on top of hands. "Who are we?"

"Lighthouse!" everyone cried.

"And what are we gonna do?"

Everyone looked confused, unsure of what she wanted from them. *Almost* everyone, that is, because Dad chuckled and said, "We're going to fucking ruin Simon Burke's entire life."

"Hell yes," Nick breathed. "I *knew* it was an awesome catch-phrase. Suck on *that,* haters!"

"We are," Gibby agreed. "We're gonna show him why messing with our family was the worst mistake he ever made. You know your jobs. You know what's at stake. Watch each other's backs. Be safe. Be strong." She grinned at them. "And remember: *we* put the *extra* in *Extraordinary*. Let's do this."

They reached the parking garage, going up to the top level of the six-story structure. A few blocks away, Burke Tower rose high into the sky, the top lit up in red, white, and blue, and an oversized screen at the front of the tower displaying a waving American flag underneath the words IN BURKE WE TRUST! The sun was setting, painting the sky in fiery shades of red and orange.

The parking garage was full. People hurried toward the stairs and elevators, carrying brightly colored streamers and signs in support of Burke, kids with their faces painted with blue stars. A few glanced their way, but mostly because of the mural on the side of Matilda, some parents glaring at them, shielding their kids from the sight of a busty woman riding a seahorse. Not exactly inconspicuous, but Nova City was filled with such oddities, a melting pot of weirdos who did that and worse.

Dad stood in front of Miss Conduct, back to the others as she lifted her hands to Dad's face. She frowned before nodding and saying, "Done and done." Dad turned around, and Nick choked on his tongue.

Dad wore a large fake brown mustache and oversized mirror shades. He looked like a seventies porn star, something Nick immediately wished he could banish from his brain. He knew a disguise was necessary in case Dad's former colleagues recognized him, but there had to be a better way to go about it.

"Well?" Dad asked. "How do I look?"

"Like you want us to follow you into an alley so you can flash us," Nick said.

"Like you own sixteen birds with complicated backstories for each," Seth said.

"Like you're the bass player in a Christian punk band called Please Us, Jesus," Jazz said, leaning her head out of Matilda.

"Like you have red satin sheets on your bed and mirrors on the ceiling," Gibby said, her head just above Jazz's.

"Like you know how to show a guy a good time," Burrito Jerry said.

"They've got a point, man," Trey said as Bob nodded. "I feel like you want to give me a body-cavity search with gloves you brought from home."

Dad threw up his hands.

"Ignore them," Cap said grumpily as he climbed out of the SUV. "A mustache makes a man. Looks good, Aaron." He held out his fist, and Dad bumped it smugly.

"Mustache bros," he said.

"Ugh," Nick said, making a face. "If this is your version of a midlife crisis, we're gonna need to decide if I can be seen in public with you. I have a reputation to maintain."

"Riiight," Dad said, wiggling his mustache. "Keep telling yourself that, kid. Burrito Jerry likes it. That's enough for me. He's got good taste."

"I think I'm falling in love with you," Burrito Jerry said seriously.

Everyone crowded at the back of Matilda, trying to look nonchalant as they blocked the view of the interior so Seth could change into his Pyro Storm costume. Gibby helped him put on his helmet, the red lenses flashing as they came online. Gibby spun around, ducking to avoid hitting her head on the roof of the van, fingers flying over the keyboard, eyes fixed on the monitor in front of her. "Lighthouse, you copy?"

"We do," Martha said, voice crackling from the speakers. "We have your position locked thanks to the button pins. Signal strong and clear."

"Good work, Gibby," Trey said, his pride evident. "I don't know how you figured all this stuff out, but it's impressive."

Gibby preened, ducking her head as she smiled.

Miss Conduct leaned her head into the van. "You heard from Chris?"

"He's online, too," Martha said. "As of ten minutes ago he was working crowd control. He'll be at the entry point making sure you get in without any trouble."

Chris's voice filled the back of the van, his voice a low mutter as if trying to not be overheard. "How long until you get here? Need to make sure I'm there. I—hold on." He raised his voice. "I'm heading over to help get people in. Tell the sergeant in case she asks." Then, lowering his voice once more, "You guys gotta hurry. What's your ETA?"

"Fifteen minutes," Dad said.

"Got it. Make sure you get in my line. We're checking purses and bags. I'll get you through."

"Will do," Nick said, turning around and hurrying back to the SUV, pulling his heavy backpack out before shutting the door. When he turned around, Pyro Storm stood at the edge of the parking garage, hands on the stone barrier in front of him. He bent over, scanning the streets and the throngs of people moving toward Burke Tower. Nick left him to it, going back to Matilda. Jazz sat on the left side of the van, hunched over, staring at the two monitors in front of her. Gibby worked furiously on her own setup, muttering under her breath.

"Jazz, you reading this?" Pyro Storm asked. On Jazz's screens, the view from Pyro Storm's helmet zoomed in, scanning over the faces in the crowd.

"Yep," she said. "When you head to the tower, keep your head pointed down toward the street. If Owen's out there somewhere, we'll find him."

"And the other stuff?" he asked.

"Working on it," Gibby said without looking away from her own screens. "I'll be ready." She shook her head. "As if that fire-wall can keep me out. Amateurs."

"Good," Pyro Storm said, and Nick peered over the side of Matilda to see him squaring his shoulders. "I'll head out."

"Wait," Nick called, shouldering his backpack and hurrying toward him. Pyro Storm turned, and Nick cupped the sides of his helmet, already feeling the heat emanating from him. He pressed his forehead against the helmet, blinking against the brightness of the lenses. "Be careful," Nick whispered.

"I will," Pyro Storm promised. "You, too. If you need me, let me know. I don't care if it ruins everything else. Live to fight another day."

"I know."

Pyro Storm nodded, stepping back from Nick. "Good to go?"

"Wait," Dad said as another group of people walked by. "Hold. Hold. Okay. Go. Now."

"Hey, Nick?"

"Yeah?"

Pyro Storm said, "It's time to burn." And then in flash of fire, he rocketed upward, faster than Nick had ever seen him fly before. Within seconds, he was a dot in the sky, high above Nova City.

Circling back to the open doors of Matilda, Nick looked in and said, "You guys good?"

"Don't you worry," Miss Conduct said, the stench of fried ozone around her as she lifted her hand, tiny arcs of electricity crawling along her fingers. "No one touches our girls while I'm around."

"Go," Gibby said, glancing at Nick. "We'll be your eyes and ears but watch your back."

"I'll just sit here being the best I can be," Burrito Jerry said. "Jasmine said she might even let me use the night-vision goggles. Can you imagine? Seeing in the dark! What will they think of next?"

"Uh, sure," Nick said. "You do you, Burrito Jerry."

He stepped back to allow Miles and Trey a chance to say goodbye to their daughters.

Once finished they joined Nick, Dad, Cap, and Bob.

"Daddy?" Jazz said, leaning her head out of the van.

"Yes, my love?" Miles said.

"You got this. Dad Squad."

He grinned at her. "Dad Squad." When he looked back at the others, he was determined. "Let's go."

They joined the massive crowd moving toward Burke Tower, sticking together as best they could. Nick kept his head ducked low, surrounded by the adults—Cap in front of him, Bob to his left, Miles to his right, Trey and Dad bringing up the rear. Dad kept his hands on Nick's shoulders, guiding him forward so Nick didn't have to raise his head.

The closer they got to Burke Tower, the louder it became. Music blasted from somewhere, the sound cacophonous, bouncing off the sides of the high-rises around them. Between that and the noise from all those moving around them, it should've been horribly distracting, but Nick thought this was like being trapped in his own head, an overloading of his senses. He'd had years to get used to it and was able to block out the worst of it, focusing on putting one foot in front of the other, keeping his breaths even, calm.

They passed by cops in tactical gear lining the sidewalks, white lettering across the front: NCPD.

"Hold up," Dad whispered. "Left. The third line. Chris is already there."

They shoved their way to the left. A dozen lines all told, moving fast, cops and security making quick work of going through purses and backpacks. Rows of metal fences gleamed in the sinking summer sun.

Sweat dripped down the back of Nick's neck as they got closer to the front, shuffling forward, then stopping. Forward, then stopping. By the time they reached the front, he was soaked, his shirt sticky with sweat, backpack heavy.

"Cap," one of the cops said as they reached the front of the line, sounding surprised. "What are you doing here?"

"Celebrating with friends," Cap said easily. "Collins, was it?"

The cop nodded, pleased. "Yessir."

"Good. You're holding up the line, Collins. Get us through so these good people can enjoy the fireworks."

"Yessir," Collins said. Cap didn't have a bag to check, and Collins waved him through, sweat dripping down the side of his face.

"Where's Chris?" Nick hissed, panic bubbling underneath his skin.

"I don't know," Dad muttered. "He was here. Can't see him."

Miles went next. Then Bob. Then Trey, who looked back at them when finished, eyes wide.

"Next," Collins said, looking at Nick. "I'll need to check your bag."

Nick froze, Dad's finger digging into his shoulders.

"You," Collins said, sounding aggravated as he pointed at Nick. "Come on. Keep moving."

"Shit," Nick whispered. "Shit, shit—"

"I got this," Chris said, appearing out of nowhere. He was in uniform, his duty belt cinched tight around his waist. "Take a break, Collins. You've earned it."

Collins looked surprised. "Morton? What are you doing here? I thought you were assigned to crowd control."

"Helping out," Chris said, and if he was nervous, Nick couldn't tell. "Don't want to you to collapse in this heat. Go hydrate. I'll cover for you."

Nick held his breath.

Collins said, "Hey, thanks. I appreciate it." He looked back at Nick and Dad, gaze lingering for a moment before shaking his head. "Officer Morton will take care of you folks. Have a great night!" He spun on his heels and disappeared into the crowd.

Nick exhaled explosively, knees weak. Too close.

Chris beckoned them forward, and it was only then Nick saw his hands were shaking. Dad pushed Nick toward him. "Backpack, please," Chris said, loud enough for the others in line to hear him. Nick handed it over, standing next to the cheap, cracked folding table Chris had put the backpack on. "Anyone watching?" he asked out of the corner of his mouth.

Nick glanced from side to side. "No."

Chris unzipped the backpack, but only halfway. Nick caught a flash of cerulean blue as Chris shoved his hand inside. A moment later, he pulled it out, zipping the backpack back up before looking in the smaller, remaining pockets. When finished, he handed the backpack to Nick. "Thanks. You're good to go." Nick started to move past him when Chris's hand pressed against his. Tiny plastic objects dug into Nick's skin as he closed his hand. "Already online," Chris muttered as he waved the next people forward.

Nick walked toward where Cap, Trey, Bob, and Miles were waiting for them, just inside the fencing. Waiting for Dad, Nick pulled out what Chris had given him, glancing down. Six earpieces, a little red light blinking at the top of each. He gave one to each of the others, who put them in their ears.

"That was close," Dad muttered, taking an earpiece from Nick, putting it in his ear. "Mobile Lighthouse, you copy?"

"Loud and clear," Gibby said, voice tinny. "You inside?"

"We are," Nick said. Dad gripped him by the elbow, leading him away from the lines of people streaming in. "Any sign of Owen?"

"Nothing yet," Pyro Storm said.

Nick turned his face upward. Burke Tower loomed ominously above them. "Where are you?"

"On the roof. Found the keycard Firestone left. She's sure this won't set off any alarms?"

"That's what she said. They've had issues with the door. Wind sets off the alarm. Faulty wiring, so they turned it off until it could get fixed. She deleted the request before the head of security could approve it."

"Let me try, just to make sure."

"Not yet," Gibby said sharply. "I'm not in the security system. It's . . . hold on."

"Gibby," Nick ground out. "We don't have time for—"

"Shut up," Gibby snapped. "We're working as fast as we can. It's more complicated than it looks. Jazz, I need you to . . . yep. There you go. Open that one. What do you—*yes*. Pyro Storm, we're in. I've got the security grid pulled up for Burke Tower."

"Copy," Pyro Storm said. "Trying the door."

"Oh man," Trey breathed. "Now I know why heist movies are always so tense. I feel sick."

"We're fine," Cap said, wiping sweat from his brow with the back of his arm. "If the alarms go off, he can get out of there and we'll figure something else out."

"It works," Pyro Storm said a moment later. "Keycard. Code to the door. It's open. Gibby?"

"You didn't trip an alarm," Gibby said breathlessly. "You're good."

Bob sagged, shaking his head as Miles patted his back. "This probably isn't helping my blood pressure."

"Come on," Miles said, jerking his head toward Burke Tower. "We need to get closer before it starts."

"Allow me," Cap said, squaring his shoulders. He marched down the street, people moving out of his way. The others followed in his wake, the crowd expanding then collapsing behind them.

The closer they got to Burke Tower, the harder it was to push their way through the throngs of people. Most were clad in some form of Burke swag: white hats with his name in red lettering across the fronts, shirts with his face on them. Signs that proclaimed him to be the savior of Nova City, along with anti-Extraordinary sentiments. Nick even saw crude drawings of Pyro Storm, face crossed out with a black X. One was carried by a kid who couldn't have been more than nine or ten years old. In the distance, above the din around them, the sounds of protestors shouting as one, voices carrying: "*NO JUSTICE. NO PEACE. NO JUSTICE. NO PEACE.*"

"This is a powder keg," Miles muttered. "I sure hope we know what we're doing."

"We do," Nick told him. "Focus. Stick to the plan."

A huge stage had been constructed in front of Burke Tower. Banners in patriotic colors hung from the front of the stage. Three massive screens—two on thick metal posts on either side of the stage, and the biggest one above it, hanging above the entrance. The stage itself was lined with chairs, a dozen in all, behind a podium stacked with microphones. In front of the stage, a line of men and women, all wearing black pants and collared shirts, yellow lettering across the front proclaiming them to be SECURITY. They stood at parade rest, their hands folded behind their backs. In front of them, metal barriers four feet high.

"Can't see it," Jazz said in his ear when he asked.

"Hold on," Nick said. He unfastened the button on his chest and lifted it as high as he could, pointing it toward the stage. "That work?"

"Got it," Jazz said. "Turn it left. Your other left, Nick. There. We're good. Can you get closer?"

"We can try," Cap said. "But we don't want to be right at the front in case someone sees us."

"On it," Bob said. "Miles, Trey, and I can do it. Cap, stay with Aaron. We'll get Nick as close as we can."

"No," Dad said, shaking his head. "We stick together. I don't want—"

"Dad."

He looked at Nick, worry clear on his face.

Trey said, "We'll watch over him."

Nick touched the back of his hand.

He gave Nick a quick hug. "Go."

The crowd began to roar. Nick whirled around, looking at the stage. People were beginning to file on, people in suits and dresses. The interim police chief in dress blues, service cap pushed back on his head. Others Nick vaguely recognized. One man caught Nick's attention. His black suit coat hugged his large frame, tie cinched tightly at his throat. Head shaved.

Anthony. Burke's driver and bodyguard, the one who'd stopped Nick on the street last spring, forcing him into a limousine where

Burke lay waiting. He jumped off the front of the stage, going to one of the security guards, tapping him on the shoulder and whispering in his ear. The security guard nodded and said something back.

Miles grabbed Nick by the elbow. "We need to hurry. Excuse me. Pardon me. So sorry. It's my kid's dream to get as close as he can. Loves politics and fireworks. You know how it is. Ah, thank you. So kind."

Nick looked back, Trey and Bob crowding behind him. He couldn't see Cap or Dad anymore. It was as if they'd been swallowed whole.

They were still at least ten feet away from the barriers when Miles came to a stop. No matter how hard he tried, he couldn't get anyone else to move.

The multiple speakers around the stage flared to life, blaring music as the three screens lit up. The crowd cheered, hands above their heads. The screens flashed with images. Nova City, seen from above, a slow, panning shot that looked as if it had been taken from a drone. People walking the streets. Construction workers with yellow hard hats, laughing and shoving each other. A teacher in a classroom, students watching her as her mouth moved silently behind the swell of music. Parents with their kids between them, all smiling at the camera.

"Simon Burke believes in this city," a narrator said over the images. "He was born here. Raised here. The blood of Nova City runs through his veins."

The screen changed, showing a white woman with red frizzy hair sitting in a park on a blanket. "Why am I voting for Simon Burke?" she asked, perfect teeth flashing as she grinned. "That's easy. Because I know he's a family man."

She disappeared, replaced by an Asian man with chubby cheeks who stood behind the counter in a bodega. "Because he understands the value of small businesses."

A Black man, working in a factory, sparks flying behind him as he stood awkwardly, hands twitching, his smile more a grimace. "Because he'll protect the working class."

And then the screen changed again, and Simon Burke appeared, standing in front of a group of people, hands animated as he spoke to them, looking loose, relaxed. Whatever he said was muted, the voice-over saying, "Simon Burke knows what it means to struggle. He knows hardship. But instead of blaming others, he accepts responsibility and strives to be better. And that is the core of his mission: to make Nova City a better place for everyone, no matter where they come from."

"Bullshit," Trey said under his breath, eyes narrowed as he glared at the screens.

The screens changed once more, this time showing Burke sitting in his immaculate office, scribbling his signature on a piece of paper. He looked up at the camera and smiled. "My name is Simon Burke, and I approve this message."

His image faded, replaced by white lettering exclaiming IN BURKE WE TRUST!

The crowd picked it up, beginning to chant over and over with an almost religious fervor.

*"IN BURKE WE TRUST!*

*"IN BURKE WE TRUST!"*

The chants dissolved into cheers as another figure walked onto the stage, waving both her hands at the crowd. She wore a sharp pinstriped suit tailored to her frame, a red tie, and black pumps, her blond hair pulled back into a tight ponytail. She looked out onto the masses before her, and for a moment, Nick thought she saw him, a brief pause before her gaze swept away over everyone else. When she reached the podium, the screens changed again, showing her from different angles.

"How the hell are ya, Nova City?" Rebecca Firestone asked, voice carrying over the crowd. "Are you ready for a night you won't forget?"

They were, if their answering cries were any indication.

"My name is Rebecca Firestone, and it is my great pleasure to stand before you tonight," she said. "In a moment, the man we're all here to see will arrive. His critics will scream at the top of their lungs that he's just another rich man who's only in it for himself and his wealthy friends. That he doesn't care about the middle class, or those who have found themselves in the grips of poverty. That, my friends, couldn't be further from the truth. Simon Burke is a man of the people, one who knows what it's like to overcome adversity . . ."

"Man," Trey whispered in Nick's ear. "I hope to hell you're right about her. She's not doing herself any favors."

"Wait," Nick whispered back, though a trickle of alarm ran down his spine.

". . . and who has never let his detractors drown out his message of unity." She smiled widely. "Simon Burke is here for you. He will always be here for you, whenever you need him. And on today of all days, Independence Day, a message: Simon Burke *will* win!"

The crowed exploded once more.

"Ladies and gentlemen, citizens of Nova City, join me in welcoming the man of the hour . . . Simon *Burke*!"

Chaos. Chaos and noise, a storm of reverence and adulation that threatened to overwhelm Nick. He blocked it out as best he could, vision shrinking to a pinpoint, fixed firmly on Simon Burke, who jogged up the steps to the stage, waving his hands as confetti shot from cannons, brightly colored slips of paper spinning through the air. Rebecca Firestone shook his hand, Burke pulling her close, kissing her cheek. She nodded at whatever he said and smiled, though it didn't reach her eyes.

The crowd continued on and on, a wall of noise that never seemed to end as Burke approached the podium. He wore jeans and a red polo shirt, buttoned all the way up to his throat. (A crime.)

"It's starting," he said, cupping his ear. "Are we ready?"

"Getting there," Gibby said, sounding harried. "How long into the speech?"

"Three minutes. When he starts talking about Extraordinaries registration, it's on."

"We'll be ready," Jazz said, though she, too, sounded nervous. "Martha? How are we doing?"

"Sending it to you now," Martha said, all business.

"Got it," Gibby said. "Crap, this is . . . complicated."

Another voice came on the line. Aysha said, "You can do it, Lola. Take a breath. Let it out. Clear your head."

"Pyro Storm?" Nick asked as Burke grinned, his face on the screens behind him.

"Moving," Pyro Storm grunted in his ear. "Seventy-second floor, right?"

"Yes," Nick said. "That's where he's put his new office." He looked up the side of the building, a wave of vertigo washing over him. "You have time. Take it slow."

"On it. Nick, get ready."

Without hesitation, Miles and Bob and Trey surrounded Nick. "Mind if I borrow that?" Trey asked the man standing next to him. "Want to get in on the action."

"Sure," the man said with a shrug. "Knock yourself out. So long as I get it back." He handed over a large cardboard sign reading BURKE FOR MAYOR! Trey lowered it in front of him, blocking the sight line between his legs.

As Nick kneeled down, sliding his backpack off and setting it on the ground in front of him, Burke began to speak. "My friends, it is my honor to stand before you today."

Nick unzipped the backpack.

"Much has been made of the past year, the trials and tribulations we have all faced. It never seems to get any easier, does it?"

Nick lifted his helmet out of the backpack reverently, setting it on the ground next to him.

"And I'll admit something to you, something that I've never said to anyone before. I've had doubts. After all, I am just one man. A man with a vision, yes, but greater men than I have had vision, only to fail."

The costume next, cerulean, with white lines.

"But I promise you, I will *not* fail."

Chucks off.

"I see a world where we are free. Where we are safe."

He rose, sliding the costume up and over his shoulders. Bulky from his shorts and shirt.

"Extraordinaries," Simon Burke said, leaning toward the microphone. "Those who think they're better than us simply because of genetic aberrations. I'm here to tell you enough is enough. We will *not* be silenced. We will *not* cower in fear."

Nick looked to the stage and saw Rebecca Firestone staring directly at him from where she sat behind Burke, off to his left. When she saw she'd gotten Nick's attention, she put her hand on her thigh, fingers spread wide.

Five.

"We will meet the Extraordinary menace head-on."

Rebecca Firestone folded her thumb against her palm. Four.

"We will never falter."

Three.

"We will stand tall and brave in the face of those who would try and take away our lives and liberties."

Two.

"You deserve to know who hides behind the masks of those who call themselves heroes."

One.

"On today of all days, one where we celebrate our God-given rights as a free people, it is my pleasure to announce the Extraordinaires Registration Act, a comprehensive piece of legislation that will—"

Rebecca Firestone—face splotchy, eyes wide—closed her fist. Zero.

Nick turned his head upward to see a figure skating down the side of Burke Tower, hurtling toward the stage, the glass of the windows cracking under their feet. It was one thing to be told what was coming, but it was something else entirely to see it for himself.

Guardian. His same costume, down to the smallest of details. Anger burst in Nick's chest, a sense of violation coursing through him. It was his mother's. It was *his*. How dare they.

Burke said, "And I promise you. This act *will* pass. We will know every single Extraordinary, no matter where they go, no matter where they try to hide, we'll find them and—"

A woman off to Nick's left screamed. The people around her lifted their heads and began to shout along with her.

Burke faltered, whirling around, looking up to where people were pointing. Still ten stories up, the figure leapt off the side of the building, flipping forward, arms spread wide. Anthony barked an order as he hoisted himself up onto the stage, going for Burke, who stumbled backward, but not before Nick saw the quick flash of a triumphant smile.

The false Guardian hit the stage, causing it to creak and groan as they rose slowly to their feet.

Burke grabbed a microphone from the podium, jerking it free from its stand, feedback squealing as Anthony tried to pull him back. "See?" Burke hissed into the microphone. "*See?* Even now, they won't let us be. Do not be frightened. You want to know the truth? Let me be the one to tell it to you. This? This is *nothing* because this is a *child*. Show yourself, you coward. Tell everyone who you really are before I do it for you."

The crowd stopped moving, stopped shoving, stopped screaming.

The figure on the stage cocked their head.

"Fine," Burke snarled into the microphone. "It's time to end this charade. The world is watching, and you will not intimidate me, *Nicholas Bell*."

The figure lowered their head, hands coming up to the sides of their helmet. They lifted it off, and there, standing on the stage, teeth bared, was Nick. The hair. The face. All of it. It was like looking in a fractured mirror.

And he was *smiling*.

"Holy shit," Trey breathed.

"That's right," Burke said. "Just as Pyro Storm was revealed to be a mere boy, the same is true about the one who calls himself Guardian. This is who they lift up? This is who they expect to save them?"

"Get *down*," Nick snarled, and without hesitating, Trey, Bob, and Miles dropped to their knees. Fake Nick raised his hand toward Burke, and cops drew their weapons, shouting, Anthony thrown to the side, Burke raising his hands as if in fear, but the real Nick was already moving. He crouched low, and with all his might, shot up, feet leaving the ground, the air underneath him pushing him up and up and up until he was above the crowd. Picturing large, flat stones in his head, Nick leapt forward, the bottoms of his boots finding solid air, jumping from one to the next to the next. The people on the stage scattered as he landed right behind his doppelganger. Simon Burke's eyes bulged from his head, and Fake Nick whirled around.

"Hey," Nick said. "Got something for ya." The doppelgänger had no time to react when Nick swung his helmet out in flat arc, smashing it into the side of the liar's head. Fake Nick stumbled, almost falling to his knees as a dazed expression settled on his face. "And *that's* called kicking your own ass!"

"Don't piss them off," Gibby warned in his ear. "Stick to the plan, Nick. Get them—"

Fake Nick moved swiftly—near silent—feet barely touching the stage as he shot toward Nick. Nick dropped his helmet and sidestepped, grabbing Fake Nick by the wrist, using momentum against him. He jerked his arm as hard as he could, flinging Fake Nick toward Anthony who was rising to his feet. Fake Nick crashed into him, knocking them both down, Anthony's legs dangling off the side of the stage as he blinked up toward the darkened sky, face awash with light from the screens above him.

"Don't," Nick warned when Fake Nick immediately started pushing himself up once more. "Stay down before I put you down again."

Fake Nick grinned. "Let's see how it plays out, yeah? It's time to take out the garbage."

Nick had barely had time to steel himself when Fake Nick tackled him, sending them crashing to the stage, wood and metal groaning under the impact. They rolled over once, twice, three times, and then Fake Nick was on top of him, knees pinning his arms to the side, hands wrapped around his throat and *squeezing*. Fake Nick raised his hips as he glared down at Nick, leaning forward, faces inches apart.

"You should've stayed away," Fake Nick whispered.

"Fake-ass bitch," Nick managed to choke out. "Didn't think this through, did you? Because if you look like me, then you probably got the junk, too. Sucks to be you."

Fake Nick blinked. "What are you—"

Nick kneed him in the balls as hard as he could. Fake Nick opened his mouth in a soundless shriek, cords on his neck jutting out. Nick didn't wait for him to recover, pressing his hands against Fake Nick's chest. Instead of pushing with his hands, he pushed with his mind, the spark growing larger, the edges rippling as if alive. The air between him and Fake Nick stuttered as it expanded, a balloon being filled with helium. Fake Nick flew back, sliding along the stage, coming to a stop at Simon Burke's feet.

Nick jumped to his feet, chest heaving, throat sore. He spat onto the stage as he rubbed his jaw. "That all you got? No other powers to use? What about the smoke? The ice? The *water*? Man, this is disappointing."

Fake Nick pushed himself up. Nick prepared for another attack and was stunned when Fake Nick turned toward the crowd, looking panicked. "Help me!" he cried. "That thing isn't me! I'm the real Nick!"

Nick snorted. "Oh, bullshit. Like people are going to fall for that. They're not that stupid."

Apparently they were, because every single cop turned toward Nick.

"Uh," Nick said, taking a step back. "Hold up a second. *I'm* the real Nick."

"Don't listen to him!" Fake Nick snapped. "He's trying to get inside your heads." He looked out into the crowd. "Dad! Where are you? I need you!"

"What! That's *my* dad, you asshole. You don't get to—"

Movement, in the crowd, as Dad and Cap, followed by Trey and Bob and Miles, reached the metal barriers, a cop turning around and pointing his gun toward them. Cap reached out and disarmed the cop neatly, ejecting the magazine and unchambering the last bullet before handing the gun back. "If you're going to point that thing at someone, you better know how to use it," Cap said sternly. "Otherwise, you're an idiot with a gun."

Dad gripped the barrier, knuckles white as he looked up at the stage. Before Nick could say anything to him, Fake Nick appeared at his side, face streaked with tears. "Dad," he said, voice breaking. "It's me. You have to believe me."

Nick shoved him hard. "Are you out of your damn mind? Like I'd *ever* cry in front of thousands of people. I'd save that for the safety of my bedroom like a normal teenager who still struggles with showing emotion in front of strangers!"

Fake Nick reached a trembling hand toward Dad. "Please. Help me. Don't let him hurt me anymore."

"Shit," Trey breathed. "I can't tell which is which."

"Are you *kidding* me?" Nick demanded. "I'm literally standing right in front of you!"

"Me, too!" Fake Nick said. "I'm standing right here!"

"What's happening?" Nick heard one of the cops ask.

"I have no idea," another cop replied. "You think we're still going to get overtime for this?"

"We better," the first cop muttered. "If not, I'm going to report this to my union rep."

"Aaron?" Miles asked. "Who's the right one?"

Dad looked between the two Nicks before him. "I . . ."

"Dad," Nick and Fake Nick said at the same time, one pleading, the other irritated beyond belief.

"I love you," Fake Nick said. "You and me, remember? We stand together so we don't struggle—"

"If you say *one more word*," Nick snarled, "I'm going to make you eat your stupid *tongue*."

Dad grinned, bright and fierce. "Nicky, *no*."

Fake Nick frowned. "What? What do you mean *no*? Why won't you—"

"Nicky, *yes*!" Nick crowed and let his fist fly. When it came down to it, it wasn't the best punch ever thrown. But the punch didn't need to be perfect, because surrounding his fist was a wall of air that slammed into Fake Nick, lifting him off the ground. Before he fell and hit the stage, Nick closed his fist, causing Fake Nick to hang suspended, feet kicking into nothing.

"Stay there," Nick said. "Or get out of it by using your other powers. Show everyone what you can *really* do. No? Nothing? Huh." He went to the podium, glancing back at Simon Burke, who stood near the edge of the stage, face red with fury. When he looked back out onto the crowd watching them with no small amount of wonder, Nick realized now wasn't exactly the best time to remember his terrifying fear of public speaking. Thousands of faces looked at him, tracking his every move. "I've had dreams like this," Nick blurted into the microphones, voice carrying and bouncing off the buildings towering around them. "Usually I'm naked and have forgotten to do my homework—"

"Nick, *focus*," Jazz hissed in his ear. "We only get one shot at this!"

"Right, right," Nick said hastily. He gripped the edges of the podium. "You want to talk, Simon Burke? Let's talk. Because that dude floating in air? That's not the real Guardian." He looked down at Dad, who nodded encouragingly. With part of his family standing below him, and the rest listening in, he said, "My name is Nicholas Bell."

"Give it to 'em, Nicky," Pyro Storm—*Seth*—whispered in his ear.

"And like my mother before me, I'm the Extraordinary known as Guardian. The *real* Guardian. I'm not here to harm anyone. Well, except for the person trying to imitate me, but that's a long story. We won't hurt you. Your kids. Your friends. Hell, not even Simon Burke. Are there douchebag Extraordinaries? Hell yes.

But there are good ones, too." He frowned. "Ew, forget I just said that. That was the same as the cop argument of a *few bad apples*. Yuck. Where was I? Right. We're not monsters. We're not evil. We're *you*." He took a deep breath. "But we're not the solution to every problem this city faces. We can't be. But we can be part of the conversation about what change should look like, same with everyone here. It'll take all of us to do that, though. It's going to be a lot of work, but I have faith we can do it if we join together. Who's with me?"

He didn't know where it started. While he wasn't exactly expecting applause, he certainly didn't think people would start to *boo* him. But that's exactly what they did, the sound growing louder and louder.

"Oh, come on!" Nick cried into the microphones. "I just bared my soul to you and you're *booing* me?!"

Someone chuckled darkly, and Nick turned his head to see Simon Burke lifting his microphone to his lips. "You tried, boy. But they see you for what you are."

"He's goading you," Gibby snapped in his ear. "Don't fall for it."

"Look at him," Simon Burke said, stepping forward, once more in control. He ignored Fake Nick still hanging safely in the air. "This is who you're asked to put your faith in? He's a child, and a dangerous one at that. There can be no unity when people like him exist."

"Perhaps you could be the one to help me with that." Summoning Jazz's powers, Nick made his eyes go as big as they could go. Not quite Disney-princess levels, but close. "I *am* just a kid. I have so much to learn. Why don't we go inside and you can teach me about how to be a better person?" He nodded toward the booing crowd. "I'm sure they'd appreciate you taking the time to set me on the right path. In the name of unity and all."

The boos dissolved, replaced by loud cheers. "Help him!" someone shouted from the crowd. "Show him the error of his ways!"

Burke smiled his politician's smile—smarmy, condescending. And knowing. "Yes. Let's talk, you and I." He looked down at the crowd. "And let's invite your father, shall we? And Miles Kensington. Trey Gibson. And who is that? Bob Gray? The uncle to Seth Gray, also known as Pyro Storm? You, too, my good man. I'm sure we have much to discuss." He frowned. "And where is Rodney Caplan? He seems to have disappeared."

Burke was right. Cap had melted back into the crowd, but Nick knew where he was going. He gripped the podium tightly. Knowing he needed to sell this as best he could, his voice wavered when he said, "Leave them out of this."

He flinched when Burke joined him at the podium. He held the microphone down at his side as he leaned over and whispered in Nick's ear. "You are the one who brought them here. Whatever happens next, remember: this is on you." Then, without missing a beat, he brought the microphone back up to his mouth. "Officers, we're all right. Stand down. It would seem I'm needed at the moment. Anthony, let's invite our guests inside."

Anthony leapt down from the stage, knocking the barrier aside, grabbing Dad, other security guards going for Miles, Trey, and Bob. They came willingly enough and no one tried to stop them from being taken. They just stood there, letting it happen, all eyes on Burke as he moved toward Nick and the podium, phones still raised, recording every second.

"My apologies for this unfortunate interruption," Burke said, smiling warmly. "Please enjoy the fireworks, I'll be back shortly." He set the microphone on the podium and grabbed Nick by the elbow.

But before Nick could be dragged away he leaned forward, knowing he'd never get the chance again to have this many people listening to him. "Queer rights!" he shouted. "Down with the patriarchy! Defund the police! Support fanfic writers!"

Burke jerked Nick away from the podium, pulling him toward the stairs. Nick dug in his heels. "Forgetting something?"

Burke narrowed his eyes. "What?"

Nick grinned at him. "Your wife, who I kicked in the nuts."

In his head, he loosened his grip on the spark. Fake Nick crashed to the stage on his knees. He lifted his head slowly, mouth twisted in a snarl.

"There," Nick said innocently.

He expected Burke to be furious. His hold on Nick tightened hard enough to leave bruises, but the smile on his face was somehow worse than any anger could be. It made Nick's skin crawl. Burke marched them across the stage, only stopping so he could kick Nick's helmet toward Rebecca Firestone, who stood wringing her hands near the steps. "Bring that with us," he ordered. "I'm sure I'll find a use for it." He escorted Nick down the steps, where three security guards waited for him with the interim police chief, a wisp of a man with enormous eyebrows and a pale face.

The chief cleared his throat. "Mr. Burke, perhaps we should let the NCPD handle this from here. I'm sure we can—"

"You'll do what I tell you to," Burke said coldly. "No interruptions, you hear me? I will see to this myself."

The man winced. "I don't think—"

"I don't pay you to think. I pay you to do what I say when I say it."

Nick nodded sagely. "Bribing the police chief. Got it." He raised his hands when they looked at him. "Don't mind me. Just taking notes. Some feedback, though, Chief. You're not half the man Cap is and it shows, you spineless coward."

"Get on the stage, Chief," Burke growled. "Give the speech of your goddamn life and trust me when I say I have eyes and ears in places you can't even begin to imagine. I'll know every word you say."

"That certainly sounded ominous," Nick said. "Threatening the chief of police. Man, you're really going all out, aren't you? *Very* interesting. I wonder what everyone else would think of that?"

"No one gets in," Burke said to one of the security guards. "And search the crowd. There will be others. You have their pictures. Find them. Detain them."

The security guard nodded. "Understood, sir."

"Anthony," Burke said. "Let's bring our guests inside, shall we? The moment any of them act out, you have my permission to deal with the offender as you see fit."

Anthony popped his knuckles. "Got it, boss."

"We're in," Gibby whispered through the mic in Nick's ear as he was shoved toward the waiting doors of Burke Tower. "Pyro Storm is ready. Cap is heading to Matilda. Watch your back, Nicky. This is almost over."

In that, she was wrong.

# 17

The ground floor of Burke Tower was eerily vacant, the security desk empty, the screens on the wall lit up with the words WELCOME TO BURKE TOWER. The sounds of their footsteps against the stone floor echoed dully around them. Lights from the event outside cast the floors and walls in an ethereal glow, shadows shifting as if alive. The last time Nick had been here, it'd been with Owen and his promises of turning Nick into an Extraordinary. It was hard to believe that had been less than a year ago.

Burke slapped a small plastic card against the panel next to the automated gate. The panel lit up green and beeped, the gate swinging open.

Instead of leading him down the long hallway toward the office where Owen had once showed Nick a secret passage to a basement floor, Burke shoved Nick toward the bank of elevators, pushing the button next to one of the doors. An up arrow blinked in white.

"Going up?" Nick asked. "Why not just go to your office down here? You remember the one. It wasn't decorated in the way *I'd* do it—too masculine for me—but you do you, boo."

Burke chuckled. "You like to talk, don't you?"

"I do," Nick said. "It's my gift. Or my curse. Jury's still out."

"Anthony," Burke said as the elevator doors opened, "if he shoots his mouth off again, or if there's even a *hint* of him trying to use his powers, put a bullet in his father's kneecap. I'm sure that'll get his attention."

Nick whirled around and saw Anthony with a small black

pistol in his hand, the barrel digging into Dad's side. "With plea-sure," Anthony said.

Nick's mouth snapped closed.

"So you *can* be trained," Burke said, lips quirking. "Good to know. Though, I suppose if I were you, I'd probably want to avoid losing yet another parent. You only have one of those left, as it turns out."

"I do," Nick said evenly, fighting against the wave of rage flooding through him. This wasn't about revenge, but holy shit, it could be. "And he has me. Where's *your* son, Burke? Talked to him lately?" He glanced back at Fake Nick, bringing up the rear with Rebecca Firestone, expression unreadable. "Hate to think you and your wife haven't been able to make amends."

"We'll find him," Burke said, pushing Nick into the elevator. "And either he'll see the error of his ways, or he won't. Frankly, it doesn't matter to me either way. A guard dog is only good until it bites its owner. After that, they have the taste for blood, and the humane thing to do is to put them down."

"Maybe consider therapy instead," Nick said as the others crowded into the elevator.

Burke sighed as if disappointed. Then his brow furrowed. Nick tried not to flinch when Burke gripped his chin, turning his head to the side. "What's this?" He plucked the mic from Nick's ear. He studied it for a moment before dropping it to the floor and stepping on it. "Anthony, check the others."

He made quick work of it as Burke pushed the button for the seventy-second floor. Once he'd taken all four ear mics from the others, Anthony crushed them in his hand, turning his palm over and letting the remains fall to the floor.

"Someone has to clean that up," Nick said mildly. "You should probably be a little more considerate of the cleaning staff."

The elevator doors slid shut, and the car began to rise, a cool, feminine voice counting off the floor numbers.

It was crowded inside the elevator. Burke. Nick. Dad. Miles, Trey, and Bob. Rebecca Firestone. Anthony. Three goons in suits. And Patricia Burke, still wearing Nick's face, mouth stretched wide. Fake Nick winked at Nick, and then his face began to bulge as if something had burrowed its way underneath. It happened so quickly, he had to blink to be sure what he was seeing.

Fake Nick was gone.

In his place, Jennifer Bell, still wearing the Guardian costume.

"Hey, kid," she cooed. "It's so nice to see you again. I've missed you. Have you missed me?" She reached for him as Rebecca Firestone looked away, her lips a thin, bloodless line, the Guardian helmet clutched against her chest. Nick didn't move a muscle as Patricia/Jennifer stroked his cheek, her fingernails scraping against his skin. "Maybe when we're done here, I can convince Simon to let you go. You won't remember much of anything—your friends, your family, your name. Just an empty husk, mind forever scrambled."

"Don't touch him," Dad snapped, but Anthony dug the gun into his side again before Dad could move.

She laughed, and it sounded nothing like Nick's mother. "Jealous? Don't worry, honey. I haven't forgotten about you." Dad stared resolutely forward, jaw tense as Patricia/Jennifer kissed his cheek with a loud smack.

"Cats," Burke said.

"Cats," Nick repeated. "Are we just . . . what. Saying things without context? I can do that. In fact, that's my jam. Ready? What is *up* with—"

"Cats," Burke said again. "Curious creatures. Little teeth. Little claws. And still fearsome hunters when required. It's instinct, you see. Something deep within them that wants to taste flesh and blood."

"Yikes," Nick said. "Didn't know we were heading toward cannibalism, but hey, who am I to judge?" He tapped his chin. "Oh. Right. I'm me and you're you, so there's a lot of judgment. You psycho."

Burke said, "Don't you ever get tired of the sound of your own voice? You're exhausting. No, I'm afraid cannibalism isn't on the table today. Cats, Nicholas. They toy with their prey. Do you know why?"

"Must have missed that Wikipedia page," Nick said with a shrug. "You know how it is. So many entries, so little time."

Burke ground his teeth together, and Nick relished it. Keep him talking. Keep him guessing. He wasn't ready for what was coming. "It's in the interest of self-preservation. They play with their conquests to confuse them, to tire them out. Makes them weaker so when the time comes to strike, there's a lower risk of injury. Retaliation."

"Oh," Nick said. Then he brightened. "*Oh*. I get it! You're the cat, and we're the mice."

"Exactly."

"That's . . . pretty dumb, if I'm being honest. I have a question. Want to make sure we're on the same page."

"Is he always like this?" Burke asked Dad.

"You mean amazing?" Dad retorted. "Yes. Yes, he is."

Nick squared his shoulders. Burke had a few inches on him, and at least fifty pounds, but he was just a man. A stupid, horrendous man, but a man all the same. He was nothing. He was no one. He was already over, he just didn't know it yet. "What happens if the prey fights back? Seems to me an animal cornered would do anything to survive."

"Of that I have no doubt," Burke said. "And sometimes they escape. I'll give you that." He pressed a hand against Nick's chest, pushing him back a step. "But the funny thing about prey is the moment they know, they're already dead. Oh, they'll still bite and scratch, but somewhere deep inside their brains, underneath all the shrieking alarms, they know they've lost."

"I don't get it," Trey whispered loudly to Bob. "He's saying he's a cat? Like, he purrs?"

"They're called furries," Bob whispered back. "People who dress up like animals and go to conventions."

"Huh," Trey said. "That's . . ." He squinted at Burke. "You get, like, whiskers and everything? Those must be a pain in the ass to glue to your face. My daughter was a cat for Halloween when she was . . . what. Six? It took *forever* to put together. Whiskers. Tail. Face makeup. Mittens shaped like little paws."

"Please tell me you have pictures," Nick begged. "I need them like air."

Trey chuckled. "Might have a few. But you can't tell her I showed you. I like having my head attached to my shoulders."

"Anthony," Burke said, and before Nick could react, Anthony hit Trey upside the head with his gun. Trey grunted and stumbled into Miles, who slung an arm around his waist, holding him up. A thin line of blood dripped down the side of his head. He wiped it away, flicking his hand so that blood splashed against the side of the elevator.

"Anthony, was it?" Trey asked quietly. "You and me, man. We're gonna have a problem."

Anthony raised the gun again like he was going to strike Trey. For his part, Trey didn't move, staring him down. Anthony lowered the gun a moment later, putting it back into Dad's side just above his hip. "Counting on it," he said.

"There are consequences for everything," Burke told Nick as the elevator neared its destination. "You haven't yet learned that lesson, but I will teach it to you if it's the last thing I do."

Nick stared at him dead-on. "It will be."


Nick stepped off the elevator into a long hallway, the ceilings vaulted, the floor covered in a thick, lush carpet. Sconces hung on the walls, and between them, a line of photographs. An entire history captured in color and black-and-white, years passing by in the blink of an eye.

A young Simon Burke—perhaps college-age or a little older—wearing an ill-fitted suit and standing next to a model of a double helix, mouth frozen open, eyes bright.

A slightly older Simon Burke, surrounded by a group of clichéd scientists, all wearing white lab coats, goggles sitting atop their heads.

Simon Burke as he was now, sitting behind his desk, the surface covered with reams of paper, a black fountain pen in his hand.

A dozen more. No Patricia. No Owen. It was as if they didn't exist to him.

Burke led the way to a pair of large oak double doors at the end of the hall, a numerical keypad next to it below a darkened panel. Burke tapped in six digits, and the doors unlocked with a click.

"I'm going to enjoy this," Burke said to Nick, hand on the ornate doorknob, silver with a raised circular pattern of little dots.

"Whatever turns you on," Nick said. "I don't believe in kink-shaming, so spread those wings and fly."

Burke pushed the doors open and walked through. Nick and the Dad Squad followed.

The floors were made up of white stone tiles. Recessed lighting in the ceiling panels, dozens of circles beaming down light so bright, it took Nick a moment to adjust. A metal desk sat in the center of the room with three monitors on top of it. Behind the desk, on the far wall, a massive painting depicting a blood-soaked battlefield, men and horses dead or dying, dark figures standing above them with swords drawn.

The left wall was entirely glass, looking out onto Nova City from a dizzying height. The buildings next to Burke Tower were lit up from the colors of the celebration below: hues of red and white and blue dancing along brick and steel and glass.

But it was the opposite wall that captured Nick's attention. To his right, a massive screen that was dark save for a spinning symbol in the middle: two letters, BP. Burke Pharmaceuticals. Below the screen, metal shelving above a counter that stretched the entire length of the wall. The same double-helix model sat at the far end. Next to it, a row of half a dozen computer monitors, all asleep. To the right of the monitors, a row of circles in the counter, small handles above each.

The last goon through the doors closed and locked them behind him. Out of the corner of his eye, Nick saw Rebecca Firestone go to the desk, setting the Guardian helmet down on top of it, the lenses pointed toward them. Nick breathed a sigh of relief. So far, so good.

Burke went to the counter on the right wall, stopping in front of the circles, touching the handles with something akin to reverence. "Patricia," he said without turning around. "Please show our guests just how serious I am."

Fake Nick was gone. Jennifer Bell was gone. In their place, a woman he'd only seen a few times up close, the last of which being a quick flash as she fled their home through a hole in the wall. Her dark hair hung around her shoulders in waves. Shadows like bruises under her eyes, skin washed out. She wore slacks and a blue blouse, the collar slightly crooked. Her fingernails were painted white. Her feet were bare. He was about to snap at her, but the words died in his throat when the back of her blouse began to ripple.

Black tendrils of smoke rose from her back, thick tentacles that moved as if alive. They rose above her head, casting shadows on the floor. She twitched, and the smoke shot forward, slamming into Dad's chest, into Bob. Trey. Miles. They were all lifted off their feet as smoke wrapped around them, pinning their arms to their sides.

What had Smoke and Ice told him?

*Mr. Burke sends his regards.*

It was true. All of it. Part of Nick had hoped that Owen was wrong, but here it was: proof. A chimera. Made up of things she'd stolen from others. Not a cure. A disease, harmful and destructive.

"Let them *go*," Nick growled as Dad's head rocked back, the smoke tightening around his chest. They'd been here before. Dad, trapped in smoke. Nick, unable to help him.

"No," Burke said coolly. "Time and time again, your family has stood between me and harnessing the powers of Extraordinaries. It's time I paid you back in full." And with that, he gripped the handle and pulled upward. A hiss, followed by a cloud of white vapor as the container rose. He moved on to the next handle, and the next, and the next.

A dozen in all, filled with what looked like brightly colored candy. Green and yellow. Violet. Blue. Orange. Black. White.

Nick had seen them before, far below where they now stood, in a lab underneath Burke Tower.

*Green is superstrength, capable of turning you into a human wrecking ball. Yellow is the power of flight. Violet is the ability to summon storms. Blue can make you become a conductor of electricity. Orange is fire. Black is smoke. Or maybe shadow. I'd stay away from that one if I were you. I'm told it's . . . intense. I wouldn't want that for you. Perhaps the blue. Or green.*

*And the white?*

*The white one is off-limits. Even for you, Nicky. It's the most unstable. It's telekinesis.*

But they weren't the only ones.

A pile of pink pills, with two yellow stripes around the top and the bottom. Pale blue, crisscrossed with a black X. Clear pills, halfway filled with liquid that sloshed. Red, but not like fire. No, this was the dark red of blood. An electric green with a light pulsing in each pill, a steady heartbeat.

Burke finished pulling up all the containers, and stood back, pride evident on his face. "And there are more," he said, answering Nick's unasked question. "So many more. These are the most stable."

Patricia had a dreamy look on her face, the shadows from her back roiling, the men suspended above her still struggling. They'd known this was a possibility. They'd planned for this, and yet Nick could barely tamp down the fury that roared in him.

"Why?" he asked. "I thought you wanted to take our powers away."

"Both can be true," Burke said, stroking the container filled with clear pills lovingly. "One doesn't negate the other. Before we go any further, where is Pyro Storm?"

"I have no idea," Nick said. "He's his own person. He can do what he wants."

"Really," Burke said. "You of all people don't know where he is."

"Yeah. That's what I said. Glad to know you can retain information."

"Nick," Dad croaked as the end of the smoke tentacle stroked the side of his face. "Not helping."

"Anthony," Burke said. "Please check the security grid. Make sure we won't have any . . . interruptions."

Anthony nodded, striding around Burke's desk and wiggling the mouse. Rebecca Firestone cleared her throat, stepping away from the desk, leaving the Guardian helmet facing toward the others. Nick couldn't see what was on the screen from where he stood, but Anthony's face lit up when the monitor awoke. Holding his breath, Nick waited as Anthony typed something on the keyboard. He frowned, typed something else, and then said, "Clear."

Burke stroked his jaw. "Fascinating. You're sure?"

"Sure, boss. No one else in the building."

Burke looked at Nick. "What are you planning?"

Nick startled when he felt a vibration against his chest. A hardened circle underneath his costume. The pin that Gibby had given them. The cameras. His was covered, but the Dad Squad still wore theirs. Burke had found the mics in their ears, but it'd made him careless.

It was go-time.

"Me?" Nick asked innocently, hand near his throat. "*Planning? I'm more of a by-the-seat-of-my-pants kind of guy." He tapped the side of his head. "Neurodiverse, remember? ADHD makes planning things hard."

"I know," Burke said. "Your parents came to me, asking for help with that and something a little . . . extra."

"When I say it, it's cute and fun," Nick said. "When you say it, it comes off sounding like you're trying too hard. Maybe leave the quips to me, yeah?"

"Talk, talk, talk," Burke said. "If you were my child, I'd have strangled you the moment you learned your first word."

"Neat," Nick said. "Though, a note, if you're open to constructive criticism. Every fic author knows you need critical feedback in order to grow as a writer. Ready? Threatening to kill teenagers is extremely shitty, and not very mayoral. Focus, dude. You're obviously proud about the pills, seeing as how you're stroking them. That's a little weird."

"The pills," Burke repeated, eyes narrowed. "Yes, I suppose I am proud of them. A feat of human engineering, temporary though the effects are."

Anthony rejoined the goons, and Rebecca Firestone stood next to the desk, arms crossed, expression carefully blank. "But it still doesn't make sense," Nick said. "Why would you make pills to give people powers when you want to cure Extraordinaries?"

"That's your problem, Nick. You're so wrapped up in the here and now that you fail to see the future. I may not be precognitive, but the future is known to me, and it is glorious." He stepped away from the pills, gaze trained firmly on Nick. "Imagine, if you will: those whose job it is to protect and serve. Unfairly maligned. Ridiculed. Powerless against those with abilities and the unending tides of social justice."

Nick frowned. "Social—holy shit. Are you talking about the NCPD?"

"I am," Burke said. "Give them the tools to do their jobs. An army of Extraordinaries weeding out those who would defy us. Finding the Extraordinaries who hide their powers, who fight back. Removing their powers, leaving them ordinary. And once we've proven our success, the entire country will be *begging* me to do the same for them. Why call a SWAT team when you could call a single Extraordinary who could put people to sleep with a wave of their hand?"

Nick scoffed. "There's no way you'll convince people that they'll be safer being protected by cops with superpowers."

"You sorely underestimate the need for security that people feel. So many of them desperately want to believe the police can keep them safe. And the police want that as well. So if I give them the power to do just that, who do you think the rest will turn to? You, a child playing a game, or the men and women in blue? And once a few of the officers get a taste of what I can offer, won't the others want the same thing? You of all people should know what someone will do with abilities like I can provide." He smiled. "You did everything you could to become an Extraordinary, not knowing it was already in your blood thanks to your mother."

"Who you had killed," Nick snapped.

The skin under Burke's right eye twitched. "Someone's been talking, I see." He nodded gravely. "That . . . was unfortunate. I don't expect you to believe me, but I did everything I could to make her see the light. That someone like her, someone like *you* needed to be studied, tested to see just how powerful your telekinesis truly is."

Stunned, Nick said, "You wanted *me*?"

"I did," Burke said. "A child, abilities passed down from his mother. The implications were staggering. Owen didn't have that. His mother was . . . well. Normal, as was everyone else in her family, as far as I could tell. And Patricia's own parents were long dead when I met her, but there's no evidence they were anything but ordinary. Seth Gray's parents weren't able to manipulate fire. So the question is *why*? What is it about certain people that makes them genetically predisposed to pass their abilities on to their offspring while others can't? The *things* I could have learned from her. From you." He eyed Nick speculatively. "Still could, in fact."

"And she refused," Nick said, skin vibrating painfully. "So you sent people after her to make sure she couldn't tell you no again."

"Collateral damage," Burke said. "She was onto me, and it was only a matter of time before she spoke. Maybe no one would have listened to her, but I couldn't take that chance."

"They would have," Nick snapped. "She would've convinced *everyone*."

"And now she can't," Burke said.

"You're a goddamn monster," Nick said coldly.

Burke sneered. "What you call a monster, others will see as a visionary. Your mother was an unfortunate—but necessary—sacrifice, not unlike Christina and Christian Lewis."

"If only she'd listened," Patricia cooed, forehead drenched in sweat as the shadow tentacles from her back quaked. Trey, head bowed, breathing heavily through his nose. Bob was pressed flat against the ceiling, face red. Miles was near Dad, but they couldn't reach each other, arms still pinned at their sides. "She could have done so much. Instead, she threw it all away with her misplaced sense of virtue. I would know. I've *been* her." She smiled up at Dad, a terrible thing with too many teeth. She arched her back, and a piece of one of the smoke tentacles holding Dad snapped off, shrinking to the size of a quarter before expanding into a thin line with a sharp point at the end, like a spear. Ice began to form at the base, snapping and crackling as it spread until the smoke had disappeared entirely, replaced by solid ice. The spear hovered in front of Dad's face, the tip inches from his nose.

Nick jumped when something exploded behind him, the bang muffled. He turned toward the windows. Green sparks fell down the side of Burke Tower. A second later, another explosion in the sky, blue and yellow, lines of fire stretching high above Nova City and illuminating the seventy-second floor.

The fireworks had begun.

Burke stepped away and stopped in front of the windows, looking down. From this high up, the massive crowd must have looked like ants. His face lit up in shades of gold and violet as another firework detonated. "Greater men than I have tried to revolutionize the force used to protect their own people," he said. "But I have something they didn't."

"A misplaced sense of grandiosity?" Nick asked. He glanced at Rebecca Firestone, who had her hand on top of the Guardian helmet. She nodded, twisting the helmet until the lenses faced Burke once more. She jerked her hand back when Burke turned around, but he paid her no mind.

"The will to see it through," Burke said. "No matter the cost. Some won't understand. They may even think me a villain—"

"Uh, yeah," Nick said. "That's because you are. I can't believe I have to be the one to explain this to you."

Burke rushed forward. Nick didn't move, refusing to be intimidated, even when Burke gripped his face, fingers digging into his cheeks. "They will do whatever I tell them to," Burke snarled. "Sheep need direction. And I will give it to them. Nova City is just the beginning. If you think I give two shits about becoming mayor, you're sorely mistaken."

Nick laughed in his face. "Oh my god. You're a freaking *cliché*."

Burke blinked, grip loosening slightly. "What?"

He twisted his face and dropped his voice mockingly. "'I will be the supreme leader. People will bow before me, and I'll take everything from them because no one ever loved me.'" He sighed, refusing to wince as Burke applied pressure to his cheekbones. "Fic villains are more three-dimensional than you'll ever be. Disappointing that real life doesn't imitate art. I'll admit you've got some skills, though. Having your wife take the form of my mom and erase our memories of her death was pretty hard-core. And then you had her train me? What was that all about?"

Burke almost looked pleased. "It was, wasn't it? What I would have given to see the look on your face when she walked through your door. And she worked with you because we wanted to know just how powerful you are. And you gave it up like it was *nothing*."

Nick rolled his eyes. "It only lasted a few weeks, dude. And for what? You thought you could tear us apart from the inside out?" He gasped dramatically. "We're way more loyal to each other than your people will ever be to you."

"Is that right?" Burke asked. "As much as it pains me to say, you're partially correct. Rebecca." He turned toward her and cocked his head. "Or should I say Lauren Underwood?"

More explosions, the room awash in whites and greens and reds. Rebecca's face pale, eyes wide as she took a step back.

"You think I didn't know?" Burke asked softly. "You're good, Lauren, but you're not that good."

"I don't know what you're talking about," she whispered, gaze darting around as if looking for an escape. The only doors were blocked by henchmen.

Burke clucked his tongue. "You were careless."

"Your father gurgled," Patricia said darkly. "When I ate his powers and then filled his lungs with water, the *sounds* he made."

Rebecca Firestone bellowed as she rushed toward Patricia, hands raised. She only made it halfway before she came to a stop as if crashing into an invisible wall. Her eyes darted from side to side, a low moan falling from her mouth. But the rest of her seemed frozen midstep, one foot slightly raised off the floor.

"The human body," Burke said. "A marvelous feat of evolutionary engineering. Funny thing about bodies, though. Sixty percent of an adult human is made of water. The lifeblood of human existence, water is. And I just so happen to have an Extraordinary at my disposal who can control water. Anthony, your spare piece, if you please."

Anthony bent over, lifting the leg of his slacks, revealing a snub-nosed pistol in an ankle holster. He pulled it free, handing it over to Burke.

"You have her?" Burke asked.

"Yes," Patricia said, but Nick could hear the tremor in her voice. Sweat now dripped off her face in rivulets, and her hands were shaking.

*You know when lightning strikes a power line?* Owen whispered in Nick's head. *It sends a charge through wherever the line goes. Sometimes, it'll knock out power all over. But most places are outfitted with surge protectors. I think she's like that. A limit to how much she can take in. Regardless of what else Extraordinaries are, we're still human. Our bodies can't handle that much energy. I think if she tried to take any more she'd . . .*

"Boom," Nick murmured. "Stretched too thin."

Burke took Rebecca Firestone's hand in his, lifting it up. He placed the gun in her hand, positioning her fingers around the grip, thumb up the side, index finger around the trigger. It was as if she were a puppet. She moaned as Burke raised the gun in her hand, pressing the barrel against the side of her head just above her ear. A tear fell from her left eye, tracing a line down her cheek.

"A terrible thing, grief is," Burke said quietly, letting go of Rebecca Firestone's hand. It stayed where he'd put it. "All-consuming. I didn't know Rebecca Firestone was depressed. I didn't know that she was crying out for help. *Had* I known, I would've done whatever I could to save her." He sighed. "Alas, she was already far too gone. She stole my employee's weapon. She put it up against her head." He smiled as Rebecca shuddered. "Pity, that." He turned away.

Too far. Though Nick thought Rebecca Firestone sucked ass, Burke had gone too far. He stepped forward, about to tell Burke to leave her alone when Rebecca Firestone made a small sound at the back of her throat. Nick glanced at her to find her watching him. She shook her head once, lifting her shaking finger off the trigger.

"A limit," Nick whispered. Then, louder, "And the rest of us?"

"By the time I'm done with you, you won't remember any of this. Patricia will see to it." He tilted his head back, smiling. "You'll join me on that stage, and the only thing any of you will be able to say is how *sorry* you are. And before you think you can break free from Patricia's hold again, a warning: I will make you kill your father."

Nick's heart banged against his rib cage. "No."

"Yes," Burke said. "I wonder how many bones a telekinetic can pull from a body before it—"

A pounding at the double doors, insistent, loud.

Burke jerked his head toward the door. "I thought I said no interruptions. Anthony, deal with whoever that is."

*Now or never.*

Anthony moved toward the door.

Patricia grunted, the smoke tendrils quivering.

Dad grimaced, twisting his head away from the ice spike dimpling his cheek.

Miles and Bob and Trey fought against the smoke wrapped around them.

Rebecca Firestone's finger twitched on the trigger.

Simon Burke turned back toward Nick.

"You underestimated people," Nick said, taking a step toward him. "And here's the thing about prey: sometimes, we fight back." He nodded toward the screen hanging on the wall. "That thing get channels?"

The pounding on the door continued, raised, muffled voices on the other side.

"It does," Burke said slowly.

"Why don't you turn it on?"

Burke hesitated, staring at Nick, who smiled at him. He went to the screen, touching it. Rows of apps appeared, and he pressed his finger against the live-news app in the bottom-right corner.

Five different boxes appeared, each showing a different angle. Four of them were from high up, looking down on the room they stood in, Patricia Burke centered in each frame. The fifth was a lower angle, showing almost the entire room. This last box had Rebecca Firestone, gun to her head, finger on the trigger. The goons with their guns drawn, Anthony still standing next to the door. Burke, standing in front of the screen. Behind him, in sharp focus, a row of containers holding pills.

And Nick standing proud and strong, center frame.

"What is this?" Burke whispered.

"*This,*" Nick said, hands curling into fists, "is how you've lost. All you've said since stepping inside this office has been broadcast to every single screen within a ten-block radius. Cell phones. Televisions. You ever gone viral before? No? Well, guess fucking *what*. Now you have. All those people, Burke. You invited them here. You gathered thousands of them, and we couldn't have planned this better had we tried. Your message is already spreading across the world. How do you think those you call sheep feel now that they know exactly the kind of man you are?"

Burke whirled around, rage filling his face.

Anthony pulled the door open, but before it could even get partway, Nick jerked his head, and the door slammed closed, followed by the sound of the lock clicking back into place. Fireworks burst outside the window, so much like the spark in Nick's head, the room a kaleidoscope of fractured color.

Nick bowed slightly, one hand across his chest, the other behind him. "And now, a catchphrase. I'm pretty proud of it. Thought it up myself and everything. You ready?" He grinned as he stood upright, looking up at the ceiling. What came next was a battle cry, a song of war. *"It's time to burn!"*

The ceiling panels expanded, cracked, breaking apart as a great burst of fire rained down, Pyro Storm at its center. He hit the floor in a crouch, flames snapping around him, the red lenses in his helmet flashing brightly as he turned his head toward Patricia Burke. "You ran away before we could finish last time. Let's go again."

And then he launched himself toward her. Patricia snarled at him, stumbling back, the smoke around her collapsing. The Dad Squad plummeted toward the floor, but before they crashed into it, Nick raised his hands. Pyro Storm collided with Patricia, knocking her off her feet right as Nick caught the Dad Squad, bodies jerking as they came to a sudden stop a few feet above the floor.

His vision exploded when a fist connected with the side of his head, breaking his concentration. The Dad Squad fell the remaining distance, Miles and Trey groaning, Bob and Dad already pushing themselves up.

Before he could recover, another fist flew toward Nick's face. He managed to grab it before it hit him. Burke's eyes widened comically as Nick spun on his heels *"Dad!"* Nick shouted midturn. "Coming your way!"

He let Burke go, flinging him toward his father. "This is for hurting my kid," Dad snarled before uppercutting Burke in the chin. Burke flew back against the bay of windows, a spiderweb of cracks snapping along the glass. Dazed, he rubbed his hand along his jaw. Nick was about to charge toward him when arms wrapped around him from behind, lifting him up off the floor.

Anthony's breath was hot against his ear. "Caught you." His big arms squeezed around Nick, the bones in Nick's chest groaning in protest as Burke approached, eyes glittering as fireworks burst behind him.

"Bitch, you *thought*," Nick growled. "Backflip of Chaos!"

Except it didn't work. Anthony was too heavy, and Nick's feet couldn't reach the floor. All he succeeded in doing was wiggling in the asshole's arms. Anthony chuckled until Nick turned his head and sank his teeth into the meat of the bicep wrapped around him as hard as he could. Anthony bellowed in pain, dropping Nick. He whirled around, only to be tackled by Anthony to the floor. The impact was immense, and Nick wheezed when the large man landed on top of him.

"Hey," Nick managed to choke out as Anthony loomed above him. "Have you met the ceiling yet? No? Let me introduce you." With all his might, he *pushed,* and Anthony flew upward in a blur, crashing into the ceiling panels, which caved in around him. Nick rolled out of the way as Anthony fell back down, hitting the floor with a terrible crunch, shards of the ceiling hitting his back. He groaned quietly but didn't rise.

Nick shot to his feet in time to see the Dad Squad grappling with the three remaining goons, Miles jumping on one of their backs, beating him upside the head with his fist. Pyro Storm ducked an attack from Patricia, ice and smoke amassing into a roiling whip, hitting the glass containers full of pills, shattering them, spilling their contents onto the floor. He responded with a ball of fire, but Patricia was already on the defense, pulling water out of the goddamn *air* in a wave in front of her. The fireball struck it, steam billowing as the water doused the flames.

Nick was about to charge toward Pyro Storm when the double doors burst open, wood splintering, hinges shrieking. More people poured in—at least a dozen—guns drawn, all wearing black security uniforms and grim expressions. Burke cried, "Kill them! Kill them *all*!" but before the new group could do as asked, Nick brought his arms back and the spark in his head flared. He thrust his arms forward, and Anthony lifted off the floor, arms dangling, head lolling as he flew across the room, striking Burke's security force, knocking them down.

"I'll do it myself," Burke snarled, and rushed toward Nick. He took three steps before a gun went off. Burke's left shoulder jerked back as blood bloomed on his shirt like a rose. He groaned, hand going to the wound, pressing down.

Rebecca Firestone said, "The next one goes in your head. They may not kill, but I have no problem with it. After what you did to my father, I'll—" She gasped when the gun was ripped from her hands and flung across the room, bouncing off a window, causing more cracks to appear.

Patricia Burke stood in the center of the room, hair billowing around her as the air begin to spin, picking up debris like a tornado. The lights above flickered, and Pyro Storm groaned against a thick column of writhing smoke that held him on the floor. "You shot him," Patricia whispered. "How *dare* you!"

She raised her hands toward Rebecca Firestone, and Nick moved then, doing something he would have never expected: protecting Rebecca Firestone *again*. And when Patricia Burke screamed, the tornado growing larger, causing the whole room to shake, he answered with his own shout. The tornado hurtled toward them, and Nick *caught it,* even as his feet slid back, the muscles in his arms burning. Hands shaking, he forced them together, and the tornado died as quickly as it arrived.

"Thanks," Rebecca Firestone whispered behind him.

"Don't mention it," Nick said, glaring over his shoulder. "Seriously. I never want to hear it mentioned again. You helped us, but you're still the worst. Now, if you'll excuse me, I have to take care of some—"

Rebecca Firestone's eyes widened as she looked over his shoulder. He didn't have time to react as her hands shot forward, gripping his shoulders and pulling them both down. A second later, a metal strut flew right where they'd been standing, slicing through the air, causing it to whistle. It embedded itself into the wall.

Nick gaped at Patricia Burke and the Lovecraftian horror bursting from her back, tentacles of smoke and ice and crystal-clear water pulling more struts from the ceiling, gutting the area above the room. Plaster and dust rained down around her.

"And now you made Rebecca Firestone save *me*?" Nick growled. "What the hell is wrong with you?"

"You're welcome," Rebecca Firestone muttered.

"I don't like you," Patricia hissed.

"Feeling's mutual," Nick said, pulling himself to his full height. More fireworks exploded outside the windows, and above the noise, he thought he heard the sound of sirens in the distance. Nick ignored this as he charged toward Patricia.

Another tentacle threw a metal strut, much larger than the first, and Nick fell to his knees, sliding along the floor, leaning back against his legs. The strut crashed into Burke's desk, flipping it end over end, the Guardian helmet bouncing off the floor and landing at Rebecca Firestone's feet. Nick was already up and moving before Patricia could throw another, and he leapt the last few feet, back bowed, fists joined together above his head.

An ice tentacle crashed into his chest, shattering, knocking him to the side. He hit the floor hard, sliding on a surface of water and hundreds of pills. The broken pieces of ice from the impact began to move toward him, crawling up his legs. Cold. So cold. He yelped, trying to shove them off, but more and more came, hitting his legs, his hips, his chest. He couldn't think. The spark in his head dimmed, lost under a wave of crippling panic.

"You shouldn't have touched my man," Pyro Storm growled, and then the seventy-second floor lit up as if the sun had crashed into Burke Tower. Nick stared in awe at the room awash in fire, spreading like wings from Pyro Storm, molten hot and almost white. Flames leaked from Pyro Storm's hands, crackling angrily, like whips made of fire.

Pyro Storm swung them above his head in circles. He snapped

one forward, and Patricia Burke fell back on her ass, spreading her legs as the tip of the fire whip slapped the floor between her thighs, leaving a smoldering scorch mark.

"Neat trick," Patricia panted. "I've got one, too." She rolled backward, legs going up and over her head, hands pushing up off the floor. She landed on her feet, head snapping up. She raised her hand, and thick beads of water shot up her forearm, coalescing in her palm as a large bubble. Pyro Storm raised his whips above his head, crossing his arms. Before he could fling them forward, he . . . just . . . stopped.

"All that fire," Patricia said. "And yet, you're still made of water, just like everyone else." She closed her fingers around the bubble in her hand, and Pyro Storm turned toward Nick stiffly, mouth hanging open. Behind him, Dad grunted and fell to his knees when a goon smashed a gun into the back of his head. Miles lay on the floor, eyes open but dazed. Trey and Bob stood above him, both glaring as more security pulled themselves to their feet.

"I . . . can't . . . control . . . it," Pyro Storm said through gritted teeth. "Nick . . . *run*." And then he attacked.

Nick yelped and rolled left as a whip of fire hit the floor, the tremendous heat almost too much to bear. He rolled right when the other whip snapped toward him, causing the stone tiles to crack upon impact.

"I'm sorry!" Pyro Storm yelled, pulling the whips back. "This isn't me!"

"I *know* that!" Nick yelled back. "Bitch, you better step the hell off my—oh shit!" He fell back onto the floor, the whip cutting the air just above his face, singeing his hair, his eyebrows. He slapped at his face, sure he was on fire. As Nick lowered his hands, Pyro Storm took jerky steps toward him, moving as if he didn't have joints, rocking side to side. The whips shrank into his palms, turning into twin fireballs. Patricia Burke stood behind him, Pyro Storm mimicking her movements: hands spreading far apart before being brought together. The fireballs combined into a single burning star.

"No," Pyro Storm ground out. "Don't . . . do this."

"You did this to yourselves," Patricia hissed. She brought her hands to her side, then thrust them forward so hard, Nick thought he heard her shoulders and elbows popping.

But that was the least of his concerns, because Pyro Storm did the same, hands holding the fireball, bringing it to his side, then thrusting it toward Nick. The fireball—at least three feet in diameter and growing bigger—shot toward Nick, leaving a line of black on the floor.

Nick screamed and raised his hands in front of him, as if that would do anything to stop his coming death. The moment before impact—the fire so bright—the spark in his head exploded. Nick felt it roll through him, traveling down his neck to his chest, his arms, his legs. He screamed as it coursed through him, the pain immense, *too much*—

And then nothing.

Nick opened his eyes slowly.

His hands, outstretched in front of him. Beyond them, the ball of fire, stationary, suspended in air, the surface moving like liquid. A little sun, and Nick had *caught it*.

"Holy shit," he heard someone breathe.

Nick stood, hands still in front of him, and the fireball moved with him. He grinned ferociously. "Now *that's* what I call playing with fire! We really need to start writing these down."

He expected Patricia to be outraged. He faltered when he saw she was smiling just as widely as he was. "Didn't your parents teach you anything? Fire safety, Nicholas."

He narrowed his eyes. "What are you talking—"

An alarm began to blare, a little red light above the doors flashing red. A split second later, water began to rain down around them from the sprinklers embedded in the ceiling. Nick was drenched almost immediately, the fireball hissing, steam pouring off it as it shrank. Knowing there wasn't much time left, he *pushed,* and, as Pyro Storm leapt out of the way, the diminishing fireball flew toward Patricia Burke.

She didn't move. The fireball grew smaller and smaller, and

when it struck her in the chest, it was the size of a quarter, barely leaving a mark on her.

"Well," Nick said. "That didn't go like I thought it would."

Water coated the floor, and when he took a step toward Pyro Storm, toward Patricia, it rose up around his boots, making it feel like he was trapped in quicksand.

Patricia raised her hands, and the thin layer of water covering the floor *lifted,* growing larger as the sprinklers continued to spray. It covered Pyro Storm, who sucked in as much air as he could before it washed over his face, trapping him inside a bubble of water.

Panic screamed in Nick's head as his chest heaved. He tilted his head back as the water reached his neck, and then he was also entombed. With his eyes open, the room took on a squirming facade, harsh lines now wiggling. He held his breath, knowing that it was futile, that he was about to drown. Burke appeared in front of him outside of the bubble, drenched, hair plastered on his head, his shoulder wound leaking blood through a ragged hole in his shirt.

"There, there," Burke whispered, voice oddly muffled through the water. "It'll be over soon."

Nick looked beyond him as if in a dream, blood rushing in his ears. Pyro Storm, head twisting side to side. Miles and Trey trapped in their own bubble, hands joined between them. Bob's head bowed, his thin hair waving around his head, air leaking from his nose.

And Dad. Dad, on his hands and knees. Dad, surrounded by goons. Dad in his own bubble, eyes wide and panicked. Then the panic faded as he looked at Nick. He smiled and mouthed, *Love you, kid.*

Nick screamed, water pouring into his mouth and down his throat, choking him. Lights began to dance across his vision, and the spark in his head began to dim.

The room darkened, and he thought he saw movement outside the windows of Burke Tower. Another firework exploded, illuminating the seventy-second floor in blues and reds.

And there, floating outside the tower, was a figure.

Nick thought, *Who . . . who is . . .*

The windows exploded inward, shards of glass flying through the air. Patricia Burke cried out when a sharp piece of glass pierced the skin of her right arm. Another cut her on the cheek, leaving a ragged line. She fell forward. The bubble around Nick collapsed, and he took in a great, gasping breath before vomiting what felt like an endless amount of water.

The figure floated through the opening, shadows amassing around him. Feet hitting the floor with a quiet splash, he moved through the room with purpose just as the sprinklers switched off, the alarm falling silent. Nick reached for him, but gagged and vomited once again. "What . . ." Nick said thickly. "Where . . ."

The figure ignored him. He ignored the security who tried to rise to their feet only to slip and fall. He ignored Anthony, who lay on his back, breaths shallow. He ignored Pyro Storm, his helmet dripping water as he spat again and again. He ignored Rebecca Firestone, her skin pale, mouth opening and closing, opening and closing. He ignored Miles and Trey, who crouched down next to Bob, who lay flat on his back, eyes closed, body limp. Trey pressed against Bob's sternum, pumping up and down. Miles bent over, pinching Bob's nose closed, breathing into his mouth, causing his chest to expand. He ignored Dad, hair hanging around his face.

He ignored his parents, Burke blinking up at the ceiling, Patricia screeching as she tried to pull the glass from her arm.

Owen Burke ignored them all. Through bleary eyes, Nick watched him cross the room, heading toward the counter against the wall. Colorful water sluiced around his feet, and it took Nick a moment to realize where it'd come from.

The pills, melting in the water.

Some had survived, a mixture sitting on the counter, protected by the remains of the containers that had once held them. Nick tried to rise as Owen picked through them as if he had all the time in the world. He lifted a yellow one. Tossed it aside. A green one. The same. Blue and orange. He paused with a white one before shaking his head. He bent over the counter. When he turned back around, he held a pile of pills in his hand.

All black.

He looked at them, a strange glint in his eyes. "You know," he said, almost conversationally, "I really do love these things."

And then he brought the pills to his mouth and swallowed them all, throat working.

"No," Nick whispered.

"There," Owen said in that same mild voice. "That should do it." He shivered. "Oh man, I almost forgot how quickly these work. Thanks, *Dad*."

Shadows began to move around him, and Owen rose off the floor, all the light that remained in the room fading as if being sucked into a black hole. Sentient blackness moved across the walls, the floor, the ceiling.

"Owen," Burke said, slipping on the floor. "Owen, *don't*."

"You don't get to tell me what to do," Owen said coldly. "Not anymore. Not after all you've done to me."

"Owen, baby," Patricia begged. "We love you. We're your *parents*. Help us. Please."

Owen looked at her, expression softening. "Hey, Patricia. Been a long time." And then a shadow coiled around his step-mother, slithering up her legs to her arms, pinning them in place. He raised his hand, fingers spread. He slowly closed them, and Patricia began to choke, eyes bulging from her head. "Missed you."

"Owen, *stop*," Nick said, rising unsteadily to his feet, the spark pulsing weakly in her head. "You don't have to do this."

Owen chuckled darkly. "I know I don't have to do this, Nicky. I *want* to."

Burke didn't go for his son. He didn't go for his wife. Instead, he ran toward the doors as if he thought he could make it. He didn't, a thick shadow wrapping around his ankles, flipping him up and over, head knocking against the ground.

Seth ripped off his helmet, falling to his knees next to Bob, whom Trey and Miles had turned over, letting him expel all the water he'd swallowed. He coughed roughly, eyes fluttering.

Dad moved around the shadows carefully, plucking the guns from the security guards.

Owen moved toward his parents, Burke upside down, Patricia lifting off the floor, the shadows wrapping around her as she tried to break free.

"Oh, look," Owen said. "I'm stronger than you. How about that? Never underestimate the power of shadows."

"Owen," she pleaded. "We only want to help you."

"Help," he echoed bitterly. "You made me this way, and when I'd served my purpose, you threw me away like I was *nothing*. Was it your idea? All those lights, always on? Do you know what that does to a person?"

He slammed Patricia into the ceiling, and then onto the floor, knocking her unconscious. As he raised her back up, her head lolled to the side, blood streaming from her nose and the gash on her cheek, splattering in the water.

The Burkes rose higher, moving slowly toward the opening left from the broken windows. Wind whipped, fireworks still going off, much louder now that the glass was gone, bursts of light that made the shadows dance.

Simon Burke cried out when shadows pulled them through the broken windows, Patricia hanging limp and silent. Burke's legs kicked into nothing as he shouted unintelligibly.

"I've dreamed of this moment," Owen breathed. "For so long. Look at me. I said *look at me*." The shadows gripped Simon's face, turning him toward Owen. "I'm your son!" Owen bellowed. "And you treated me like I was expendable. And she just stood by and let it happen. She did nothing to stop you from hurting me. From *experimenting* on me."

"I'm sorry," Burke retorted, face red as he hung upside down.

"You're *sorry*?" Owen laughed. "You have no idea what sorry means. But I'll show you. I'll show all of you."

"Don't," Miles said, taking a shaky step forward. "Owen, you don't want to do this."

"He's right," Bob said, pushing himself off the ground, Seth helping him up. "You're only going to make things worse for yourself."

"I don't *care,*" Owen snarled. "He deserves everything he has coming to him, and more."

"Maybe," Trey said, Bob leaning on him as Seth's eyes narrowed. "But if you do this, you won't be able to take it back. It'll follow you for the rest of your life."

"It's not too late to stop this," Dad said, casting a glance at Nick. "Parents make mistakes, Owen. All the time. I would know. You can be better than he ever was. Break the cycle."

"Mistake," Burke gasped. "They're right. That's all it was. A mistake. Please, Owen."

Nick could see the gears turning in Owen's head, as if he was listening. As if they were getting through to him. Taking a chance, Nick rushed toward him, Dad and Seth shouting his name. He dropped a hand on Owen's shoulder, squeezing tightly. Underneath Owen's shirt, movement, like he was covered in thousands of bugs. Nick recoiled, watching thin tendrils of shadow peek out from underneath Owen's clothes. "They're done," Nick told him. "Everyone has already seen them for who they are. Let them go."

Owen hesitated. "That's what you want?"

"*Yes.*"

"Can you fly?"

Nick blinked. "What? Owen, why are you—"

Owen looked back at him over his shoulder. He smiled, the whites of his eyes filling with black. It leaked down like tears, crawling up and down his face, forming a black helmet with a thin visor across his eyes. His clothing rippled as it was swallowed by shifting shadows. It took only seconds, and when it was done, Owen stood before him in full costume, a glittering star symbol on his chest. "My name . . . is *Shadow Star.*"

From behind them, Trey shouted, "Nick! *Shakespeare.*"

The shadows around Patricia and Simon Burke disappeared. They fell.

Nick didn't think. He shoved Shadow Star to the side and launched himself out the seventy-second floor of Burke Tower. His father screamed his name, but it was lost in the wind roaring around him.

Patricia and Simon Burke plummeted, the ground below rushing toward them. Nick folded his arms at his sides, slicing through the air.

He closed his eyes. And there, waiting for him in the dark, his mother. She held out her hand. In it, a ball of light. A spark. *Her* spark.

"Fly," he whispered back, and pushed her spark and his together. They combined, and their dazzling light rushed through him, warming him from the inside out.

He opened his eyes. The ground was getting closer as Nick reached out his gloved hands toward Simon and Patricia Burke. Too far away to grab, but the spark was there and he pushed with everything he had. The pain that tore through his head was enormous. But as soon as it arrived, it was gone, and something else flooded through him, something bigger, stronger.

"I am extraordinary," Nick said to the wind.

The air below Simon and Patricia Burke rippled, concentric circles that expanded like ripples in a lake. The Burkes hit the air, slowing, the stage *right below them,* but it was enough, and Nick grabbed Simon's hand, grabbed Patricia's elbow, and pulled as hard as he could, the muscles in his arms straining.

And then everything stopped. The wind. The blood rushing in his ears. Everything.

Nick looked down.

He was floating horizontally above the stage ten feet below, Simon and Patricia Burke hanging from his hands. Burke looked up at him with wide eyes. Patricia's head was bowed, her hair hanging around her face. They were heavy—too heavy, really—but Nick had them.

He dropped another few feet and let them go. Patricia hit the stage hard, rolling until she came to a stop near the edge, her arm hanging off the side, limp and unmoving.

Burke landed on his side, the wood creaking as he rolled over onto his back, looking up at Nick with a dazed expression, the sounds of the frightened crowd muted as if coming from a distance.

Nick floated above him. He lowered himself toward Burke, stopping a few feet above, studying the man who'd tried to take everything from him. Because in the end, whatever else he was—villain, monster, murderer—he was still just an ordinary man, hands raised as if to ward Nick off.

"Everyone knows who you are now. What you think of them. What you tried to do. You lost."

Burke rose to his feet, looking for an escape. But the cops were gathering on the sides of the stage.

"He's a murderer," Nick said, lowering himself to the stage, voice carrying across the crowd. "He had my mother killed, and she wasn't the only one. He's hurt so many people. We've proven what he is. The rest is up to you." He leaned forward. "My name is Nicholas Bell. I'm a seventeen-year-old with ADHD who also happens to be queer as balls. And like my mother before me, I'm the Extraordinary known as Guardian. Now, if you'll excuse me, we have one more villain to stop."

He looked down at the cops surrounding the stage. Relief, then, when Chris walked up the stairs, glaring at Burke. Nick stepped away from the podium as Chris crouched down next to Patricia, fingers against her neck. "She's alive," Chris said quietly. He pulled his hand back. "You all right?"

"Not yet," Nick said.

"You heard the man," Chris barked, pulling out a pair of handcuffs from his duty belt. "Get moving."

But none of them did. They just stood there, looking wary, confused.

Before Chris could snap at them, another figure landed on the stage, causing the crowd to shout. Pyro Storm, fire dancing around him, wisps of smoke rising from his shoulders. In his right hand, he held the Guardian helmet. Nick barely had time to react before Pyro Storm practically tackled him, hugging him tightly. "You did it," Pyro Storm whispered in his ear. Over his shoulder, Nick grunted in surprise when he saw *civilians* climb onto the stage, surrounding the Burkes, keeping Simon from escaping. Chris followed them, snapping cuffs on Burke before moving on to Patricia.

"I did," Nick whispered back. "I have no idea how, but . . ." He stepped back, looking up the side of Burke Tower. "Is my dad okay? The others?"

"Everyone is okay, but I think you're going to be grounded until you're thirty."

Nick sighed. "Yeah, that sounds about right."

Pyro Storm handed him his helmet. Nick slid it over his head, the lenses bursting to life. WELCOME, GUARDIAN, the words read in front of his eyes. "Mobile Lighthouse, you copy?"

"*Nick?*" Gibby and Jazz said at the same time.

"Hi! How are you?"

Silence.

Then, Jazz: "I'm going to stab you so hard, and you will *thank me for it*," while at the same time, Gibby said, "You're the stupidest person I've ever met, oh my god. Why are you *like* this?"

"Secret lair here," Martha said, voice crackling in the speakers. "We agree with Jazz and Gibby, just so you know. We're going to hug you, but then we're going to yell at you. It's going to be very loud, but you will sit there and take it."

Guardian smiled despite himself. "Yeah, yeah, I love you guys, too. It's not over yet. We have to stop Owen. He took more of the pills. I don't know how strong he is, but we need to get to him before he hurts anyone."

"On it," Jazz said, all business even as Gibby continued to mutter about the ridiculousness of boys. "Where do you think he's going?"

"I don't . . ." He groaned. "Never mind. I *do* know where because he's an idiot and thinks this should come full circle."

"What do you mean?" Pyro Storm asked as Burke shouted he was being *framed,* it wasn't what it looked like, *get your hands off me, do you have any idea who I am?* "Where would he—McManus Bridge."

Guardian nodded. He shot up off the stage, rocketing through the air as if it were the easiest thing in the world. Laughing joyously, he glanced back down in time to see fire spreading underneath Pyro Storm's feet before he, too, rose from the stage.

They flew up the side of Burke Tower, spinning around each other, a double helix of fire and air in their wake. "You're *flying!*" Pyro Storm cried.

Twisting his body, Guardian thrust his feet against the side of the building. With all his might, he pushed *off* it, glass shattering, metal shrieking as he flew across the sky, heading toward McManus Bridge, Pyro Storm close at his heels, a trail of fire streaking behind them.

# 18

McManus Bridge was in chaos. Vehicles backed up on either side, gridlocked, the middle of the bridge blocked by an overturned city bus. People had left their cars behind, faces turned up toward the looming mass of shadows that roiled above them. Others were helping the passengers from the bus, pulling them out through broken windows. Smoke poured from the front of the bus, and Guardian saw a lick of fire shoot out from the hood. Someone shouted that it was gonna blow, *get back, it's gonna blow!*

"We have to help them," Guardian said, and without waiting for a reply, hurtled toward the bridge. He landed hard, the jolt shooting up his legs, but he hit the ground running, hearing Pyro Storm right behind him.

They reached the overturned bus and found a heavyset man standing on it, leaning down, looking through a broken window. Pyro Storm went to the front of the bus as Nick jumped on top of it, landing next to the man. He startled but recovered quickly, saying, "I can't get them out. Her kids won't leave her."

Guardian looked down into the bus and saw a young woman, two children clutching her as they wailed. "Are you hurt?" he called down.

The kids stopped crying, looking up at him with wet eyes, their mouths hanging open. They couldn't have been more than eight years old. The mother said, "Leg stuck. I can't get out. My kids. Please help them."

"I'm going to help all of you," Guardian promised. "Just hold on, I'll—"

"*Nick!*" Pyro Storm cried.

Guardian raised his head in time to see a goddamn *Buick* flying toward them, flipping end over end, the headlights still on, momentarily blinding him. He grabbed the man next to him by the front of his shirt, pulling him down. The Buick flew over them, the heat from the undercarriage immense. It landed with a crash on top of empty cars on the other side of the bus, the collision of metal causing a cascade of sparks, windows imploding, glass bouncing off the ground. Nick lifted his head slowly to see Shadow Star hovering high above the bridge, the shadows around him growing larger.

"Fire's out!" Pyro Storm shouted. "Help them. I'm going after Owen." He shot up into the sky, flames bright.

Guardian glanced at the man. "Get down. I'll get them." Without waiting for a response, he rolled forward through the broken window, landing a few feet away from the woman and her kids. The bus groaned around them, but he paid it no mind. The woman's leg was pinned under a seat that had broken off.

The kids—a boy and a girl—flinched as he approached, turning their faces against their mother's chest. "It's all right," Guardian said. "I promise. I'll get you out of here, okay?"

He reached for them, only to be knocked to the side when something struck the bus, causing it to slide along the bridge. A moment later, another collision and the sound of breaking metal. The bus lurched at a dangerous angle, the rear rising up, purses and backpacks raining down around him, mixed with shards of glass. Guardian turned toward the front of the bus, and through the windshield, saw the dark river below them.

The bus was sliding off the edge of the bridge.

"Oh, shit," Guardian breathed.

The woman shrieked, and Guardian whirled around. The little girl fell toward him, sliding along the aisle of the bus with a wail. Hanging off a seat, Guardian caught her, wrapping an arm around her waist. Her legs kicked, hitting his thigh. "I got you," he told her, trying to get her to calm down. "What's your name?"

"Alma," she whispered, bottom lip trembling.

"Alma. Awesome name. Hey, Alma. You ever gone on a piggyback ride before?"

She nodded, face slick with tears and snot. "I do it with Daddy."

"I bet he's the best at it, but can you do it with me? I know you're scared, but I got you, okay? Hold on tight. We're gonna rescue your mom and brother."

He helped her around his back, her arms and legs tight around him as the bus slid farther, the rear windows illuminated by flashes of orange and red. Fire. Whatever Pyro Storm was doing, he hoped it'd be enough to distract Shadow Star.

He started toward the woman and boy when the bus lurched again. "Hold on," Guardian told the girl. "This is gonna go fast. You ready?"

"Ready!" Alma said, practically choking him.

The bus had reached the point of no return, tilting up and up as Guardian ran up the center aisle. Without stopping, he raised his hand, blasting the seat off the woman's leg, sending it flying out a shattered window. As she and the boy began to slide toward them, Guardian caught them, the impact jarring, almost knocking him back. Without hesitating, he turned his hand toward the side of the bus. The side of the bus twisted, metal and plastic bulging outward before breaking completely, leaving a large hole. He pulled the woman and the boy through it, all of them stumbling when they hit the ground just as the bus slid over the side of the bridge and disappeared from sight. A moment later, a great splash sounded as the bus hit the river.

Hands on him, then, and Guardian jerked his head to find the man helping Alma off his back, the woman and the boy reaching for her. "I'll get them outta here," the man said, face pale. "Go help your friend."

"Boyfriend," Guardian said automatically.

"Oooh," Alma said as her mother brushed grime off her cheek. "He has a *boyfriend*."

"Thank you," the woman whispered, the boy hugging her leg. "We'd have gone over if it hadn't been for you."

"Go," Guardian said. "Quick. Don't stop running until you're off the bridge."

The man grabbed the little boy, lifting him up, taking the woman by the hand and pulling her and Alma away. They weaved in between the cars.

He looked up and saw Pyro Storm and Shadow Star locked in battle. Pyro Storm slammed into Shadow Star's midsection, flying them both into one of the bridge's towers, the suspension cables quivering loudly. One of the cables snapped, whipping into an abandoned SUV, practically splitting it in half.

Pyro Storm pulled back, and right when Guardian thought he'd done it, that he'd knocked Shadow Star out, a thick shadow shot forward, wrapping around him. Pyro Storm exploded, the light from his fire burning the shadow away. He turned and flew down toward the bridge, landing next to Guardian. Part of his costume was torn, one of his lenses cracked and dim. "He's strong," Pyro Storm panted. "Stronger than he was last time."

"This isn't like last time," Guardian said. "You have me. There's two of us and one of him. We can—"

Shadow Star pulled himself from the ruined towers, shadows rising.

They seemed endless as they surrounded him, blotting out the sky. He appeared to be made entirely of darkness, the star symbol on his chest blacked out, body writhing as if covered in coils of snakes. Massive columns of shadows grew around him, at least a dozen in all.

Through the darkness above Shadow Star, a blinking light, followed by the *whump whump whump* of spinning blades. A helicopter, the Action News logo on the side barely visible.

Shadow Star whirled around just as the helicopter's spotlight turned on, a harsh beam of light that struck him dead-on, causing his shadows to fade. He shot up toward the helicopter, which banked sharply to the right. He flew underneath it, away from the spotlight, and shadows wrapped around the landing skids, causing the helicopter to shudder. Bending backward, hands above his head, legs curled behind him, Shadow Star cried, "*Catch!*"

He hurled the helicopter down toward them, landing skids snapping, blades spinning.

Before Pyro Storm could react, Guardian shoved him out of the way. He raised his hands as the helicopter filled his world. The blades tore through the air, and as it fell toward him, Guardian could see the pilot's face through the cockpit window, mouth open in a scream, hands wrapped around the cyclic, trying to pull the helicopter back up.

The spotlight was blinding, and Guardian raised his hands, calling upon his spark. It was waiting for him, and the air around him began to ripple. He ground his teeth together as he slid backward, the thin muscles in his arms and legs straining. Knowing he was about to be crushed—or worse—Guardian closed his eyes.

The sound of the helicopter—engine racing, blades whirring—was the only thing he heard, wind slapping against him.

But the impact did not come.

He opened his eyes.

The helicopter hung suspended above him, nose tilted down, blades spinning a foot from Guardian's face, the spotlight shining on him from his chest down to his feet. The pilot gaped at him, and behind him, another man holding a large camera pointed at Guardian through the windshield.

"Behind you!" Pyro Storm yelled, and Guardian looked over his shoulder to see his shadow, the spotlight causing it to stretch long behind him. The shadow rose from the ground, taking shape—head and torso, hips and legs, arms rising. It started toward him but took a staggering step back as a ragged hole appeared in its middle, an arc of fire bursting through.

"I'll handle it," Pyro Storm snapped as he flew by Guardian, sizzling the air as his fire built around him.

Guardian crooked his fingers, and the helicopter dropped

a few more feet, the pilot and cameraman shouting inside the cockpit. He managed to lower the helicopter to the ground, where it scraped along the pavement in a shower of orange sparks. It tilted to the side, blades striking the ground, breaking apart, metal splintering and flying off the bridge into the water below. The shrill alarms inside the cockpit faded into quiet beeps as the cameraman and the pilot peered out through the cracked windshield.

"Get out of here," Guardian snarled at them. "Keep running until you're off the bridge!"

The pilot started nodding, but then his eyes widened. "Look out!" he cried, voice muffled, but the warning clear.

Guardian whirled around to find Shadow Star standing behind him. "Heya, Nicky," he said cheerfully. And then he backhanded Guardian across the face, causing him to fly back into the helicopter, grunting painfully as the nose dug into the small of his spine. He hit the ground on his knees, leaning forward, hands on the ground as he tried to suck in air. Everything hurt, and sweat dripped into his eyes.

He didn't have the strength to fight when Shadow Star gripped the sides of Guardian's helmet, pulling him up and up until his feet left the ground, kicking into nothing. Shadows snaked around his helmet as he slapped at Owen's hands, his mind a storm of panic. Behind Shadow Star, Pyro Storm lay on his back, covered in writhing black that pummeled him over and over.

"Flying?" Shadow Star asked, sounding amused. "Shit, Nicky. You got some new tricks since last time we were here."

"Why are you doing this?" Guardian gasped as he covered Owen's hands with his own. Behind him, the faint sounds of feet slapping against the ground. Hopefully that meant the pilot and cameraman had managed to escape.

"Because I can," Shadow Star said easily. "And even more than that, I *want* to. You're so wrapped up in thinking you're a hero because you saved my parents, even knowing they hate you. Your righteousness is exhausting." He shook his head. "What's the point of trying to help people when they don't want you to? When they'll turn around and spit at your feet? Aren't you tired of giving your all only to have it flung back in your face?"

"No," Guardian snapped. "If there's even *one* person who needs help, then we're gonna be there." Shadow Star's grip on Guardian's helmet tightened, and inside, Nick heard the material beginning to groan. A flashing red word appeared in front of his eyes: WARNING. WARNING. WARNING.

"I suppose that's one way to look at it," Shadow Star said. "But, for the sake of argument, here's another: they want something to be scared of? *I'll give it to them.*"

The pressure on Nick's helmet increased immensely, causing him to groan. Black spots began to dance across his vision. He blinked slowly when a voice came from the speakers inside the helmet. "Hold on, kid. We're coming. Don't give up."

"Dad?" Guardian whispered as his helmet creaked. "Is that—"

But whatever else he might have said was lost when his helmet *collapsed* around his head, digging into his skull, his ears. Shadow Star grunted as he broke it apart, and hot air washed over Nick's face, hair matted down against his forehead. The remains of his helmet fell to the ground.

Shadow Star slammed him back against the helicopter, Nick's head knocking against metal, bright lights flashing across his vision. Dazed, he watched Shadow Star bring his fist back, shadows crawling along his knuckles, forming a sharp point aimed at Nick's right eye.

And then Shadow Star was on fire.

He screamed, letting Nick go, causing him to slump to the ground. Shadow Star waved his arm wildly, slapping his other hand against the flames that burned along his arm. The smell of burned hair, burned *skin* filled Nick's nose, thick and noxious. His vision clearing slightly, he saw Pyro Storm stalking toward Shadow Star, fire roaring around him in ever-increasing waves.

"You've had this coming," Pyro Storm growled, lifting his leg and kicking him in the sternum. Fire exploded at the impact, shredding the symbol on his chest as he flew back against an abandoned garbage truck. It rocked as he slumped to the ground.

"Nick," Pyro Storm said, rushing toward him. He knelt down, cupping Nick's face. "You all right?"

Nick nodded, wincing as Pyro Storm helped him up. If he thought everything hurt before, it was nothing compared to the way he felt now. Nothing seemed to be broken, but he was going to pay for this later.

If there was a later, because as soon as he stood upright, he saw Shadow Star standing in the road, the goddamn *garbage truck* floating above him, held aloft by shadows. "Let's try this again," Shadow Star said. "Catch!"

Nick yelped, grabbing Pyro Storm by the shoulders and pushing down as hard as he could. They collapsed to the ground as the garbage truck flipped over them, one of the large wheels almost clipping Pyro Storm in the head. It hit the edge of the bridge, snapping cables before disappearing over the side.

"Dammit," Shadow Star said. "I really need to work on my aim. Let's try something else." He dropped to the ground, palms flat against the pavement on either side of him. The bridge made a terrifying groan as the ground beneath them began to rumble. A large crack in the asphalt raced from Shadow Star toward them as more cables snapped, the tower above them beginning to sway.

Pyro Storm grabbed Nick by the hand, pulling him up. They jumped over the widening split in the road, and Pyro Storm bellowed, "Hold on to me!"

Nick jumped on his back as Pyro Storm shot his hand forward, a line of fire stretching along the ground. Pyro Storm leapt on top of it, sliding along the rail, weaving in and out between the cars and trucks. Nick glanced over his shoulder and screamed when he saw shadows chasing after them, flipping vehicles off either side of the bridge. He had a feeling of weightlessness as the rail of fire ran up and *over* a motor home, stomach rising to his throat before falling back down as they descended the other side.

"We have to end this!" Nick shouted in Pyro Storm's ear. "We can't let him hurt—*shit*!"

Four columns of shadows split the asphalt apart in front of them, rising up before collapsing on top of the rail of fire, snuffing it out. They were moving too fast to stop in time, and at the last second, Pyro Storm leapt over the shadows. Nick looked down in time to see a black column shoot up, slamming against Pyro Storm's legs, sending them both spilling to the ground with a jarring impact. Nick rolled end over end, breath knocked from his chest as he and Pyro Storm crashed into the grill of a tow truck. The truck groaned, its ramp shooting out and hitting the ground, the top end still hanging off the truck.

Before Nick could push himself to his feet, Pyro Storm grabbed his arm, holding him still. "No," he hissed. "Don't. Cavalry's coming."

"Then they better hurry," Nick wheezed as Shadow Star moved toward them, whistling as if he had all the time in the world.

"They'll be here," Pyro Storm said grimly. "When I tell you to, get down."

Shadow Star stopped ten feet away from the truck. "Is that it?" he asked, head cocked. "Is that all you've got? Thought it'd be at least a *little* harder to beat you."

Pyro Storm snorted. "You'd think, right?"

"How's it going, Owen?" Nick asked, stalling for time. "You don't look so good." This was a lie. His visor had cracked, his costume still smoking, but he seemed much better off than Nick and Pyro Storm.

"Oh, I'm doing just fine," Shadow Star said, sounding almost breathless. "The pills. I can feel them. What they're doing to me. Watch."

He spread his arms like wings, and his shadow rose behind him, towering high above his head. It formed arms and legs and reached down, settling its massive, disjointed hands on Shadow

Star's shoulders. Black leaked from the fingers, crawling along Shadow Star. The costume re-formed, the star symbol intact, the tears in his costume stitching back together. The crack in his visor disappeared. Once the repairs were completed, the shadow rose back up, looming.

"Really need to learn how to do that," Nick muttered. "Remind me if we don't die."

"Will do," Pyro Storm said, squeezing his hand. "Get ready."

"There," Shadow Star said. "That's much better." He shook his head. "Scared me for a moment. A little too close for comfort. But I'm stronger than you are. Always have been. Always will be. It's over. At long last."

"Yeah, yeah," Nick called to him. "You're the bad guy. Blah, blah, blah. Heard it all before. Get some new material." He narrowed his eyes. "But I swear to god, if you start spouting my fanfiction back at me again, we're gonna have a problem. I wrote that with limited information, and I have many, many regrets because of it."

"Five," Pyro Storm whispered, and Nick saw Rebecca Firestone in his head, counting down silently with her fingers.

"Nah," Shadow Star said. "I'm done with all of that. I'm just gonna kill you instead."

"Four."

"Before you do," Nick said, "lemme clear something up."

"What's that?" Shadow Star asked, taking another step toward them, his shadow moving with him.

"Three."

"You've tried to kill us repeatedly. You tried to kill your parents."

"I have," Shadow Star said. Another step.

"Two."

Nick nodded. "Okay, cool. Just making sure we're on the same page."

Shadow Star stopped, frowning. "What? Stop stalling. You're embarrassing yourselves. I've won."

"Except," Pyro Storm said, "you've forgotten one thing."

"What's that?" Shadow Star asked, his shadow shifting above him.

"One," Nick whispered.

Pyro Storm said, "Matilda." And then he pulled Nick down as hard as he could. Both hit the ground as the sound of a roaring engine filled the air. Nick looked back underneath the tow truck in time to see headlights flashing right as a van hit the ramp of the tow truck, causing it to shudder and lurch forward, the front right tire nearly running over Nick's leg. The van rolled up the ramp, the tires clipping the cab as it launched into the air.

Nick stared up in wonder as the van flew above them, the undercarriage sparking. He heard Burrito Jerry shouting above the cacophony, "*FLY, MY LADY, FLY!*"

The headlights struck the towering shadow, causing it to rear back as the lights burst through it, creating holes in its body as the van reached its apex. The headlights turned down toward the ground, slicing the shadow thing right down the middle. Shadow Star raised his hands and screamed as the van fell toward him. At the last second, the shadow thing collapsed around him, cocooning him in a black ball.

The front of the van struck the ball head-on. For a moment, Nick thought it'd flip over, but the van crashed back down on its tires, the back two splitting and deflating. The black ball was knocked back down the bridge, bouncing like a pinball from one car to the next, stopping against the guardrail, shadows swirling around it.

The back doors of the van flew open with a snarl of electricity, and Miss Conduct jumped out, eyes glowing blue, the curls of her wig bouncing. She was followed by Gibby and Jazz, who pushed by her, rushing toward Nick and Pyro Storm. Nick laughed wildly when Cap came out next, thinking of clown cars.

Jazz and Gibby reached them first, Jazz going to Guardian, Gibby helping Pyro Storm to his feet. "Anything broken?" Jazz asked, running her hands up and down Nick.

He winced when her fingers touched his sides. "Don't think so. What are you doing here?"

"Saving your asses like we normally do," Gibby said, Pyro Storm leaning heavily against her.

"You shouldn't be here," Nick told them frantically. "It's too dangerous. Owen is—"

"About to get the shock of his whole damn life," Miss Conduct said fiercely. "He's not ready for what's coming." She turned away from them, one foot behind her as if she was getting ready to run.

Nick looked at all of them, confused. "*What's* coming?"

Cap grinned at him. "A quick but comprehensive lesson on why you should *never* mess with our kids."

Nick was about to ask what the hell they were talking about when Bob Gray jumped out of the back of the van. He winked at them, raising his hand, palm toward the sky. He snapped his fingers, and a bloom of fire burst from his palm, illuminating his face.

Pyro Storm said, "What. *What.*"

Bob stepped to the side as Miles Kensington jumped out. He looked no different, moving with ease. No different, that is, until he went to an overturned car and ripped the bumper off as if it were nothing. Settling it against his shoulder, he nodded at them.

"That's my *dad*!" Jazz cheered.

Trey Gibson followed, eyes glittering. He stood behind Matilda and turned his face skyward. Above him, out of nowhere, clouds formed, thunder rumbling inside them. Nick watched in wonder as twin tornadic spirals descended from the clouds, the wind loud, cars rocking.

"That's *my* dad," Gibby said, and Trey grinned at her.

Aaron Bell was the last, and when he saw Nick, he said, "Hey, kid. You did good. We'll handle it from here." He looked around, and on the ground near his feet were large shards of glass from the broken windows. Nick stared dumbfounded as Dad jerked his head, the glass rising from the ground and circling his head, the sharp points catching the light from Bob's fire.

Matilda revved to life, Burrito Jerry backing her up out of

the middle of the bridge, the flat rear tires slapping against pavement. Once out of the way, he leaned out the open window, slapping his hand against the door. "Do it now?"

"Now," Trey agreed.

Burrito Jerry grinned. "Rock on. Let's make sure I say this right." He cleared his throat. "Who's gonna kick some shadowy ass?"

Bob's fire spread along his arms. Miles tapped the large bumper against his shoulder. Trey's spouts grew larger, pulling up dark river water. Dad raised his hands, and the glass he'd raised from the ground snapped together, forming a glittery ball that spun slowly above him. They posed for a long moment, their powers on display. And then, as if the situation couldn't get any more ridiculous, they all shouted, *Dad Squad!*"

"What in the actual fuck," Nick breathed.

"They watched," Gibby said proudly as the Dad Squad—for *some reason*—continued to pose like they had all the time in the world. "They learned. While they were training you, they saw what it took to do what you do. The power. What's needed to control it. The pills, Nick. They took what Burke made, but instead of using it against innocent people, they're going to finish the fight." Her smile was feral. "We thought we were alone. We weren't. We never have been."

Jazz nodded. "It's temporary. They only took one each, just to be safe. The ride over here was . . . interesting. Daddy accidentally ripped up one of Matilda's seats. Bob almost lit my eyebrows on fire."

"Sorry about that!" Bob called over, molding his fire into a ball, tossing it from one hand to the other. "Thought it'd be more like a lighter than a flamethrower. Boy, was I wrong." He almost dropped the fireball, looking sheepish as he caught it before it fell. "Still takes some getting used to."

"Stay here," Miss Conduct said. "We'll handle the rest." She bowed dramatically, face only a foot above the ground, without bending her knees. Nick still wanted to be her when he grew up. "Miss Conduct will deal with the evil twink, with assistance from the DILF Squad."

"Dad Squad," Nick corrected automatically.

Miss Conduct stared at him. "I said what I said."

"Wait," Pyro Storm said, and they all looked at him. "Let me get this right. Four adult men and a drag queen are going to take on the teenager who's trying to kill us?"

"Yes," the Dad Squad and Miss Conduct said at the same time.

He shrugged. "Okay. Just wanted to make sure we're all on the same page." He sagged back against the tow truck.

Trey looked at the others around him and nodded. "Ready? Let's do this thang."

"Ooh, hold on," Miles said, gripping the bumper lying on his shoulder. "Before we go. I've been working on a little something called a catchphrase."

"How do you do, fellow kids?" Jazz muttered fondly, rolling her eyes.

"Oh my god, *yes*," Nick whispered. "I'm here for *all of this*."

Miles puffed out his chest. "What superpower do you get when you become a dad?"

Nick frowned. "Uh, that's not a catchphrase. It sounds like the setup for a terrible—"

"Supervision," Miles said. "Get it? Because we *supervise* our—"

"Dads, *no*," Nick and Gibby and Seth and Jazz said.

"Dads, *yes*!" the dads shouted, and they turned toward where Owen had landed . . .

. . . only to find him gone.

"Where'd he go?" Miss Conduct asked, joining the Dad Squad as Jazz fussed over a cut on Nick's head, Gibby's arm wrapped around Pyro Storm's waist. Cap watched over all of them, mustache twitching.

"Did he run?" Trey asked, his waterspouts swirling on either side of the bridge, misting over them, like a thin fog.

"I don't *run*," Shadow Star snarled, stepping out from behind a minivan farther down the bridge. His hands were curled into fists, shadows growing around him once more. "It's better you're here. Now I can wipe you *all out and*—"

"One chance," Cap said, glaring at Shadow Star. "I'm telling you now, Owen, we're giving you one chance to stand down."

Shadow Star shrieked as he charged them, his shadows slamming into the ground, propelling him forward. He only made it two steps before Trey clapped his hands together. The waterspouts spun furiously, hitting either side of the bridge and climbing on *top of it*, picking up glass and metal, a chaotic storm that Shadow Star couldn't get through. He made a strangled noise as the strong winds lifted him up, body twisting, shadows floundering.

Miles stepped forward, lowering the bumper and tapping it against the ground. "Aaron, on my word, hit me with that thing. You hear me?"

Dad nodded, moving off to the side, the glass ball glittering above his head. Shadow Star spun upside down in the waterspout, and Miles said, "Wait for it. Wait for it. *Now.*"

Dad thrust his hands forward, and the glass ball shot toward Miles, who swung the bumper like a baseball bat. He grunted when glass met metal, and the ball hurtled toward Shadow Star. It struck him in the chest, glass exploding around him, surrounding him in little shards.

"Miss Conduct!" Trey shouted. "You're up!"

Electricity snarled as Miss Conduct stepped forward. White-hot lightning flew from her fingertips, striking the shattered glass and water. The electricity snapped across the water with a burning sizzle, fusing the glass around Shadow Star, trapping him inside. For a moment, Nick thought that was it, that it was over, finally, at last. But then Shadow Star screamed, and the glass ball detonated into powder, the waterspout swaying, starting to diminish.

"Huh," Miles said. "Didn't expect that."

"Amateurs," Bob muttered, taking a step forward, belly jiggling slightly. "Let me show you how it's done." The fireball began to grow in his hands, flames licking his fingers. "Seth, are you watching? Look at this! Pretty cool, right?"

"Very cool," Pyro Storm agreed.

"Yeah," Bob said. "I thought so, too. Now I just have to figure out how to throw the darn thing."

"Bob!" Dad yelled. *"Duck!"*

Bob immediately dropped to the ground, twisting over onto his back as Shadow Star flew toward him, and right when he was above the fireball, Bob pushed it *up*. The fire hit Shadow Star in the stomach, flipping him over. He hit the pavement, skidding toward the tow truck. He was up before he stopped sliding, rushing back toward them, hands outstretched, mouth hanging open.

"Our turn," Gibby said, stepping away from Nick and Seth. "Jazz?"

"Oh, I've been waiting for this," Jazz said. Raising her voice, she cried, *"Cap!"*

Cap stuck out his foot right when Shadow Star passed him by, causing him to trip. He stumbled forward, momentum carrying him. Before he could recover, Gibby crouched low in front of him, then threw herself up. Her shoulder hit Shadow Star in the stomach, his breath exploding from his mouth in a wheezing grunt. Not to be outdone, Jazz stepped forward as Gibby moved out of the way. She cocked her fist back and let it fly. Her knuckles collided with Shadow Star's bared teeth, knocking him back against the guardrail. For a moment, Nick thought he'd go up and over the railing, but he managed to keep from falling.

"Punching doesn't hurt as much as I thought it would," Jazz said as Gibby snorted. "I hope I get to do it again soon. Maybe even in the next few seconds, because Owen doesn't seem to get it yet."

Shadow Star rose unsteadily to his feet and stalked toward them, but Miss Conduct moved in front of him. "I don't like hurting other queer people," she told him. "But for you, I'll make an exception." She clapped her hands together, and electricity arced around her. When Shadow Star threw a clumsy punch, she sidestepped it easily, slamming her glowing hand into his back, causing him to seize, teeth grinding together. Electricity coursed through him, shredding his costume, revealing lines of tan skin. The costume struggled to re-form as he took another hard step forward. Miss Conduct crouched low as she spun, leg kicking out, hitting the back of his knees. Shadow Star fell forward, landing facedown on the ground.

Miss Conduct rose above him, glaring. "If you know what's good for you, you'll stay down."

He did not, apparently, know what was good for him, because he started to push himself up. He laughed harshly, head bowed. "You think . . . this is enough . . . to stop me?" He raised his head, looking directly at Nick. "You were *wrong*."

"Heard you liked to play catch," Dad called, and the *sound* Nick made when he saw his father standing on the bridge was something he wasn't proud of. It came out in a high-pitched wheeze, similar to a tire deflating, but he thought he could be forgiven for this, seeing as how Dad had a red Mini Cooper floating above his head. "Catch *this*."

The Mini Cooper flew toward Shadow Star, who screeched as he dove to the ground. The car bounced off the bridge only a few feet from Shadow Star's head, flipping over him and into the water below.

"Oops," Dad said. "Hope that was insured." He looked at Nick. "Whenever you damage someone else's property, you need to own up to it. Did anyone get the license plate?"

"Maybe now's not the best time," Nick said. "Seeing as how Owen *won't stay down*."

"You're damn right I won't," Shadow Star snapped as he pushed himself up once more. He looked a little unsteady, hands shaking, panting heavily. "You think you're all enough to stop me? You're *not*. I could do this forever. I will . . ." He groaned, wrapping his arms around his stomach as his eyes squeezed shut.

Nick took a step toward him, only stopping when Pyro Storm grabbed his wrist. "Don't," he whispered harshly. "It's a trap. He's trying to catch us off guard."

"Something's wrong," Nick said, never looking away from Owen. "He's . . ."

Shadow Star collapsed to his knees, head bowed in front of him.

Pyro Storm—*Seth*—tried to hold Nick back, but he pulled free. Dad called his name as he rushed toward Shadow Star. Falling to his knees, Nick hesitated before putting his hands on either side of Shadow Star's helmet. Lifting it off, he tossed it aside.

Owen Burke blinked slowly, dazed, eyes unfocused. Nick gasped when he saw Owen's skin was almost translucent, black shadows swirling underneath. "The pills," Owen whispered. "It hurts, Nicky."

"I know," Nick said, touching the side of Owen's face. He recoiled when Owen's cheek *bulged,* a shadow trying to force its way through. Owen had done so much to hurt them, to hurt others. He'd taken lives, stolen people away from their families. He had to be stopped. But no one deserved this. "We can help you. You don't have to do this anymore. You're not your father. You're not Patricia."

Owen smiled weakly. "You think?"

Nick nodded.

Owen stared at him for a long moment. He turned his face into Nick's hand. "We had something once, didn't we?"

"We did," Nick agreed quietly. "For once in your life, do the right thing."

"If I say no?" Owen asked, eyes narrowed.

A chill ran down Nick's spine as he sat upright. "Then I'd say there's ten of us. One of you. You can't win against those odds."

And Owen said, "Maybe not. But I can sure as hell try."

He did. He tried. Shadows burst from his back, but they flickered angrily as they whipped around. One hurtled toward

Nick's face but stopped inches from the tip of his nose. Nick didn't move, didn't blink, and when Seth's arms wrapped around his chest, pulling him away, he didn't try to fight it. Instead, he felt a strange sense of grief wash over him, knowing no matter what any of them did or said, it was already too late for Owen.

The shadows trembled as Owen clutched himself, face contorted. He brought his hands up to his head, gripping his hair, and the *scream* he let out would haunt Nick for years to come. It echoed across the ruins of the bridge. Seth breathed heavily in Nick's ear, his grip around his chest tight. But Nick barely felt it. He barely felt it because of Owen's legs. They were *dim,* translucent. Same with his hips. His chest. His arms. His face. Owen held out his hands in front of him, and his fingers began to fade, little wisps of shadows rising like smoke from the tips.

"What is this?" Owen whispered.

"The pills," Dad said, appearing next to Nick and Seth. He looked exhausted, horrified. The lines on his face were deeper than Nick had ever seen them. "You took too many, Owen. There's always a price to pay."

Owen shook his head. "No. *No.*" He took a step toward them. And then another. And then another, but then he could walk no more because his lower legs turned to shadows, unable to support his weight. He fell to his knees, settling back on his haunches. Owen smiled at the night sky and spoke his last words.

He said, "I . . . am . . . *Extraordinary.*"

His face, his teeth and tongue, dissolved into shadows. The rest of him followed, and his body burst silently in a puff of black that swirled away, caught in a warm breeze that spread all that remained of Owen Burke, like ash over an ocean.

He was gone.

Seth let Nick go as he turned toward his father, grabbing him as tightly as he could. Nick felt something in him break, and he clutched at his father as tears fell.

Hands on his back. His hair. Words whispered from his

friends, his family, familiar, sweet and soft. Dad whispered in his ear, "We've got you, kid. We've got you."

Nick didn't raise his head when the sounds of sirens filled the air, people approaching from either side of the bridge, calling out. He closed his eyes and held on for dear life.

## 19

**Fic: The Truth**
**Author**: Guardian
**Chapter 1 of ?**
**4,782 Words**
**Pairing**: Guardian/Pyro Storm, Nicholas Bell/Seth Gray, Lola
  Gibson/Jasmine Kensington, Minor Nicholas Bell/Owen
  Burke, Owen Burke/Himself
**Rated**: PG-13 (and I better not get any shit for this, you
  weirdos!)
**Tags**: Idiot Boys in Love, Super Queer Girls, Pining, Dad
  Squad, Lighthouse, A Guy Called Burrito Jerry, Real Person
  Nonfiction, Autobiography, Happiness, Sadness,
  Somewhat Anti-Rebecca Firestone, Violence, All the
  Catchphrases, ADHD Is a Superpower, Neurodiverse
  Unite!

...............................................................................

### Chapter 1: We Are Done Hiding

I have a story I want to tell you. Most of it is pretty unbelievable, but
stick with me, okay? It's probably going to go on for far too long, and
you might even think that I'm full of shit, but I promise every word
that follows is the truth. Right now, I'm sure there are journalists all
over the world cursing my name as they read this, especially since I
refused to be interviewed after all that happened. I was even con-
tacted by publishers wanting me to write a *book* about the last few
years. Ridiculous, right?

I refused because I wanted to tell my story *my* way. And what could be better than writing it down and releasing it for free on our be-loved fic site? Take *that,* capitalism!

A few things about me before we start: I am seventeen years old. I'm a student at Centennial High in Nova City (home of the Fighting Wombats!). I'm queer. I have ADHD and it's not the death sentence I once thought it was. Some of the smartest people I know (hi, Jazz and Gibby!) have told me time and time again it's my superpower and that no one thinks like I do. I believe them because they're smarter than the rest of us combined. My brain *is* my superpower, but it's not the only one I've got.

My name is Nicholas Bell. You might know me as ShadowStar744 or PyroStormIsBae, both monikers I used to write fics on this site (and the first person who gives me crap over my ShadowStar744 fics will be yeeted into the sun). But I have another name, one you've undoubt-edly seen spread across every news channel, every newspaper across the world, given there's apparently nothing else going on. Someone I love with all my heart (hey, Seth! you're the best!) once did the brav-est thing I've ever seen. He removed the mask and revealed the Ex-traordinary underneath, knowing there would be people who hated him simply for existing.

I was scared for him. I've seen what people are capable of. And honestly, I was scared for *me,* knowing what I could do. I felt like a coward letting him go through it alone. I didn't have the immense courage he did, and though I wanted nothing more than to join him, I couldn't bring myself to do it.

But I'm done hiding.

My name is Nicholas Bell. I'm the Extraordinary known as Guard-ian. And this is my manifesto.

My mother, Jennifer Marie Bell, once held the same moniker. It's mine now, and I hold it with pride, honoring her memory. She's gone. That hurts to write, after everything we've been through.

Here are a few other things you should know about her.

She was kind.

She was honest, even if the truth was hard to hear.

She loved my father, her husband. They met when they were in college. It's the only hetero meet-cute I'll tolerate (straights, you've had *enough* of those): she was on a ladder in the NCU library, trying to reach a book from a top shelf. She slipped, and who just happened to be walking by when she did? Yep. My dad. He didn't so much catch her as break her fall, and he said that the first time he saw her face, he knew she was it for him.

And like me, she was telekinetic. But that's not all she was. She was so much more than her ability to move things with her mind. If I can impress upon you one thing, it would be this: she was an Extraordinary, but she was also my mother. I miss her every day, and everything I am, everything I do, is because of her.

Now, let me tell you about my dad, Aaron Bell.

If you live in Nova City, you probably know that name. Shortly after my mother died, my father—an NCPD detective—struck a witness who was being cruel and saying things about Mom. Instead of being fired, he was demoted. But that only lasted for a few years. After the Battle at McManus Bridge Part I (yes, this is probably a thing some underpaid intern thought up; if it'd been up to *me*, the title would have been much longer and with many more exclamation points), he was assigned to lead the newly formed Extraordinaries Division. It was his job to keep track of the Extraordinaries in Nova City.

But he should have been fired. Or he should've quit. No matter what was being said to him, putting his hands on someone was the wrong thing to do. Dad knows I'm writing this. He knows I'm leaving nothing out because it's important for you to hear the truth, as ugly as it can be.

He's not a cop anymore. He quit when Rodney Caplan did. Too little, too late? I don't know. You won't hear me arguing one way over the other, but I know my father. I know the type of man he is. He's trying every day to become a better person. And I'm going to be there to make sure he continues to do that, while also making sure I do the same. We owe it to each other, ourselves, and our friends and family to do the best we can.

I have friends. (Yes, yes, I'm bragging.) Gibby and Jazz. Two women who have helped to shape who I am today. Both of them are rad. Protective. Badass. They are two of the best people I've ever had the pleasure of knowing, and I'm so lucky to have them in my corner. The love they have for each other is inspiring, and we should all try to be like them.

I could say that if you mess with either of them, you'll face the rest of us. That's true. But if you mess with Gibby, then god have mercy on your soul because Jazz is coming for you.

Gibby was the rightful valedictorian of her graduating class, only to be stripped of the title because she made the decision to help others at the Attack on Centennial High (I *see you*, Nova City School District, trust me on that!).

You've probably seen the viral clip of Jazz from last month at that meeting, standing in front of the school board, taking them to task for not allowing Seth Gray to return to school. Though many people spoke that day on both sides of the issue, it was Jazz who struck at the heart of the matter, telling them in no uncertain terms that if they didn't allow Seth Gray—AKA Pyro Storm (more on him in a moment)—to return for his senior year after being kicked out the spring before, she'd (and I quote):

". . . make your lives a living hell. Do you know what Seth did? Do you know the courage it took? Because I don't think you do. Even now, you're sitting there, some of you gaping at me, others muttering under your breath—*you*, sir, yes, you. Care to say that a little louder? No? That's what I thought. You say you're trying to protect the other kids in your district, but if you'll look at the folders I provided, you'll see the signatures of over six *thousand* of these same kids in the Nova City School District, all of whom are demanding that Seth Gray be allowed to return for his senior year. We may be young, but our voices are important. It doesn't matter who is or isn't an Extraordinary. In addition to Seth being allowed back at Centennial High, we demand a full apology not only to Seth and Nick Bell, but to Lola Gibson, too, whom you railroaded out of her rightful spot as valedictorian of her graduating class under the guise of an investigation, the results of which have never been made public. And before you accuse me of taking something away from someone else, you'll see a note attached to the petition from Matthew Rogers, who was made valedictorian over Gibby. He writes that had he been in possession of all the facts, he would have refused the title of valedictorian. You're *adults*. Do your damn jobs."

(I clapped so hard, I thought my hands would fall off.)

A week later, the school board released the following statement:

*Against a tide of misinformation, we want to be clear that we value each and every one of our students. Though we typically avoid commenting on individual students given that privacy is paramount, we are making an exception today. Seth Gray will be invited back to Centennial High for his senior year. We will not be making any further comments at this time.*

Did you see the apology in there? An acknowledgment that Gibby was wronged? Yeah, me neither. But wait, there's more! Half the school board resigned fifteen days after their nonapology. Trey and Aysha Gibson—parents to Gibby—were appointed to the board for the foreseeable future, along with a few other parents who are ready to fix what's broken. Things are going to change and while it won't be easy, if anyone can do it, it'll be them.

Remember these names: Jasmine Kensington. Lola Gibson. I have a feeling you'll be hearing about them quite a bit in the future.

Which brings me to Seth Gray, AKA Pyro Storm.

I can write thousands of words about him. Hell, I already have—see *A Pleasure to Burn* (yes, I will finish it!).

Seth's my hero. He's always been there, holding my hand, helping me breathe. He's lifted me up when I was at my lowest. And even when I get certain . . . *ideas*, he's never made me feel stupid, or that my opinions didn't matter.

I could tell you so many things: How he looks when he's sleepy (so *soft*). How he tries to be strong for the rest of us, and sometimes needs to be reminded that we can be strong for him, too. I could tell you how smart he is, how brave, how selfless. A leader. A trailblazer. A man who is going to change the world.

I'm the luckiest queer dude in the world, because he chose me. If I may get a little sappy (fair warning: it's probably only going to get worse from here, and I regret *nothing*), Seth Gray is the better part of all of us. I love you, dude. Always.

This manifesto is called *The Truth*, which is what I will give you. About us. About Simon Burke. About Patricia Burke. About Owen Burke, who was once my friend.

That being said, Owen was a villain. He killed people. He hurt many others, including me, my friends, my family. You won't hear me making excuses for him. The families of the people he harmed are owed better than that.

But Simon and Patricia Burke bear an equal amount of responsibility. They did things to their child that no parent should ever do.

I have no doubt that some of you reading this are angry with me. Some of you might even fear me. Burke didn't create the divisions between us; they were already there to begin with. He merely harnessed them to further his message of hate and vitriol, stoking the fears that many of you were already feeling.

If you were a supporter of Simon Burke—of which there are still many—I'll say this: if there ever comes a time when you need a hero, we'll be there.

And last, a message to Extraordinaries, both known and unknown: We see you. We know you're scared. We know you think you have to hide, and if that's what's best for you, then do what you need to in order to protect yourselves. I wish I could tell you it's going to get easier from here, but that would be a lie. There are always going to be people who hate you for what you are, what you represent.

But there are more supporters than you think. We're here. We're with you. We have your backs. You don't have to go through this alone. We will be the lighthouse, the beacon, guiding you home. One day, the world will see you for just how extraordinary you really are. But until then, reach out if you need to. I promise we'll listen.

(Unless you're evil, then we'll just kick your asses, so.)

Next week, the real story begins in Chapter 2 (unless I'm slammed with homework, ugh, *why*). There will be danger! Romance! Skwin-kles Salsagheti and crickets smashed against pillows! Heroes born, and villains rising! I hope you're ready, because I'm just getting started. Stay tuned!

# CREDITS

Endings can be difficult, especially when you've spent as much time with a group of characters as I have with Nick and Seth and Jazz and Gibby. For years, I've had Nick shouting in my head in all his ridiculous glory, and I know how lucky I am that I got to tell his story in its entirety. He's quieter now. I know that means his story—at least one that I'll tell—is over, but I will never forget the time I got to spend with him in Nova City. Like many of my characters, I know he's fictional and yet, he feels real to me. I will miss him forever.

That being said, I did not go through this journey alone, so let's take a look at everyone who helped bring the Extraordinaries to life. They deserve just as much—if not more—credit for getting these books out into the world.

Deidre Knight is my agent. Chances are if you've read any of my books over the last few years, you recognize that name. Back in the day—oh lord, did that hurt to write—even before *The House in the Cerulean Sea*, Deidre read *The Extraordinaries* and saw something in Nick and company that made her want to sell the hell out of the book, and in turn, the series. She did, and it's because of her—and everyone else at the Knight Agency—that you got to read these books in the first place. Elaine Spencer handles all the foreign rights to my novels with the Knight Agency, and I'd be lost without her. Thank you.

Ali Fisher, my editor, was the first to read *The Extraordinaries* at Tor Teen. I remember Deidre telling me it's not about how many rejections an author gets because all it takes is *one* person seeing the value in the work. Ali was that person. She saw what I was doing with *The Extraordinaries* and not only ran with it, but made each book better than it has any right to be. Thanks, Ali.

Also on the editing side is associate editor Kristin Temple. She is a tireless cheerleader and never makes me feel like a dork for asking questions that have obvious answers (usually within the same email I'm asking questions about—yikes!). Thanks, Kristin.

I've always been a vocal champion of sensitivity readers. They are the unsung heroes of the publishing industry and should be lauded much more than they are. Margeaux Weston and Jon Reyes provided wonderful notes on *Heat Wave*. The book would not be where it is without them, and I am eternally grateful.

Saraciea Fennell and Anneliese Merz are my publicists, and they too don't always get the credit they deserve. Though many people have helped me get where I am today, Saraciea and Anneliese are the reasons my name gets put out there in the first place. I firmly believe that any success I've had over the past few years is because of them and their tireless work on my behalf. Also, though they don't know it, they absolutely demolished my fear of public speaking *because they keep making me speak in public*. Funny how that works. Thanks, Saraciea and Anneliese.

The higher-ups are President of TDA and Tor Teen Publisher Devi Pillai; Vice President, Director of Marketing Eileen Lawrence; Executive Director of Publicity Sarah Reidy; Vice President of Marketing and Publicity Lucille Rettino; and Chairman/Founder of TDA Tom Doherty. These are the people who let me tell the stories I want to tell. They know how important queer narratives are and have been wonderful champions of my work.

Anthony Parisi is the marketing lead. He—and his team—come up with some of the best marketing events for each of my books, and I'm blown away by his empathy, kindness, and seemingly inexhaustible work ethic.

Isa Caban works with Anthony as the marketing manager, and I still wish I could be as rad as she is, though not for lack of trying.

An additional marketing lead is Becky Yeager. Though she mostly works on my adult books, these are my acknowledgments, and I can thank whoever I want. Becky, you are amazing, and if anyone tells you otherwise, send them to me. She also does ad promo, which is something I know nothing about, so I bow to her.

Sarah Pannenberg and Andrew King, the digital marketing coordinators, run the Tor Teen social media accounts. They both understand the value of a good gif (pronounced with a hard g, you weirdos), and I am extremely appreciative of that. Thanks, both of you.

On the production side of things, you have production editor Melanie Sanders, production manager Steven Bucsok, interior designer Heather Saunders, and jacket designer Lesley Worrell. See how pretty this book looks? That's because of them. Thank you. Also, David Curtis has done the artwork for the entire series and made the reversible covers for the US releases of the series. Before *The Extraordinaries* came out, I floated the idea of having "variant covers" like they do in comics. David took the idea and ran with it, making something uniquely Nick. Thanks, all.

Michael Lesley did the audiobook. I've worked with Michael for years across many books, and there's a reason I brought him on to this series: He's one of the best audio narrators working today. He *is* Nick (as he is Sam and Justin and Paul and Sandy and Josy). We should consider ourselves lucky that we get to witness his talent.

Thank you to Lynn Schmidt, Mia Gardiner, and Amy Miles for beta reading. They get to see the books before anyone else (and usually with instructions from me to CUT CUT CUT). They dig through the messes that are the first drafts and tell me how to make them readable. Thanks, ladies.

And last but certainly not least, to you, the reader: Thank

you for reading these books. I know endings are hard. But I've learned that it's not always about the end; instead, it's about the journey. Thank you for going on this journey with me. It means more than I could ever say.

TJ Klune<br>March 5, 2022

(Did you really think I'd end this without *one more thing*? Because guess what? There's one more thing. Turn the page, won't you?)

# LATER

He couldn't get his stupid bow tie to work. No matter what he did—how many times had Seth shown him over the years? a dozen? a million? something like that—it still ended up going wrong halfway through, one end longer than the other, dangling limply down his chest. The bow itself looked like a messy pile of fabric sitting under his throat. He was on his sixth try and somehow, it looked worse now than when he'd started.

"Why won't you *work*?" Nick growled at his reflection.

His suit—Jazz-approved—was a deep navy blue, the tailored jacket with black lapels, the slacks tight against his butt and thighs. If he farted, he'd blow his dress shoes off and hit someone important in the face. He hoped it wouldn't be the officiant, a severe woman who was *not* a fan of Nick, if the number of times she'd rolled her eyes when he'd met her was any indication.

Underneath the jacket, a crisp white button-down with blue stripes. The black bow tie was supposed to be the finishing touch, but it was obviously broken.

He looked away from the mirror when a knock came at the door. "It's open!" he called, hoping it was anyone but Seth. He didn't want the love of his life seeing how he couldn't even tie a freaking bow tie, especially on today of all days. Not that he'd give Nick any crap for it, but Seth had been tying his own bow ties since he was seven years old. What did it say about Nick that he couldn't do it now at the age of twenty-six?

Thankfully, it wasn't Seth. Dad opened the door, leaning his head in. His hair was shot with gray, the lines around his eyes and mouth a little more pronounced than they'd once been. Still, somehow, Dad wore his age with grace. He was as handsome as ever, and when he saw Nick frowning at his reflection, he smiled, shaking his head. "Figured something like this was happening."

"Yeah, yeah," Nick muttered. "I wanted to use my powers, but figured I'd probably end up strangling myself. Again."

(Long story—suffice to say, Nick was *not* allowed to use his powers while dressing himself. The last time he'd tried—a year ago—it'd turned into this whole thing involving a pair of chaps, an angry villain called Steamroller, and an apology to the entire country of Norway. That had been a weird Easter, but thankfully, Norway had accepted his apology, and Steamroller had decided to give up his life of crime and now helped inmates getting their GEDs while serving twenty years for trying to disrupt the Nova City power grid.)

Dad stepped into the bedroom, shutting the door behind him. He wore his black suit well. He'd gained a little weight over the past few years and it looked good on him. Dad seemed . . . relaxed. Happier. Therapy helped. That was a big part of it, but it wasn't the only part.

Her name was Yolanda Jimenez. She worked as a veterinarian. They'd met on the streets of Nova City in front of Caplan, Bell & Bell, the offices of the private investigation agency that Nick and Dad had continued after Cap retired, keeping the name the same to honor their friend. She came over a few days after the opening, bringing with her a welcome basket filled with pastries and coffee from a bakery in the neighborhood. Nick had been putting the finishing touches on his small office—really nothing more than an oversized closet—hanging pictures of his friends and family next to his NCU diploma. He'd paused when he heard the bell ring and the front door open but ignored it when he heard Dad raise his voice in greeting.

When he'd come out twenty minutes later, Dad and Yolanda had been standing near the front desk, Yolanda laughing, Dad blushing. She was a stout woman with shiny black hair and an expressive face. Nick liked her immediately, especially when he saw she was capable of giving his dad shit, but not in a mean way.

"This is my son," Dad said awkwardly, waving his hand, looking a little out of his depth. "Nick. He's my partner in the agency."

"Hey, Nick," Yolanda said, smiling warmly. "Heard about you. Guardian, yeah?"

Both Dad and Nick stiffened. People could be . . . weird around him.

"Yeah," Nick said slowly. "That's me."

"Good for you," Yolanda said. "Thanks for helping out."

And that was it. She'd turned back to Dad and told him about some of the other businesses around them. Most were cool, she said, and they'd formed a tight little community who watched each other's backs. She invited Dad and Nick to a meeting of all the business owners the following week, and left shortly after, telling them if they needed anything, she was only a few doors away.

And the look on Dad's face when she'd gone—wondering, confused—had let Nick know exactly what he was thinking.

They'd gone to the meeting, and wouldn't you know? Yolanda had saved them a couple of seats near the front. By the time they left, Nick had made sure Dad had her phone number, and she his. "Just in case he needs to call you for anything!" Nick called as Dad dragged him away. "Like for vet advice even though we don't have pets. Ooh, or what about a *date*? Dad? *Dad*. Stop pulling me!"

Dad had yelled at him when they'd gotten back to the office.

Nick had smiled through it and asked, "Are you finished? Because you should call her."

He had (two days later, saying that he didn't want to seem too eager), and the rest, as they say, was history.

Dad crossed the room as Nick turned back toward the mirror, frowning at the stupid bow tie. He sighed when Dad stopped in front of him, arching an eyebrow. "I think I need help."

"Looks like," Dad said. "You nervous?"

"Understatement," Nick muttered as Dad began to fix the bow tie. "This is a big deal. I don't want to screw this up."

"You'll be all right," Dad said. "One foot in front of the other. There, see? All done." He walked around Nick, standing behind him and putting his hands on Nick's shoulders.

Nick gaped at the mirror. "How did you do that?"

Dad chuckled. "Don't need powers, just takes a little practice."

Nick let out a slow breath. "Big day."

"It is," Dad agreed. "You ready for it?"

"Think so. Just want to get it right, you know?"

"I know, Nicky," Dad said, squeezing his shoulders. "But you'll be fine. You know what you're going to say?"

Nick groaned. "Mostly. I tried writing it down, but it didn't come out like I wanted it to. Kept getting distracted." His ADHD—that part of him he once despised—hadn't disappeared as he'd gotten older, but that was okay. He was in control. He had the tools. Medicine. Meditation. Even then, he still had days when he felt like he was vibrating out of his skin, but that was part and parcel of being neurodiverse. He didn't let it stop him from living. It was only a small part of the greater whole that was Nicholas Bell.

Dad grinned. "Gonna wing it, huh? That'll be . . . fun. You want me to step in if you start talking about the mating habits of turtles?"

"Please," Nick said, relieved. "Though I think they're probably expecting that."

"Of course they are," Dad said, stepping to his side. They stood in front of the mirror, watching each other in their reflection. "Not too shabby. I can't believe we're about to—"

Nick said, "I wouldn't be here if it wasn't for you."

Dad sucked in a breath, looking away, blinking rapidly. "Oh, hey, you don't have to—"

"Thank you," Nick said, turning toward his father. "Thank

you for loving me. Thank you for protecting me. Believing in me. Thank you for being my dad."

"It has been my honor," Dad said roughly, gathering Nick up in a tight hug. "You and me, kid. Always."

They stood there, holding each other, the sunlight of a cool November morning filtering in through the window.

They found Seth pacing in front of a pair of double doors, looking slightly panicked. On the other side of the doors, a loud murmur of voices of those in attendance. In a room off to their right, a burst of laughter from those waiting to make their entrance. It was almost time.

Seth deflated slightly when he saw them. "There you are. I was getting worried. We have to—holy *shit*, Nicky."

Nick grinned at him, spreading his arms and turning a slow circle. "Pretty good, right? I mean, it's no dead magician's suit, but it'll do. Did it all myself with absolutely no help."

Dad coughed pointedly.

Nick winced. "Okay, maybe a *little* help."

"Bow tie?" Seth asked, a slow smile spreading across his face.

"Bow tie," Nick agreed.

Seth kissed him with a loud smack. "You look amazing. I know I saw the suit earlier, but this is . . . wow."

"You, too," Nick said. Seth was wearing a suit that matched Nick's down the smallest detail, aside from one little difference. On the lapel of his suit coat was a red-and-orange pin in the shape of a flame. A gift from a girl he'd saved years ago from a high-rise fire.

As Seth blushed, Nick could see the boy he'd once been. Oh, the curls were still there, and he had that same fiery spark in his eyes, but the man before him—once a boy on the swings with chocolate pudding on his lips—was a grand sight to see. Even though they'd been together for years, Nick still pinched himself every now and then at how lucky he was. He'd been given the awesome and slightly terrifying responsibility of carrying Seth's heart, something he did not take for granted.

(It also helped that they were *amazing* at butt sex. Seriously. The first time had been a bit of a disaster—waaaay too much lube, so much so that it'd been like a human Slip 'N Slide— but every time after? Holy shit, they should've gotten awards for some of the stuff they did. Seth could be very imaginative. Nick felt bad for the people who couldn't have sex while flying. It was really something else.)

"I'm going in before this gets weird," Dad muttered somewhere behind them. "Nick, I will remind you that you're in public. Indecency laws are still a thing. Seth, make sure—"

Nick turned slowly to look at him.

Dad threw up his hands. "I can't believe you—fine. *Dr. Gray,* please make sure Nick keeps his pants on. You, too." He gave them a stern look, though it seemed as if he were fighting a smile as he went through the doors, the sound of the crowd on the other side rising and falling as he closed the doors behind him.

Seth groaned. "Nick, you don't have to make him call me that. We *talked* about this. I still have a bit to go before I even have my PhD, and then it's just more school. I'm not a doctor of anything yet."

He did, but Nick was absurdly proud of his partner. Seth had been working his ass off to get where he was, long days and even longer nights. But he knew what he wanted to do, and Nick had supported him, knowing what he was working toward, and how important it was. The plan was for Seth to finish out his PhD before moving on to medical school with a specialization in psychiatry. Once done, he wanted to become one of the first to work primarily with Extraordinaries, those who needed someone to talk to about life, superpowers, and what it meant to exist in a world where many people were still scared of people like them.

"We *have* talked about this," Nick told Seth. "You're gonna get there, dude, helping people who need it most." He kissed Seth's cheek. "Besides, you know how hot it makes me, *Dr. Gray.*"

Seth rolled his eyes fondly, the tips of his ears turning pink. "Yeah? You like that?"

"A lot," Nick breathed. "Hey, we have a few minutes. What say you and I find an empty closet and I'll show you just how much?"

Seth made a face. "That wasn't as romantic as you seemed to think it was."

"It wasn't meant to be," Nick assured him. "I just want to put my mouth on your—"

"Later," Seth said, and the heat in his eyes made Nick shiver. "Promise."

Nick believed him. Seth had never led him astray, and though the odds had been stacked against them—who *really* found the love of their lives in high school?—they'd stuck together.

Which was why he'd come to a decision, one that made him deliriously happy and deliriously nervous in equal measure. Tucked safely away in the back of the hallway closet in their small apartment was a box. And in that box, a ring that Aaron Bell had once worn, given to him by Jennifer Bell. Nick was working up the courage to give it to Seth. Soon.

(Three days from now, he will, only to be stunned when Seth bursts out laughing, telling him to stay right there. He'll rush back to their bedroom, leaving Nick gaping after him, reappearing a moment later with a similar box in his own hand. In this box is a ring once worn by Jeremy Gray, his father. Seth will say he'd been waiting for the right moment to propose, and they'll laugh. They'll cry. They'll hold each other close and the rings will absolutely be the wrong size, but it won't matter. The next day, they'll tell their family, and everyone will agree it's about damn time.)

"Later," Nick said, taking Seth's hand in his. "We should—"

The double doors opened, and an usher stuck his head out. When he saw Nick and Seth, he said, "I think we're ready."

"On it," Seth said, pulling Nick toward a room off to the right. Seth knocked on the door before pushing it open. Inside, a group of people in matching outfits—all blue—looked at him.

"You all good?" Seth asked. "Looks like we're about to start. Can you get in the order we practiced? Line up in front of the entrance and wait for your cues."

The people inside nodded, standing up from their chairs, smoothing out their suits and dresses, a few fixing the flower crowns sitting on their heads as they filed out into the entryway.

They left them to it and went to another door just down the hall. Nick knocked this time. "Hey, it's us. You ready?"

"Come in," a voice called out.

Nick pushed open the door, and inside found Trey and Aysha Gibson standing with their daughter, Congresswoman-elect Lola Gibson.

*Congresswoman-elect,* Nick marveled as Gibby smiled at them. It'd been close, the election a few weeks before, a nail-biter right down to the last minute, but Gibby had emerged the victor. Representing the Fourteenth District, she was one of the youngest people ever elected to the office. The wedding party was made up of many of her staffers, people whom Gibby and Jazz had hand-selected for their ideas, their desire to create change. Gibby's opponent—a six-term incumbent—had decried her age, saying that she was far too young and inexperienced to represent her district. Not only had he tried to make it about her age and her platform of police reform, he'd used her relationship with Pyro Storm and Guardian to say that she was no better than Simon and Patricia Burke, the former now incarcerated in a maximum-security prison upstate for the rest of his natural life, the latter at a facility that once housed her son. "She has *Extraordinaries* at her beck and call," the douchebag had argued in their final debate. "What is she going to do when her first bill fails in committee? Sic her pet Extraordinaries on us?"

Gibby had smiled (the one smile that Nick *knew* meant she was about to ruin the douchebag's life) and said, "At least I'll have submitted a bill for consideration, which is more than you've done in the entire time you've been representing Nova City." She then proceeded to provide a point-by-point take-down of the incumbent's lack of action in his years in office. By the time the debate was over, even her most ardent critics had begrudgingly admitted that she'd wiped the floor with her opponent.

Still, it'd been close, and when the election had finally been called in her favor, they'd all been frazzled. All, that is, except for Gibby, who looked up at the screen in wonder and said, "We did it."

With tears streaming down her face, Jazz said, "No, Gibby. *You* did it."

Apparently, a newly elected congresswoman didn't seem to mind being tackled by her friends and campaign-manager fiancée, which was good, seeing as how that's exactly what happened.

Now, standing in the room with her parents at the Kensington home, Gibby wore a smart suit, similar to Nick's and Seth's: blue and black, her long tie cinched firmly at her throat.

"You look so good," Nick said. "You put the rest of us to shame."

She laughed, looking down at her suit. "This old thing?" She smiled again, but it trembled a little. She cleared her throat. "Have you . . . uh. Have you seen her? She okay?"

Nick grinned. "I have. As Jazz's man of honor, it was my duty to tell her she looks beautiful, though she didn't need to hear it from me. She's very, *very* excited."

"And as *your* man of honor," Seth said, "you look perfect, Gibby."

Gibby nodded, obviously relieved, but before she could speak again, Trey promptly burst into tears. "She does, doesn't she?" he sobbed, Aysha smiling warmly at him, squeezing his hand. "The best thing ever."

Gibby laughed quietly. "Thanks, Dad. I . . ." She shook her head. "I guess it's time, huh?"

"It is," Nick agreed. "You need a moment? I can tell them to wait a minute if you do."

She shook her head. "No. I'm ready." She laughed again. "I'm so, so ready."

The wedding itself was small. Family, friends, staffers, all sitting on chairs in the backyard of the Kensington home, next to the pool where electric tea candles floated. An archway had been built at the end of the yard in front of the audience, covered in vines and blooming flowers. When the doors opened and the first of the wedding party went through, people turned toward them, all smiling.

Music played from speakers, wordless, soft. The air had a bit of a chill to it, but not unpleasantly so. Nick and Seth waited for their turn, knowing they'd be among the last to walk through, standing with Gibby and Jazz.

When their cue came, they stepped out into the backyard, walking down the long carpet that divided the audience. Nick nodded at Mary and Rodney Caplan, Cap's mustache twitching as he grinned at them, tossing them a wink. He laughed when he saw Chris and Mateo Morton's three-year-old son squirming in Chris's lap. Luis was not a fan of sitting still, and when he saw Seth, he shouted, "Papa, it's *Fire Guy*!"

Everyone laughed as Seth flushed. Luis was Pyro Storm's biggest fan.

Chris sighed and said, "Yeah, kiddo. It's Fire Guy."

Burrito Jerry sat with his boyfriend, Derek, and their girlfriend, Amy. Both adored him. It'd been Amy first, then Burrito Jerry had picked up Derek in Matilda when he'd needed a Lyft, and they'd all been inseparable ever since. So much so that Burrito Jerry had repainted Matilda, turning the scantily clad figure riding a seahorse into Derek (still scantily clad, of course), with Amy and Burrito Jerry riding their own seahorses behind him. It was . . . a lot, but they were happy, and that was all that mattered.

Dad and Yolanda sat near the front, hands clasped between them as Dad smiled widely, eyes glistening.

They reached the front, the officiant nodding at them, mouth twisting a little when Nick said, "If you need me to take over, just let me know. I got you, Melissa."

"Thanks," Melissa said dryly. "But why don't we just let me handle it."

They took their places on either side of her, the wedding party lined up behind them.

And then the music changed, and Gibby walked out of the house into the backyard, her parents at her side. She looked determined, and when they reached the front, her parents took turns hugging and kissing her, whispering words meant only for her. When finished, they went to the empty chairs in the front row, standing with everyone else to wait for the last of the wedding party to come through the doors.

They didn't have to wait long.

Arm in arm with Miles and Joanna Kensington, Jazz walked out into the backyard, and everyone gasped. Nick had already seen her—her long white flowing dress, the flowers braided into her hair—and so he looked at Gibby, wanting to see the exact moment she saw her wife-to-be.

He was not disappointed. Gibby's jaw dropped, and she exhaled explosively. "Oh my god," she whispered. "She's . . ." A tear trickled down her cheek.

"Told you," Nick whispered, ignoring Melissa's pointed glare.

Jazz moved slowly, so slowly, in fact, that when they were halfway down, Jazz's face scrunched up as she declared, "Okay, this is fun, but we need to move *faster.*" Everyone burst into laughter as she dragged her parents toward the front, Miles almost tripping over his feet.

She didn't wait for her parents to give her away. Instead, she launched herself at Gibby and kissed the ever-loving *hell* out of her. "I accept," she said, peppering Gibby's face with kisses. "I do. I am your *wife*. We are *married*."

"Not quite," Melissa said, amused. "But sure, why not."

Jazz didn't seem to want to let Gibby go, but then Gibby didn't either. They finally broke apart, hands clutched between them.

"Let us begin," Melissa said, opening the leatherbound book she carried. "We have come together today to celebrate two people who wish to pledge their lives to each other." She smiled at Jazz and Gibby, but they only had eyes for each other. "I will read from—

"*Aha*!" a thunderous voice bellowed from above. "I've got you *exactly where I want you*. Prepare to suffer my wrath!"

Everyone looked up.

A figure floated down toward the ground, decked out in a makeshift costume consisting of a snowsuit, at least seventeen rolls of duct tape, and a bicycle helmet, complete with stickers of unicorns on the sides. His cape—what looked like a comforter he'd taken from a bed—billowed around him as he touched down in the middle of the audience. At the center of his chest, a symbol that looked like it'd been ironed onto the front of the snowsuit: a predatory bird with wings spread and sharp talons.

"Oh boy," Trey said. "You're gonna regret this, man. Probably a better idea to turn and walk away."

"I *won't*," the man snapped. "I never back down from a fight!"

Trey shook his head. "All right. Don't say I didn't warn you." He glanced at Aysha, sitting next to him. "I've never been to a wedding *and* a funeral at the same time."

The man sneered at him, his teeth bared. He looked to be in his forties, and thin as a whisper. He posed in the yard, hands on his hips as everyone stared at him. "Like I'm scared of a little fire or telekinesis. I can do things you haven't dreamed of. There's a new Extraordinary in town, and I will bring Nova City to its knees." He jutted out his chin. "They call me . . . Commander Hawk. With one piercing cry, I can summon birds of prey that will do what I tell them to, up to and including ruining a wedding!" He frowned as he looked around. "Why aren't any of you screaming or running for your lives?"

"Because we know what's about to happen to you," Trey

called from his seat. "You were warned. What happens next is all on you."

Commander Hawk scoffed. "Didn't you hear what I said? I'm not afraid of fire and telekinesis. Pyro Storm and Guardian? More like Pyro . . . something and Guardian . . . something else." He frowned. "Okay, that wasn't good. I'm a little nervous."

Seth sighed. "It's not me or Nick you need to be afraid of."

Commander Hawk blinked. "What do you mean? Who else am I supposed to be scared by?"

"Us," Jazz said, eyes glittering dangerously. "Gibby, if you please. This idiot is interrupting our special day."

"Your wish is my command," Gibby said. And with that, she charged forward.

Commander Hawk barely had time to back up before Gibby kicked him in the nuts. He shrieked, face turning white, the cords on his neck thick as he bent over, clutching his junk.

Jazz hiked up her dress and moved quickly. Gibby dropped to a crouch, and Jazz rolled over her back, the hem of her dress fanning as her right foot shot out, her heel striking Commander Hawk in the throat. He made a strange noise—*urk!*—as he began to gag, stumbling back, helmet askew on his head. Gibby rose and finished him off by kicking him squarely in the chest, knocking him off his feet, skidding along the ground. He came to a stop, dazed, as wedding guests peered down at him.

"I . . . have . . . so . . . many . . . regrets," he whispered.

"And stay down," Jazz snapped. "If you do, maybe we'll let you have cake later. But if I hear one more word from you, I'm gonna stab you and I won't be made to feel bad about it on my wedding day." She grinned suddenly. "Wow. I get the whole bridezilla thing now."

"I knew we needed those extra forks," Miles said, puffing out his chest. "Glad I asked for them."

"I got it, Jasmine," Burrito Jerry said, rising from his chair. "You get married. I'll make sure he doesn't interrupt anymore."

He stood above Commander Hawk, frowning down at him. "Hey, guy. That wasn't cool. Queer-girl weddings are the best weddings. I should know; I've been to six of them."

"My *testicles*," Commander Hawk wheezed. "They're . . . *inside me*."

"Yes, well," Burrito Jerry said easily, "that's no one's fault but your own. Come on. Get up. You can sit by us. Meet my boyfriend and girlfriend. Amy's a paramedic, so she can tell you if your testicles will ever lower again. Fun fact! They probably won't." He helped Commander Hawk up, and thanked the usher who hurried forward with another chair. He forced the would-be villain to sit, which caused him to groan and cup his groin. Burrito Jerry sat down next to him and gave a thumbs-up to Jazz and Gibby.

"Did I smudge my makeup?" Jazz asked as Gibby led her back up to the front.

"You look as beautiful as ever," Gibby assured her.

"Oh, good," Jazz said as she took her place in front of Melissa, who looked like she didn't know quite what to make of what she'd just witnessed. "We still have pictures to take when we're done. He's not allowed to be in any. He doesn't match with the rest of the wedding party. Nick, your bow tie is crooked."

"Please don't kick me in the junk," Nick said, trying to straighten his bow tie. "I need it for later. Seth, tell her."

Seth did not. Instead, he said, "Remember Nick's twenty-first birthday party?"

Gibby laughed. "I'd forgotten about that. Those three douchebag Extraordinaries who burst into the bar and tried to say they were holding us all hostage." She shook her head. "Nick was so drunk, he flew into the ceiling."

"I meant to do that," Nick snapped, and everyone in the audience laughed. "What? I *did*!"

"Sure, kid," Dad said. "Whatever you need to tell yourself."

Nick crossed his arms and glared. "It worked. I stopped them, didn't I?"

"You did," Jazz said. "I've never seen grown men scream

like that before. To be fair, though, you did throw up all over them." She shuddered. "All that shrimp and tequila. It's no wonder they gave up immediately."

"Can we please focus?" Nick said through gritted teeth. "Seems like we were doing something before we were interrupted."

"Oh, right," Gibby said. "Melissa, we apologize. You were saying . . ."

Melissa gaped at her.

"We told you this might happen," Jazz told her, patting her hand. "It's why we paid you extra. You good to go, or should we have someone else take over?"

"Yes," Nick whispered fervently. "I *knew* getting ordained online wasn't a waste of time, no matter what anyone said."

"Eh, screw it," Gibby said. "Melissa, if it's all right with Jazz here, why don't you just say the magic words and let me kiss my wife."

Melissa sighed and said, "By the power vested in me by the state of—"

"You may kiss the bride!" Jazz exclaimed, and later, they would see the exact moment captured by the photographer. Nick pumping his fists above his head, mouth open in a frozen shout of happiness. Seth smiling, one of his curls hanging down on his forehead. Melissa, standing in the background, eyes wide, book forgotten in her hands.

And Jazz and Gibby, of course. Gibby, cupping Jazz's face, kissing her sweetly as her wife smiled so brightly, people would say it was like looking directly at the sun.

It was this picture Nick and Seth would hang in their home (right next to an old photograph of a woman and her son standing at the edge of a sea, a lighthouse in the distance), surrounded by a dozen others from a life well lived.

As Jazz and Gibby broke apart, as the cheers washed over them, Nick looked at Seth and was floored by the soft expression on his face. Seth must have felt Nick's eyes on him, because he turned his head slightly and smiled. *I love you,* he mouthed.

And as Nick mouthed back the same, Seth's smile widened, fierce and dazzling.

He turned his face toward the sky as the thunderous applause continued on and on.

"We're extraordinary," Nicholas Bell whispered as he closed his eyes.

And breathed.